Praise for
Beach House Reunion

"Readers . . . will be enthralled. . . . Authentic, generous, and heartfelt!"

—Mary Kay Andrews, *New York Times* bestselling author of
The High Tide Club

"This atmospheric novel depicts a lush sanctuary that draws in the needy and provides heartwarming inspiration."

—*Library Journal*, starred review

"A beautiful novel and a fantastic read that is perfect for the start of summer."

—*RT Book Reviews*

"Fans of Elin Hilderbrand and Mary Kay Andrews will adore this tender and openhearted novel of familial expectations, new boundaries, and the power of forgiveness."

—*Booklist*

"Monroe's trademark mix of environmental awareness, coastal nostalgia, and gentle wish fulfillment should be catnip for the hoards of recreational readers who've made her a *New York Times* bestseller."

—*Wilmington Star-News*

Praise for
Beach House for Rent

"Reading this novel feels like a long, luxurious trip to the beach. Mary Alice Monroe writes gorgeously, with authority and tenderness, about the natural world and its power to inspire, transport, and to heal."

—Susan Wiggs, #1 *New York Times* bestselling author

"Mary Alice Monroe understands that a house is never just a house. . . . Monroe's singular ability to blend the natural world with the emotional world allows for a gorgeous novel, wondrously both bittersweet and also life-affirming. The story reveals its secrets with shorebirds and human hearts at the center of its graceful axis. No one else tells an insightful and powerful story quite like Mary Alice Monroe—and in *Beach House for Rent*, you won't be able to stop reading—for even that glass of sweet tea."

—Patti Callahan Henry, *New York Times* bestselling author

"Fans of Mary Kay Andrews and Mary Simses will adore this novel of simple pleasures, shifting priorities, and the power of self-discovery. Tender and inspiring with a touch of romance, it's just the thing to fill an empty beach bag."

—*Booklist*

"A charming and poignant story ideal for summer reading."

—*PopSugar*

"A skilled storyteller who never lets her readers down . . . [Mary Alice Monroe] makes Isle of Palms come enticingly alive, calling all readers to this garden of paradise which is just ripe for a visit. Mary Alice Monroe creates characters that you wish/hope could be real people so that they could become your friends. And you feel if you could visit the lowcountry they would be there waiting."

—*Huffington Post*

Also by Mary Alice Monroe

Beach House Memories
Beach House for Rent

LOWCOUNTRY SUMMER SERIES

The Summer Girls
The Summer Wind
The Summer's End

A Lowcountry Wedding
A Lowcountry Christmas

The Butterfly's Daughter
Last Light over Carolina
Time Is a River

Mary Alice Monroe

Beach House
Reunion

GALLERY BOOKS

New York   London   Toronto   Sydney   New Delhi

G

Gallery Books
An Imprint of Simon & Schuster, Inc.
1230 Avenue of the Americas
New York, NY 10020

First Gallery Books trade paperback edition March 2019

GALLERY BOOKS and colophon are registered trademarks of Simon & Schuster, Inc.

For information about special discounts for bulk purchases, please contact Simon & Schuster Special Sales at 1-866-506-1949 or business@simonandschuster.com.

The Simon & Schuster Speakers Bureau can bring authors to your live event. For more information or to book an event, contact the Simon & Schuster Speakers Bureau at 1-866-248-3049 or visit our website at www.simonspeakers.com.

Manufactured in the United States of America

10   9   8   7   6   5   4   3   2   1

The Library of Congress has cataloged the hardcover edition as follows:

Names: Monroe, Mary Alice, author.
Title: Beach house reunion / Mary Alice Monroe.
Description: First Gallery Books hardcover edition. | New York : Gallery Books, 2018. | Series: The beach house
Identifiers: LCCN 2018002826 (print) | LCCN 2018006126 (ebook) | ISBN 9781501193316 (ebook) | ISBN 9781501193293 (hardcover : alk. paper) | ISBN 9781501193309 (trade paperback : alk. paper)
Subjects: LCSH: Domestic fiction. | BISAC: FICTION / Contemporary Women. | FICTION / Family Life. | FICTION / Romance / General.
Classification: LCC PS3563.O529 (ebook) | LCC PS3563.O529 B46 2018 (print) | DDC 813/.54—dc23
LC record available at https://lccn.loc.gov/2018002826

ISBN 978-1-5011-9329-3
ISBN 978-1-5011-9330-9 (pbk)
ISBN 978-1-5011-9331-6 (ebook)

To Kathie Bennett, with great love and gratitude.

Chapter One

In the spring, mature loggerhead females steadfastly swim thousands of miles through the Atlantic to nest in the region of their birth. The females repeat this journey every two to three years.

ALL ROADS LEAD *home.* That thought mingled with the soothing sound of Debussy as Cara descended from the majestic highlands of Tennessee toward the sultry lowcountry of South Carolina. Her brand-new red station wagon wound its way past racing rivers and creeks that flowed south to the ocean, past billboards advertising fireworks, fruit stands, deserted gas stations, and tumbledown antiques shops. Signs of spring—yellow jasmine blooms against lush greens—dotted the countryside. From time to time a flock of birds would fill the sky, and she would crane her neck to watch them migrating north. A short laugh escaped her lips. *We are all heading home to nest*, Cara thought.

She stretched her long legs as best she could while driving in skinny jeans. The cuff of her white cotton shirt was stained with coffee from a quick swerve. Everything had been too fast in the past few weeks as she scrambled to pack up and move home—too many fast decisions and too much fast food. And here she was, journeying the same stretch of road again. Going home never seemed to get easier. She glanced into the rearview mirror as the passing years flashed in her mind. How many times had she made this journey back to the Isle of Palms?

At forty, she'd driven back from the chilly North to seek refuge at her mother's beach house in the sultry South, as listless as a rudderless ship. Primrose Cottage had been her sanctuary, as it had been her mother's before her. A special place by the sea to recharge one's batteries and find renewed purpose. At fifty, she'd buried the past and left again, looking for a fresh start. Now, three years later, like the loggerhead sea turtle she was named for, Caretta was returning to the only place she'd ever considered home.

She leaned slightly to the right to glance in the rearview mirror again. Her dark eyes were smudged with fatigue and had a few more lines around the corners. She wasn't a child any longer, or even a young woman. Each decision she made now had rippling consequences. Cara felt her resolve stir. She needed to be home now, more than ever.

~~~~~

LINNEA WAS SO done with the four-lane I-26. She'd sped along that endless stretch of highway from the University of South Carolina in Columbia to her home in Charleston so many times in the past four years that she could drive it in her sleep. And there were some trips that had come dangerously close to that. Red Bull could only do so much. This was her last one, however. She'd graduated at last, and after a final round of parties, she'd crammed everything she could into her blue convertible Mini Cooper and headed home.

At last she exited in Charleston. If she'd been a tourist, she would have followed the main road and got caught in the horrid logjams on East Bay, Meeting, and King Streets. Every time she came home, there was another hotel going up in the city. Traffic was a nightmare. She tapped her fingers on the steering wheel and swore the whole peninsula was going to sink in the next flood.

But, having been born and raised in Charleston, Linnea was no stranger to the city. She made a sharp right, then shot down Broad Street toward the water, ducking down narrow alleys only locals knew about—bumpy cobblestone roads lined with parked cars. After two more turns, she veered sharply into their driveway on Tradd Street, then slammed on the brakes. Panting and clutching the wheel, she stared at the imposing black iron gate and exhaled in relief that she hadn't hit it. Her father would have tanned her hide if she'd damaged that elaborately curved and exorbitantly expensive ironwork.

"Oh, Mama . . ." she muttered as she collected her wits. Her mother had complained for years about how the tourists brazenly peeked into their walled garden or even through the windows. While gardening one Sunday morning a few months ago, her mother had turned her head to see a strange man standing inside their enclosed garden taking pictures as free as he pleased—

including one of her bent over pulling weeds. She'd screamed at him, but he'd only laughed and strolled away. Her first call was to the police and the next to an ironsmith. Of course, being Tradd Street, it had to be a skilled craftsman who could create an elaborate, Charleston-worthy gate in the style of Philip Simmons. Daddy'd had a fit when he saw the bill.

"Hell, Julia," he'd argued, "that fella just took a picture of your best side."

Mama had won the argument, of course, as she had with each improvement of the grand house on Tradd.

Linnea had completely forgotten about this when she turned into the driveway. Staring at it now, she had to admit that it was imposing, if annoying.

She dug through her purse and pulled out the slip of paper with the combination her mother had e-mailed to her. She raised her sunglasses, then carefully punched in the numbers, and with a gratifying click, the great gate smoothly split open. Linnea felt pretentious driving through and wondered if that was exactly the effect her mother had hoped for. After all, she did love panache.

Linnea parked in front of the stately cream stucco house and tapped the horn twice in announcement of her arrival. Manicured ivy climbed the walls of the garage along trellises—her mother wouldn't allow an untidy mess—and flowers exuberantly tumbled from classic Charleston window boxes. Linnea was always proud to bring her friends to her house near the famous Charleston Battery in the golden perimeter known as South of Broad. The handsome Greek revival never failed to impress with its gracious three-story piazza. But, in the end, it was just home.

She ran her fingers through her blond hair, which fell smooth and straight to her shoulders, the same cut she'd worn some version of since high school. She swiped on a bit of rosy lip gloss and blush to cover up the effects of one too many graduation parties the previous week. God knew, her mother had binocular vision when it came to telltale red eyes.

Linnea climbed out of the car and smoothed out her floral swing skirt. One of her passions was vintage clothing, especially from the 1950s. No sooner had she closed her door than her younger brother trotted around the house from the garden.

"Cooper!" she called out. Her knight in shining armor was coming to carry her luggage.

Cooper Pringle Rutledge was wearing baggy beige shorts frayed at the hem and a stretched-out Porter-Gaud T-shirt. He was in that adorable stage she liked to call a man-child. At eighteen, he was tall and long-legged like his aunt Cara. Like her, he took after the Rutledge side of the family with his thick, dark hair and eyes and his strong jaw and proud nose. He looked like a young John Kennedy. In contrast, Linnea was a tintype of her grandmother Olivia. Petite, blond, and blue-eyed, she fit the stereotype of a southern belle, even if the expectations chafed her.

Cooper trotted toward her with his friendly, gangly gait. He was restless, like his father, always tossing a ball in the air, rushing from place to place, playing sports, and perfecting his game. Linnea was more solitary. She preferred to read, sew her own vintage-style clothes, or walk outdoors and observe nature. The Tortoise and the Hare, her mother had called them growing up. The fact that Linnea was mad for sea turtles made the description apropos.

"Hey, Sis," Cooper called out. When he reached her side, he bent to kiss her cheek. "Nice to have you back."

"Nice of you to *not* make it to my graduation."

Cooper ducked his head with a wry grin. "Yeah, about that . . . sorry. It was the big Porter-Gaud–Bishop England basketball game."

"Bigger than my college graduation?" she asked, her words ringing with doubt.

"Yeah, well, I'm on the team." He looked up at her, eyes twinkling. "We can make it up when you come to my graduation next week."

Linnea could never stay mad at him. She socked him in the arm. "Yeah, well," she replied, teasing his phrasing, "I'll see if I can make it. I've got a lot of parties and all. . . ."

They laughed, both knowing she wouldn't miss it.

A shiny black pickup truck pulled up, dwarfing her car. She was blinded by the amount of chrome on the grille. The big engine rumbled loudly, and inside the cab she saw four boys she'd watched grow up since the first grade. She greeted them all warmly, congratulating them all on somehow managing to graduate high school.

"Gotta go," Cooper called out as he climbed into the truck—probably the driver's graduation gift.

Linnea was flabbergasted. "What? You're leaving? I just got here!"

He shrugged with an endearing grin, and she couldn't help but laugh. *That boy's smile is going to get him into trouble someday*, she thought as she called out, "Thanks for helping me with my luggage!"

The truck's engine roared with a show of testosterone and whipped out of the driveway. Before it squealed down the street, she heard Cooper bark out to a friend, "Shut up, that's my sister!"

Linnea shook her head and wondered what kind of trouble her brother was going to get into this time. Mama had called her just last week, worried to leave Cooper home alone for her graduation since Missy Bond's house had just been trashed by a graduation party.

She wiped away the perspiration forming along her brow. It was four o'clock on a steamy May afternoon. Summer had come early this year. The azaleas had bloomed in February, and it was already hitting the nineties. Early springs and late winters seemed to be the new normal.

She almost burned her fingers opening her trunk. "Thanks a lot, Cooper," she groaned upon seeing it packed to the gills. As she began tugging out the boxes, though, she heard the rumble of the garage door opening.

Rescue came in the form of her father.

"Daddy!"

"Hey, baby girl! Welcome home!"

She set a box down on the cement and hurried into his embrace. Her daddy, Palmer Rutledge, took after his mother's side. Like her, he was blond and blue-eyed. In bare feet he reached five feet eight inches, but most of his shoes boosted his height another inch. Being relatively short was a sore point between him and her aunt Cara. She was tall and dark; he was short and blond. Palmer claimed their mother got the genes mixed up.

He was a handsome man, dependably clean-shaven and well

presented in his usual uniform of polished shoes, a pale polo, and tan trousers. Looking at him in the full sun, Linnea could see his hair was thinning on top. His belly was fuller, too. But it was his ruddy cheeks so early in the day that concerned her. In his hand was a thick-cut crystal glass half-filled with ice and a brown liquid she'd bet good money was bourbon.

"It's a little early for a cocktail, isn't it?"

He squinted and shook the ice in his glass. "I got home early to see my little girl and now she's busting my chops?"

"Sorry, Daddy. I'm just teasing," she said quickly, though it wasn't true. When her parents had come up to Columbia the previous weekend for her graduation, Linnea had been shocked at how much her father drank. He downed bourbon like water, morning and night. When she'd mentioned it to her mother, Julia had simply tightened her lips and shaken her head, both in resignation and refusal to discuss it.

"Look at you," he said, holding her at arm's length. "I swear, you look more like my mama every day." He smiled wryly at her skirt. "Or maybe it's just 'cause you're wearing her clothes."

"Hey, Daddy," Linnea said with a teasing pout. "I made this skirt myself."

"It's right pretty," he said, and gently tapped her nose. "Just like you."

Palmer looked around as he walked toward her car trunk. "Where's Cooper? I sent him out here to fetch your luggage."

Linnea followed him. "He took off when a truck full of his friends pulled up. Lord, all those babies are becoming men already. Unleashed on an unsuspecting world."

"I swear, that boy's never around when you need him. He's perfected the art of the dodge."

"At least he made it through high school."

Her father made a face. "Thanks to a handshake and a hefty donation. Cooper never took to school like you did. He hasn't the sense God gave a mule."

"Oh, he's smart," Linnea countered, reaching into the trunk. Defending her little brother was second nature to her. "He's just lazy." She pulled out a box and handed it to her father. "And he sure is cute. The girls must be going crazy."

Palmer rubbed his jaw to hide his smile. It was obvious her father doted on the boy. "Can't shoo 'em away with a flyswatter." He narrowed his gaze on her. "What about you? You've got some fish on the hook I should meet?"

"Nope," Linnea said, turning back to the trunk.

"Why not?" he replied, hoisting the box. "You're as pretty as they come. I used to sleep with a shotgun by my bed when you were in high school for all the tomcats crying at your window."

She didn't reply because it was true. In high school she'd been an incorrigible flirt. With experience, however, she'd grown choosier.

Palmer started walking toward the house. Over his shoulder he called, "You're not getting any younger, you know."

Linnea felt the drag of the suitcase. "I'm only twenty-two! Hardly an old maid!"

"Your mama married me at your age." He set the box by the door with a thunk. "Graduation in May. A bride in June."

She wanted to say, *And look how well that turned out*, but she wasn't that stupid. Linnea just parked the luggage by the door, turned on her heel and walked back to the car to carry the last vestiges of her college life into her childhood home. With each step, she felt her family's expectations closing in around her.

~~~~~

THE SKY WAS as black as tar by the time Cara left the mainland to cross the Connector Bridge to the island. Few stars shone through the night, the moon was hidden by clouds, and the vast acres of salt marsh were as inky as the sky. Ahead, tiny red lights blinked on the island's water tower, and here and there golden light shone from a few houses. At last, she'd arrived.

"Isle of Palms."

The name slid from her mouth in a sigh. The gentle name of the small barrier island off the Charleston coast was synonymous with home to her. A sun-kissed place where visitors came to feel the caress of salt-tinged breezes, dip their toes into the warm waters of the Atlantic, and stare out over the expanse of sea and sky. Here they could escape from the sometimes overwhelming strains of a hectic life beyond the marshland. Her mama used to say that barrier islands protected the mainland from the storms. But in truth, the marshes protected the islands from the stress of the mainland.

Life was different on the islands. The pace was slower, the summer wind stronger. And that threat of losing all possessions during the hurricane season had taught Cara early that true joy came from loved ones, not loved things. Knowing that helped her feel free.

Cara flashed back to one particular blustery night when a tidal surge from a hurricane had pushed past the dunes to race through the house. She and her mama had huddled in the attic crawl space, clinging to each other while the water rose higher and higher. On that terrible night, Lovie had held her hand, looked deeply into her eyes, and told her she was leaving the beach house to her, because Lovie knew Cara understood the power of the beach house as a sanctuary.

And it was true. Cara had always been happy at the beach house. Her best memories had been born on this island. She prayed that many more happy memories were yet to be forged. She felt buoyed by an air of expectancy.

Out in the ocean's swells, the female loggerheads were biding their time, poised to swim to the beaches and begin the summer saga of nesting. Cara hoped it would be a good year, with lots of nests and thousands of turtle hatchlings to scramble to the sea. In a few weeks, the tourists would also return, swelling the island population to more than double. The summer was a busy time along the southeastern coast, but Cara wouldn't rent her beach house this summer. Or ever again.

This time, she was home to stay.

She turned west onto Palm Boulevard, then slowed when she passed the small gray-brick house on the creek that sat tucked behind a giant live oak tree. She'd spent ten happy years in that house with Brett. A stab of bittersweet memories hitched her breath. Widowhood was a lonely state of being. She'd worked fiercely to create a new life in Chattanooga, but after three years, she still mourned. Now a strange car was parked in the driveway.

With a quick sniff, Cara gripped the steering wheel and drove on. *No looking back*, she told herself. She hadn't returned to this island to wallow in the past. She'd come to build a new future, one filled with hope. Turning seaward, she drove the final few blocks. Anticipation thrummed in her veins the closer she got to home. Then she saw it: Primrose Cottage.

The pale-yellow house sat perched on the dune in the shadows of the starless night, dwarfed by the imposing mansions on either side, as small and demure as the wildflower it was named after. A few of the postwar cottages still remained on the island, nostalgic reminders of a quieter time long gone. Back when a nearly impassable maritime forest dominated the northern end.

Cara drove up the short, pebbled drive and came, at long last, to a shuddering stop. She leaned back against the headrest and breathed deeply, letting the sensation of miles flowing beneath her subside. "I'm home," she whispered, feeling the impact of the words radiate through her body. Home at last.

The porch light shone bright over the ocean-blue door, a beacon of warm welcome.

"Thank you, Emmi," she said, as a small smile of gratitude eased across her face. Emmaline Baker Peterson had been her best friend since childhood. She'd lived next door during the summer months for as long as Cara could remember. Cara knew she'd find milk, bread, and eggs in the fridge; fresh linens on the bed; and windows open to the evening breeze.

A whimpering noise from the backseat immediately brought her to attention. Cara swiftly glanced again in the rearview mirror. She smiled when she saw the sweet face staring back at her. The baby girl's large, dark eyes blinked sleepily under her dark brown curls as she yawned widely. Then her legs began to kick, and her plump hands moved in agitation as she started whimpering again. Cara jumped into action. The precious child had slept for hours with nary a peep.

"I'm coming," Cara said, and quickly released her seat belt. She swung open the car door and stepped out into the moist, balmy air. She paused a moment, breathing in the welcoming scents of wildflowers and sea after hours in the cramped, air-conditioned car. But another whimper sent her scrambling to the rear door.

"I'm here," she crooned as she lifted the year-old child into her arms, bringing her tight against her breast. The baby smelled of milk and soap and something intangible God put there in His wisdom to protect the innocents. She kissed the top of her head, feeling the delicate strands of hair graze her lips. Soft as a prayer.

"Welcome home, Hope!"

~~~~~~

CARA BALANCED THE baby on her left hip as she struggled to find the right key to the front door. On the ground was a box with a chirping bird inside. The baby was slipping, and her arm strained to maintain her grip. At last a key slid in and the lock clicked. With a gusty sigh, she pushed open the front door and hoisted Hope higher on her hip. "We're here," she said, and stepped inside.

She immediately felt the welcome of the beach house. All was in readiness. The floors had been washed, furniture dusted, flowers set in vases. She could smell the oil soap. A small table lamp shone golden light across the living room. Not a chair or painting was out of place. All was just as she'd left it three years earlier.

Cara was humbled by her friend's thoughtfulness. After a long day's drive, she didn't have to open the door to a steamy, stagnant, and stuffy house. She always had so much on her mind, projects and endless to-do lists, so when a friend took the time to do something thoughtful to make her life easier—better—just because she cared, Cara had to stop and remember that life was so much more than a job's progress or a list of accomplishments. Life, if lived well, was enjoying random acts of kindness that elicited joy from giver and receiver alike. Each time she was reminded of this, she vowed to try to be a better giver than a receiver.

This was one of the reasons she'd returned to this beach house on Isle of Palms. Cara needed the help of her friends and family to learn how to be a good mother to Hope.

And I need the security of this little house, she thought as she surveyed the small rooms. The beach house was not grand, but it had loads of vintage charm. A row of windows overlooked the breadth of the Atlantic Ocean and gave the house an open, airy feeling. Even now when the ocean was cloaked in the evening's velvety blackness, she could hear the gentle roll of the waves through the open windows, as soothing as a cat's purr.

Even though the beach house was now hers, in her mind it would always be the cottage of Olivia Rutledge, Lovie to all who knew her. It had changed little over the years. The art on the walls had been painted by her mother's friends, local artists. The same ruby and blue Oriental rugs colored the wood floors. Even the plump upholstered furniture was Lovie's. When Cara took it over, she didn't want to change a thing; she'd simply freshened it up. She'd painted the walls a soft ocean blue with crisp white trim, replaced the Palm Beach-y chintz with durable white fabric, and removed the countless knickknacks her mother had in every nook and cranny.

"What do you think?" she asked Hope with a gentle squeeze. "Shabby chic, but not too shabby, eh?"

The baby looked back at her with wide, uncomprehending eyes. Chuckling, Cara kissed her cheek. "Well, we look a bit shabby after that long drive. And," she added with a sniff, "you smell like you could use a change. Let's freshen you up. How does that sound?"

She went out the front door to pick up the bird box. Her canary, Moutarde, skittered about but didn't utter a sound. She set the box on the table, then made a beeline to her childhood bedroom down the hall. She paused at the door, stunned by the transformation. Her old black iron bed was gone, and in its place was a brand-new white crib dolled up with pink floral sheets and ribbon-trimmed blankets. Where her painted wooden desk had once sat was a cushy white upholstered rocking chair with pink piping and a small bookshelf filled with children's books. Cara laughed aloud at seeing the sweet green-and-pink-shaded lamp—it was a sea turtle. Emmi had raised two boys but had always wanted a girl.

"She must've had a field day fixing up your room," she told Hope as she laid her on the changing table. She chatted with the baby to distract her from getting her diaper changed. "You're going to love your aunt Emmi. I've known her since I was just a bit older than you. No one has a smile like Aunt Emmi." Cara envisioned her friend's wide, Carly Simon smile. "She's going to make you laugh. Oh yes she will," she added, tickling Hope's belly and eliciting a giggle. "And smother you with kisses." She nuzzled Hope's cheeks. Cara had never known what joy a baby's laughter could bring.

"And your Aunt Flo," she continued, reaching into her baby bag and pulling out footie pajamas. Cara still felt clumsy in her newfound motherhood and secretly feared she was doing something wrong. For her, it was all trial and error. "Aunt Flo will tell you the best stories," she said as she lifted Hope into her arms. "Most of them about turtles. She used to take care of me when I was your age."

Cara set Hope inside the crib, noting the quick frown of disapproval that flashed across the baby's face. "It's okay," she crooned. "Just stay here and play with this turtle." She placed a stuffed toy in Hope's lap. "I'll be right back."

Hope immediately began to protest, lifting her arms and crying to be picked up. Cara's heart pinged. She couldn't bear to hear Hope cry. "I just have to get the suitcases," she explained with a hint of panic. "I'll only be a minute."

Hope was having none of it. Her cries followed Cara down the hall and out to the car. They spurred her on like stings from a whip. She dragged suitcases, bags of baby supplies, and personal belongings out of the rear of the car and up the gravel drive and front stairs, not pausing for a breath and working up a sweat. She dragged in the last bag and plopped it on the kitchen counter, winded.

"No wonder only young women have babies," she muttered.

She cast a weary glance at the pile of brown bags littering the kitchen, but a boisterous cry from Hope focused her anew. "A bottle," she muttered, and rushed to the kitchen sink to fill the teakettle. "Mama's coming!" she called out as she set it on the stove.

As the water heated, Cara put her fingertips to her temples to calm herself. She had adopted Hope in February, and with that single decision she'd once again changed her life. The past four months had been a steep learning curve for a woman in her fifties who had never had much to do with children. A single woman at that. Cara was never one to let the moss grow under her feet, however. Once a decision was made, action followed.

She'd given notice to the Tennessee Aquarium that she was resigning her position as the PR director—a job she'd loved—and made plans to move home to Isle of Palms to raise her child. Despite her seeming confidence, there were times, such as now, when the professional businesswoman was a complete and utter klutz.

The baby began howling. From the box on the dining room table she heard the worried peeps from her bird. With mounting hysteria Cara ripped through her carefully packed bags in search of bottles and formula. She tossed bottles, nipples, and tops onto the counter and finally found a matched set. But her success was short-lived. Opening the formula tin was like breaking into Fort Knox. Especially with her shaky fingers. Just as she pried off the stubborn lid at last, the kettle whistled, and jolting forward to grab it, she bumped the open jar of formula powder. She watched in horror as it plummeted in slow motion to the floor, exploding white, powdery milk all over the clean hardwood.

Cara gasped and stared disbelievingly at the mess. "No, no, no," she cried, dropping to all fours and scooping what she could back into the container. As soft and fine as talcum powder, the disrupted formula created milky clouds in the air.

In that ignominious moment, all the stress of the baby's incessant crying mixed with the strain of quitting her job in Tennessee, packing up their things to move to South Carolina, and the long, exhausting drive came crashing down on her. She slid her long legs across the floor, leaned against the counter, and brought her powdery hands to her face as her cries blended with the baby's.

Who did she think she was fooling? She was hopeless when it came to mothering. An utter and complete failure. She was a fifty-three-year-old career woman. Her résumé was great for a PR executive, but she'd never bag a job as a mother. She couldn't even make a bottle without screwing up.

At moments like this, her greatest fear would surface. *Was it a mistake to adopt Hope?*

Help me, Mama, she cried into her hands.

The baby's cries pierced through her desolation. Cara was never one to wallow in doubt and self-pity. Her nature was to get things done. And that bottle wasn't going to make itself. She finished scooping up as much formula as she could and dragged herself to her feet. She washed the powder from her hands and face, and with a determined swipe of her nose on her sleeve, she started anew to prepare the bottle. She worked quickly, with steady hands, but as she shook the bottle, she suddenly noticed the house had gone quiet. She froze. Hope had stopped crying.

Cara turned on her heel and rushed to the bedroom. She screeched to a halt at the door and sucked in her breath. Fear fluttered in her heart. But as she slowly exhaled, the fear dissipated and wonder took its place. It was as if time were standing still. A hazy white light shimmered near the crib. Hope was standing, clutching the railing. No longer crying, her face bore the sweetest grin of pleasure as she cooed and babbled at the glowing light beside her.

And in that shimmering light Cara saw her mother, or rather, a ghost of Lovie. Transparent yet real. There was no mistaking her. Lovie's hair was pulled back in her usual chignon, her profile serene as she gazed at the child. Then, in a breath, her mother turned her head and looked up.

Cara felt the unspeakable power of a mother's gaze. The light seemed to enter her soul, permeate her being, and warm her. Reassure her. Comfort her. Lovie smiled, and Cara felt the weight of her hopelessness lift from her shoulders. In that miraculous instant, she knew she was going to be all right.

Then, in a blink, the light disappeared, and Lovie was gone.

"Mama?" she called out. Cara suddenly wondered if she'd imagined it all. She shook her head and looked down at Hope. The child gazed back at her with innocent eyes.

Cara hugged the little girl and crooned softly as she rocked her in her arms. The room was filled with the scent of jasmine. Her mother's scent.

"Thank you, Mama."

Chapter Two

The scientific name for loggerheads is Caretta caretta. *It is the third largest of seven sea turtle species, including the leatherback, olive ridley, hawksbill, flatback, green sea turtle, and Kemp's ridley.*

THE MORNING SUN crept into the room like a thief, slipping through openings in the plantation shutters and stealing away precious moments of sleep. Outside her window a cardinal sang his dawn song as strident as a bugle's call, signaling the start of a bright spring day. Cara plopped a pillow over her head with a groan. Every muscle ached from the push of packing and the long drive. Plus, Hope had awoken three or four times in the night. She was teething, poor dear, but they were both paying the price for it. Cara yawned. Even her bones ached. She wanted to sleep for hours.

No sooner did drowsiness slide over her again than she heard a short cry from Hope. Cara held her breath, hoping it was a passing whimper and she would be able to go back to sleep. But no . . . the dulcet tones of Hope's cries soon joined the birdsong. She groaned again. *This* song she couldn't ignore. She tossed off the pillow and covers, then dragged herself out of the cushy bed.

Her mother's four-poster was high off the ground and dominated the room. The floors and trim were dark wood, but everything else was white—the walls, the lace curtains, the crisp bed linen. Unlike the rest of the house, where paintings covered the walls, only one hung in this room. It had been her mother's favorite, commissioned when Cara and her brother, Palmer, were very young. In it, two children played together on the beach, building a sand castle with a bucket and spade, the boy with white-blond hair, the girl's dark. The island had been a paradise for Cara and her brother growing up, and she intended to pass on that lifestyle to her own daughter.

She rose and went to the bathroom to splash cool water on her face. She glanced in the mirror as she patted her face dry, then lowered her hands and studied her reflection. She let her fingers comb through her very short hair. Seeing the new style still had the power to startle her. She'd worn her thick, dark hair to her shoulders, or longer, all her life. It was a glossy mane, an enviable feature and arguably one of her better ones. When she'd adopted Hope, however, she wanted to make a different statement. Cutting her hair short seemed a powerful way to embark on a journey of personal transformation. What better way to begin than with the literal cutting off of the old and starting anew?

Hope was standing in the crib, her arms outstretched, when Cara arrived. She paused, her heart beating quicker. She never failed to be amazed that this sweet baby wanted *her* and accepted *her* as her mother . . . despite her ineptness. Cara brought the baby close to her, kissing her cheeks that were still flushed and warm from sleep. *Ah, yes,* she thought. *This makes waking up at dawn worth it.*

She changed Hope's diaper, grateful it was just wet, and managed to fasten all the snaps and buttons without caffeine. She plodded into the kitchen, then stopped and surveyed the mess of scattered bottles and spilled formula from the night before. She took a deep breath.

"Our first day home," she told Hope with a gentle shake of encouragement. "Let's make it a good one."

After a few clumsy attempts at keeping Hope from rummaging through the bags, she managed to get the high chair set up and Hope strapped safely in. She set a few Cheerios in front of her, then began to clean the floor and counters, still groggy from lack of caffeine.

Suddenly the kitchen door flew open and an elderly woman breezed in. Her bright white hair was cut short, and she wore brown nylon cargo pants and a green TURTLE TEAM T-shirt. Her blue eyes were as bright as a torch, and she was all smiles.

"Caretta!"

"Flo!" Cara exclaimed, her hand at her heart. She shouldn't have been surprised. Flo had freely strolled into her kitchen for as long as she could remember. Her mother's best friend, Flo Prescott was like a second mother to Cara and Emmi, especially since both of their mothers had passed. Cara ran into the old woman's arms.

"You scared me half to death!"

"Welcome home, baby girl," Flo said, her soft arms wrapping

around Cara and patting her on the back. She leaned back and gently shook Cara's shoulders, her bright eyes shining. "Took you long enough."

Cara took a moment to absorb the shock of Flo's aging. Her skin was paler, her short hair wispy at the crown, and the sharp gleam in her eyes dimmed. It had only been a year since she had last seen her . . . but in that short time, Flo had aged dramatically.

"Hey, girlfriend!" Behind her a younger woman with fiery red hair and a wide grin entered with beckoning arms. This one hadn't changed at all.

"Emmi!" Cara ran to her, lingering a moment in her best friend's tight embrace, comforted by her familiar scent. She was transported back to childhood. School was out, she'd just arrived on the island, and the first thing she did was run straight to Emmi Baker's house. They'd squeal as they ran into each other's arms and hug as if they'd been apart for ages instead of one school year. Now women, they still hugged each other with the same enthusiasm.

"Lord, I've missed you," Emmi said into her ear with a squeeze.

"It's so good to see you both again. I've missed you, too," Cara said, pulling back. Emmi was already lightly tanned and her nose and cheeks were sprinkled with freckles. They were the same age, born only a week apart, and when Cara saw the wrinkles forming around Emmi's eyes and on her forehead, she knew Emmi was spotting them on her face as well. Thanks to L'Oréal, neither of them showed any gray. Emmi's hair was the same Scottish red. The only change was the additional pounds she'd gained each year since menopause that seemed to settle in her hips. *Broad in the beam*, as Lovie used to say.

Emmi scrunched up her face. "You haven't changed a bit. Except for your hair. You cut it!"

Cara's hand flew to her cropped hair. "I needed a change. What do you think?"

Emmi crossed her arms and narrowed her eyes as she considered it. "Very Anne Hathaway of you. You still look sensational, damn you. With your bone structure, you can pull off that short hair. Me? I'd look like Howdy Doody. If he had big hips."

Emmi's big smile and laugh were so infectious that Cara had to laugh too.

"I've put on almost ten pounds this year," Emmi told her with a pat on her belly. "I started watching TV and stopped exercising. But the turtle team season has started and I'm out on the beach walking every day. It'll drop off."

"If you lay off the wine," Flo muttered.

"Never!" Emmi fired back with a laugh. "Speaking of which," she said to Cara, "there should be a few bottles in the fridge."

"I can't thank you enough for all you did to get the house ready. I didn't get in until very late, and it made all the difference in the world to have a clean house and fresh sheets."

Flo just waved her hand in friendly dismissal. "Pshaw. It was nothing. You'd do the same for us. Now, enough talk. Where's that baby?" Her sharp gaze darted around; spotting the baby, she clapped her hands together. "Look at you!" she exclaimed, making a beeline toward Hope. "Aren't you precious? Give me some sugar."

Cara watched with uncertainty as Flo bustled toward the baby. Hope's eyes widened and her lips quivered. Flo was a dear, but her personality could come on a little strong sometimes.

"Don't pounce. You'll scare her!" Emmi admonished.

Flo stopped and looked back, confused. But it was too late. Hope scrunched up her face and wailed.

Cara rushed to pick her up and soothe her. It wasn't how she'd hoped this first meeting would go. She wanted Flo and Emmi to love Hope just as much as she did.

"She's tired," she said by way of excuse. "Neither of us got much sleep last night. She's teething and must've woken up half a dozen times."

"Oh, honey, no worries. It's just the strange place," Emmi said. "She doesn't know where she is, is all. She'll get used to it." She laughed. "In time." She bent at the waist and spoke to Hope in high-pitched baby talk. "Well, hey there, butter bean. Aren't you a pretty thing? I'm your aunt Emmi. I've been waiting to meet you. We're going to be the best of friends."

Cara watched as Hope listened, eyes wide and clutching Cara's robe. She rewarded Emmi with a shaky smile.

"Well, lookee there," Flo said with a shake of her head. "I guess I am a tad loud for babies."

"Hope just needs to get to know you," Cara was quick to reply. "Soon she'll be running over to your house like Emmi and I did. And you'll teach her all about the sea turtles, like Mama would have."

Flo took a seat at the table and rested her elbow on it. "I expect *you'll* be teaching her all about the turtles. You're coming back on the turtle team, aren't you?"

Cara puffed out a breath. "In time," she replied, hedging.

"The time is now," Flo said matter-of-factly. "Season's already begun. We've got three nests already."

"Three already? We don't usually get any till *maybe* next week."

"We had the earliest nest on record. April thirtieth."

"April?" Cara repeated, stunned.

"So, we're off and running." Flo paused, and shrugged wearily. "I'm not as up-and-at-'em as I once was. Moving a bit slower now. Emmi could use some help on the team."

Cara felt Hope's body meld into hers, as though she'd always belonged in her arms. This little one had changed her every decision.

"I don't know," she said in a tone that implied *no*. "Mornings are pretty unpredictable with Hope. I can't just tell her to wait for breakfast."

"Why not?"

"Flo!" Emmi said with a guffaw. "What you know about babies wouldn't fill a thimble." To Cara she added, "I think we should let her babysit one morning and see for herself."

Flo shot Emmi a withering look.

"You'll both have ample opportunities to babysit," Cara said, putting Hope back into the high chair. After a few squawks, Hope relinquished her grip on Cara's robe, and soon her chubby fingers were grabbing Cheerios. Cara brought her hand to her throbbing head. "I can't make a decision until I make coffee."

Emmi rushed to the sink. "I'll make the coffee. You sit."

"Thank you. I *am* tired. Everyone always tells you how glorious it is to have a baby. How cute they are. How fulfilling. And that's all true. . . . But no one tells you how *hard* it is physically. It's been a grueling few months. Honestly, when I look back, I can't believe how completely my life changed in such a short span of time. Utterly and completely changed."

Emmi filled the kettle, then put it on the stove to boil. "We really don't know very much about it."

"And we've got a lot of questions," added Flo. She indicated the child with a thrust of her chin.

"I'm sure you do. Let me get Hope settled before I launch into my story." Cara ran her hand through her tousled hair and sighed. "It's a long one and complicated." She rose.

"I'll do it," Emmi said. "Just tell me what you want done."

"It's easier if I just do it myself." Cara went to the counter and mixed dry baby cereal with formula as Emmi gathered mugs, pulled cream from the fridge, and scooped tablespoons of ground coffee into the paper filter. Cara couldn't help but notice how Flo stayed seated and was gently tapping her fingers on the high chair to amuse Hope. Years back, Flo would've been a tornado in the kitchen, pushing them aside to get the tasks done.

Soon the heady scent of freshly brewed coffee filled the air. Cara carried a steaming mug in one hand and the baby's bowl in the other. Emmi carried two more cups and handed the one with lots of milk and one teaspoon of sugar to Flo, her familiarity a product of the two women sharing the house next door for more than ten years.

Cara spooned cereal into Hope's mouth, and for several minutes the women watched in silent amusement as the little girl opened her mouth eagerly, fists clenched, for every bite.

Flo said, "She looks like a baby bird."

"She has a good appetite," Cara said a bit smugly.

"Count your blessings," Emmi said. "For as tall as my boys grew, they were finicky eaters. Mealtimes were battles."

Flo chuckled. "Well, you won the war. You raised some strapping fellows."

Emmi smiled with satisfaction. "I did." She sipped her coffee.

Emmi's older son, James, was a surgeon living in Chapel Hill. He was married and had made her a grandmother. "How old is Jamie now?"

"I have to think," Emmi said with a short laugh, and counted on her fingers. "Thirty-one."

"You have a thirty-one-year-old son," Cara said, bringing another spoonful to Hope's open mouth. "And here I am raising a one-year-old. It's rather daunting. And that makes John . . ." She paused, doing the math. "Thirty?"

"Last month."

"What I want to know is how you found this sweet baby to adopt," Flo said. "You don't tell us anything until that phone call announcing you'd adopted a baby girl. You could've knocked me over with a feather."

"What do you mean?" Emmi asked. "Cara always wanted to adopt. Don't you remember? It was Brett who didn't want to." She darted a look at Cara, gauging how she reacted to the mention of Brett's name.

"I did," Cara said in a calm tone. Hearing Brett's name was still a pinprick in her heart, but after three years she could handle it. "But that was while I was married. After Brett died, I didn't pursue adoption. As a single older woman, I didn't think I had much of a chance."

"That's not true," Flo said. As a former social worker, this was her area of expertise. "I'm long retired, but I keep up in my field.

More people are adopting later in life than ever before. Age is no barrier, except you still have to be twenty-one."

"So I learned. . . ." Cara let her fingertips gently smooth back the soft curls from Hope's face. "Hope found me." Cara spooned the last bit of cereal into Hope's mouth, dabbed away the mess with the bib, then wrestled her out of the high chair and into her lap.

"Let me hold her," Emmi said, setting down her mug. She came over and smiled at the baby, hands out.

No one could resist Emmi's smile. Cara was convinced that was what had snagged the boy both of them were angling for in seventh grade. Hope fell for the charm too and went willingly into Emmi's arms.

"You didn't pursue the adoption?" Flo continued. "Then how . . . ?"

Cara paused, gathering the pertinent details of the long and emotional story. "I met this young woman while working at the aquarium. She was an intern. Pretty, vivacious, a bright girl. She was interested in nonprofits, particularly in PR, so she latched on to me." She smiled in memory of the girl she'd grown fond of over the year. "We got along well—you know how I love mentoring young women: Toy, Heather. And then Elena. That was her name. In a way, each of them was like a daughter to me. I guess that makes me the proverbial wise old crone." She laughed and looked down at the channel-set diamond wedding band she wore on her right hand now. Her smile faded, remembering how this story ended.

"Elena shadowed me for several months, and we grew quite

close. Neither of us knew many people in the city. She was from Mexico; did I mention that?"

The two women shook their heads.

"But her English was flawless. We would have lunch together at work, and once we even went to a Spanish guitar concert together. Then she just disappeared." She lifted her shoulders. "No good-bye, no note. Nothing. I was hurt, I can't lie. But I wrote it off to the callousness of youth."

Hope made a noise, but Emmi gave her the spoon, which she promptly inserted into her mouth.

Cara continued in a somber voice: "It wasn't callousness at all, though. I should have known that wasn't like Elena." She paused. "It turned out she was pregnant. Apparently a one-night stand with some American boy she thought was cute. She drank too much. . . ." She shrugged and lifted her palms as if to say, *You know the rest of this story.*

"'Apparently'?" asked Emmi. "You don't know?"

Cara shook her head. "I never talked to Elena. Never saw her again. One day last January I got a message from Social Services. They told me that Elena had died after a car crash and that she had a daughter. They contacted me because Elena had listed me as next of kin at the hospital."

"Next of kin? But . . ." Emmi tilted her head. "Can she do that? You're not related."

"Apparently she can."

"Next of kin is a legal term," Flo explained. "But . . ." She turned again to Cara. "The agency seeks first to place the child with family, a relative. Didn't she have parents? Grandparents?"

"She does. In Mexico. Elena was in the country illegally, so it slowed the investigation down. Eventually they tracked her family down through the school she was enrolled in in Chattanooga. Turns out they're a well-to-do family, and I'm sure they were heartbroken by the news. But according to the agency, they were ashamed that Elena had had a child in America and cut her off."

"Imagine cutting your child off in a foreign country," said Emmi. "There's nothing my boys could do that would make me that kind of angry."

"We don't know what really happened," Flo said. "They may have offered to fly her home, put the baby up for adoption."

Cara spoke again. "Poor Elena. Whatever they said, she didn't feel like she could go home, and she remained here as an illegal alien. Trapped between a rock and a hard place. Pregnant, alone, and then with a new baby. It must've been very hard. She worked as a maid at a hotel." Cara exhaled heavily. "Now that I'm taking care of Hope, I swear, I don't know how she managed."

"Horrible. Sad," Flo said, her eyes flashing. "I've seen that happen far too often."

"That was pretty much Toy's story," recalled Emmi. "Her parents gave her the boot and Lovie took her in."

Cara remembered the bumpy road she'd traveled with Toy Sooner, her mother's caretaker, when she'd arrived at the beach house after leaving Chicago. She'd been jealous of their relationship at first, but in time she came to feel like Toy's older sister. She adored Toy and was an aunt to her daughter, Little Lovie. That sweet child had filled a deep void in her and Brett's life during the years they'd tried for a child of their own.

"I only wish Elena had tried to contact me. I'd have helped her. I remember how tough it was when I first left home. My parents had abandoned me. I felt I was on my own with no one looking out for me."

"You made it," Emmi said with admiration.

Cara nodded. She didn't think she could ever fully explain to her best friend how hard and lonely those years of being young, alone, and without support had been and what they had cost her.

"Look how far Toy has come," Emmi added.

"I'm sure Elena could have too. But she'll never have the chance now. . . ."

The women lapsed into silence, each brooding over the sadness of the situation.

Flo scratched her head. "I'm trying to get this straight. The agency tried to place the baby with relatives first. And no one claimed her? No uncles or aunts?"

Cara shook her head. "No one."

"So they contacted you."

"Yes."

"Extraordinary." Flo smirked. "I'm guessing they did an assessment to determine you were, as they say, fit and willing?"

"Oh, yes," Cara replied with an eye roll. "Honestly, I didn't think I'd pass the grade. A single woman in my fifties. On the one hand, getting older isn't easy on the ego. But on the other hand, I can be proud that I'm financially stable and"—she lifted her brows in mock modesty—"relatively mature. We older parents have devoted decades to building careers and are now ready to say yes to being parents."

She took a long sip of her coffee and set the mug back on the table. "And a lot of us are women like me who've spent years trying. Infertility treatments, waiting and waiting, only to be disappointed. The heartbreak. The money spent. The years wasted. All those years dreaming and hoping. Then giving up. And then suddenly this . . ." Even now, after all these months, the realization had the power to give her pause. "This opportunity to be a mother came out of nowhere. I was speechless. A deer caught in the headlights. I swear I couldn't breathe for days while I agonized over the decision."

"But why?" Emmi asked. "You'd wanted this for so long. It was a gift."

"I wasn't sure if I was up to the task."

"Why didn't you call me?" asked Emmi, her voice gentled.

"I couldn't. I didn't want to call anyone. This decision I had to make alone."

"I guess I can see that," Emmi said softly.

"I had a lot to think about. Was I too old? What would I do about my job? Could I afford it? Did I want to be a mother at my age? When Brett died, that dream died with him. I was trying hard . . . so hard . . . to move on. To make a new life for myself."

Emmi reached out to place her hand on Cara's arm in unspoken understanding.

"Then one night I had this dream. It was so real, like watching a scene in a movie, only I was in it. Mama, too. I could smell her perfume." She looked at Emmi and Flo to gauge their reaction. The two women had leaned forward, listening intently. "It was during the hurricane, that last summer with Mama."

"Ah, yes," Flo said in a breath of understanding.

"The tidal surge had pushed into the house, and the water was rising foot by foot. I'll never forget walking through the blood-warm water in the middle of the night, worrying about snakes or God knew what else. We were sitting in the dusty, steamy attic space, holding on to each other while the wind screamed and tore at the roof overhead and the inky waters rose higher in the house."

Cara shivered in memory.

"But despite the storm's fury, Mama was as calm as the eye of the hurricane." Cara could feel again her mother's arms around her. "I heard her voice as clear as a bell in my dream. She told me the same thing she did that night. She spoke in that same raspy voice. Remember that?"

"Of course," said Emmi.

"It was from all the coughing," added Flo.

Emmi prodded, "So what did she say?"

Cara wiped her eyes, remembering. "I'm sorry. I'm just tired."

Emmi reached for her hand. "We miss her too."

"That night I asked Mama," Cara continued, "'How will I find my happiness? How will I know?' Mama cupped my face and smiled. I swear, in my dream I felt the force of that smile enter my soul like a beam of light. It gave me strength, filled me with faith. 'You'll know, my precious,' she told me. 'One day you'll look up and see it—and just know.'"

She looked at Flo and Emmi, silent and thoughtful.

"When I awoke the following morning, I was filled with a sense of peace. Like a storm passing, my mind was clear. Later that day I met Hope for the first time. It might sound strange, but it felt predestined. I looked at her and I just knew she was mine."

"Oh, Cara . . ." Emmi said.

"And I knew I had to come home. I want to raise Hope here, at the beach house where I've been happy and where I hope she will be too. Here, with you." She squeezed Emmi's hand. "And you." She looked over to Flo and met the older woman's blue gaze. "And Toy and Ethan, Heather and Bo, Palmer and Julia, Linnea, Cooper. You're my family. I need you. And so does Hope."

"It takes a village," Flo said in summary.

"We're here. Right next door. And our door's always open."

Cara nodded, taking a resolute breath. "I know."

"By the way, did you name her Hope?" asked Emmi. "Because it's kind of perfect."

Cara shook her head and looked at Hope, her dark brown eyes never wavering from Cara's. She felt the love for her child pumping through her veins. "Elena named her Esperanza. 'Hope' in English."

Emmi smiled. "Like I said. Perfect."

Chapter Three

*Loggerheads have gorgeous reddish-brown carapaces and get
their name from their massive heads and strong jaws that
can crack hard-shelled creatures like conch, crab,
clams, mussels, and sea urchins.*

IT WAS STRANGE living back under her parents' roof. For the last
four years, Linnea had lived an independent life. She liked
being able to do what she wanted, when she wanted. That freedom
had been hard-won from her hovering parents, and she wasn't willing to relinquish it.

Although, she thought with a glance around her room, *it is a
beautiful prison*. Linnea was lying on her back, legs crossed, on her
four-poster rice bed. Their house on Tradd Street was a historic
gem. Her grandmother, Lovie, had restored it from near ruin back
in the 1960s when she and her grandfather, Stratton, bought it.
Lovie had returned the great house to its original state of elegance.
She'd expanded the gardens, too, and to this day, the house was on

the city's garden tour schedule. When Linnea's father inherited the house from his parents, her mother had upheld Lovie's standards. Julia truly loved the house and had not only maintained it but also updated it with impeccable taste befitting the treasured family antiques. Her daddy was always complaining about the cost, but Linnea knew he was proud of the family home.

Linnea's room had once been her aunt Cara's. Her mother had redecorated it with gorgeous wallpaper covered with creamy white magnolias. She also had her own bathroom with vintage black-and-white linoleum that she'd begged her mother to keep. Cooper slept in his father's childhood room down the long hallway with a guest room in between—which suited her just fine. The house was divided into "the upstairs" and "the downstairs." Though never spoken, it was understood that the upstairs was spared her parents' purview, since their master suite was on the main floor.

Linnea stretched out on her mattress, closing her eyes. Her head was still spinning and her mouth felt like it was filled with cotton after last night. The long string of graduation parties was continuing in Charleston as more of her high school friends returned home from colleges all across the country. Texts were blowing up her phone. She opened her eyes and checked her texts.

Dale back! Party at the Darling at 8

Going to the darling? Can I borrow your red Louboutins?

Leslie's is on SI. Bring wine . . . lots of wine

She found the endless round of parties to be just a continuation of the college weekend binge drinking. Only it seemed to be a perpetual weekend. They were blending one into the other—lots of drinking, laughing, acting like high school students again. She could predict what the next round of parties would be. Dale's would be a private dinner party for twelve in a private room in a restaurant thrown by his exuberant parents, who were thrilled he'd been accepted to med school. Then it was on to Jessica's family beach house on Sullivan's Island. The cottage would be crammed from porch to rafter.

Linnea had had way too much to drink at last night's party. She usually wasn't a heavy drinker, but last night, Darby Middleton had shown up. They'd been serious in high school and he'd been her escort to her debut at the St. Cecilia Ball. But their parents' calculated efforts and not-so-subtle hints, like showing how beautiful her new monogram would be, helped split them up. They went their separate ways in college—he to Sewanee and she to USC. Last night, however, Darby had looked even more handsome than she remembered. Unfortunately, he ruined the impression by getting too handsy in a dark corner. She'd remembered him being a good kisser, but something was missing. As with the parties, Linnea had grown bored and pushed him away.

She and her girlfriends had ended up crashing on the spare beds of the beach house like a pile of puppies rather than risk driving home. She'd risen at the crack of dawn, drunk gallons of water, then made her way back to Charleston. Thankfully the iron gates didn't squeak. She'd tiptoed into the house as quiet as a mouse, careful not to awaken her parents, then spent the day in her room, sleeping and drinking coconut water for hydration.

She put her arm over her eyes to quiet her throbbing temples. She was finished with these endless parties. She felt restless, but she wasn't sure what her next step should be. She was a college graduate. She was supposed to be a grown-up ready to tackle a nine-to-five job, Monday through Friday. The trouble was, she couldn't find a job in her field and she had no idea what to do without one. Should she seek an internship? But she'd done that, and it felt like just postponing her leap into the real world. Marriage was not even on the table, much to her mother's despair. Maybe grad school? But she hadn't a clue what area to focus on. She'd been searching for a job for months. Organizations wouldn't hire her because she didn't have experience, yet no one was giving her a job to *get* that experience. It was all such a merry-go-round and so very frustrating.

The dinner bell sounded. Linnea groaned. She hated that dinner bell. Her mother had brought back an enormous cowbell from Switzerland and thought it was a clever way to call the children to dinner. It might've been clever when Linnea was ten years old, but at twenty-two, it was insulting. She pushed herself up on her elbows. Her mother would bang that damn bell until she came running.

"Coming!" Linnea called out, then grimaced as pain ricocheted through her head. There wasn't enough water and aspirin in the world to flush this hangover away. With an aggrieved sigh, she slid from her bed and walked into her bathroom. She splashed cold water on her face, relishing the shock to her sluggish system. She stared back at her face, pale and wan, from behind the towel. She looked terrible. Her blue eyes were traitorously red-rimmed and puffy. She rummaged through her makeup drawer for eyedrops and a bit of brown shadow. Then she added blush to her cheeks and even applied lip gloss. Finally, she ran a brush through her blond hair and pulled it back with a clasp. She had to pass her mother's radar. She slipped a green vintage sundress over her head and while she did up the front buttons slid her feet into sandals.

The bell rang again, more persistently this time. Linnea turned off the light, but instead of going directly downstairs, she took a detour to check on her brother. She raised her fist in the air to knock, then paused to sniff. There was no mistaking the scent of pot. She knocked once and swung open the door without waiting for a reply. In the darkened room her brother slept like the dead, snoring and stretched out on his belly, his feet hanging over the side of the mattress. Apparently, the dinner bell hadn't registered through his haze. She crinkled her nose at the stench of stale alcohol.

"Cooper. Get up," she said, wiggling his foot. "It's dinnertime."

He waved her away drunkenly. "Go away."

"It reeks in here."

No reply. She wiggled his foot again but only got a grunt for a response. At least he was alive. She drew closer and gave his shoulders a hard shake.

"Whaaat?"

"Get up. It's dinnertime."

"Don' wann any," he slurred.

"What time did you get in last night?"

"One," he mumbled against his pillow.

"That's not too late."

"Afternoon."

"What?" Linnea was stunned. "You stayed out all night?"

He only grunted in reply.

"Mama's going to kill you."

"She knows."

Linnea felt frustration bubble in her veins. If she'd dared stay out all night in high school, she'd have been disowned.

"I went fishing." Cooper turned to his side. His dark curls fell over his thick brows, covering his bloodshot eyes.

Linnea smirked. She knew fishing and hunting weekends at the lodge were nothing but excuses for the boys to go out to the country and drink themselves senseless. God help anyone fool enough to put a gun in their hands. She hated to think what would happen.

"Well, come on, then. You need some food in your stomach."

He groaned and fell back on his stomach. "Can't. Sick."

Linnea looked around the darkened room. Clothes were strewn upon the floor, drawers were spilling over, and dirty dishes cluttered the desk. It smelled like a sty. A flicker of worry brought her closer to sit on the edge of his bed.

"Hey," she asked in a gentler tone, "are you okay?"

"Yeah."

"Look at me."

"Go away."

"I'm serious. Look at me."

Cooper groaned again, more from annoyance, but he complied, raising himself up on his elbows and opening his eyes. He stared at her with bug-eyed exaggeration.

"See?"

Linnea peered into them and was satisfied the pupils were not dilated. "Okay," she said, "but slow down on the drinking. You look like shit."

He smiled lazily. "I love you too."

She shoved him gently, smiling. "So," she said, trying to start a conversation. "How are you? Really."

Cooper pushed the thick curls from his face and shifted to sit back against the bed frame. "Okay," he said on a long yawn. "Glad to be out of school. I need a break. Soccer was tough. Basketball was the bomb."

Linnea knew sports were important to Cooper, so she feigned interest. "Go Cyclones. What college sports will you play?"

Cooper's face darkened. "I don't know. I was recruited by USC for soccer."

"That's great!"

He shrugged and picked a nail. "I'm going to the Citadel."

"Oh, well then, go Bulldogs."

"Yeah."

He seemed despondent, but it could've just been the hangover. "Are you excited to begin college? Get out of the house?"

"No." He snorted. "I'll just be on the other side of town."

"Yeah, but you'll still be out."

"I'll be a knob."

Linnea couldn't help her outbreak of laughter. "Sorry," she said, covering her mouth. That was the term for freshmen at the Citadel. He'd have his head shaved and live a military lifestyle. And the hazing of knobs was legendary. This was the first she'd heard that he'd chosen the Citadel. She'd been asking her brother about his college decision for months, but he'd been evasive.

"What made you decide on the Citadel?"

Cooper stared at his hands. "Dad decided."

The humor fled. "Oh. But you agreed, right?"

"I did what I was told."

"Oh, Coop," she said.

Linnea studied her baby brother. He looked like the perfect jock and privileged boy, but he had a soft underbelly. Under his nonchalant façade, she knew he felt things intensely. And he avoided confrontations. Cooper was a team player, a trait that helped in sports and popularity, but took its toll in his personal life. Sometimes, though, like now, she wanted to give him a swift kick in the butt.

"It's your life, Coop. You're not a kid anymore. I mean, you're the one going to college."

"Not college. The military. I'm going to the Citadel." He spat the name out with venom.

She stared at him. "You don't want to go there?"

Cooper's face flushed with anger. "No, I don't want to go there!"

She was taken aback. Cooper was slow to anger. "Then why did you apply?"

"I didn't choose it. Dad did! I wanted to go to USC and told him that. Even got some scholarship money for basketball." He released a short laugh. "If you could go there, why couldn't I?" He shook his head. "That's when I got the long lecture about how Rutledge men go to the Citadel. How he went, and Granddad went, and how I damn well was going too."

Linnea felt her blood boil. She'd thought she had it bad when she fought to go to a university out of the South. The battle had been fierce but Linnea didn't give in and had enlisted Aunt Cara's support. Cara always had a special influence over her father.

"Coop, you should've fought harder. Just tell Daddy you want to go somewhere else."

"Yeah, like that's going to happen."

"Why not? I told him. He had a hissy fit but he came around in the end."

"You were always able to go toe-to-toe with him. I just . . ." He shrugged. "It's not my style."

"They would've come around."

"You don't get it."

"Get what?" She heard the challenge in her voice.

"You think you have it so hard as a woman in the South. Try being the only son. My whole future is mapped out. I'll graduate from the Citadel, get my MBA, and work for the family business. I'll probably even live in this house for the rest of my life."

"First of all, that's ridiculous. We don't live in colonial times. Secondly, boo-hoo for having to live in this house."

Cooper just flopped back down on the mattress and put his arm over his head. "Whatever."

"Hey, don't shut me out. I'm on your side."

He didn't respond.

"Do you want me to talk to them?"

"It won't do any good. He has his heart set on my going."

"So what?"

Cooper swallowed hard. "I don't want to disappoint him."

"But—"

"Just let it drop, okay?"

She gritted her teeth when the bell clanged again.

Cooper snorted. "See?" he said, peeking out from under his arm. "Things don't change."

Linnea wanted to climb back into her own bed too. But she'd been trained to put on a starched smile and engage in chitchat for dinner. She feared Cooper was more right than she'd given him credit for. She rose and headed for the door but turned to deliver a parting shot.

"Look at you, ignoring the bell. You're braver than you think."

~~~

HER LONG, MANICURED hands lightly grazed the mahogany railing to steady herself as Linnea slowly made her way down the stairs, past the portraits of her Rutledge ancestors. The Rutledges were a proud family who were among the founders of the city. Her pedigree granted her entry into Charleston's most exclusive societies. But she couldn't help but feel the subtle pressure such a heritage placed on her shoulders. It was as if each pair of eyes down the staircase followed her every move. Linnea felt Cooper's fatalism weigh her down. What young woman—or man?—wanted to be held hostage by antiquated rules?

Palmer was already seated in the rose-colored dining room when she entered. His pale blond head peppered with gray was visible over the *Charleston Post and Courier*.

"Hi, Daddy," she said as she approached.

He lowered the paper and smiled. "Hi, baby. Where've you been all day?"

She kissed his offered cheek before sitting in the chair to his left. "In my room. Reading."

"On a beautiful day like this?"

She glanced out the window to see a brilliant blue sky beyond the palm fronds. "It's a good book."

He laid his paper on the table and looked at her appraisingly. "Any luck with the job hunt?"

Linnea felt the throbbing in her temples intensify. She picked up her napkin and laid it across her lap, buying time. "Daddy, it's only been a week."

"Have you been looking?"

"Of course."

He lifted his brows.

"I *have* been looking. Really. Even while I was back at USC. There just aren't that many jobs out there for environmental studies majors. Especially for someone without experience. How am I supposed to get experience if no one will give me a starting position?" she asked and hated the whine in her voice.

Environmental studies was all she'd wanted to do, ever since she'd been christened a junior turtle lady by her grandmother Lovie and Aunt Cara. Linnea had done well enough in biology, chemistry, and geology. Her real interests, however, lay less in lab research than in policy and interpreting research findings for the public.

Her father leaned back in his chair. "Bring me up to speed, honey. Where've you been looking?"

She took a breath, trying to organize a coherent answer in her foggy brain. "Well, I'm checking for openings online every day. I'm looking in South Carolina, of course, but I'm extending my search to other states too."

"Not too far, I hope."

"Daddy, you can't be on my case to get a job if you won't let me look anywhere other than here. There's a world outside of South Carolina, you know."

"Not one that matters."

She smirked and didn't rise to the bait. "I've sent my résumé out to a lot of organizations."

"Like who?"

She knew this terrier wasn't going to drop the bone. She reached for her water and took a small sip. Resigned to continuing the discussion, she listed the usual suspects: "The Department of Natural Resources, U.S. Fish and Wildlife, the Audubon Society, Ducks Unlimited, the Coastal Conservation League . . ."

"You know you won't make a dime working for a nonprofit."

"Well, that's not the most important thing I'm looking for in a job."

"It should be."

Linnea pinched her lips. Comments like that hit her viscerally. She wasn't the type to sit back and take an insult, even a perceived one. How many toe-to-toe arguments had she had with her father over the past years in this very room? Linnea had known he'd never pay for a college out of the South. So they'd compromised. He'd conceded on her choice of major, and she'd conceded on the University of South Carolina. It had been an uneasy peace. But as far as her mother was concerned, the argument was moot. All that really mattered to Julia was that Linnea find herself a suitable husband, marry, and settle in Charleston.

Linnea picked up her salad fork and twirled the tips of the prongs into the white linen tablecloth. "I've also been researching companies that need an environmental consultant."

"Well, that's more like it," he said, leaning back in his chair. He grabbed his cut-crystal tumbler and swirled the bourbon before taking a long sip. "Now, explain to me what that means, exactly."

"Well," she began, frustrated because she'd already explained this to him, "I would help a company assess how a development project might affect the water, soil, air, or wildlife in the area. They're called environmental impact studies. There are lots of professional roles I could play." She laid her fork on the table, neatly lining it up with the dinner fork. "You know, Daddy, I heard about that project you invested in. You know, the one in the Upper Peninsula?"

Palmer narrowed his eyes and swirled his drink. "What about it?"

"I didn't realize how enormous the project is."

"What'd you hear?"

"It's running into some trouble with environmental issues. Which is exactly what I'm talking about. My job would be to explain the project's positions to the public. To pave the way for better understanding. Maybe you could put in a good word for me. I'd love to get an entry position on their team."

Palmer scowled as his face colored and shook his head. "They've got an army of so-called environmental consultants already, and I don't know what the hell they're doing. Wasting our money, from what I can tell. The damn project is still stalled." He took a long swallow and finished the drink.

"What we need is a damn good lawyer." He skewered her with a loaded gaze. "Maybe you could go to school for *that*, huh? We could use a good lawyer in the family."

"Let Cooper do that."

A flicker of frustration crossed his face. "I don't know that he's got the stuff to be a lawyer." Her father set his glass on the table and looked around. "Speaking of the devil, where is that boy?"

"He's upstairs in his room. He's sick."

"Sick? Or hungover?"

She shrugged and said nothing.

He looked up as his wife entered the room carrying a platter of roast beef. Their cook, Belinda, followed with a platter of vegetables.

"Julia, do you know our son is lying hungover in his room? *Again?*"

Julia set the beef in front of Palmer. "He's just feeling poorly."

"Uh-huh. For the third time this month."

"Oh, it's just graduation. You know boys," she replied, taking the platter from Belinda and setting it on the table. "They have to sow their wild oats. You did the same at his age. And your daddy before you." Julia looked pointedly at Linnea. "Look at you, sitting at the table while I serve. Go in the kitchen and fetch the red rice and beans."

"Yes'm," Linnea muttered, and rose too quickly, feeling a wave of dizziness sweep over her. She clutched the back of her chair.

"What's the matter with you?" Palmer asked, concerned. "You sick too? Hell, maybe Cooper isn't hungover."

Her mother looked at Linnea with accusation. "I do believe our daughter has the same sickness our son does."

Palmer looked from Julia to Linnea. "What? Are *you* hungover?"

"I'm fine," Linnea replied quickly. "I just got up too fast, is all."

"Don't you be lying to your father," her mother said. "I happen to know you came tiptoeing back into the house in the wee hours of the morning. I hear everything." She turned to Palmer. "Your darling daughter didn't come home last night."

Linnea's blood chilled as she watched her father's face pale. She cast a withering look at her mother. *Thanks a lot.*

Palmer tossed his napkin on the table. "You didn't come home?" he bellowed. "Where the hell were you?"

Linnea unwittingly took a step back. "I was at Jessica Linton's," she said, trying her best not to sound rattled. "She had a party at their beach house. I just stayed over."

"Were there boys at that party?"

"Oh, for heaven's sake, Daddy. I'm twenty-two. Of course there were boys. Or men, rather. What's the big deal? They're all nice guys I went to high school with. You know most of them. Everyone's coming home after graduation and we're all just glad to see each other again." She looked at her mother. "Darby was there. I spent most of the time talking with him. We had a nice catch-up."

Her mother's eyes glittered, and Linnea saw with satisfaction she'd played the right card. *That ought to quiet her for a moment*, she thought.

Her father didn't care that it was Darby Middleton of *the* Middletons. All he heard was there were men at the party.

"And you spent the night." He said these words in a low, rumbling voice, which she found more frightening than his shouts.

"Not with the boys," she said lightly to diffuse the tension. "With the *girls*. After everyone else left, a few of us decided to crash." She counted off on her fingers: "Jessica, Lane, Delancey, Ashley, and me. It was, you know, like a sleepover."

Her father seemed placated. "Nice girls . . ." he muttered, picking up his napkin.

Her mother clasped her hands. "Why didn't you call to let us know where you were? Do you know how worried I was? I almost called the police."

The truth was, no, she hadn't thought of calling her parents; it had never crossed her mind. "I'm sorry I worried you," she said, and meant it. "But I am twenty-two."

"I don't care how old you are!" her mother snapped back. "You're an unmarried woman. Your reputation will be ruined if you stay out all night. This is a small town. Word gets out."

"What about Cooper? He was gone all night. All weekend! And we all know he wasn't fishing or hunting."

"It's different for boys," her father said.

"That's so nineteen-seventies," she fired back.

"What's that supposed to mean?" her mother asked.

"It means you're using the double standard you grew up with. But that's not true anymore. I'm an adult. And *I* can drink legally." She paused and lowered her voice. "Last night I drank too much. I admit it. It doesn't happen often. I knew better than to get behind the wheel. It was a responsible decision," she argued. "I thought you'd be proud of me for not driving."

"I'm not happy you didn't call," her father said.

Linnea exhaled with relief. Her father's tone told her he wasn't angry.

"You shouldn't worry your mother."

"You're right. I'm sorry."

"Promise me it won't happen again," her mother said in a calmer voice, trying to restore peace at her dinner table.

"I promise," Linnea replied in a rote manner.

"Well, then," her mother said. She took a breath, pulled out a chair, and slid elegantly into it. She made a show of smoothing her napkin on her lap. "I think we're done with that conversation. Hardly suitable discussion for dinner. Let's enjoy our meal."

"Excuse me, please," Linnea said, rising. She set her napkin on the table. "I really don't feel well. I'll be in my room."

Hearing no arguments, she hurried back up the stairs, past the gauntlet of stern, disapproving looks from the portraits. Closing the door, she leaned against it.

She'd only been home a week and couldn't wait to leave.

Chapter Four

The female loggerhead is wary as she sits in the surf and scans the beach under a dark sky. Is it safe to leave the protection of the sea and venture forth across the sand? In the water, she is a powerful swimmer, but on land, a cumbersome, slow-moving creature. Instinct urges her on. Should she nest here or move on?

T HE BEACH HOUSE was still dark. The sun hadn't yet risen. Even her canary was a puffball in the cage, sleeping on one leg. Cara sat in front of her computer, a cup of steaming coffee to her left. In the past two weeks as she'd settled into the beach house, she'd been trying to establish her at-home work schedule. It turned out that the only times she could work were early in the morning before Hope awoke and late in the evening after she went to bed. The problem was, Cara was so exhausted by that point that she fell asleep.

It had been risky to leave a secure position with benefits, but the benefits of living near family outweighed any others. She had a reputation for excellence and was willing to take the chance. While working for Brett's ecotour business, she'd been her own boss. She'd learned to be disciplined with her work hours and used that discipline now to find time to work around Hope's erratic and demanding schedule. Today she was sending out her résumé to two firms that had shown interest. *Fingers crossed*, she thought. Money was tight and she had to make do.

She smiled as she pulled up her files. *Make do* was a phrase her mother used to say. Despite the Rutledge family wealth, her father, Stratton, had kept his wife on a miserly budget. It wasn't until years later that Cara had learned how punitive her mother's budget was, especially concerning anything to do with the beach house. It had been Lovie's, passed down to her from her parents before she married. All the other properties—even their home on Tradd Street—had only Stratton Rutledge's name on them. He'd been a controlling man, and it drove him crazy that Lovie refused to sell her beach house. Likewise, when Palmer had assumed control of the family finances he, too, had badgered his mother to sell the house. And later, Cara. That, he soon learned, was futile.

Lovie had always told Cara that the beach house was her own "little slice of heaven." The small cottage was her sanctuary where she could hide from the slings and arrows of Stratton's mental abuse, the social demands of Charleston, and the burden of caring for the large house South of Broad in the city. On the island she could live a simpler life with her children. Stratton hated coming to "the shack" on Isle of Palms. He'd rather have sold it and bought a house on Sullivan's Island, where his friends had houses. Over the years he'd stopped coming altogether. They both preferred it that way.

Thus, each summer Lovie and the children spent three glorious months free from Stratton's tyranny. They had no schedules or social engagements. If the children wanted to play on the beach all day, they could. If Cara wanted to sit in the shade to read for hours in her pajamas, she did. The meals were simple too. Lovie went to the docks to buy fish off the boat; grits were a staple in the house; and strawberries, blueberries, peaches, and vegetables came from farmers' markets. Even though they lived on a shoestring, whenever they did something extravagant, Lovie would just laugh and say, "Oh, we'll make do," as she paid the sum.

Cara leaned back in the chair and smiled, remembering those golden years. They'd gone by quickly. Everything had changed when Cara graduated from high school. She'd started making plans of her own—plans that didn't correlate with those of her father.

It came to a head during an epic battle when she was only eighteen. Cara had left her home, Charleston, and all she knew and headed north. She was on her own without one dime to rub against another. But she wasn't afraid. She was hell-bent on succeeding. She was smart, and more, she was a hard worker.

Her first job had been as a receptionist at Leo Burnett, a major advertising firm in Chicago; gradually Cara had earned her way up the ladder to become an account executive, getting her college degree after years of tedious night school. And then, suddenly, it was over. After twenty years of mainlining work at the expense of her personal life, she'd been ignominiously let go in a major power shift at the agency.

That was when she'd come home to her mother. Once again,

Cara had rebuilt her life, giving up the bright lights of the city for the moonlight and sunshine of the lowcountry. She'd met and then married the love of her life. She'd been happy. Then, just when things were going smoothly, her husband had died in a cruel twist of fate, and Cara was alone once more. She'd picked herself up off the floor and left the lowcountry to find new meaning in her life. And she'd ultimately found it in the form of a twenty-three-pound little girl. For Hope's sake, she would be careful and make do until she landed a few more clients. Her decisions for the future would always put Hope in the forefront. With her daughter, Cara would never be alone again.

This thought gave her the motivation to shake off the sleepiness and focus on the tasks at hand. Fatigue was never good for one's work ethic.

An hour later, she heard the faint sound of Hope's call: "Mama!"

Cara lowered her head into her palm. *Not yet*, she thought. Hope wasn't supposed to awaken for another hour. Cara had two conference calls scheduled for later in the day and needed to prepare. Hope was teething and had woken four times in the night.

Beside her, Moutarde heard the cries and began chirping with excitement, hopping from perch to perch. Cara closed the computer and rose to fetch her daughter.

By 10 a.m. Hope was changed, dressed, fed, and playing on the floor. Cara knew this peace was short-lived. Soon Hope would be crawling to a new location, trying to stick her finger in an electrical socket or some other such dangerous game. Cara needed coverage for her phone calls. With desperation she reached for her phone and dialed the only person who she knew could help.

"Hello?"

"Emmi? It's me. Cara. Listen, I have to get work done and I'm just not managing with Hope crawling about. She wants me to play with her all the time and she isn't napping."

"You sound frazzled."

"I'm just so tired. She gets up at the crack of dawn and wakes up during the night. I need sleep. But I need to work more. Emmi, do you know someone I can call to babysit?"

"Oh, gosh, Cara. I've been out of that game for a long time. And"—she rushed on—"I can't. I have to go to work."

"I know you can't. I was just hoping you knew someone who might babysit. Or just take pity on me for a few hours?"

"What about Heather?"

"I wish. She's out of town."

Emmi exhaled heavily after a moment's thought. "I'm sorry, I can't think of anyone. Most women I know are either working or volunteering."

Cara sighed. She needed someone today if she was going to get those résumés out and be ready by the deadline. "What about Flo? Is she busy today?"

"Flo? Honey, Flo's eighty years old."

"So? She seems plenty sharp to me. Certainly capable of watching a small child."

There was a long pause. "I don't know," Emmi replied slowly. "It might be too much for her." She lowered her voice. "Here's the thing . . ." She hesitated again. "Flo's . . . not herself."

"What do you mean?"

"Well," Emmi began uncomfortably, "you remember Miranda, don't you?"

"Flo's mother? Of course I do."

"Do you remember how she started to wander off looking for turtles? And how Flo would get all worried and we'd all run out and search the beach?"

"Good Lord, Emmi. Is Flo wandering off?"

"No! Not yet, anyway. But she forgets things more."

"We all do!" Cara felt enormous relief. "She's just getting older."

"True," Emmi replied with a light laugh. "I can't remember names at all anymore. I recognize the person, but the name? Gone. But," she continued in a more serious tone, "it's not just names with Flo. Her mind wanders too. Honestly, I just don't know if it's safe to leave a baby with her."

"I won't leave the baby with her. I'll be in the next room. I just need another pair of eyes. Someone to play with Hope so I can work."

Emmi sighed. "I guess that's okay. Anyway, she's in the kitchen. Hold on. I'll fetch her. Oh, wait, I almost forgot. I'm having a little party tomorrow night. Just family and friends. I want to welcome Hope."

Cara was touched. One more proof she'd made the right decision in returning home. "That's so thoughtful. Thanks, Em."

"You know me. I love a good party. Now, hold on. . . ."

Cara watched Hope while she waited. Her daughter had crawled over to the base of the large birdcage and pulled herself up to a stand. She began banging the cage with her palm, sending Moutarde fluttering.

"No, no, Hope," Cara said, hurrying over to pull her away. "Don't touch the birdcage."

She picked Hope up, eliciting a howl of protest. Cara felt a spurt of worry that maybe Flo was too old. She set Hope in front of the pile of toys. "Here, baby girl. Play with your fun toys!" No sooner did she let go of her than Hope was crawling right back to the birdcage.

"Hi, Cara!"

At the sound of Flo's strong, assured voice, Cara felt a wash of relief. Emmi was just a worrywart.

"Good morning, Flo!" Cara said into the phone as she hurried to grab Hope before she reached the cage. "How are you feeling?"

"As well as can be expected at my age."

"Good. Good," Cara said, rocking Hope on her hip.

"What can I do ya for?"

Cara took a breath. "I was wondering. Do you have any free time this morning? I'm desperately trying to get some work done, but with Hope awake, I can't focus. Would you be able to watch her? Just for a few hours?" She couldn't keep the pleading tone from her voice.

There was a pause as Flo considered the request. "Well, now . . . I'm not as quick on my feet as I once was. And it's been a while since I did any babysitting."

Cara heard the hesitancy and plowed forward. "I only need you to keep an eye on her while I work. You'll be in the next room, and I'll be here the whole time."

"Well, then, I think I can manage."

"Oh, thank you, Flo!"

"Happy to help. What time should I be over?"

Cara sighed. "As soon as you can."

~~~~~

A FEW YEARS earlier when Heather had rented the house, Cara had converted the ocean porch into an art studio and aviary. Cara had been slightly jealous of the great, light-filled space; now that Heather wasn't renting the house any longer, Cara had followed her example and set up a desk, a few bookshelves, and her canary cage on the porch and claimed it as her office. Once she got Flo and Hope settled in the living room, she sat at her desk and sighed with relief. *At last.* Soon her fingers were tapping away on the keyboard.

Within a few minutes, Hope was crying. She heard Flo's high-pitched voice trying to cajole her to be quiet. The problem was, Flo didn't cajole very well. Hope was having none of it, and her crying only intensified. Cara closed her eyes and counted to ten. *If I could just get one good hour* . . . She checked her watch, mindful of her phone appointments.

She reluctantly pushed back her chair and went to the living room; Flo was sitting on the floor and trying to keep Hope from crawling to the porch. It was kind of funny. Flo had never married or had children. She wasn't the domestic type.

"Maybe I could take her for a walk?" Flo offered. "She knows you're in there, and there's no holding her back."

A memory of Miranda wandering the beach searching for hatchlings flashed in Cara's mind. But Flo seemed just fine. Older, yes. But Alzheimer's or dementia? No.

"That sounds like a good idea. Hope loves the outdoors."

As predicted, Hope quieted the moment the breeze kissed her skin. She lifted her face and smiled widely. Cara slathered her with sunblock, put on her sun hat, and buckled her into her stroller.

"Have a nice time. Not far, though," she added.

"Get some work done," Flo shot back.

Cara laughed and crossed her arms as she stood at the end of the driveway and watched Flo and Hope meander away at a leisurely pace. Then, checking her watch, she hurried back to her office.

~~~~~

MORE THAN AN hour later, Cara's last phone appointment was finished. She set the phone on the desk and cocked her head to listen. The house was strangely quiet. Only Moutarde's occasional peep broke the silence.

Cara furrowed her brow. It didn't take an hour to walk around the block. She got up and walked to Hope's bedroom, thinking Hope might be napping. No one was there. Walking faster, she went out to look across the deck, then farther out onto the beach. She saw no one. Her heart began beating a little faster as she went out the front door, grabbing her phone en route. First she went to Flo's house, but no one was there. Picking up speed, Cara power-walked around the block, craning her neck. It was a beautiful spring day on the island. The sky was a peerless blue and dotted with white clouds. Birds chattered in the trees, and an occasional wind ruffled her hair, the kind of soft breeze Hope loved.

Her thoughts raced faster than her steps. *Where are they? Was I wrong to let Flo babysit? Could she be lost in her own neighborhood? She's lived here for eighty years!* She was almost running by the time she turned the final corner toward Flo's house and caught sight of a woman and a stroller in the distance.

Relief flooded her as she hurried toward them, trying to catch her breath. Flo was leisurely smiling under her turtle team ball cap, and Hope was blissfully asleep in the shade of the canopy.

"Hey there," Flo said as she drew closer. "Beautiful day, isn't it?"

Cara's mouth was dry. "Where were you?"

Flo straightened, and her face registered Cara's sharp tone. "I was walking the baby, like you asked."

"For so long? I said a short walk."

"Well, we made a stop at the beach."

"You took her to the beach?"

"Whyever not? She loves it! In fact, the only time she squawked was when I lifted her up to put her back in the stroller." Flo smiled. "You should've seen her. At first, she wasn't sure what this *sand* was, scrunching it up in her hand. Then she tried to eat it, of course. Thank heavens I was quick enough. She loved grabbing handfuls of sand and letting it slide through her fingers. Spent at least fifteen minutes doing just that." She chuckled softly. "This child's a lowcountry baby, that's for sure and certain."

Cara was taken aback. Hope loved the beach? She wished she had been there to share her first visit. Why hadn't she taken her? What had been more important?

"I've been so focused on getting the house settled, I didn't get to the beach yet."

"Honey, take it from me. Life's too short to only do work. From the moment of birth, babies are poised for leaving. Before you know it, this little tyke will be grown and packing up to go to college or move to some other state, and you'll only have your memories to hold close."

Cara was quieted by the advice. "I don't really have a lot of choice in the matter. I have to earn a living."

"Of course you do. You'll find a way. Most mothers do. But really, Cara, what did you come here for if you don't go to the beach?"

Cara couldn't help but laugh. "You're right, of course."

"I know it," Flo said with a smug smile. She gazed at the baby. "I gave her a bottle, and she fell asleep lickety-split. Look at her," she said with warmth. "As content as a cat with a belly full of cream."

Cara looked down at her daughter. Hope's long lashes rested against her full cheeks, pinkened slightly by the sun. With her dark hair and rosy lips, she looked like a tiny, perfect Snow White.

"You know," Flo said, looking up again at Cara, "it struck me several times how much Hope looks like you."

Cara was surprised by this. Delighted. "Like me?" When she looked at the baby, all she saw was glimpses of Elena.

"With her dark hair and eyes. For sure. And she sure loves you. Even when she was having the best time, she'd look for you and ask, 'Mama?'"

"You can't know how much it means to me to hear that."

Flo's eyes glittered. "Did you get your work done?"

It was just like her to deflect emotion. "I did. Thanks to you. Really, you're a lifesaver."

"Happy to do it. Hope's a real charmer."

Cara took a deep breath and asked, "So, are you free again tomorrow?"

"Aw, honey, this was more exercise than I've had in months!"

"You wouldn't have to walk her every day."

Flo slowly shook her head. "I'm not strong enough—or fast enough anymore. Sure, I could help you out in an emergency, but for every day you need someone who has the energy to play with her. Someone young who likes children."

Cara sighed. "Do you know anyone like that?"

"Not anymore. I used to when I did social work. That's how I found Toy for your mother. But I've been out of the system for too long. Don't worry. You'll find someone." Flo began pushing the stroller up the driveway. "For now, though, she's asleep, and I'm still here. Run and get some more work done. Oh . . ." She turned back. "Don't forget the party tomorrow night."

"Of course. What should I bring?"

"The guest of honor, of course. Hope!"

Chapter Five

Under the cloak of night, the loggerhead drags her three-hundred-pound carapace in a tank-like crawl across the beach to the dunes. It is a long, perilous journey for her. She leaves deep, unmistakable tracks in the sand as she plows forward to fulfill her destiny.

WHEN CARA SAW the pink balloons fluttering in the air, tied to the iron gate of Emmi's house, she felt her heart swell. She really and truly was being welcomed home with her daughter.

Although Emmi's house was just beyond her driveway, Cara packed like she was going across state lines. Diapers, bottles, wipes, a change of clothes, a blanket, myriad toys. She piled baby and accoutrements in the stroller and headed for the door—then stopped short. She'd forgotten the wine. Cara didn't have food to share—she hated to cook—but she could always be counted on for a good bottle of red.

The night air held that perfect blend of warmth without humidity that she called *island balmy*. Though it was six o'clock, the sun was still high in the June sky. Hope had been napping, so she was running late for the party. She plowed the stroller through the crushed-shell driveway she'd just had put down. When she crossed into Emmi's front garden, she heard the laughter of children coming from the street. Turning, she spotted Toy, sporty in a pink summer top and denim short shorts that showed off her tanned legs, walking up the driveway with her two children. Her left shoulder sagged with the weight of the bag she was toting. Her blond hair was long now and pulled back in a ponytail that made her look even younger than her thirty years.

Then there was Little Lovie. Cara's heart flipped, and her lips automatically turned up at the sight of the child she'd watched grow from infancy. Her goddaughter had sprouted from a chubby-faced girl into a coltish, beguiling thirteen-year-old with the same smattering of freckles across her nose and wispy blond hair as her mother. Behind her was a mischievous boy of about five who was poking at her bottom with a bird feather. Cara shook her head, smiling. She'd peg him as a Legare any day, with his lanky build and curly brown hair just like his daddy—and his being a dickens. He stopped poking his sister, distracted by Flo's garden gnome.

Toy spotted her and squealed, "There you are!" She hurried forward, tottering on her espadrilles under the weight of the bag. "Let me see that baby!" She rushed a kiss to Cara's cheek, gingerly set down the plastic bag that held a covered dish, and, eyes gleaming, bent to look at Hope. "Oh, she's precious!" she crooned. "She has your coloring. I've been dying to hold her since the moment I saw her picture." She turned her face toward Cara. "May I?"

"Of course. If she'll let you. She's a bit clingy with the move and all."

With the hands of a practiced mother, Toy had Hope unbuckled and in her arms in no time. She rocked her gently from left to right on her curvy hip. Little Lovie and Danny clustered around her, big eyes studying the baby.

"Can I hold her?" asked Little Lovie.

"Not here, honey," Toy told her. "Maybe when we get inside where you can sit. She's pretty heavy."

"I can lift her," Little Lovie assured her mother, embarrassed by the implication that she was too young.

Her spirit was what Cara loved most about Little Lovie. Her fearlessness and belief in herself. She was a born naturalist who loved bugs, sea turtles, dogs, chickens—any critter, really—more than dolls or jewelry. Brett had taken a special liking to her and treated her as the child he'd never had. Maybe because he was the one who'd found Toy during the worst of Hurricane Brendan and got her to the hospital for Little Lovie's birth. Her knight in shining armor; there'd been a special bond between them.

Ethan came walking up the drive, the muscles in his forearms straining under the weight of a big blue cooler. Cara felt the chill of a ghost run down her spine. With his brown hair salt-stiffed and sun-kissed and his chambray shirttail hanging out over his frayed khaki shorts, he looked so much like Brett at that age. She flashed back to a Fourth of July party well over a decade earlier. It was the summer she'd fallen in love with Brett. He'd walked up this same driveway, larger than life, his eyes the color of the sky, carrying a cooler full of crabs, just like Ethan now.

She felt the quick stab of sadness she always did when something brought Brett to mind. But those pangs were less frequent now and the pain less sharp. She didn't have time to wallow. Ethan spied them standing there and, grinning, set the cooler down with a thunk.

"They're real beauties," he said proudly, lifting the lid. The cooler was filled to the top with ice and shrimp in the shell. He reached in and grabbed a handful of long white bodies, which hung from his fist by their long whiskers. His grin widened. "Take a look!"

"They're huge!" Cara exclaimed.

"Yep. Right off the boat. I'll pop the heads and cook 'em up. I hope y'all are hungry."

The children were dancing on the balls of their feet, and Danny reached out to touch the shrimp.

"Not yet, Danny," Ethan said, putting the shrimp back in the cooler.

"But I want to help," he whined with a defeated slump.

"Well, come on then," Ethan said, flipping the lid shut. He bent and lifted the heavy load with a grunt. He leaned forward for a perfunctory kiss from Toy, then walked off, preceded by his children, who clamored to open the door for him.

Cara heard laughter emanating from inside. "We might be the last to arrive," she said. Turning, she saw Toy's gaze following her family.

"You're happy," Cara said as a matter of observation. She was smiling. It felt good to see her friends happy and doing so well.

"Very." Toy kissed the top of Hope's head and began gently rocking her once again. "And it's nice to see you happy again too."

"I'm getting there."

Toy studied her face, then said, "I can tell. You look good. I don't mind saying we were all worried about you. You got too thin. By the way, I love your haircut."

Cara's hand automatically went to her hair. "Do you?"

"I do. Really. It's very cool. Young."

Cara smiled. "I need some cool in my life now."

Toy looked away, and Cara sensed a shift in her mood. When Toy met her gaze again, Cara caught the worry shining in her blue eyes. "What?"

"I'm pregnant."

"Congratulations! How wonderful!"

Toy took a breath. "It's a surprise, I'll tell you."

"But a happy one, right?" When Toy didn't respond, Cara said, "Or is it?"

"Not a problem," Toy said hesitatingly. "It's just . . ." She rocked the baby a bit more vigorously. "I've just been offered a big promotion at the aquarium."

"Well, congratulations again!"

Toy took the praise in stride. "It'll mean I'm no longer director of the sea turtle hospital," she explained.

"Oh." Toy was passionate about sea turtles, loggerheads in particular. "Are you comfortable with that change?"

"I have to be. I'll still be involved with turtles, of course, but I'll branch out to other areas. Education, sustainable seafood, plastics in the ocean, climate change. All important areas I can dig my teeth into."

Cara thought the job sounded challenging. Something she wouldn't mind doing herself. "What's the job title?"

"Conservation director. It's a newly created position. They said they had me in mind when they designed it," she added with a faint blush of pride. "Because education is a major component, I'll go out to the community to speak a lot. Which means a lot of travel and late hours. That's going to be hard to do with a family."

"It's a lot to juggle."

Toy took a breath. "Right. I don't know if—" She stopped when the front door opened.

Flo stuck her head out. "What y'all doing out there? Stop yakking and come in. Folks are waitin' to see the guest of honor! And by that, I mean that baby!"

"Be right there," Cara called back. Flo waved in acknowledgment. When the door closed again, she turned back to Toy. "You were saying?"

Toy kicked a pebble. "We can talk later."

"Let's talk now. It's important. You don't know if . . ." she led.

"I don't know if I can do all that with a new baby." She shook her head with a shrug. "Who am I kidding? I know I won't be able to do it."

"But you've been trying to have another baby for years."

"We stopped trying last year. Then, bingo." She laughed. "Wouldn't you know it?"

Cara felt a pang at the irony. "When Brett and I stopped trying, I used to pray I'd miraculously get pregnant like that. You hear those stories." She laughed shortly. "And the miracle happened to you." She reached out to touch her arm. "And it is a miracle."

Toy bumped her shoulder gently against Cara's. "You got your miracle too."

Cara smoothed Hope's hair. "I did."

Cara had been Toy's mentor, an older sister, even a surrogate mother after Lovie died. She'd been the one to dispense advice. But now they seemed more like equals. The twenty-year age difference melted away. In fact, Cara felt she was the one who needed advice from Toy.

"I understand, I really do," Cara said. "I'm trying to figure out how to work at home and make a living with a baby too. At least you have Ethan."

"And he's been great," Toy was quick to say.

"He's happy about the pregnancy?"

"Over the moon."

Cara smiled. Of course he was happy. Ethan came from a large, boisterous family and made it no secret he wanted more children. He'd adopted Little Lovie without a second thought and loved her like his own.

"Well, then," Cara said with undisguised relief. "I'd say you had your answer. You'll have to do what women have done for centuries. Make it work."

Toy snorted and handed Hope back to Cara. "Thanks. Spoken like a woman who's been a mother for, what, six months?"

Cara laughed. "Five, but who's counting?" The front door opened, and Emmi appeared in a pink apron. Her red hair was piled atop her head in a bun and she waved her pink-tipped fingers in the air.

"What's taking you two so long?"

"Lucy, I'm home!" Cara called out, and Toy barked out a laugh.

"Ha-ha," said Emmi. "Now get your butts in here. The party's waiting for you!"

Cara walked into a home that had been transformed by fairy lights and pink crepe paper. A side table draped in a white table-cloth with pink polka dots held a large tiered cake decked with pink and lavender flowers, surrounded by champagne flutes. The next table was covered with gifts.

"Oh my. They went all out," Toy said with wonder.

"I didn't expect all this!" Cara exclaimed and suddenly felt sheepish for being late.

Toy went directly to the dining room table to add her covered dish to the groaning weight of platters and bowls. Drawing near, Cara saw the requisite pimento cheese sandwiches and deviled eggs, red rice and beans, pickled okra, a selection of salads, and fried chicken. A large wooden serving platter in the center of the table waited, she knew, for the steamed shrimp.

On cue, the kitchen door swung open and Ethan emerged with the steaming pot of shrimp, guests filing in behind him. Exclamations of welcome echoed throughout the room. Cara smelled the sweet scent of shellfish and Old Bay seasoning, heard the laughter, and felt herself light up with happiness. Immediately she was surrounded by such love—her brother Palmer and sister-in-law Julia, along with Linnea and Cooper. Heather and Bo Stanton were back in town with their new towheaded son, whom she'd yet to meet; he looked to be close in age to Hope. Finally, there were Flo and Emmi. Her nearest and dearest, her family. They'd been there for her through the good times and the bad. She'd loved them all before, but now, alone with a baby, she treasured them. Through a veil of tears, Cara felt humbled with gratitude.

With the huge influx of attention, Hope began to cry. Emmi

rushed forward to scoop her up, cooing softly, and someone handed Cara a glass of the champagne.

The party was under way.

~~~~~

THE SKY HAD turned indigo, and most of the guests had left. This was Cara's favorite time of a party, when the din died down and meaningful conversations could be held without interruption or straining to hear through the noise. She'd had such a lovely time, but now she could finally stop smiling at all the congratulations. Like a bride, her cheeks hurt.

Flo and Emmi would've made a caterer proud by how quickly they'd cleaned up and packed away the food. They'd sunk into the couch and kicked their shoes off, and were chatting, glasses in hand and heads tilted toward each other, no doubt sharing impressions from the party. The oohing and aahing over Hope had tuckered her out, so she was asleep upstairs. Cooper and Danny looked like Mutt and Jeff, playing a game in the TV room, shoulders hunched over controllers. She felt kindly toward Cooper for taking the youngster under his wing.

Over by the table Palmer was embroiled in a heated discussion with Ethan about the new baseline and setbacks of property for the islands. Palmer's Sullivan's Island home was caught in the crosshairs, which was going to make his insurance premiums soar. Ethan had his arms crossed and a beer in his fist, rocking on his heels as Palmer dominated the conversation, gesturing broadly.

Suddenly Palmer bellowed, "No, no way! You crazy, boy?"

Cara swung her head around to catch her brother reaching out to steady himself on the back of a nearby chair. From the corner of her eye, she saw Linnea look up sharply, her heavily lined eyes shining with embarrassment. Cara's heart flinched with sympathy. How many times had she died a thousand deaths hearing her father's drunken outbursts? She searched the room for Julia, who was usually good at cutting Palmer off before he got out of hand. But she was walking toward the kitchen with a tray filled with dirty glasses, apparently unconcerned.

Linnea turned back to Little Lovie and with forced cheerfulness engaged the young girl in conversation to distract her from Palmer's behavior. Cara looked at Linnea with fresh eyes. Her niece had become a woman, she realized. As poised and pretty as her mother. But in truth, she was a ringer for her grandmother Lovie! Linnea had the same petite bone structure, blue eyes, and fair coloring. Cara smothered a laugh. The resemblance was all the more remarkable since Linnea was wearing a shirtwaist dress in the style of the 1950s. Her hair was in a ponytail pinned back with pink clips. It took confidence to pull off that look, Cara thought with admiration.

"For you." Julia was at her elbow, handing her a cup of coffee.

"Why, thank you. It smells heavenly," Cara said gratefully. Then, nodding toward Palmer, she said, "I think he could use a cup. Maybe two."

Over the rim of her mug Cara saw Julia glance at her husband and her lips tighten in annoyance. "He wouldn't drink it," she said, and sipped the coffee herself.

"I hope you're driving," said Cara. "Or Cooper."

"Cooper's had too many beers. As usual, it's up to the women."

"Speaking of women, I've been meaning to ask you something all day. I'm in desperate need of a nanny. Do you know of anyone you can recommend? Or an agency?"

"A nanny? I thought you were staying home with the baby."

"I am," Cara replied a bit defensively. "But I'm trying to work from home too. I'm not getting much done with Hope underfoot. She just wants my attention all the time."

"I remember those days," Julia said wistfully. "The best days. Before you know it, they don't care about your attention at all. Cara, honey, are you sure you want to work? This time is precious. It goes by so fast."

Julia had had the luxury of staying home with her children without having to worry about supporting them. She was oblivious to how tender a subject it was for a woman who had only herself to depend on.

"I don't have a husband," Cara said. She couldn't help the sting that came out with that painful statement. "I have to provide for us."

Julia looked a bit nonplussed. "I didn't mean—"

"I know you didn't," Cara said, putting an end to this uncomfortable topic.

"Cara, I'm so proud of you. I'm not sure I would be so brave as to adopt a child on my own."

Cara appreciated her sister-in-law's support and tried to explain. "The problem is, I quit my job so I could come home and raise my child myself. To be near my family and to provide a loving network. In order to do that, I'm trying to get my fledgling consulting business off the ground so I can stay home with Hope." She exhaled. "But I still have to get work done. And that's not going to happen if I don't get childcare."

"Have you looked into day care?"

"What's the point of staying home if she's not there, though?" Cara shook her head, frustration pitching her voice a little louder: "I just need a good babysitter."

"How much babysitting do you need? A couple of hours here and there? Or something regular?"

"Regular," Cara replied. "As many hours as I can get."

"So, you're looking for a nanny."

Nanny, babysitter . . . Cara didn't have a clue what the difference was, other than a nanny sounded more upscale than a babysitter.

"Sorry, I'm not sure I know the difference."

Julia explained: "A babysitter takes care of your child for a few hours at an hourly rate. You call her when you want to go out to dinner or a movie. More short-term. A nanny, on the other hand, is a full-time caretaker who is more involved with the child, arranges schedules, helps with household chores, prepares meals. She's almost part of the family."

Cara said, "I guess what I need is a nanny, then."

"Well," Julia said with a grimace, "nannies can be quite expensive. All that time and personal investment . . . Perhaps you just need someone part-time?"

"I'm getting desperate. Where can I find someone to babysit Hope in my home for a few hours every day while I work?"

Across the room, Linnea raised her head toward them. "Aunt Cara, did you say you're looking for a babysitter?"

Cara turned toward Linnea. "Yes. Do you know someone?"

Linnea rose to her feet. "'Scuse me a minute, precious," she said to Little Lovie. She walked over to join Cara and Julia, who watched her daughter over her mug.

"I'm interested."

Cara blinked, caught off guard. She couldn't believe she could be so lucky. Still, this was her niece. She wanted Linnea to move forward with her own ambitions, especially at this point in her life.

"But, Linnea, you just graduated from college. Aren't you looking for something in your field?"

"Yes, but I've been searching for weeks," Linnea explained, a hint of her frustration leaking into her voice. "I'm afraid it's going to take more time than I had expected. Frankly, I'd like to make some money while I'm looking."

"I won't be able to pay you a nanny's full-time rate," Cara said honestly. "I need someone who can sit for me during the day. I'm flexible with hours. A routine matters the most to me." She looked at her niece with affection. "I doubt you'd be interested in what I could afford."

Linnea was not deterred. "Does the job include room and board?"

"Why, yes. If you'd like. In fact, I'd prefer it."

"Good. Because I'd really love to stay with you at the beach house this summer. I'm sure we could work out an arrangement we could both afford."

Cara released a short laugh of surprise. "But are you sure?" she asked, not wanting to get her hopes up. "You'd be Hope's nanny? Or babysitter, or whatever you wish to be called."

Before Linnea had a chance to respond, Palmer was at her shoulder, his face scrunched up.

"What's this I hear? Something about you being a nanny?"

"Yes, Daddy. Cara's offering me a job!" Her tone implied she expected him to be pleased.

"Hell, girl, I didn't send you to college for four years to be no nanny!"

Linnea turned away in a show of pique.

Palmer shot out his arm to grab her. "Don't you walk away from me."

Linnea jerked back her arm. "Let go!"

"Palmer," Julia said in horror.

Palmer immediately opened his hand to release her and weaved back two steps, shamefaced.

"Daddy!" Linnea said accusingly, scanning her forearm for marks.

Cara stood in shock as a deep-rooted anger rose up within her and old memories resurfaced. She looked over to see Flo and Emmi watching from the sofa, equally shocked. Flo met Cara's gaze and signaled her with a quick, stern shake of her head: *Stay out of it*. Cara clenched her cup and told herself this was between father and daughter. Besides, there was nothing she could say that wouldn't make her look selfish about getting Linnea's help.

She was relieved to hear Julia jump in.

"Oh, for pity's sake, Palmer," she said with more annoyance than Cara had ever heard from her in public before. "You don't know your strength when you've been drinking. You've been after

Linnea to get a job. Until she finds one, this makes sense. A job's a job. And she won't be lying around the house all summer."

"If it's any job she wants, she can work in the office with me," Palmer said belligerently.

"I'm right here, you know," Linnea said. "You don't have to talk about me like I'm out of the room." She turned to her father. "I don't want to work in your office. I have no interest in the business and it'd be a waste of my time. I'd much rather be at the beach house with family and take care of Hope, and I'd be helping out Aunt Cara. Plus . . . Daddy, this might be the last time I get to stay at the beach house for a whole summer. You know I love it here. I used to stay here with Grandmama Lovie."

Palmer shook his head and put his hands on his hips. "I swear, not only does she look like my mother, but she sounds like her too."

"Is that a bad thing?" Cara asked gently.

At the mention of their mother, the steam of his fury was released in a long sigh. "I suppose not."

Relieved at the sudden shift in mood, Cara gently bumped his shoulder with hers. "I miss her too."

She almost told him she'd seen Lovie's ghost, but held back. He'd been drinking. She didn't want him to get all emotional. Instead she told him the simple truth.

"I'm in a pinch and I'd really be grateful to have Linnea for even a little while. If she gets any opportunity to work in her field, I'll be the first to encourage her to take it."

Palmer looked at her, and she saw in his eyes that her big brother once again wanted to help her.

She nudged his shoulder gently. "Think back to when *you* were twenty-two," Cara said. "If you had a chance to work in a warehouse downtown or in a cottage at the beach for the summer, which would you choose? And before you answer, remember that I have strong memories of you riding the surf every day." She pointed toward the ocean. "Right out there. Despite those fancy silk Tommy Bahama shirts you wear now, you're a surfer boy through and through." She bumped his shoulder again.

Palmer released a reluctant smile. "All right. But just for the summer. And you save your money, hear?" he told Linnea, pointing a finger her way. "I don't want you cryin' to me to help you out come fall."

"I won't," she fired back, but she was smiling.

"So," Cara said, turning to Linnea, deflecting another argument. "You're my new nanny?"

"Yes, ma'am," she replied, grinning.

"When can you start?"

"Is tomorrow too soon?"

Chapter Six

The loggerhead uses her front flippers to clear a spot in the dry sand. Then she uses her hind flippers to dig a hole some twenty inches deep before laying 80 to 150 leathery eggs. When done, she refills the nest, then tosses sand to camouflage it from predators.

As soon as she got home, Linnea went directly to her bedroom closet and pulled out a box tagged TURTLE TEAM from the shelf. She was filled with a renewed sense of purpose. The opportunity to be a nanny for Cara was a gift from the gods. It wasn't the job she was looking for, but it was a job nonetheless that swept away the cloud of uncertainty that had hovered since graduation. With the major perk of being able to spend a summer at the beach house, the place of her best childhood memories.

She set the box on the bed, sweeping off a layer of dust from the lid. It'd been years since she'd opened this. She smiled at seeing her old turtle team T-shirts in assorted colors, along with a few pairs of indestructible nylon fishing pants. Her team uniform.

Most of them she'd never be able to fit into again, but one or two of the later ones were promising. She pulled out a spring-green shirt, children's size eight. She brought it to her nose and caught the faint sweet scent of soap. But in her mind she smelled the sea. . . .

~~~~~

"LINNEA, HURRY ALONG, child!"

"Coming, Grandmama Lovie!"

The rising sun created a tapestry of colors on the beach. This was eight-year-old Linnea's first summer on the turtle team. Her parents were letting her stay weekends with Grandmama Lovie and Aunt Cara at the beach house. Time at the beach house was the best part of her week.

This morning she was bent at the knees watching Aunt Cara and Emmi at the turtle nest retrieving eggs and putting them into the red bucket. Lovie had decided that the nest was in a bad place for the eggs because it was below the high-tide line and the water would wash over the eggs, destroying them. So while the team opened the nest, Lovie was scouting for a good spot for the new nest. That's where she was going now.

Linnea ran through the hot sand to catch up with her grandmother. She was the best teacher and knew the most because she'd been a turtle lady long before there were teams. Aunt Cara said she was the original turtle lady on Isle of Palms and Sullivan's Island. Linnea was proud to be her granddaughter and felt privileged to be the first junior team member. She couldn't touch the eggs or the hatchlings because she wasn't permitted by the Department of Natural Resources, but the team gave her lots of other jobs.

She caught up with Lovie standing in front of a dune, her hands on her hips as she studied it. Lovie was so thin now Linnea didn't think she weighed much more than she herself did. Lovie wore nylon pants and a long-sleeved TURTLE TEAM shirt, even though it was hot outdoors. On her head was a white floppy hat.

"Come take a look," Lovie called to her, waving her closer.

When Linnea drew near, Lovie pointed to the dune.

"Here's what I'm looking at. See that nice open patch of sand, the spot without any sea oats? That's good because the roots won't interfere with the nest. And it has a nice slope so the hatchlings have a clear path to the sea. Best of all, I know who lives in that house and she'll keep the lights out. What do you think? Is this a good spot to put the nest?"

"Yes!"

Lovie's face softened to a smile and her blue eyes shone with pride. "Good girl. Now, help your old grandmother down," she said, reaching out for Linnea's arm. With a bit of effort and a spell of coughing, Lovie got to her knees on the dune. "Run and fetch my bag, would you, sugar?"

She ran as fast as her feet would take her. Linnea treasured these private moments with Lovie. She just knew a lesson was coming.

Lovie rummaged through her canvas bag and pulled out a large shell, as big as her hand. The rounded shell was symmetrical and unbroken. A real treasure.

"This is a cockleshell," Lovie told her. "And it makes the very best tool for digging a nest." Lovie bent over and scooped out a shell full of sand. She continued this, one scoop after another, several inches down.

"That's a good start," Lovie said a bit winded, and sat back on her heels. "Now let's see you try."

"Me?" Linnea asked, incredulous. She hadn't imagined she'd get to dig.

"Of course. You're on the team, aren't you? The trick is to turn your wrist slightly when you scoop. Think of the mama turtle. She uses her back flippers. The left dips to scoop up about a cup of sand, then the right, over and over to about twenty inches deep. So we have a ways to go. Go on, then," she said encouragingly.

The shell was a beauty and it fit Linnea's palm perfectly. Linnea began to dig, scooping one shell-full after another until she was almost shoulder deep in the sand. By the time she'd finished, Aunt Cara and Emmi had arrived carrying the red bucket full of eggs.

"Looks good!" Cara exclaimed. "We've got one hundred twelve eggs."

"Cara," said Lovie, "you might want to round out the bottom of the nest to make room for the eggs. Linnea did a good job."

"Here's the shell," Linnea said, offering it to Cara.

"Oh, no, that's your shell," Lovie told her. "I found that one especially for you."

"We all have our own," Cara said, and lifted hers for Linnea to see. "But that's a good one you've got."

While Cara bent over the nest to finish the digging, Linnea went to sit beside her grandmother. Her mother had explained to her that Lovie wasn't well and she needed to rest. That this was Lovie's final summer. Knowing that made each day with her special.

"Grandmama Lovie, why doesn't the mother turtle come back to take care of her eggs till they hatch? Like a bird does?"

Lovie sighed and looked out over the sea. This morning the ocean was serene, rolling in and out in its predictable manner.

"Because a turtle is not a bird!" Lovie answered simply. "For a turtle, it is normal to lay several hundred eggs over the summer. She knows not all of the hatchlings will survive, but the few that do will keep the species alive. A bird has two or three chicks. A dolphin only one calf. Each animal has its own unique instinct for survival. Turtles are more than one hundred and eighty million years old, so that's a long time to develop very strong instincts. The mother turtle knows that when her eggs hatch, her hatchlings will hear the loud voice of their instincts telling them to run to the sea as fast as they can. And when they reach the water they swim, swim, swim without stopping until they reach the Gulf Stream where there are big floats of seaweed called Sargassum. The hatchlings hide in there from other fish predators until they're big enough to venture out into the ocean. Instinct tells them what to eat, where to go, who to run from."

"What do my instincts tell me?"

"Well, do you ever hear a voice in your head that tells you to stop doing something? Or a funny feeling that something's off and you should be careful?"

"You mean like the 'uh-oh' feeling?"

"Yes, exactly. Intuition guides us and the wise person listens."

"So the turtle listens to her instinct to go back to the sea."

"That's her home. Her shell is very heavy and she has to drag it across the beach to lay her eggs. But once she's back in the water, she's free of gravity and can swim fast and quite gracefully."

"Would she die if she stayed on the beach?"

"She would. So would her hatchlings. This is why we try to help their chances to get to the sea as fast as possible."

Linnea was silent for a while. She finally worked up the courage to ask the question that had been niggling in her heart for weeks.

"Grandmama Lovie, are you going to die?"

Lovie turned her head to look into Linnea's eyes. Her gaze was thoughtful. Loving.

"Yes, dear girl. I am. We all will die someday, of course. But my time is coming soon."

Linnea felt her heart break at hearing from her grandmother's lips what had seemed impossible to believe when her mother had told her.

"Oh, Linnea, don't cry!" Lovie said and bent to wrap her arms around Linnea and draw her close to her breast.

"But I don't want you to die."

Lovie rocked her and kissed the top of her head. "Don't be sad. A part of me will always be with you. You have my genes. My goodness, you look just like I did at your age."

Linnea sniffed. "Really?"

"It's quite remarkable."

"And I love turtles like you do."

Lovie laughed lightly and rocked her again. Linnea caught the scent of Lovie's perfume and felt the bones of her chest against her cheek. Even though she was frail, Linnea felt her grandmother was still strong.

"Yes, you do," Lovie replied with affection. "You know," she added, "my going away is like the mother turtle going into the sea."

Linnea looked at her doubtfully. "How?"

"You could say I've spent a long time on the beach. I've had my babies, and I've been blessed to see my grandbabies. Oh, Linnea, it's been a good life. And now it's time for me to crawl back to the sea. I'll huff and puff a bit," she added with a slight cough that Linnea knew was from the cancer. "But when I get to the sea, I'll welcome it. I'll take a breath, and slip under a wave, and I'll be home again."

"You mean heaven?"

"Yes," Lovie replied on a sigh. "So you see, it's not sad at all."

"But I'll still miss you," Linnea said with a pout.

"Oh, precious." Lovie held her tighter. "See those eggs that Cara's putting into the nest? In about sixty days those eggs will hatch and the hatchlings will scramble out and hurry to the sea. In thirty years, one of the females will come back here to lay her nest. And you can be here to take care of her babies. You see? You'll be doing my job for me. Around and around the cycle of life goes. It's really quite beautiful."

"I'll be here waiting, Grandmama Lovie. I promise." Linnea hugged her grandmother with a child's fervency. "I'll be here for you. . . ."

~~~~~

LINNEA HELD THE small T-shirt to her chest and felt a rush of love for her grandmother. She'd slipped away at the summer's end. But every summer since, when the sea turtles returned, Linnea thought of Lovie.

"I'm coming back to Isle of Palms, Grandmama," she whispered. "Like I promised."

~~~~~

LINNEA AWOKE AT the sound of shouting. She blinked heavily, rousing further. *Oh, yes* . . . She recognized the voice with a yawn. It was her father. *Annoying*, she thought. It sounded like he was really riled. She rubbed her fingertips over her eyes, yawning again, then pushed back her covers and rose to investigate. She opened her bedroom door and peered out. The volume heightened, and she could hear how truly angry her father was. The lights were all on downstairs, and shadows stretched out across the floor. Whatever was happening was a big deal. Her fingertips grazed the cool staircase railing as she scurried down to the main floor.

Clutching the newel, she paused at the bottom of the staircase where she could see her parents. They were standing side by side just inside the living room doorway, looking at someone she couldn't see but knew was Cooper. He must've done something really bad this time. Her father's face was red, he was jabbing his finger, and she could almost see the spittle flying across the room.

"You need the discipline of the Citadel, boy. Now more than ever. It'll make you a man!"

"I don' wanna . . ." The words slid into unrecognizable muffling.

Linnea's hand flew to her mouth. Her brother was slurring his words badly.

"You're so drunk I can hardly understand what you're saying," his father roared. "Stand straight, son, and look at me, hear?"

"Palmer . . ." her mother countered in her low, soft voice, and reached out to put her hand on his arm. Palmer rudely brushed it off.

Her mother ignored him and stepped out of sight, presumably closer to Cooper. "It's late," she said in a calm voice. "Let's go to bed. We're all overtired, and tempers are short. We can talk about this in the morning."

"I want this settled now," Palmer ground out. "This isn't one of his pranks. The boy got a DUI. That's major. It's on his record. This could ruin his chances of getting into the Citadel." He took a step closer to Cooper, almost out of view. "How could you do this to me? To your family?" He swayed slightly as he stretched out his arm and pointed at his son again. "I'm going to have to pull in a lot of favors for you."

Linnea leaned forward to catch Cooper's muttered words. She couldn't be sure, but she thought he said, "I'm not asking you to." Linnea willed her brother to just be quiet. Not to fan her father's flames of fury.

But Palmer heard and it sent him off on another rant.

Linnea put her hands over her ears and climbed back up the stairs. She couldn't listen to any more. Her stomach was roiling, and her heart was beating fast. Cooper had really blown it this time, and her father had a right to be angry. How could Cooper be so stupid and careless? But she couldn't muster any anger. This went beyond that. All she felt was a bone-chilling fear.

She slipped back into her room, closed the door softly, and leaned against it, absorbing the dark, soothing quiet. She was deeply shaken. Sure, there'd been lots of arguments in their house. Most families shouted at one another from time to time. It was nothing to be proud of but still in the realm of normal. But tonight, her father's fury had reached a new level of intensity. It had frightened her. And tonight, Cooper had reached a new low. That frightened her more.

She pressed her ear against the door. The shouting had stopped downstairs. She closed her eyes, weary, and pressed her forehead against the door. She hoped everyone had just gone to bed like her mama had suggested. These family dramas were draining. She didn't wait long before she heard heavy footfalls coming up the stairs, then Cooper's low, drunken voice.

"I'm sorry. . . ."

Her mother's soft voice followed wearily: "I know you are, honey. Come on, now. Oh, Cooper," she said, her voice shaking with heartbreak. "What am I going to do with you?"

"I'm sorry, Mama."

"Let's just get you in bed so you can sleep it off."

Linnea heard the bedroom door close. She sighed, then padded across the dark room and climbed back into her bed. She felt bone-weary and heavyhearted. She laid her head against the soft, cool pillow and closed her eyes. The tears felt hot on her face.

She was the older sibling. She'd defended Cooper, made excuses for him, was his champion, and picked him up when he fell down. And then she'd grown up and moved away, leaving him to fend for himself. She'd never worried about him. He always seemed to roll with the punches. He was popular and laid-back. She'd thought he was happy.

The young man she'd come home to was a different person. His smile was there, but his usual good humor was missing. He was drinking a lot too. Way too much. Her parents were right to be upset, but yelling at him wasn't going to help. They had to loosen up on the pressure. They had to listen to him.

Linnea squeezed her hands into fists. She wanted to help but felt powerless. It reminded her of when Cooper was little and got sick. She'd hung around his room and worried. There wasn't anything she could do. Except watch and wait.

She would watch and wait now too. She wouldn't leave him. She made the only decision she could. She wouldn't go to the beach house tomorrow. She'd call Cara and tell her she'd come when she could.

Chapter Seven

Loggerheads are found all around the world. They are the most abundant of all sea turtle species in U.S. waters and nest on the southeastern coast of the United States, mostly Florida. But their numbers worldwide are decreasing. Pollution, trawling, and development have kept this ancient mariner on the threatened species list since 1978.

WHERE DID THE *week go?* Cara wondered as she ran her hand through her hair. She stood staring at a wall calendar made by a member of the turtle team. Each month featured a color photograph of the loggerhead turtle season. For June it was a photo of a woman's cherry-red-painted toes in the sand beside two tiny hatchlings as they scrambled to the sea. And Isle of Palms and Sullivan's Island already had nineteen nests. It gave her hope that the loggerheads were trending upward. She paused, thinking again of the irony that nothing made her feel more like she'd arrived home than the sea turtles. As a girl, she'd been jealous of her mother's devotion to the turtles. As a woman, she'd taken her mother's place on the team.

The sea turtle nesting season heralded summer on Isle of Palms. Across the marshes, schools had released the children. Teachers and parents both sighed in collective relief that another year was done. Colleges were out, and families from across the country—the world—were planning vacations to the lowcountry. The floodgates were open, and already the bridges to the islands were jam-packed with traffic. Colorful towels lay scattered on the beach like confetti.

When Linnea had called and said she'd begin working the following week instead of immediately, Cara was disappointed. She'd been so eager to start the new routine. She had so much work to do. On reflection, however, she'd decided to take this gift of a week as vacation time with Hope. She'd been so frazzled when she'd arrived: the move, the drive . . . all while learning to be a mother. Yet day by day, she'd fallen into island time and felt more relaxed. Plus, she'd discovered that when she was relaxed, Hope was too. She wasn't as clingy now as she had been those first days.

"You're going on your first turtle duty," she'd told Hope when she lifted her from the crib that morning. The sun was barely up, but Cara had volunteered for today's walk to help a fellow turtle team member who was ill. She applied a heavy dose of baby suntan lotion on Hope's body, put on a broad-brimmed sun hat, and packed up a beach bag with lotion, water, sippy cup, towels, and snacks.

Cara made her way down the narrow beach path as nimble as a pack mule. All around her the dunes were cloaked with colorful wildflowers and vines. When she was young, these dunes had stretched far back to her beach house and she would be able to see the great expanses of the ocean from the street. After Hurricane

Hugo in 1989, new mansions had formed a glamorous wall along the street and nary a peek of blue ocean could be spied between them. It seemed to her that constructing the houses even closer to the water was a dare from the builders to the ocean to strike again. She chuckled to herself. She knew who'd win that contest.

Which was another reason she was so grateful to Russell Bennett for purchasing the plots of land in front of her beach house. She pushed the stroller along the beach path that traversed the property. Russell Bennett had cleverly, deliberately set aside two plots on the island for conservation. No one could build on them. He'd done it to set an example for others. The fact that he'd purchased them in front of her beach house wasn't lost on her. Russell Bennett had been the love of her mother's life. And she was his. She liked to believe that, had he lived, they would have found a way to be together. Fate was against them. As were the constraints of their time. They were both married to others when they fell in love, and divorce was a scandal. That he loved her, there could be no doubt.

For he'd left a third plot of land in Lovie's name with enough money in an offshore trust to provide for it. It was all very neatly done. Very hush-hush. And it was her mother's greatest secret. One she'd kept all her life for fear of scandal. She wouldn't allow her love affair with Russell to appear tawdry. The only ones who knew of the land were Cara, Flo, and the offshore bank. After Lovie's death, that plot of oceanfront land had been inherited by Cara. Along with the beach house.

Cara reached the beginning of the beach path and paused to catch her breath before hiking the sandy path with Hope in her arms. She looked back over her shoulder. Across the lot she could see the beach house, sitting prettily in the distance, surrounded by waving sea oats and wildflowers. She chuckled. If her brother ever found out about the land she'd inherited, he'd split a gut. Palmer had been searching for ways to buy the land given to conservation for decades, and failing that, he'd been angling for Cara to sell the beach house. His plan was to build a house on the site and make big profits for both of them.

Cara would never do that, of course. For her the beach house was a sacred place, just as much as it had been to her mother. There was no amount of money that would tempt her to sell it. She'd traveled off, true. But her name was Caretta. And like the sea turtle she was named after, she came home to nest. And this time, she wasn't going to leave.

Her muscles burned as her heels dug into the soft sand while carrying the added twenty-three pounds of Hope. *Shame on me for not walking more,* she chided herself. There was no excuse for being a hermit while living on the beach! At last she reached the end of the path and stood at the top of the dune. She lifted her chin, breathed deep the salty air, and stared out at the water. Sky and sea blended together at the horizon line to create a seamless blue so vivid she heard her breath release as a sigh. Cara had always come to the sea to relieve stress, to gather her thoughts, to recharge her batteries. It was a great peace she felt in every cell of her body.

Hope felt it too. She was smiling, her eyes dancing with happiness. Buoyed with joy, Cara hoisted her up higher in her arms and continued down the dunes to the beach. This early in the morning, there were only an older woman in a pink jogging suit walking her chocolate Lab off-leash and a young man jogging close to the surf.

She carried Hope to the shoreline and set her down, expecting her to balk at the strange feel of the sand. But this child was a little turtle. Hope didn't hesitate at all. She crawled straight for the sea. Cara was right behind her, laughing, as Hope scrambled like any hatchling into the waves. When a gentle wave slapped her face, she didn't cry; she laughed! Cara scooped her up in her arms and twirled her around, relishing the sound of her laughter.

Brett would have loved this, she thought, then squeezed Hope tighter.

~~~~

THE FOLLOWING DAY Cara took Hope to the park. She sprayed insect repellent on both herself and Hope. The mosquitoes were so fierce and big this summer she was sure one could carry Hope off. She loaded up the stroller with the bag of bottles, biscuits, and diapers, and they were off on another adventure.

The traffic on the island wasn't too bad midweek. She cruised along Palm Boulevard, seeing neighbors planting flowers and crews mowing. She took the S turn by the church and soon turned inland into the shade of towering live oak trees lining the street. At the end of the road young boys were clustered around a baseball diamond in the grass. The tennis courts were filled too. She heard the muffled grunts of serving. It was a perfect morning to be outdoors. The sky was blue, the humidity low, and the temperature not too hot. She lifted Hope from the stroller and made her way across the soft playground mulch to buckle her into a swing. She gave a hearty push and was rewarded with a gurgling laugh from Hope.

A sweet-faced girl no older than five walked up to the bigger swing. With her long pigtails slipping out of their elastics, a smattering of freckles, and the scab on her knee, she looked like Pippi Longstocking. She climbed onto the seat and kicked her legs mightily, but the swing barely budged. Cara looked to the other side of the park where a young mother was strapping an infant into a carrier.

"Want some help?" Cara asked the girl.

The little girl nodded gratefully. Cara walked behind her and gave her a couple of good pushes to get her going. She smiled, listening to the young girl's laughter as she flew high into the sky.

"Are you having a good time?" Cara called out to the little girl.

"Yes!" she called back.

"What's your name?"

"Jessica."

Looking over again, she caught the mother's eye. The woman smiled and waved gratefully. Cara felt a first flush of inclusion into the motherhood club.

"Is that your mama over there?"

Jessica looked to where Cara pointed, and nodded. "Yeah. She's with my baby brother. He cries a lot."

She pushed the girl a few more times and then returned to Hope. When the girl's swing slowed once more, she climbed down, already bored. Jessica hung around a few minutes longer, hanging on the poles, watching them. Then she pointed to Hope. "Is that your baby?"

"Yes. Her name is Hope."

"Are you the baby's grandma?"

A little part of Cara's self-esteem withered with her smile. She didn't think she dressed differently or looked much older than the child's mother across the playground. She was shocked that an innocent question could make her feel so insecure.

"No," she replied. "I'm her mama."

"Oh." The little girl's perplexed look quickly disappeared, her curiosity sated. When her mother called her name, Jessica took off running, calling, "Bye!"

Cara was relieved to see her go. The sweet child had suddenly become annoying. Cara chided herself for being sensitive. She had to face the fact that though she might feel like that thirty-year-old mother, she wasn't thirty anymore. She looked again at Hope in the swing. *Was* she too old? she worried. Would her daughter ever look at her and wonder why her mother looked older than her friends' mothers?

Hope was smiling gleefully, kicking her legs, demanding another push.

Cara couldn't stop the smile that bloomed on her face. At least for now, Hope didn't care if she was young or old. Perhaps years from now, when she was in school, she might wonder. Cara knew that the day would come when Hope would have many questions. Including who her birth mother was.

Cara gave Hope another push. She would deal with those questions later. For now, these precious moments were fleeting. She took a cleansing breath, and looked out across the park. A tall man was pushing a stroller toward them across the great expanse of grass. He was nattily dressed in dark jeans and a blue-and-white-checked shirt rolled up at the sleeves. Though he was youthful in appearance, his salt-and-pepper hair hinted he was either a grand-father or an older parent, like her. Except, she thought with cha-grin, he probably had a younger wife . . . a trophy wife. She tried not to stare as he approached, but something about him seemed vaguely familiar. He was wearing aviator sunglasses, which made it harder to tell if she knew him. She absently gave Hope another push.

Then he looked her way. When their gazes met, she felt sud-denly embarrassed for being caught staring. But then a wide grin of recognition stretched across his tanned face, and he picked up the pace. As he drew closer, Cara was stunned. Unless she was mis-taken, he was Heather's father, David Wyatt. She hadn't seen him since that pelican release on Sullivan's Island, was it three years ago? In a flash she recalled his thoughtfulness that difficult sum-mer. He was a good father to Heather, and it appeared he was a good grandfather to Rory as well. And, she thought with a be-mused smile, he was just as good-looking as she remembered.

She waved her hand in greeting. "Well, look who's here!" she called out. "What are you doing in my sandbox?"

David laughed and called back, "This is our Wednesday morn-ing hangout. Rory and I have a couple of good swings, toss back a bottle or two, then head for home."

His voice was unusually pleasant and low. It was one of those small, telling details she sometimes pocketed away. David parked the stroller beside the swing set and removed his sunglasses. His rich brown eyes shone with warmth, and for the second time that day, Cara suddenly felt like an insecure teenager. He was even *better*-looking than she'd remembered. His thick head of dark gray and white hair sharply contrasted with his tanned skin and thick black brows. Cara felt a stirring of attraction she hadn't felt in many years. Not since before Brett had died. She'd lost interest in other men after his death, and this first flush surprised her.

"Seriously," he said. "It's good to see you, Cara. Though I almost didn't recognize you." He touched his head. "Your hair's shorter."

Cara's hand flew to her head. "Oh, that . . ." She raked her fingers through her dark hair, glad she'd decided to put a pair of small gold hoops in her ears at the last minute. "I needed a change."

"It's a nice change," David said. Then he glanced over at Hope. "Speaking of change, Heather told me you have a daughter. Congratulations."

"Thank you."

"She's a beauty."

Cara was relieved to have an excuse to bring her attention back to Hope. "She is. And congratulations to you too," she added, indicating Rory. "It seems both of our lives have changed since we last saw each other."

His grin widened. "Boy, have they."

"Rory is about the same age as Hope, right?"

"He's a little over a year. Fourteen months."

"Hope is coming up on her first birthday on the eighteenth. I'm still waiting for her to take her first steps."

"Rory took off before he hit a year," David said proudly. "We have to keep an eye on him. He's suddenly into everything."

She allowed him his boasting rights. It was surprisingly pleasant to be chatting about the children instead of politics or making awkward chitchat. In fact, David was surprisingly easy to talk to. She remembered that about him, how he readily made anyone feel at ease. He lifted Rory from the stroller, and Cara noticed the strong lines of his physique. He had the trim body of a man who exercised regularly. He settled Rory in the second baby swing and came around to stand beside Cara. They pushed the children side by side at a companionable pace.

"How long are you here for?" she asked, thinking she'd like to invite him to dinner, along with Heather and Bo, of course.

He tilted his head, and his eyes glimmered with amusement. "I live here now. Hadn't you heard?"

"No!" she replied, her jaw slipping open.

"I retired from my law practice, sold my house, and moved here. Bought a house on Dewees. In fact, the kids live with me now." He laughed.

"Really?" Cara was astonished. He'd retired? She didn't think David was even sixty. Plus, she couldn't imagine Heather living in the same house as Natalie. Heather despised his second wife, and the feeling was mutual. "Dewees is so isolated. I can understand Heather moving there. And Bo. Even you. But Natalie didn't strike me as the outdoorsy, nature-loving type."

His smile fell, and he shook his head. "She wasn't. Turned out she wasn't my type, either. We're divorced."

Cara shot an involuntary glance at his ring finger. The gold wedding band was no longer there.

She smiled ruefully. "Well, this certainly is a day for catching up." She paused to digest the information, using the time to give Hope another gentle push. "Frankly, I'm amazed that choice bit of gossip hadn't reached me." She gave another push. "Though I have to say, I'm not surprised."

David skipped a beat. "Apparently no one was. Except me. No fool like an old fool and all that."

"Not so old."

He slanted her a glance of appreciation.

"Besides," Cara added, "Natalie was a clever manipulator."

"She didn't fool you."

Cara shrugged lightly. "I'm not easily fooled. Plus, I was on Team Heather."

"You were," he said as his gaze swept over her. "I always appreciated that. She blossomed under your care."

"I can't take any credit for that. Heather worked hard for her success. Art is a tough business to make a mark in. But don't forget, she took good care of me too. Those were some dark days." His expression told her he remembered. "Heather's a remarkable young woman. You must be very proud."

"She gave me Rory. She can do no wrong."

"How do *you* like living on Dewees? Quite a change from a city like Charlotte."

"I love it. I've finally got the time to do things like learn the names of birds and plants. I've become quite well versed on alligators too." He laughed. "The folks on Dewees are genuine. And quite social. We come out for the occasional party or town event. But all of us like our privacy and respect that. And my house is an architectural gem. The previous owners were looking to sell just as I started looking. I fell in love at first sight. Had to have it. And it's Heather's favorite house on the island, so that was another big selling point. I bought the furniture too, so it was an easy move. You'll have to come see it."

"I'd love to." She could imagine him slipping into a new house, a new lifestyle, with ease. Little seemed to faze this man.

His face was handsome, but not in a pretty way. More interesting, with his deep-set eyes, thick brows, and high, bold cheekbones. His features and height gave the impression of strength. She imagined he was formidable in the courtroom.

"Do you miss practicing law?"

He shook his head. "Not at all."

"Still, a bit of a culture shock living on an island without shops or restaurants, or cars, for that matter?"

"Yes," he agreed. "It was at the beginning."

"What do you do to fill your days? You were so busy in Charlotte."

"I'm busier than ever. Bo's in high demand on the island, and his carpentry business off-island has him out a lot. Heather's receiving a lot of commissions for paintings. Plus, she's preparing for her first show. So, with the two of them in the thick of their careers . . ." He shrugged. "I sort of slid into taking care of Rory. That boy keeps me busy."

"You're a manny!" exclaimed Cara.

His brows rose. "A what?"

"A male nanny. A manny," she explained.

A slight flush colored his tan cheeks as a crooked smile slid onto his face. He shifted his gaze to his grandson. "Yeah, I guess that's my new job title. Long hours, no pay, but lots of benefits."

She found his confidence enormously attractive.

"How about you?" he asked, shifting the spotlight. "Are you a full-time mom these days? Or working?"

Long answer or short answer? she wondered. She could tell Hope's enthusiasm was waning, so opted for the short answer. "I'm the sole provider, so being a full-time mom isn't an option. I'm doing consult work now and seeing how that turns out. I lucked out last week. My niece is coming to live with me this summer to help me out with Hope. I still want to be hands-on, but I can't focus on my work when she's tugging at me. I'm still searching for a balance."

"Heather still worries about being away from Rory too much, but since she has dear old Dad taking care of him, she's feeling less guilt. I hope . . ."

"I'm told mother guilt is a universal emotion."

"Neither of you should feel guilt. As for Heather, this is her moment. In the art world, they don't come often. She has to take it. And we get along just fine, don't we, pal?" he asked, rubbing his fingers through Rory's blond hair.

Hope started whining in the swing, indicating she'd had her fill of this ride.

"That's my cue." Cara slowed the swing and lifted Hope into her arms. She smoothed a dark curl from Hope's forehead, then touched the spot with her lips. "Okay, baby," she crooned. "Mama's taking you home."

David moved closer and bent to look into Hope's face. "I know she's adopted," he said, "but she's your spitting image. Especially her eyes."

Cara could never hear that compliment enough. "I'm flattered to be compared to a baby. My ego took a solid hit today. Before you got here, a little girl asked me if I was Hope's grandma."

"Ouch!" David laughed. "No offense to the little girl, but she's crazy. You don't look like anyone's grandmother." He snorted and said in an offhand manner, "Hardly."

"My self-esteem has been reassured," she told him. She couldn't deny the current flowing between them. Tall, chiseled features, intelligent—he was her type. Still, she didn't feel comfortable getting flirtatious with David. He was Heather's dad, after all. She moved Hope to her other hip. "And now, I must go. My boss is getting hungry."

"Let me help you," David said, and went to fetch the stroller. He held it steady while Cara put Hope back inside. When she was settled, David stepped back and said, "I was serious about having you come see the house."

When she turned to face him, he asked, "When can you come?"

Cara was nonplussed by the suddenness of the invitation. "To Dewees?"

"That's where the house is," he said.

"I have Hope."

"And I have Rory." He smiled that easy smile that lowered the tension. "We'll make it a playdate."

She had to laugh. That was a new one. She'd told herself she wasn't going to flirt, but he was on a full-court press. Plus, a playdate seemed harmless.

"A playdate sounds perfect."

"Great. When? Tomorrow?"

"Are you always this pushy?"

"Only when it matters."

Cara took a breath. "Let's make it the day after tomorrow. Hope has a doctor's appointment tomorrow, and she'll be cranky after her shots."

"Friday it is, then. I'll put your name on the list as my guest for the nine o'clock ferry and meet you at the dock with the golf cart."

"Sounds like a plan."

For a moment, neither spoke. There didn't seem to be anything left to say.

She turned away and called out, "Bye, then!"

He raised his hand in a wave. "See you."

Pushing the stroller, Cara began the long trek across the playground to the parking lot. She knew if she turned to look back, she'd see David hawking her every step.

Chapter Eight

Her nest laid, the loggerhead makes the long trek
back to the sea. She will never return to the nest. A reptile,
the turtle follows the biological model called predator glut, over-
feeding the predators so a few offspring survive, ensuring
the species, too, survives. It is estimated only one in one
thousand hatchlings will live to maturity.

CARA HAD ALWAYS believed the lowcountry showed itself best
from the water. The Dewees Island ferry slowly motored
down the narrow inlet from its dock on Isle of Palms, past impressive mansions with long docks that stretched out to the water and
the Isle of Palms Marina with its fleet of Coastal Ecotours boats,
small pleasure boats, and ocean-fit yachts.

Cara sat with Hope on her lap inside the ferry on a horseshoe-
shaped, padded bench. Beside her was an older woman carrying an
insulated bag of groceries and a bouquet of spring flowers, obviously an island resident. She chatted amiably with the captain.
Across from her a man in an appliance repair uniform sat checking
his phone, oblivious to the beauty outside his window. Two others

in outdoor work clothes looked out the windows and seemed to be enjoying the change from reaching a job via highway traffic to a boat trip along the Intracoastal Waterway.

It was an exceptionally beautiful day. Once out of the no-wake zone, the captain opened the throttle, and the engines roared. The windows of the ferry were open, and salty breezes ruffled Cara's hair and caressed her cheeks as the boat picked up speed. Hope's eyes widened at the noise, but she sat quietly and stared out the window as they raced across the crystalline water. The ferry wound its way through the Intracoastal Waterway, banked on either side by lush, spiky grass that stretched out for acres. Cara spied a long line of pelicans flying so low in formation that they seemed to skim the tall grass. She caught sight of other birds as they flew over the salt marsh but only recognized the oystercatcher with its flashy black and white coloring and bright red bill. Heather, she knew, would be able to name them all and tell her a bit about each. Cara turned her gaze to the white ruffled wake of the boat, hoping she might catch sight of a dolphin riding the waves.

It felt like she was traveling to another world. *What would it be like*, she wondered, *to cut myself off from the mainland and be accessible only by boat?* She imagined life's stresses would diminish. Or would new stressors be added? She could see Heather and Bo being perfectly suited to such a lifestyle. They appreciated a simpler life, apart from the crowds. Cara, on the other hand, was accustomed to the instant gratification of convenience. She'd lived much of her adult life in Chicago, where everything she needed was at her fingertips. Moving to Isle of Palms had been a significant slowing down for her. *Could I go one step further and be con-*

nected to shops only by a boat ride? Could she raise a child there? Her thoughts turned to David. He was such a vibrant man, accustomed to fast-paced city living. How did he do it?

She'd have her answer soon, she thought as the boat slowed down. She turned to look out the window and saw they were approaching a small island. A long wooden dock led to a wide covered deck with a large green sign that read: DEWEES ISLAND, S.C. WELCOME.

The mighty engines lowered to a growl and a whiff of diesel permeated the cabin as the captain guided the boat into position beside the dock. Cara watched the deckhand toss ropes ashore, then nimbly jump from the boat to the dock to tie them to the pilings. Done, he jumped back aboard the boat to lower the landing platform. Around her the passengers were on their feet, queuing at the door. Cara joined them, grabbing her bag and firming her grip on Hope.

Cara felt a welcome, bracing gust of sea air that caused the ferry to rock. She grabbed hold of the railing as overhead a laughing gull cried out its mocking call. Cara's mama used to call her a laughing gull when she was young because of her dark cap of hair and her loud voice. She chuckled at the memory and looked at Hope.

"What kind of bird are you?" she asked. Considering the child's wide-eyed curiosity and quiet, observant manner, Cara said, "Not a gull, that's for sure." She kissed Hope's forehead. "Something sweet. We'll have to ask Aunt Heather for suggestions."

She stepped out onto the long ramp from the boat to the dock, where a cluster of people waited. She immediately spotted one man whose salt-and-pepper head rose taller than the rest. He wore sunglasses and a pale-blue fishing shirt. And in his arms he carried a baby. He raised a bronzed arm in an arc of welcome and called her name. Two women near him turned toward the passengers, curious to see who he was calling. *Perhaps they find him attractive too*, she thought with a slight smile.

Cara smiled wide in acknowledgment. David walked around the two women and met her as she reached the top of the landing.

"David Wyatt," Cara said warmly. "And Rory! How nice of you to meet us."

"Of course. Have to teach my boy manners. Let me carry that," he said, taking her bag with his free arm. "Your ride is right this way." He guided her through the covered dock and past the two women, who scrutinized her with brazen curiosity.

"I think you have a few admirers," she told him sotto voce.

David quickly looked over his shoulder. A bemused smile stretched across his tanned face. "Just neighbors," he said.

Uh-huh, Cara thought, but didn't press. She certainly understood the women's attraction. David was a handsome man by any standard. But here on Dewees, clearly in his element, he was especially magnetic.

A long line of thirty or more golf carts was parked at the edge of the landing. How anyone could spot their own cart when they returned from the boat was beyond Cara. But David had no trouble leading them to a large navy double-seater with two car seats already strapped in.

"Your limo awaits you," he said with a flourish.

"My . . . you went to a lot of trouble."

"Golf carts are our main means of transportation here. We

keep them charged and ready to go. It's safer in the back, if you and Hope want to hop in. Rory and I will take you on the scenic route."

After they were all strapped in, David slapped a black Panthers ball cap on his head.

"Panthers fan?" she asked.

He turned to look back over the seat. "Of course. You?"

She laughed. She wouldn't know one team from the next. "I love 'em all," she replied evasively.

"Spoken like someone who doesn't watch football."

"Guilty as charged."

"Did you bring a hat?"

"Forgot it."

"Then you won't mind wearing this one." He reached down to pull a hat out of his bag and handed her a purple ball cap with an orange tiger logo. Looking at it, Cara felt her heart twinge. She knew this logo well. Brett had gone to Clemson.

"Go Tigers!" she exclaimed and put the hat on her head.

As she put on her sunglasses, David deftly backed the long cart out of the narrow parking spot, and they were on their way. Cara had been to Dewees many times, but each time she was struck anew by the island's seemingly untouched beauty. Most of the houses were hidden behind a thick barrier of trees and shrubs, leaving a small footprint in the natural vegetation. Pine trees, tallow, and massive live oaks lined the roads, creating a ragged canopy of shade. Butterflies hovered over wildflowers, and birds sang in the trees. There was an abundance of wildlife, and Cara felt as though they were the only ones on the island. She understood exactly why shy Heather would love living here.

David slowed and pointed to the left as they passed a small lake. Birds of different sizes waded near the shoreline. She recognized the white egrets, then gasped with delight when she spotted the unmistakable rosy pink plumage of a few roseate spoonbills. Heather had told her about them, but she'd never seen the elusive bird . . . until now. They were like flamingos, with flat bills. Both elegant and comical. *A beguiling combination*, she thought, utterly charmed.

Thank you, she mouthed when he turned his head to meet her gaze. He smiled with satisfaction, turned toward the front once more, patted Rory, and then they were off. The little cart moved in its bumbling manner over ruts and small rocks in the dirt road. The second time he stopped, David stepped from the cart. He waved for Cara to get out as well, smiling.

"Come take a look." When he saw her turn to Hope, he said, "Leave the children buckled up. It's right over here. It'll only take a minute."

Cara was reluctant to leave Hope in the cart. Mosquitoes buzzed by. Cara was wearing thin jeans and a long-sleeved white shirt, but Hope was in a summer dress and a sunbonnet. Cara reached into her bag and pulled out a light muslin blanket and covered the baby's body. She checked on Rory—he had long sleeves and pants. Satisfied, she climbed from the cart. David reached out and took her hand, leading her only a few feet from the edge of the road. He slid his hand to her shoulder and guided her to stand in front of him, then pointed. Cara tried to adjust to the feelings racing through her with his body so close to hers. She followed the direction of his finger and saw a large pond just beyond the brush. Insects flittered in the steamy haze, and a few egrets waded along the mud banks. In the middle of the pond was a large floating dock. And in its center, resting like a log, was an alligator.

"It's enormous!" Cara exclaimed with a short laugh.

"That's Big Al," David told her, pleased with her reaction. "He's a celebrity on the island."

"I've never seen one so big."

"Not surprised. Seeing a big bull like that one is rare. Trouble is, since it's legal to kill alligators in South Carolina, we're losing our mature ones. That's a surefire way to decimate a population, especially since this is an animal that takes a long time to mature and breed. That bull over there is at least thirty years old."

"He's lying like a statue out there. And those yellow-bellied sliders next to him don't seem to mind him at all."

"That's because he's digesting his food. As a reptile, he needs to regulate his digestive system. See how he keeps his mouth open? I used to think that was threatening until I learned it's their way of regulating body temperature. Like a dog panting."

Cara glanced at him. "You've become quite the encyclopedia."

He chortled and scratched his ear. "I've got a lot of time on my hands," he said with characteristic modesty. "I've always wanted to study this stuff but didn't have the time."

Cara looked over her shoulder to check on the children.

David noticed and took a step toward the cart. "We should get back. Only wanted to introduce you to Big Al. Alligators generally keep to themselves, but they wander. Al's never threatened a resident," he said, then paused. "But once I saw him walking toward the water with a whole raccoon dangling in his jaws. So it's good to keep dogs leashed and children close. And don't ever try to feed a gator. Not if you want to keep your arm."

"Noted," she said with an exaggerated shiver.

He laughed lightly and helped her into the cart.

"Time to get these cuties home," David called out as he turned on the motor.

"Good idea."

The cart was off again, bumping along the road. She turned her head to check on Hope when they bounced over a rut. She was proud her little girl only laughed.

They rounded the picturesque island to the ocean side. Along both sides of the dirt road, narrow driveways just wide enough for a golf cart were marked with wooden number signs and the names of the owners. The roads all disappeared into the brush. At last David turned off at one marked WYATT & STANTON. The drive meandered into a shadowy enclave of woods and over a small wooden bridge across a rivulet of water to a wide graveled courtyard. Before them loomed a tall house of dark wood and glass with levels that jutted off at angles. It seemed to be part of the forest surrounding it.

"I know this house!" Cara said, reaching forward across the seat to touch David's shoulder. "This is the house Bo worked on a few years back. He created the porches and . . ." She paused to look over the property. "There! I knew it. That's the tree house he built."

She heard him softly chuckle. He stretched his long arm over the seat and removed his sunglasses to meet her gaze. "Yep, this is it." He turned back to the house. "It's a gem. How could I not buy it?"

"I can't believe you got *this* house. However did you manage it?"

"The usual way," he said with a modest shrug.

"Don't be coy. How did you buy this particular house, and knowing how much it meant to Bo and Heather?"

"Pure luck," David admitted. "I came here and started looking for a house. Judy Fairchild—do you remember her? She's the real estate agent and mayor of the island. Wonderful lady. Anyway, she knew of one that might go on the market. She made a phone call, and as it happened, the owners were indeed considering selling. When it turned out to be this house, I knew it was fate. I didn't fool around looking at other houses. I made a good offer, and they accepted."

Cara studied him, liking him more. "Knowing that Bo and Heather loved the house."

David shrugged again. "I loved it too. And the bonus was the owners were downsizing to move to a retirement community, so they sold it furnished. It was a turnkey move."

"If I recall, the furniture was uniquely chosen for the house. And quite special."

"True. They made sophisticated choices that suited me. In the end, we were pleased with the way it all turned out. I brought a few personal items from Charlotte, of course. But for the most part, it's pretty much as you remember. Let's go in."

They disembarked, releasing the babies from their seats.

"There's an elevator, if you want it," David offered.

"I could use the exercise."

"That's how I feel. Especially with an extra twenty-five pounds in my arms. Who needs a gym when you carry weights around all day, right?"

"Right," she agreed with a laugh. Babies in arms, they walked up the long flight of stairs. Cara paused at the two landings lined with planters along the way. Thankfully it was cool in the woods. All around her birds chirped and darted. A flash of blue made her heart jump. She hadn't seen an indigo bunting in years. At the top, the massive, carved-wood front doors made a stunning statement, flanked by two stone planters filled with coleus and greenery.

Once inside, Cara turned around, mouth agape, enjoying the dramatically jutting ceilings and tall windows, which created the feeling of living among the trees. The décor was as she remembered, simple and spare. Her eyes widened at the George Nakashima chair in the foyer. Yes, it was very much the remarkable house she remembered.

David took her on a brief tour, moving through the halls and pointing out this and that in his rich, low voice. She thought how well the strong lines, the elegance, and the ageless quality of the house suited the man.

The sounds of canaries chirping caught her attention as he led her up to the second floor. "Aha! How are the canaries?"

"They love it here."

"They must. It's like living outdoors. Does she still have both birds?"

"More!" He laughed. "You know Heather. She's passionate. Now she's gotten into breeding them. We had babies last spring." He rolled his eyes and began walking again. "I'll let her show you the happy families later." David stopped to ask her, "You wouldn't want another bird, would you?"

Cara laughed and shook her head. "No, Moutarde is quite territorial. He'd get jealous."

"Let us know if you change your mind—please."

Cara laughed again, enjoying his acceptance of Heather's passion for birds. She thought again what an intrinsically kind man he was. They reached an outdoor porch, and David opened the door. Cara sucked in her breath when she saw the long wooden walkway that extended from the porch to a small turret house nestled in the trees.

"Bo was so proud of this," she said, appreciating the tree house's design. "I still think it looks like something fairies might live in."

"Most people say that it stirs the imagination."

"What couldn't the imagination create in a room like that? You know," she said, remembering, "this is a telltale moment."

"How so?"

"Bo built the turret house for the previous owners. But when we toured, we all shared what *we'd* use the room for if we lived here. Each answer was different."

"What'd you want to do with the room?"

She thought back, seeing in her mind a gorgeous desk in the center of the room. "I wanted a desk. What an office it would make."

He laughed. "Of course."

"I wouldn't mind going to work in there!" she said a bit defensively. "Bo wanted a bed."

She caught his eye, and they exchanged a long, amused look.

"And Heather," Cara continued, "wanted to put an easel in the room."

"Shall we see?"

"I'll bet *you* put a desk in it," Cara said with a teasing glance.

"Come on, then."

The turret house was the size of a garden cottage and built like a fortress. David turned at the door, and his gaze met hers.

"Want to take a guess?"

"No. Open it!"

He swung open the door with a *swoosh*. Inside the wood-walled room she saw that Heather's wish had come true. Her easel was set up in the center of the room. Everywhere else—stacked against the walls, hanging on walls, piled in corners, and covering the floor—were canvases. Trees, water scenes, portraits of Rory, but most of them birds—shorebirds, wading birds, songbirds. Cara went to the easel and inhaled with amazement. Heather was in the process of painting a trio of roseate spoonbills. They clustered together in the water, their reflections shining back at them. The light in the feathers was ethereal. Cara stared at the painting for several minutes, taking in the beauty. But Hope's wiggling to get down broke her concentration.

"She's so talented," Cara breathed.

"I think so. Then again, I'm her father."

Cara studied the canvas on the easel. "The quality of light in her paintings . . ." She paused. "She's growing. Getting better."

"Yes," he said with a father's pride.

She looked up at David. "You say she's having a show?"

"At the end of the summer. She's working hard."

"I'd better get in early with my bid." She indicated the painting on the easel. "Will this one be for sale? I'm quite taken with it."

"You'll have to ask her."

"I will. But I don't want her to give it to me. She's too generous. I already have one of her pieces from the first stamp collection over my mantel. But if I can afford it, this one has my name on it. You know, my mama liked to collect the art of people she knew. She used to say that when she looked around the house at her paintings, she felt surrounded by friends." Cara smiled. "I've always liked that. And as a result I've inherited some paintings that have gone way up in value over the years."

Hope whined in her arms. "Oh no. She's beginning that limp body thing that makes her dead weight. We've kept these two locked up for too long. Where can we let them run?"

David shifted Rory to his other side. "Follow me. I've planned adventures."

The morning flew by with fun activities for the children. They spent a luxurious hour, just the four of them, on the deserted beach. The sun dazzled in a clear sky. Hope and Rory kicked their legs in glee while Cara and David dipped them in the ocean. They sat under the shade of an umbrella while the two toddlers endlessly poured sand from one container to another. After a bath and lunch back at the house, the babies fell asleep without a fuss.

"I'd offer you a glass of wine, but—"

"—we're on baby duty," she finished for him. She suddenly felt very tired. A glass of wine would have put her to sleep.

"I've got iced tea. Sweet or unsweetened?"

"Sweet. Thanks."

She curled her long legs up onto the cushions of the long, ice-blue sofa in the great room, leaned back, and closed her eyes. She heard David's footfalls, the opening of the fridge, the clinking of ice. A few minutes later she heard his voice beside her. Her eyes flew open.

"Oh, thank you." She sat up and reached for the glass. It felt cool in her hand, and she took a bracing sip of the tea. "I needed that. I can't remember the last time I played so hard," she said with a light laugh.

"It's times like these when I understand why people have kids young."

"I'm going to start walking every day and lifting weights."

David moved to sit in the pale-blue cushioned chair across from her. He took a long drink, and then asked, "So, how are you settling in?"

"Pretty well. I have to remind myself I'm not here for a few weeks' vacation but forever."

"I remember that feeling. Especially right after I retired from my practice. I felt guilty for sleeping in or reading the paper instead of rushing off to work." He paused. "That feeling passes."

She took another sip, then ventured the question that had been niggling at her. "Aren't you a bit young to retire?"

David leaned back. "My law practice was a big part of my life, I admit. An important and challenging part. But it wasn't all of my life. I have other business ventures. Investments. And I've taken on a few more." He laughed lightly. "You met one of them."

"Ah yes, Rory. He takes a considerable amount of your time."

"He does for now. I'm enjoying the summer with him. But we have Miss Sara come three days a week. She's Rory's official nanny."

"Oh, I see," she said. "You don't babysit every day?"

He shook his head. "Just two days a week. And that's only when Heather needs me. A bit more now. I'm on board for this summer while she prepares for her show. And I enjoy it. I didn't spend much time with Heather when she was growing up, even though she is my only child. I was building my career, always working. Most men in that stage of life are caught in that spiral," he added, not by way of defense but as a matter of fact. "My wife, Leslie, was a stay-at-home mom. She did everything." His face softened at the memory. "She was a wonderful wife and mother. Creative and full of heart. Heather was such a shy child. We didn't understand she had an anxiety disorder. She had few friends and didn't get invited to many parties, so Leslie would have these big birthday parties for Heather every year. Heather, of course, dreaded them."

Cara sympathized with Heather's reticence at parties. Not because she herself was shy—quite the opposite. Cara was strong-minded and never reticent about voicing her opinions, more because back in high school, she'd found the parties pointless. Cara had always been an academic. She'd excelled in business. And she'd found that she didn't need many friends, just a few true-blue ones.

Cara sipped her tea, realizing that she and Leslie were polar opposites. If Leslie was David's type, she thought, then she wasn't. But then again, neither was his second wife.

"You must miss Leslie."

"Of course. She'll always be in my heart. As I'm sure Brett will be in yours." He paused. "But I've had a long time to find peace and acceptance. Heather has too, at last." He rose to get the pitcher from the table and topped off Cara's glass. The ice clinked in the silence.

"Would she have liked this house, do you think?"

David straightened and paused, pitcher in hand, tilting his head in consideration. "I never thought about it," he said. "I don't know if she'd have left her house in Charlotte. She'd designed it, decorated it. It was traditional and comfortable. Lots of curtains and wallpaper. And she loved her gardens. . . ." He looked around at his modern house, lost in thought.

"I don't think you could say Natalie was the domestic type."

He barked out a short laugh. "No." He shook his head ruefully. "No, she wasn't."

"Do you think you remarried too quickly?"

David brought the pitcher back to the table and sat in the chair, crossing his legs. He didn't answer.

Cara looked at her glass. "I'm sorry. I don't mean to pry."

He placed his hands on his thighs. "No, it's not that. I don't know the answer," he replied honestly.

"Natalie just seemed so different from how you describe Leslie."

"She was."

There followed a long silence.

"You see," David began again, "you don't pick up where you left off when your spouse dies. That's the first thing you learn. Though," he added, "learning that takes time and quite a few agonizing dates." They both chuckled. "Anyone you date is going to be a different person, with his or her own likes, dislikes, strengths, flaws. It's a different relationship. New. I started out looking for a clone of Leslie. It doesn't take long to figure out it doesn't work like that. With Natalie, there was a spark. She was very accomplished. Beautiful." His lips slid into a rueful smile. "She flattered me." He flipped his palms up. "Who knows?" he said with a shrug. He leaned back, grabbed his glass, and took a drink. "Apparently, I did marry too quickly."

"I'm only curious because I'm struggling with the whole starting life over thing," she told him. "Widowhood is such a limbo. Even the name is horrible. 'Widow'—makes me think of a deadly spider. It's been almost three years." Saying it still gave her pause. There were days she had to think long and hard to recall what it felt like to be with Brett. On other days she still thought he was alive and expected him to walk into the room or make a comment.

"I've made a life for myself . . . without him. The old saying that life goes on isn't just a cliché. Hope filled a huge hole in my heart. With her, I have purpose again." She paused. "Being home, though, has flushed out a lot of memories that lay dormant. Little things spark a memory. They come from nowhere and catch me off guard." She sighed. "But the pain isn't as sharp. That means something, I suppose."

"Sure it does," he said gently. "Every step forward matters."

She knew he wasn't preaching, but speaking from experience. "I'll remember that."

Cara felt they'd both said more than they felt comfortable sharing and turned to another subject.

"So," she said in an upbeat tone. "Now you live on Dewees Island. That's quite a change. Do you ever feel isolated here, so far from other people?"

He shook his head. "I take the ferry in several times a week. I often go to Charleston. And I still travel quite a bit. Sometimes it feels like I don't spend enough time here, enjoying the quiet."

"And those other projects you're involved in. Do they take up much of your time?"

"As much as I care to give," David said. "I enjoy managing my investments. It's rather like playing a game of chess. Both chess players and investors know that strategy is key. Each piece has a role to play. One has to look into the future and calculate the moves, the offense and defense."

She raised a brow. "How's the game going?"

"So far, I'm winning."

Cara thought of David being able to make an offer on this house that the owners couldn't refuse, of his early retirement, his support of Heather, his world travel, and realized his wealth had to be considerable.

"You'll have to give me some tips," she told him in a wry tone, adding, "Once I have money to invest." She swirled the ice in her drink. "For now, I'm trying to build up my consult business. If you know of anyone, send them my way."

It was a good place to end their conversation. They both turned their heads at the sound of a baby crying. They looked at each other and smiled reluctantly, and suddenly David no longer appeared a successful lawyer, but a younger, freer man.

A second cry echoed through the cavernous rooms.

"Back to work," David said.

As they headed toward the bedroom to fetch the babies, Cara considered how much they had in common. She wasn't the same person she'd been three years ago. Nor was he. They'd both lost partners. They'd both been alone, and now fate had designed that they both had a new baby in their lives.

Although this was a playdate for the children, she was surprised by how much they'd learned about each other.

And by how much she liked David Wyatt.

Chapter Nine

*Loggerhead hatchlings are less than three inches long when
they emerge, but those that survive to adulthood grow into
three-foot-long, three-hundred-plus-pound adults.*

THE BEACH HOUSE had a long history as a haven for women,
and Linnea felt their spirit the moment she stepped inside.

"Welcome!" Cara exclaimed, pulling her indoors. She wrapped
her long arms around her, and Linnea caught the scent of limes
and flowers in her perfume.

Pulling back, she looked up into her aunt's face. At five feet
four inches, Linnea was a good four inches shorter than Cara. Her
aunt was still quite thin but looked more alive and healthy than the
last time she'd seen her. She had the glow of an early tan and a
blush of greeting on her face as her eyes danced with joy.

Linnea dropped her bag on the floor and took a sweeping

glance around the beloved house. She felt a flush of gladness sweep through her. It was as though she'd left a dark room and stepped into the sunshine.

"I'm back!" she said exultantly.

"You look wonderful."

"You look happy."

"I *am* happy," Cara said with confidence. "Hope and I both. Especially now that you've arrived. Come in and make yourself at home." She grabbed hold of the suitcase.

"Where's my girl?"

"Napping." Cara rolled her eyes. "I hope. I've made such a fuss." She lowered her voice to a whisper. "I'll just bring this to your room. We can duck out. You know what they say about sleeping dogs and children."

Linnea followed Cara to the spare room across from Hope's nursery. She knew the room had once been her daddy's. Cara, in typical fashion, had redecorated it to be more comfortable for Linnea. She'd brought back her old black-iron bed, the one Linnea had always slept on when she came here. It was covered with fresh white matelassé bedding, and perched on top was a large stuffed turtle that had been Linnea's in childhood.

"You still have it?" she exclaimed. When Cara shushed her, she added in a whisper, "How did you keep it all these years?"

"Your grandmother Lovie never threw anything away. I used to chide her for it. Now I'm happy she didn't. I'm slowly going through the storage unit and finding all sorts of treasures."

"If you find any of her old clothes, let me know."

Cara's gaze swept Linnea's white shorts and 1940s-style top.

On her feet were a great pair of seventies-era sandals she'd found in Columbia.

"I'd forgotten you love vintage clothing. Oh, honey, I found some really choice items of Lovie's. Dresses, skirts, even some of her old turtle team shirts. I couldn't squeeze in them, but you look to be the same size. I was just going to take them all to Goodwill."

"No!" Linnea exclaimed without thinking, immediately cringing and putting her hand over her mouth. They froze while Hope stirred in the next room . . . then smiled when silence returned. She whispered, "Please let me see them?"

Cara laughed softly. "Of course. Now, let's sneak out of here. You don't want to meet cranky Hope."

Linnea didn't think there was such a creature as "cranky Hope." She soon learned that that was not true.

~~~~

LINNEA THOUGHT HOPE was a beguiling girl with her limpid brown eyes and wispy dark brown curls against her light skin. After the baby woke, Cara gave Linnea a tour of Hope's nursery, where the stash of diapers, clothing, et cetera, were stored, then on to the kitchen to find baby supplies, and finally the living room where she stored the toys.

"It'll take a few days for you to really get used to being here and create a routine," Cara told her. "I suspect you'll both need a few days to adjust. I thought I'd go out and run a few errands. Give you two some time to get acquainted without me in the way."

"I'm sure we'll be fine," Linnea told her, smiling into Hope's face. "We're best friends already, aren't we?"

Hope stared back at her doubtfully from her mother's arms. Cara was wearing a long, flowing skirt and a tank top with a chunky necklace and espadrilles. Linnea, on the other hand, was dressed for babysitting in short yoga pants and a T-shirt and was barefoot. She'd pulled her hair back and her face was scrubbed clean.

When the appointed hour arrived, Cara tried to pass Hope over to her, but Hope began shrieking and clinging to Cara. Linnea felt nervous, wanting to make a good impression. Babies, she quickly learned, didn't care about impressions.

"I'm sorry—" Linnea began, frustrated at her own ineptness.

"You don't have to apologize," Cara said. "Babies cry when they want something. Either they are hungry, which she isn't. Wet"— Cara made a quick check of Hope's diaper—"and she isn't. Or sleepy, which she isn't. So it simply means she wants something."

"You."

"Yes, I'm afraid so." Cara exhaled, thinking. "Maybe if we get her started playing with her toys," she suggested. "The power of distraction."

The two women sat on the floor and began playing with the building blocks and small dolls until Hope grew engrossed. Cara quietly rose to her feet and tried to slip away, but Hope's radar picked it up. Immediately she swung her head around and called out, "Mama," abandoned the toys, and began crawling after Cara.

Linnea desperately tried to distract her. She frantically wiggled the doll in her hand and called Hope's name, all to no effect.

They repeated this pattern two more times before Cara, growing exasperated, finally said, "I think we should just tear the Band-Aid off. You take her in your arms and I'll say a quick good-bye. I'll go out to do my errands. Eventually she has to learn that Mama has to work and Mama will come back." She followed her own advice with action, and shortly the door closed behind her.

Linnea realized in the next few minutes that she really knew nothing about taking care of babies. She'd babysat when she was younger, but the children could walk and talk. Babies were another world. Hope cried and cried and couldn't be comforted. Linnea tried interesting her in toy after toy, but Hope only grew more frustrated. Her face was pink and tears flowed down her cheeks. Linnea felt helpless. When Hope crawled to her mother's bedroom door and sat there crying piteously, Linnea's heart broke.

She began to wonder, *Is there something wrong with me?* She'd always thought motherhood would come naturally. She'd had no idea that it could be so agonizingly hard. Or that she'd feel not only frustration but fear. What was she doing wrong? She ran to get her laptop and googled how to handle a baby crying. Scanning the list, she found she'd already tried most of the helpful tips. The one that hit home reassured her to stay calm.

Linnea thought Hope would self-soothe and tire of crying eventually, but twenty minutes later she was only gaining steam. The walls were closing in on her with Hope's screams echoing. The canary, of course, thought the crying was marvelous and was singing his heart out. It was mayhem. Linnea was near to bursting into tears herself.

What would Cara do? Linnea wondered. Then she knew it was time to take charge.

"Come on, sugar," she called out in a cheery voice as she made her way through the pile of toys scattered across the floor to Hope, who'd pulled herself up and was standing at her mother's door. "We're going outside!"

She picked up the stiff-legged child and first wiped her face of tears, kissing her frequently. She slipped into sandals, grabbed the beach bag of supplies, and carried Hope out the porch door into the sunlight. It was another in a line of gorgeous summer days on the island. The sun was shining in a clear sky, and it was neither too hot nor too humid. Linnea saw the blue ocean's soothing, rolling surf, and immediately she felt the tension lessen. The serene, twinkling water stretched out to infinity.

Then it struck her—Hope had stopped crying! No longer stiff, the child had relaxed comfortably into her arms. Her dark eyes, a bit puffy from crying, were calm now as she looked out toward the sea. A whisper of a breeze ruffled her soft curls and, blinking, Hope smiled at the sensation.

Linnea's heart bloomed with love for her. "You're a kindred spirit, aren't you?" She squeezed the baby. "Let's go to the sea. It's calling us!"

Linnea put sunscreen all over both of them, then carried Hope along the narrow beach path, pointing out all the wildflowers and grasses on the dunes as they walked by. "There's yellow primrose. That was your grandmama Lovie's favorite. That's morning glory, my favorite. And be careful of the prickly sandspurs. They hurt so badly! I'll tell you a story Lovie told me.

"There used to live here the most beautiful small parrot called the Carolina parakeet. The sweet, colorful birds ate the nasty sandspur seeds. The seeds were toxic, and cats that ate the parakeets died. So it helped with the wild cat population too. Oh, those parakeets loved the sandspur seeds! But the Carolina parakeet is gone now. Isn't that sad? There used to be flocks of two to three hundred. Can you imagine such a sight?" She sighed and looked at the sky, imagining a colorful flock. "Hunting, deforestation, and disease destroyed every single bird. They're all gone. And see the sandspurs everywhere? They are the parakeets' revenge!"

She laughed lightly, remembering Lovie's laugh. Being here again, surrounded by the dunes, the beach, especially during turtle season, Linnea felt Lovie's presence and was comforted by it.

Hope began kicking her legs in excitement once they hit the beach. She was saying, "Beesh, beesh." Linnea laughed again at the child's precociousness. "You're saying 'beach,' aren't you? Well, okay. Let's get to the beach!" She trotted quickly across the sand to where the sparkling sea rolled up to meet the shore.

It was a glorious morning of dipping in the water, squeezing sand in hands, letting Hope crawl anywhere she wanted, and helping her walk in her unsteady gait. The child was fearless. It was a joy to watch. The freedom and the sea were a tonic for them both. Their spirits soared like the pelicans flying overhead, and Linnea knew that morning beach walks would be paramount in their routine for the summer.

When at last they returned to the beach house, Linnea found Hope to be sweet and compliant. There wasn't a mention of "Mama." She bathed Hope and changed her into clean clothes. She sang nursery songs to her while she prepared lunch, and afterward brought her to the couch to read books. Hope loved books and was eager to learn new words.

Linnea didn't remember how many books she read aloud. The last story she remembered was about a bunny in a great green room, a moon, mittens, and kittens. The last words she remembered saying were "Goodnight, noises everywhere."

~~~~~

CARA RUSHED HOME, worried that she'd spent too long away. She'd finished her errands, then was surprised to receive a phone call from a prospective client. She'd pulled into a coffee shop for an impromptu conversation that resulted in new business. Cara felt like she was soaring on wings all across the Connector to the island. She did worry, however, how the two were faring on their first day alone together. She'd checked her phone a hundred times for any SOS texts from Linnea, but there were none.

When she entered the beach house, all was quiet. She looked at her watch. It was Hope's naptime. When she stepped into the living room, she had to stifle the laugh. There on the sofa she saw Linnea fast asleep with Hope cuddled in her arms. Like two peas in a pod.

And more, Cara breathed in the comforting, heady scent of jasmine.

~~~~~

AFTER THE BEACH trip, Linnea's transition into the beach house went seamlessly. In just one week, she and Hope were fast friends.

Cara purchased a beach stroller that would allow Linnea to go on turtle team walks with Hope.

After two weeks, Linnea and Hope had developed a routine. Cara was able to go into her office and work without Hope crying to be with her. Linnea could hear her fingers tapping on the keyboard and the murmur of the occasional business phone call. Everyone felt at ease with the new arrangement. Proof of its success came the afternoon that Hope cried when Linnea left.

Early one morning Linnea was walking at a brisk pace along the shoreline, pushing Hope in the new stroller. One of her first jobs as a junior turtle team member had been to carry a plastic bag and pick up trash left behind on the beach. It had taught her at an early age to always toss garbage into the containers and never litter. Plastic was a scourge of the oceans. For her morning walks, she continued the tradition and carried a trash bag on the corner of the stroller.

It was a quiet morning on the beach. Only a few surfers were waiting for a wave in the fairly calm sea. Two spaniels chased balls tossed into the ocean. But she came to a sudden stop when she spied a long trail of tracks scarring the clean sweep of sand from the high-tide line all the way up to the dunes. Turtle tracks! Her heart pumping, she picked up speed. As she neared, she saw the unmistakable pattern the flippers made in the sand. She followed them, climbing the soft incline to a large circular section of disturbed sand at the top of the dune. Looking out again, she could see the outgoing tracks cross the incoming and continue all the way to the shoreline. She'd bet money there were eggs here.

Linnea wasn't a permitted member of the team, so she couldn't do anything more. She took out her phone and dialed Emmi's number. Emmi was the team leader. She answered on the second ring, and Linnea reported her discovery.

"Congratulations on finding your first nest this season," Emmi told her.

"Hope's first nest ever!"

"We'll be right there."

Now there was nothing for Linnea to do but wait for the team to arrive. Pushing the stroller, she idly followed the tracks back to the sea, noticing that this sea turtle must've had some barnacles on her undercarriage, judging by the pattern in the sand in the middle of her tracks.

In the distance she spotted a mother and daughter strolling along the shore in the early morning sun, gathering shells. The little girl, maybe five or six years old, was bent over inspecting a shell before racing to show it to her mother. When they drew near, the girl spotted the turtle tracks and, with a squeal of excitement, ran toward Linnea as her mother followed.

"Are those turtle tracks?" she asked, eyes as wide as the sun rising beyond her.

"Yes, they are."

"Are you a turtle lady?"

Linnea was wearing the season's T-shirt and ball cap, which made her a walking advertisement. "Yes, I am."

The girl's mother caught up to them, tote in tow. She had the wholesome prettiness of young mothers, freckles smattering her cheeks from the sun.

"Isn't this exciting, Willa?" the girl's mother asked her. She looked to Linnea. "Willa loves turtles. She reads books about them all the time," she added proudly.

Linnea looked at the young girl. She had long brown hair and freckles, like her mother. Her eyes were full of wonder and curiosity. Linnea could recall being mad about sea turtles at Willa's age. The summer she'd become a junior turtle team member was a memorable summer for all, it being the last summer of Lovie's life. Linnea always felt a glow of satisfaction that before she died, her grandmother had known her granddaughter would follow in her footsteps.

The following summer, Aunt Cara had stepped in to lead the team and taken Linnea under her wing. Her parents had let Linnea live with Cara and Brett in Lovie's beach house for the summer, kind of like camp. "Only better—Camp Beach House is free!" her daddy used to joke. At sixteen Linnea became an intern for Brett's Coastal Ecotour boat and fell in love with the lowcountry's other marine life as well. Brett had taught her how to drive a boat and follow the tides. He was a natural teacher and loved nothing more than sharing his knowledge of the sea and its inhabitants. Linnea's love affair with the lowcountry's wild places had grown as she did.

It was inevitable that all those summers on Isle of Palms would shape Linnea's career path. She didn't think it was too much of a stretch to say they'd changed her life. By the time she was eighteen and headed for college, she knew she would end up working in environmental science. Lovie and Aunt Cara and Brett had impressed upon her the importance of giving back and making a difference with her life.

She looked at the young girl and felt a responsibility to encourage her. To help her see that she had an important role to play.

"When will the eggs hatch?" Willa asked.

"The mama turtles are just laying the nests now," Linnea explained. "It takes forty-five to sixty days to incubate. So the nests won't start to hatch until sometime in July."

Disappointment flooded their faces.

"But isn't it exciting to see the tracks? You came to the island at an excellent time. You found a nest! Look up there," she said, pointing out the dunes. "Last night a mama turtle crawled ashore and laid a nest there. I only just found the tracks. Do you know what kind of sea turtle laid this nest?"

Willa shook her head. Linnea looked at the mother. Her eyes were as wide as her daughter's. *Nature makes children of us all*, Linnea thought.

"A loggerhead?" the mother replied with all the excitement of a prize student.

"That's right. Let me show you the nest. Follow me." Linnea walked them up to the nest, explaining the nesting saga on the way. She took her time showing them how the turtle reached the top of the dune, described how she dug down to deposit her eggs, then showed the sprinkled sand, explaining how the mother threw sand to hide the nest from predators. The body pit was well marked and allowed their imaginations to soar.

"If you wait here a little while longer, the team will be here to check out the nest and find the eggs."

Willa bounced on her toes in excitement while her mother mouthed a heartfelt *thank you* to Linnea.

A short while later, Linnea spied Barb, a team member, coming up the path with her camera hanging from her neck. Behind her Emmi and the other members of the team plowed through the soft sand, on duty. There were hugs among friends Linnea hadn't seen in several years, and introductions to new members of the team—Cindy, Jo, Crystal. In the rear of the group walked a surprise.

"Cara!" Linnea exclaimed.

"Emmi called," Cara yelled back.

Hope immediately turned toward her mother's voice and began calling out, "Mama!" Cara reached the stroller and pulled Hope into her arms, kissing her cheeks.

"I couldn't miss Hope's first turtle nest! This is a milestone in our family."

"Linnea," Emmi said, approaching. "Since you found the nest, would you like to probe for the eggs?"

Linnea was stunned by the offer. She'd only just joined the team again after years away. "I haven't done it in years."

"Well, it's time to get back on the horse. Besides . . ." Emmi handed her an envelope.

"What's this?"

"Open it."

Linnea looked around to see all the other team members smiling. Curious, she opened the envelope and pulled out the slip of paper. She gasped at reading it.

"This is my SCDNR permit!"

"Yes, it is. And here is your probe stick," Emmi said, handing her the narrow metal rod the team used to locate eggs deep in the sand. It was the prize possession of a team member. "Now you can probe for the eggs and do everything else the team does. You already know how. You never forget."

Cara added, "You learned from the best."

Linnea accepted the probe stick with reverence. "You can't know how much this means to me." She couldn't put all the emotions into words. How being back on the turtle team, working with these dedicated women, teaching Hope and then Willa and hopefully many more curious young of all ages, she felt again the passion that had brought her to study environmental science years ago.

Suddenly, with a brilliant clarity, Linnea knew what she wanted to do with her degree—and more, her life.

"Thank you," she said, realizing that sometimes a few words said the most.

Chapter Ten

Female loggerheads have great endurance. During the three months or so that a female loggerhead breeds, she will travel hundreds of miles to nest, lay thirty-five pounds (sixteen kilograms) of eggs—or more—and swim back to her home foraging area, all without eating anything significant.

AFTER A LOVELY dinner of poached salmon, salad, and biscuits with a crisp chenin blanc, Cara put Hope to bed while Linnea cleared the table, stacked the dishwasher, tidied the counters, and picked up the last of the toys. The days flowed by and they'd fallen into this pattern, which turned out to suit them both. While she did the dishes, Linnea heard the water splashing in the tub while Hope got her bath, then the melodic tones of Cara's voice as she changed her into pajamas and sang Hope to sleep.

Linnea lingered in the kitchen to bake a few healthy snack cookies. She loved to cook and bake, unlike Cara, and enjoyed reigning over the kitchen. Cara was a grateful recipient who let

Linnea plan the menus and cook anything she wished within reason, footing the bill.

She knew her aunt was struggling financially. But Cara always made her feel like they were well-off and never let her worry if she wanted a good piece of fish. "Life is too short to eat badly," she always said. Cara had worldliness, a self-confidence and straightforwardness that Linnea admired. One always knew where one stood with her. There was no subterfuge or false smiles, like with Linnea's mother.

Her father had often told her that though she looked like her grandmother, in fact she was a lot like his sister, her aunt Cara. He usually said this whenever she argued back or "gave him lip." Linnea chuckled, relishing the comparison. This summer she vowed to be more confident and unafraid to trust in her choices, just like her aunt.

She hung the towel on the rack, flicked off the lights, and walked across the living room, intending to watch a little television. A noise on the windward deck caught her attention, so she detoured through the sunroom and slid open the sliding door. She spotted her aunt sitting on the deck in her robe with her long bare legs up on a spare chair, a glass of wine in her hand. On the teak table were a bottle of wine, a spare glass, and a flickering candle. It was a balmy, sweet-smelling night, perfect for sitting outdoors.

"Am I disturbing you?"

"Not at all! I was waiting for you. Sit down. Want some wine? I have a glass for you."

"Why, thanks. Love one."

She poured a glass for herself while Cara moved from her

chair to pull a large old-style steamer trunk toward her. Linnea drew near, her curiosity piqued.

"First of all, I'm loving the old steamer trunk."

Cara smiled mischievously. "You're going to love what's in it more. Go ahead. Open it."

Cara sank back in her chair and watched as Linnea set her wineglass on the table and approached the chest. The aura of Christmas was in the air. She pulled out the lock and lifted the lid. The smell of mothballs tickled her nose. The trunk was filled with women's clothes. Linnea reached in and pulled out a sage cotton shirtdress with white piping that looked like it was from the 1950s.

"Oh, it can't be!" Linnea exclaimed. "Are these Lovie's clothes?"

Cara had to laugh at her expression. "Only the best. She saved all her favorites and the designer clothes. There's quite a collection. She was tiny, but so are you. I'm thinking you'll find some winners in there."

Linnea was beside herself. This was a treasure trove! She dove in and began pulling out skirts, one more beautiful than the last. Tops and sweaters and— Oh! She unfolded a cocktail dress with a twirl skirt that was breathtaking. Linnea put it against her body and spun in a circle.

"Cara, I can't believe you're giving all of these to me! Thank you! I love them."

"Who else would I give them to? They belong to you."

"I'm going to spend every free minute tomorrow trying each piece on. We'll have a fashion show."

Cara stretched her legs back out on the opposite chair. "I remember whenever we came back from a shopping trip on King

Street, Mama would have me show my new clothes to my father before dinner. She called it the fashion show." Cara smiled. "Those are some of the happier memories with my father."

Linnea put the clothing back into the trunk and closed it with a sigh of contentment.

"You look like the cat that caught the canary," Cara said.

"Don't let Moutarde hear you say that, but yes, I'm content." She picked up her glass and clinked it with Cara's. "Here's to the best summer."

"I'll drink to that."

"The baby is asleep?"

"Blissfully," Cara replied. "What's that heavenly scent wafting from the kitchen?"

"Those healthy cookies you liked so much."

"What have I done to deserve you?"

Linnea laughed, pleased at the comment. "You gave me a boatload of vintage clothing, for starters. But mostly, you let me stay here." She breathed deep, catching the faint lemony scent of the primroses. "It's strange, but I feel more at home here than at Tradd Street."

"It's not strange at all. I've always felt the very same thing. As did Lovie. That's why she came here as often as she could."

"I thought it was just to escape her husband."

Cara smirked. "That too. But it was so much more. The lifestyle here is more let-your-hair-down relaxed. You feel it driving over the Connector, don't you? The vast miles of cordgrass cut through by snaking water, then you reach the apex and suddenly . . ." She sighed as though feeling what she was describing.

"You see the Atlantic spread out before you and you think, *Is it blue today? A stormy green?* Then all at once you feel like a delete button has been pressed on all your stress and worries, and for that moment you feel serenely connected to something much bigger than you. And it happens every time. If you just take the moment to look."

Linnea could see in her mind's eye exactly what Cara was describing and felt the serenity by association.

"That's all true," Linnea said. "But for me, being here is so much more."

"How so?"

"It's hard to put into words. I've been away from the beach house for four-plus years. Yet in that time I kept the dream of doing something meaningful in my life, like Lovie taught me. She used to say I should feel passion for whatever I chose to do. That way I'd always love my work. You know better than anyone I had to fight with Daddy to declare environmental science as my major. It was the right choice. I have a good science foundation to better understand the issues. Now I have to find the path that best suits me and my interests and talents to use my education. I know I'm not suited for lab or fieldwork. But I came home in a quandary about what I really want to pursue. I've applied for jobs in environmental PR, but nothing's come up. It's hard to find an entry-level position."

"I think you'd be very good at that."

"But, oh, Cara," she said with feeling, "since I've been here, I've remembered how much I enjoy being with people. Sharing what I love. Brett taught me that, too. Being on the turtle team and teaching the children, I realized something very important. I know what I want to do with my life."

Cara leaned forward, listening intently.

"I want to be involved in public education. I love seeing the awe and hope in people's eyes, feeling like with each person I talk to or influence, I'm lighting a candle of hope. I know that sounds dream-filled, but I've seen the reactions myself. People *do* care. They want to help. To make a difference. This is important, especially now." She fell silent a moment. "I just have to find the best way for me to do that."

"That will come from experience," said Cara. "And luck. Sometimes, if you're lucky, you fall into the right place at the right time. Or you find *a* job that leads to the *right* job. And, of course, there's always volunteering. We're all in this together."

"Right." Linnea heartened at this. "Like everyone else, I'm worried about climate change. Every day we hear about the catastrophic effects on the planet. But here on the island, I can see the changes for myself. And I worry. What if the high temperatures create more female turtles than males? Why are we having early season starts? And I pick up so much more plastic trash than I used to. It's everywhere." She took a sip of her wine. "I'm going to start narrowing my job search. I feel empowered knowing what I want to do."

"I have every confidence in you."

"Thanks, Aunt Cara. That means a lot. You've always been there for me."

"Oh, Linnea," Cara said quietly. "You're young. You have your whole life ahead of you."

"So are you."

Cara laughed and looked into her wineglass. "Not so young . . ."

Linnea shifted in her chair, moving closer. Cara, at fifty-three, was as vibrant and attractive as a woman ten years younger. Nothing about her slender figure, glossy dark hair, and elegant clothes implied age.

"You still have a life ahead of you. Especially with Hope in it. And maybe someday you'll find love again."

"Love?" Cara shook her head. "I don't know if I can ever love anyone the way I did Brett."

"No," Linnea said, treading carefully. She traced her finger around the rim of her glass. "But you can love someone else differently, because that person will be different."

"You know, someone else told me the same thing."

"Because it's true—this isn't India, you know. You don't have to throw yourself on the funeral pyre. You'll always love him. I'll always love him. You know, when I was young, I'd see you two together and pray that someday I'd fall in love like that. I can't imagine how hard it must be to let a love like that go. But, Cara, Brett left. Through no fault of his own, but he's gone. And I know that if he were here tonight, he'd tell you to live your life. It's too short to waste a single day. Now I pray that you find someone new to love."

Cara ran her fingers through her short hair. Looking down, she said by way of confession, "I *have* met someone I find attractive."

Linnea was surprised by this. Cara could be so discreet. "Who?"

She lifted her gaze. "David Wyatt."

"Heather's father?"

Cara made a face. "That makes it awkward, doesn't it?"

"Not at all. It's just a coincidence. So . . . what's he like?"

"The first word that jumps to mind is kind."

"I'm sold."

Cara laughed again and shook her head. "I don't know why we're even talking about this. I can't imagine dating anyone again. It feels like a betrayal to Brett. It's too soon."

"It's been three years, Cara." Then it hit her. "You mean you haven't dated anyone else yet? Not in Chattanooga?"

Cara shook her head. "Not that I wasn't asked. But I had no interest."

"Wow," Linnea said. She couldn't imagine a dry spell of three years. "I loved Brett like a second father, you know that. And you've always been a second mother to me. So this doesn't come lightly. . . . Cara, I honestly feel Brett would want you to date again. He wouldn't want you to waste away, pining for him. You're too vibrant. Too beautiful. Cara, you deserve another chance at love."

Cara didn't respond, but she looked at Linnea with a new vulnerability. Linnea felt she was truly listening, as though the tables had turned and now Linnea was the one dispensing advice. For the first time, it felt to her that instead of a mother-daughter relationship, they'd morphed into two women friends.

Cara poured herself another glass of wine, then took a sip. Linnea could see she was already composing herself, reining in her emotions. There would be no tears.

"You can wear one of those new dresses to Emmi's party," she said.

"What party?"

"This weekend at her house. A barbecue."

"There's another party at the Social Club?"

Cara laughed at Linnea's nickname for Emmi's house. "Her son is visiting from California. Well, actually it's more than visiting. He's moving in temporarily. Emmi is thrilled and wants us all to meet him."

"Doesn't Emmi have two sons?"

"That's right. James and John."

"Not very creative with names, was she?" Linnea joked.

"It was something to do with the apostles," Cara replied, then waved that topic off. "James is married, goodness, four years now. He's the eldest. Emmi's very proud of him, and with good reason. He graduated from Duke Medical School and practices somewhere near there. I can't remember his wife's name, but they already have a son. I think he's two already."

"James is the perfect son," Linnea quipped.

"So it seems."

"And what's the one who's going to be at dinner like?" Linnea asked with idle curiosity.

"John is the younger son. He's not an academic. More of a maverick."

"'Maverick' as in an unreliable eccentric? Or unconventional?"

Cara chuckled. "The latter. John's just more laid-back than his brother. When James was in the library, John was out surfing. Emmi tells me John is super smart, but not conventional smart.

More entrepreneurial. I remember when Emmi used to complain that the teachers said John didn't live up to his potential in school."

"That's what the teachers always say about Cooper. They're trying not to say he's lazy."

"In John's case, I suspect he was bored. His report cards were so-so, but he aced his SATs. Near-perfect score. He went to Stanford."

Linnea set down her glass, impressed. She'd earned all As in high school, but her SAT scores were only average. The tests were the great equalizer.

"That's impressive. Stanford . . . So what does he do now?"

"He's into computers. He went to California for college and never came back. I think he lives in San Francisco now. Or did."

"If he was doing so well, what's he doing back here?"

"I don't know. Emmi loves to toot the horn about her sons' successes. Which is only natural," she hurried to add. "But she can be very hush-mouthed about any problems. Since I haven't heard, I'm guessing it's not good. But," she said on an upbeat note, "Emmi's thrilled to have her baby back home and wants to call the clan together."

"I'm hardly the clan." Linnea picked up her glass. "I don't think I've ever met him."

"Yes, you have. At that Fourth of July party Lovie held that last summer. We decorated the house with fairy lights, there were mountains of food, and Flo's mother Miranda went wandering the beach."

"Oh, yes," Linnea said, a smile flitting across her face at the recollection of that very special night. "A turtle nest hatched that night. The first I'd ever seen."

"That's right."

"But I don't remember Emmi's sons. Cara, I was only, what? Eight years old?"

"Was it that long ago?" Cara asked with a sad shake of her head. A wistful, then sorrowful expression crossed her face. "That was a wonderful night," she said softly. "I can't blame you for not remembering. The boys were teenagers with better plans for the Fourth than to come to their mother's friend's party. Emmi must've twisted their arms. They obliged, stuffed a few burgers in their mouths, and split. But, Linnea, surely you've seen them come and go from Emmi's over the years?"

Linnea shrugged. "If I did, they didn't make much of an impression."

"Well, you'll meet the mysterious John Peterson at the party."

"Is he good-looking?"

Cara laughed. "I haven't seen him in years."

"But you said he surfs?"

"He did. Devotedly."

"That's on my bucket list this summer. I've always wanted to learn, and for the life of me I can't imagine why I never did. I mean, the ocean's right out there! My dad taught Cooper, but not me." She frowned. "It's that double-standard thing again."

"Why didn't you ask Brett to teach you? He loved to surf."

"I don't know," Linnea replied with remorse. "I guess he taught me so much already."

"He would have enjoyed teaching you. He loved you, you know. Like a daughter."

Tears flooded her eyes. "So silly," she said, sniffing. She reached for a napkin. "I was afraid you might burst into tears at the mention of Brett, and here I am, weeping like a baby."

"Don't start, or I will."

"I'm okay. . . ." She wiped her eyes and laughed at herself. "I'm such a crybaby. I cry in movies, reading a book, even watching a Hallmark commercial."

"I just had a brilliant idea. Come with me," Cara said, swinging her legs to the ground and rising. "Watch your step."

She led Linnea down the dark steps to the ground and around the corner to the leeward side of the house. She flicked on the light to illuminate the area under the front porch where they stored the strollers, bicycles, garden equipment, and such.

"There it is," Cara said, and made her way toward the far corner of the storage space. She had to dodge spiderwebs and move a bicycle. She rested her hand on a long blue and white surfboard, pausing in private thought. Then she turned to Linnea. "This was Brett's surfboard. I don't know why, but I just couldn't sell it with his other things. Maybe because he'd had it for such a long time and loved it. And maybe because when I see it, I remember how handsome he looked riding the waves." She smiled at the memory. "I know he'd want you to have it."

"I couldn't . . ." Linnea said, deeply touched.

"Let's not do that back-and-forth dance," Cara said. "I want you to have it. Use it! That's what a surfboard is meant for. It'd make both of us happy."

"It's in such good condition."

"Brett was meticulous about his tools."

"I'd love to have it. Thank you. I can't wait to try it out."

"Maybe John can teach you."

"What's to teach? I just take the board out and hop on, right?"

~~~~~~

LINNEA ROSE WITH the sun, eager to ride the waves on her new surfboard. She applied a thick coating of high-SPF lotion while looking out at the rosy sky. She slipped into her bikini and a rash guard and flip-flops, then tied her blond hair back with an elastic. She moved quietly, not wanting to stir the sleeping baby.

The house was dimly lit with the first rays of the sun as she creaked across the wooden floors. The house was dear to her, at no time more than in these early hours when the world still slumbered. The toys were neatly stacked, but she knew it was only a matter of time before Hope had them splayed across the floor. Soon the scent of coffee would fill the air, the phone would start ringing, and the day would be off. But for now . . . all lay in wait.

Opening the front door, Linnea stepped out into the morning's promise. She made her way down the stairs to the storage area under the porch, where the surfboard sat near the entrance. She imagined Brett coming down these same stairs, fetching his board, and going out to the sea. The board was much heavier than she'd imagined and so long that she could hardly manage to carry it along the beach path to the ocean. She felt like a mother sea turtle dragging a heavy shell, stopping frequently along the way to catch her breath.

But at last she made it, and she took great gulps of the fresh breeze as she stared out at the ocean. She felt a surge of exhilaration. It was her favorite time of day on the beach, when the sun cast a rosy tint on the dark water and the sand. For those few precious moments, the effect was otherworldly. There was no time to waste, however. Two surfers were already out in the ocean, bobbing on the waves like pelicans. It was a perfect day to begin surfing.

She'd gone on the Internet to watch a few how-to videos on surfing and felt prepared. The swell was a few feet high, which by South Carolina standards wasn't too bad. She hoisted the surfboard the final feet to the water's edge. The air was a bit chilly, which made the water feel cooler. *Refreshing*, Lovie would call it. Standing with her feet in the water, Linnea felt a sudden rush of doubt. She really didn't know a thing about surfing other than from a quick Internet search and a lifetime of watching others. This was something she'd always wanted to learn, right? Cooper had learned at the age of ten. How hard could it be?

"Here we go," she said aloud, and set the board on the water. She clumsily lay down on the board and clung to the sides as it rocked wildly. "Whoa," she exclaimed, trying not to fall off. Once it settled, she cautiously began to paddle with her arms. At first she seemed to go back more than forward. She put some muscle into the effort, and gradually began inching forward. She was beginning to feel good about her progress out toward where the two other surfers sat on their boards, waiting for a good wave. Each small wave set her back a bit, but she kept going. Then she caught sight of the first wall of blue water. Her eyes widened, and she gripped the sides of the board as the wave slammed into her. She went rolling off the board and was sent spinning in the wave, hurtling toward the shore.

Linnea sputtered to the surface and scrambled to stand in the sand. She caught sight of the two men poised atop their boards, coasting effortlessly, just as another wave slammed into her, knocking her over a second time. Gasping, she staggered to a stand, wiping the hair from her face since the elastic had sailed away. She looked around frantically, searching for her surfboard. She spotted it bobbing in the current, taking off down the shoreline farther away from her. *Oh, no, Brett's board!* In a panic, she pushed through the thigh-deep water, swinging her arms to catch it.

A tall man rushed into the surf to grab her board. She waved in acknowledgment, so grateful that he held it for her while she pumped through the water toward him. He was tall, with the deep tan of a surfer. His longish hair was a deep auburn, but the sun had bleached the tips a golden red. The closer she got, she saw that he wasn't a college kid but a man, maybe late twenties or early thirties, and very good-looking. She reached up to smooth her wet hair from her face.

A crooked grin eased across his face. "I think this belongs to you," he said as she drew near.

His eyes were a piercing green with whites that contrasted sharply with his tan. She felt the power of them sweep her body and sucked in her stomach.

"Thanks," she said, taking hold of the traitorous board.

"Major wipeout."

"Yeah," she said, and had to laugh. She looked up and wanted to tell him it was her first time out on the board, but he shook his head and laughed.

"See ya," he said, and walked away with a backward wave.

He was laughing at her, she realized, feeling like a little girl just dismissed. Her blush deepened. *Major wipeout.* She closed her eyes, unable to imagine how ridiculous she must've looked getting knocked down before even making it to the breakers—twice!

She watched as he trotted back to his own board and picked it up from the sand as though it weighed nothing. He waved to the other surfers, then jogged into the sea and slid onto his board like an otter. His strong arms dug deep into the water and made short work of the journey out. She put her hand over her eyes to watch how he seemed to lift himself and the board over the oncoming wave to glide over it and just kept plowing out to where his friends sat on their boards beyond the breakers. It was beautiful to behold.

She looked at the long surfboard and felt again the sting of his laugh. Maybe there was a lot more to learn about surfing than she'd figured. But this morning's embarrassment and the sting of the surfer's laugh, rather than discouraging her, only fueled her fire to learn.

Chapter Eleven

Despite living in the ocean, turtles cannot breathe underwater.
They are reptiles. Like the mammals dolphins and whales, they
have to surface from time to time to breathe.

IT WAS A perfect night for a party. Long tables covered in blue-and-white-checked tablecloths stretched across the flagstone patio. Hurricane lanterns flickered in the dusk. Linnea stood at the gate and heard the low murmur of conversation broken by occasional laughter. Squinting, she scanned the yard to see who was there.

Flo walked around carrying red wine in one hand and white in the other, refreshing everyone's glasses. Emmi manned the barbecue. The scent of pork ribs wafted in on the breeze. Linnea had been exhausted by parties, but this one promised to be a special evening with women she'd grown up among.

Linnea's plan was to stop in and say hello to everyone, meet

Emmi's son, then quietly slip out in time to go to a gathering at Jessica's family's beach house on Sullivan's Island. She was wearing the sage-green shirtwaist dress from Lovie's collection, which showed off her tiny waist and long, slim legs. Her hair was loosely pulled back, and her sun-kissed skin was free of makeup except for her dewy pink lips and a swipe of mascara.

Her game plan set, she scanned the patio for Cara and spied her sitting at a table with Hope in her lap, beside a handsome man with dark gray hair sprinkled with white. Heather walked up to him and handed off Rory. He held the boy high in the air like an airplane before settling him in his lap. He must be Heather's father, she realized. So he was the man Cara found attractive . . . Linnea looked closer at his dark, bushy brows over beautiful brown eyes, his ruddy tan and outdoorsman appeal, and readily understood Cara's attraction. He didn't look like Brett, but he was the same type. At least physically. And unless she was mistaken, there were sparks flying between him and Cara. Linnea walked into the party, her steps a bit wobbly in her strappy sandals as she made her way across the crooked flagstones directly to Cara. With a knowing smile, she was introduced to David Wyatt. He was both charming and handsome; and though fiercely loyal to Brett's memory, a part of Linnea hoped that Cara might at last end her mourning and find happiness with someone like David.

～～～

AS LINNEA MADE her rounds at the party, she caught up with Heather and Bo, who still acted like newlyweds. From the moment she'd met Heather, they had instantly connected. They were almost the same age and she'd sensed a kindred spirit in Heather. They shared a love of nature and wildlife. As they chatted, Linnea was impressed once again by how much Heather knew about birds, both shorebirds and songbirds. When she invited Linnea to come along on a birding expedition at Bulls Bay, she jumped at the chance. They talked for a long time and could've talked for hours more, but Heather heard her son fussing across the patio.

"I'd better find Rory and pack up," Heather said. "We have a ferry ride back to Dewees."

Linnea thought just getting to know Heather had made the party worthwhile. She glanced at her watch; time to make an exit herself. She was heading toward the gate when she heard male laughter coming from the upstairs back porch. She glanced up. Under the dim yellow light of the outdoor lantern, she caught sight of two men, each with a beer in hand. They were both tall, but the younger one was leaner in tight jeans and a black T-shirt that didn't hide his broad shoulders.

Curious, she grabbed her purse and thought maybe it was wise to go upstairs and fetch a drink before leaving. She quickly applied a fresh coat of lipstick, then climbed the stairs.

The light on the porch was dim, but she could readily see that the older man was Heather's father. The second man had his back to her. But his hair gave him away. It was a deep red, brushed back from his tanned forehead. She froze.

The younger man suddenly turned his head to look over his shoulder, as though realizing he was being stared at. Their gazes locked. Linnea sucked in her breath.

"You!" she exclaimed.

"You!" he replied, and broke into a wide grin. "The girl who can't surf."

She felt her cheeks burn. Her heart beat fast, as if she'd just suffered an electric shock. His eyes . . . they were the most piercing blue-green color. She actually felt shaky. She wasn't prepared for this kind of jolt tonight. She collected her wits, not wanting to appear—again—like some silly schoolgirl. She couldn't hold her own fiasco against him.

David cleared his throat. "Excuse me, I want to say good-bye to Heather and Bo."

Linnea waited until David disappeared down the stairs. She turned to John. "Thank you again for saving my board."

"Out on the water, we have each other's backs," he replied. "I didn't see you go back out."

"As you said, it was a major wipeout. And I didn't want to be a joke." She pursed her lips and raised a brow.

"I wasn't laughing at you," he said. "But it was pretty funny."

Linnea flushed again, but couldn't stop her laugh. "It was my first time on the board."

"Really?" he asked in sarcasm.

Linnea strategically stepped closer to the cooler, opened it, and peered in. She glanced back over her shoulder to find he was still looking at her.

He stepped forward and asked, "Can I get you a drink?"

She licked her lips and tucked a wayward lock behind her ear. "I'd love a water, but all I see are beers and soda."

"They're all hiding in the bottom. Hold on." He bent at the

waist and plunged his hand into the ice. She noticed that his arms were deeply tanned and muscled, and the edge of a tattoo peeked out from under his shirtsleeve. She tried to make out what it was as he rummaged through the ice, but glanced away when he straightened again, a dripping bottle in his hand. He grabbed a paper napkin and wiped off the water, then unscrewed the cap and handed the bottle to her.

"Thank you," she said, looking into his eyes. "Nicely done."

"Comes from years of waiting tables."

Holding his gaze, she brought the bottle to her lips and took a long sip, feeling the cool water slide down her throat. His face was finely chiseled, his dark-red hair long without being shaggy. And his eyes . . . their intensity was smoldering. Smiling inwardly, she thought, *Let the games begin.*

She tilted her head and asked, "Do you surf a lot?"

"Every day the waves are there. I was surprised how good the waves were this week, considering the forecast. I guess that storm out in the Atlantic had more of a bump than I anticipated." As he brought a beer bottle to his lips he asked, "And you?"

"Obviously I'm not a surfer. Yet. I was trying out a board my aunt just gave me. I've always wanted to surf. I'm on the turtle team, and I walk this stretch of beach every morning and see the surfers out there and wish I could join them."

"You're a turtle lady?"

She didn't miss the tease in his eyes.

"I am indeed," she replied, and allowed him his laugh. "They've been my passion since I was a little girl. My aunt Cara taught me everything I know."

His expression shifted into surprise. "You're Cara Rutledge's niece?"

She put out her hand. "Linnea Rutledge."

Caught in the game, he smiled and reached out to take her hand. "John Peterson. Nice to meet you."

"I thought as much."

His expression changed. "Wait . . . I've met you before."

She looked at him doubtfully.

He pointed at her playfully. "It was at the Fourth of July party at Lovie's house. Years ago." He laughed. "You had those long pigtails with enormous red-white-and-blue ribbons."

Linnea drew herself up. "It *was* the Fourth of July."

They smiled at each other, taking each other's measure.

"I'm sorry to say I don't remember you."

John put his hand over his heart. "I'm wounded."

"I was eight years old."

His smile turned devilish. "You aren't eight anymore."

Linnea was enjoying the flirtation. She sipped her water. "Nope."

"And you live next door." It was a statement, not a question.

"Actually, I live in Charleston. I'm babysitting Hope for the summer." Then, realizing that sounded a bit lame, she added, "I just graduated from USC, and it's my final summer on the beach before I join the nine-to-five work world."

"Good move. Then we'll be neighbors," he said, obviously pleased with the notion.

"Word on the street is that you're moving in here."

He looked chagrined. "I'm not moving back in with my mother," he explained, then added, "Not exactly. I'm working on something right now and needed a place to crash."

"What are you working on?"

"A computer program. Top secret. Can't divulge. I wouldn't want to have to kill you."

"Very funny. How long will you stay on the island?"

He shrugged. "Hard to say. It depends on how long the project takes. I'd like to be back in San Francisco by September."

"I wish I knew where I'd be in September."

"Tell me."

"I'm job-hunting."

"What are you looking for?"

"Something in environmental science."

"That's a hot career in California right now."

"So I hear."

"You should look out there. San Francisco, especially. Everyone is environmentally conscious, and there are a lot of new startups. In fact, I know of a company that—"

"There you are!"

Linnea swung her head around to see Cara standing at the top of the stairs. Her face was slightly flushed from the exertion and her cheeks had a lovely glow from the wine.

Cara walked closer, her arm out in greeting. "I see you've met John," she said in a knowing tone.

I'm not going to blush, Linnea told herself. "Yes. Just. It seems he remembers me from Lovie's party years ago."

"Really?" Cara cast her gaze on John. "You and your brother ran out of there so fast I'm surprised you remember meeting anyone."

"Bad manners. Forgive my teenage hormones," he said.

"All's forgiven because you've made your mother very happy by visiting her. *All* of us are happy to see you again."

Linnea smiled stiffly and sent Cara warning flashes with her eyes.

"Well, I've just come to say good-bye," said Cara. "Hope will be up at dawn."

John and Linnea watched Cara disappear down the stairs. In the garden below, Flo and Emmi were bringing in the last of the dishes. There was an awkward silence.

So much for my plans to leave early, Linnea thought. "I'd better go."

John held out his hand. "I'll walk you out."

Linnea looked at him for a moment, then set down her water bottle and grabbed hold of his strong, tanned hand. They walked down the stairs to the gate, a short distance that seemed to take forever in her mind.

"Well, good night," she said, opening the gate.

John put his hand on the gate, stilling it. "You said you wanted to learn to surf?"

Linnea's insides jumped. She leaned back to look at his face. His eyes seemed to reflect the moonlight. "Oh, yes."

"The surf's supposed to be decent tomorrow. I'll pick you up at seven."

Linnea turned and walked back to the beach house, thinking that was the best pickup line she'd ever heard.

~~~~~

THE FOLLOWING MORNING Linnea awoke to a high-pitched *ding*. It took a minute for her brain to fight its way through the fog before she clumsily grabbed her phone. Blinking her dry eyes, she read the text.

I'm here. Come on out.

She gasped and glanced at the time. It was seven on the dot.

She leaped from the bed, wide awake at the prospect of her first surf lesson. She couldn't believe she'd forgotten to set the alarm. She stumbled in her haste to slip into her bikini and put on the rash guard; not to waste time, she slipped her thin cotton sleep shirt over her like a cover up. As she hurried from the room, she stuck her feet in flip-flops and grabbed an elastic from the dresser top. Running down the hall, she hand-combed her hair and pulled it into a ponytail. Hope was still sleeping, and, judging from the silence in the master bedroom, so was Cara.

She flung open the kitchen door, expecting to see John. But no one was there. Linnea stepped outside and looked around. The air held that lovely early-morning freshness that would dissipate as the sun rose higher. Across the driveway, she saw John in his swimsuit and a pale-blue and black rash guard, already working at fastening the two surfboards to the back of his white Ford pickup. It was an oldie but goodie, covered in dents, spots of rust, and bumper stickers, prominent among them a Tom Petty decal across the rear window. She walked over to Emmi's driveway.

"Good morning!" she called out.

"Morning," he called back, not turning his head as he worked the straps.

"We aren't going to surf right out here?" she asked, wondering why he was loading his truck.

He finished tightening the straps and faced her, slapping dirt from his hands. "No, only the best for your first lesson. We're lucky there are some decent waves today. Beginner's luck. This is Isle of Palms, after all. Not California. The waves here are slim pickings."

She scratched her head lazily, waking up more. "Do I have time to make some coffee?"

"Nope. We need to catch the waves." He paused and took a moment to really look at her, from head to toe, amusement sparkling in his eyes. "You look like a little girl, all scruffy and no makeup."

That was the last thing she'd expected him to say. She felt a bit embarrassed. "I didn't have time to primp."

"I like it," he said. "You look like Gidget. You're probably too young to know that movie."

Linnea smiled, delighted at the analogy. "I've always loved that movie. I'm kinda shocked you know it."

"My mom . . ." he said with a slanted smile. "I liked the surf scenes."

"I don't remember how I first watched it. I was probably just trolling channels on a lazy summer day, but I fell in love with the movie. I wanted to be Gidget. She wasn't trying to catch a boy. She wanted to learn how to surf and be accepted as one of the gang."

"Well, Gidget, you're going to learn now. Let's go."

"Wait! My beach bag. I need to get a towel and suntan lotion."

"I've got lots. Hop in."

He seemed determined to get to the waves, and who was she to argue? She hurried to the passenger side of the truck and climbed in. The inside was as well-worn as the outside. The seats were torn, and the floor was coated with a thick layer of sand. He tossed her a bottle of water.

"Thanks," she said, twisting the cap. She was quiet as they drove north along Palm Boulevard. In the shadowy light, she admired John's strong, straight nose, high cheekbones, and pale reddish-brown lashes. He didn't have his mother's wide mouth. His lips were actually rather thin and surrounded this morning by dark auburn stubble that she found sexy. Seeing his bed head, she didn't feel badly for not brushing her hair. She smiled and looked out the windshield. And why bother? They were going to get wet in a few minutes anyway.

There wasn't much traffic on Palm until they made the S curve. Traffic slowed as a line of cars with surfboards strapped to their roofs searched for parking spots on the green grass that lined the road. It seemed everyone knew one another. Surfers gave one another knowing nods and waves, some stalling traffic to share a few words. No one seemed to mind. She watched, fascinated. She'd had no idea that there would be this many people here. In college, everyone was sleeping in at this hour. There was a whole other world she hadn't known existed during the dawn song.

John found a spot at Thirty-First Avenue and parallel-parked on the grass with dexterity. Large houses formed a wall between the street and the ocean beyond, blocking the view. She could hear it, though, and was eager to get out.

"All right, li'l lady," John said, turning off the engine. He met her gaze and smiled encouragingly. "Let's do this." Reaching across the seat, he dug into a bag at her feet and pulled out a tube of suntan lotion. He tossed it to her. "Don't be skimpy."

Linnea was grateful. Going out on the ocean without high-SPF lotion would've been a disaster for her fair skin. John looked in the rearview mirror and applied a thick white cream on his nose, cheekbones, and collarbones. When he was done, he handed her the stick.

"Seriously?" she said, scrunching up her nose. "That looks like war paint."

"I don't mess around. The sun's rays are for real out there."

Linnea looked at the SPF dubiously. Determined to be a good student, she moved closer to him to look in the rearview. They were touching shoulders, and she was aware he was watching her as she delicately dabbed the white lotion on her nose and cheeks. She screwed the top back on the stick and handed it to him. He studied her face critically.

"May I?"

She nodded.

He leaned close and gently applied a thick stripe of zinc down her nose and along her cheekbones, then playfully dabbed at her chin. When he tucked his finger in the collar of her shirt, he paused to look into her eyes, checking if it was okay for him to proceed. She felt the air thicken between them and nodded.

John gently stroked a line of lotion on one collarbone, then the other. Even though it was an innocent, straightforward gesture, it felt enormously intimate. Linnea felt her neurons inflame as the roller moved along her skin. Finished, he looked again into her eyes, so close she could feel his breath on her lips. She saw desire swimming in those pools of green and knew her own eyes reflected that emotion.

"That's better," he said, releasing her shirt and leaning back.

She breathed again in the cooler air.

John tossed the lotion into the bag and said, "Would you mind taking that?"

She was happy to have a job to do.

They got out of the truck, and John tucked the keys under the front driver's-side tire. Around them other cars were jostling for spots while still others whizzed by. She heard car doors slam and greetings shouted as men and women, all carrying surfboards, headed to the beach. John knew the routine. He moved swiftly and efficiently, removing the straps from the boards and carrying each one from the bed of the truck to the grass.

"Where's the bag?" he called, arm extended.

Linnea hurried over with it. He reached in and pulled out what looked like a bar of white soap.

"First lesson," he said, holding up the bar. "This is surf wax. And these," he said, dropping to his knees, "are called longboards."

Indeed they were. Each board had to be nine feet long. John waved her closer.

"You take this surf wax," he said, moving over the boards, "and spread a layer of it on the board to create a good grip for your feet. That's so you don't slip off while riding the wave. You rub it on, like so."

She watched his shoulders move and his tanned muscles flex.

"You want to make sure there are no slick spots." He leaned back on his haunches and scanned his board. Satisfied, he pointed to her white and blue board. "All right," he said. "Have you named your board yet?"

"Named it? No. It was Brett's board."

"It's yours now. You develop a kind of bond with your board. At least, I do. If you love the sport, you'll spend a lot of time on it. You and the board will go through a lot together."

Linnea stared at the board, searching her brain for the right name. "It's a boy board, of course," she said, thinking that it came from Brett. "And it's big. . . ."

"How about Big Blue?"

She smiled. "I like it. Big Blue it is."

"Treat him well, and he'll give you the ride of your life." He handed her the wax. "Do the honors."

She grabbed the bar of wax and shifted to her knees. The dry crabgrass mingled with tiny bits of gravel that dug into her tender skin. But she wasn't going to complain. She began rubbing the bar in even strokes across Big Blue, pushing hard to get a good spread. At last she straightened and looked at him for approval.

"Good job," he told her.

She felt inordinately pleased.

"Okay, then." John rose effortlessly and stuck out his hand to help her to her feet. Then he picked up his board, and tucked it under his arm as though it were a feather.

Linnea looked at Big Blue, remembering how clumsy she'd been with it before. He waited. Determined, she bent to pick it up. She struggled, and it was hardly graceful but she somehow managed. The board was heavy, but what made it unwieldy was its length.

John watched her with a grin on his face.

Her temper sparked. "You've got long arms," she told him crossly. She teetered but finally managed to get a solid grip. When she turned to face him, the back of the longboard smacked into the side of his truck.

She gasped and looked at John, grimacing. "Sorry!"

He laughed, setting his board down. "I don't think one more bang will make a difference on that old truck." He took her surfboard in his arms.

"Okay," he said in a calm voice, and looked squarely at her. "The secret with surfing is to always be centered. On the board, when you're in the water. On land when you're carrying the board. And always"—he gently tapped her forehead with his fingertip—"in your head."

She listened, nodding in understanding.

"If it's difficult to carry the board under your arm—because it *is* a big board and you aren't so big," he said with a smile, "then you can carry it over your head. Like this." He lifted her board with enviable ease and lowered it to rest on his head.

She was not convinced.

"Now you try."

Linnea was game. She centered herself, took a deep breath, then hoisted the board up with a grunt. John helped her this first time to rest it on the top of her head. To her surprise, it didn't feel too heavy, and once she got the weight centered, she felt in control.

"Hey, I can do this," she called out, pleased with herself.

"If you're sure . . ."

"I'm sure. But let's go! I'm not that strong."

John gave her a thumbs-up. "Okay, Gidget. It's not too far."

Trailing John down the road toward the beach, Linnea concentrated on keeping the giant board balanced on her head. Still she couldn't help but notice his muscular body. As they crossed Palm Boulevard, she noticed the passing drivers enviously watching the surfers. Usually she was the one sitting behind the wheel. She was the surfer now, and the thought made the surfboard suddenly feel a bit lighter.

The narrow beach path was tough going while balancing the nine-foot board on her head. She kept her gaze straight ahead, carefully moving one foot past the other, praying she didn't step on a sandspur and end up in a heap in the sand. Linnea's arms were shaking by the time she felt the first salt-tinged gust of ocean air. She laid her board on the sand with a heavy sigh of relief. She looked over to see John standing with his hands on his hips, looking out over the water. Turning, he waved her over to his side and slid his arm around her shoulders.

"See that cluster of surfers out there?"

She nodded, feeling a thrill at knowing she'd soon be out there with them.

"That's what we call the break. They're waiting a few strokes ahead of where the wave's going to break." He pointed. "Now watch. . . . In a few minutes a wave will build."

She watched as the line of surfers got their boards into position. The water swelled behind them, blue and bulging.

"There they go!"

She felt his hand tighten on her shoulder as he pointed out the action. "They paddle hard to catch the wave. Then it peaks. There! See it?" She nodded. "That's what you wait for. That's when you hop up and catch it. 'Cause if you do, you get to ride the wave."

Linnea felt his excitement in the tension of his muscles, heard the thrill in his voice. She almost felt that she too was one of the surfers gliding across the water. It was poetry in motion. She leaned against him.

"Wow" was all she could say.

He squeezed her shoulder and looked down at her. "Think you want to try?"

She leaned back in his arm, and their gazes met. "Oh, yes."

"Then there's only one more question to ask." He released her and put his hands on his hips. "Are you regular or goofy?"

Linnea laughed and shook her head, wondering if he was joking. "Huh?"

"I'm serious. Get on your surfboard like you're paddling."

"You want me to lie on the board? Here on the sand?"

"Yep. Get on the board," he said, ushering with his hand.

"You're the teacher." Linnea lay belly-down on top of the board and looked up at him, waiting for him to tell her what was next.

"Okay," John said, coming close. "When I say, 'Pop up,' jump up on the board, one foot in front of the other. Almost like a warrior yoga pose. Don't think about it. Just do it. Ready?"

"Ready."

"Pop up!"

Linnea sprang to her feet, holding her arms out for balance in a yoga pose, and looked to John. "Like that?"

"Just like that." He looked down at her feet. "Okay. You're regular."

She narrowed her eyes at him.

He pointed to her right foot. "See your foot? Right foot forward is goofy. Left foot forward is regular."

"So is regular good?"

"There's no good or bad. The flow of surfing is for everything to be natural. You don't want to conform to any preconceived formation. Just do what comes naturally. So, my friend, you're naturally a regular."

"And you are?"

He grinned. "Goofy all the way."

She offered a crooked smile. "Figures."

"Now that we know that, we're going to take this leash"—he knelt on the sand and picked up the leash connected to the board—"and wrap this Velcro band around your right ankle."

She felt his hands attach the strap around her ankle.

"You have skinny ankles," he said.

"I heard that a good surfer has big feet for balance."

"If that were true"—he lifted his foot into the air—"I'd be pretty good."

"You know what else they say about a man with big feet?"

He met her gaze and said with a straight face, "Big feet, good surfer." They laughed. "But unfortunately, that's not true. If anything, I'm guessing a little thing like you would be able to find her center of gravity on that big board better than a big clod like me."

"Is that supposed to be encouraging?"

"It is. But there's only one way to find out. Come on, Gidget."

"Okay, Big Kahuna."

He paused and looked at her askance. "Big Kahuna? I'm not that much older than you."

Linnea just shrugged, pleased he understood the reference.

The water reflected the shimmering blue of the sky. Because the waves were so good today, a line of surfers already sat bobbing at the break, their laughter echoing in the wind like birdcalls. Linnea hoisted her board and stepped into the ocean. She gasped at the chill of the first splash and, laughing with excitement, held tight to Big Blue as they crossed the shallows. The water reached John's hips, and his body glistened with water.

Later, they stretched out on the boards in the deep water. John paddled his board closer to her.

"You remember the last time you tried to paddle through the waves?"

Linnea groaned and said with exaggeration, "Don't remind me!"

"I'm going to get you over them, don't worry. There are two different ways to get past the white water with a big board like this," he said. "If it's a small wave, you do what we call the push-up. That's best for the waves here. You start by getting a lot of momentum. Head straight for it. If you're angled or sideways, the white water will knock you off your board." His brows lifted but he held back his smile. "I think you remember that. As you approach the breaking wave, push up so the wave rolls over your board and underneath your chest."

He pushed himself up on the board. She didn't miss his arm muscles flexing.

"If the wave is more powerful and you find yourself facing a wall of white wash, you grab the sides of the board like this, and do the turtle roll."

She laughed. "I like the sound of that."

"I thought you would. For that, when the wave hits, you flip upside down, hanging on to your board while the wave rolls over you. Then you pop back up. You shouldn't have to worry about doing that here. For today, let's just concentrate on the push-up method."

"I think I can do that."

"Oh, yeah," he added, tugging at the leash on his ankle. "Here's why you need the leash. First, it might just save your life. You get tired, you get pounded by the waves. And sometimes rip currents take you for a ride. With your surfboard, you'll stay afloat. And one of these leg ropes will prevent your surfboard from hitting your fellow surfers. That's a biggie. And finally"—he smiled—"if you have a leash, you won't spend most of your surf time chasing after your surfboard. You can't be sure some nice guy will be around to grab it."

She smiled, remembering. "Got it."

"I think that's it." He looked out to scan the water. "Here comes one."

She caught sight of a blue wall heading toward them and her muscles tightened.

"Push up!" he shouted.

Linnea gripped the sides of her board, feeling her stomach clench. As the blue wave hit, she sucked in her breath and pushed herself up on her arms. A rush of cool water flowed under her. She exhaled with a shout of joy, thrilled to her core. The ocean awakened her, leaving her feeling invigorated, confident, like she belonged here. She grinned and searched for John. He was close, smiling at her, giving her the thumbs-up. Then he pointed and she saw another wave coming. She followed his example and started paddling again, harder. She pushed through this one too, riding over it and laughing when the water rushed by.

"You're doing great!" John called out.

At last they made it to the break where a line of other surfers waited. She tried to sit up on the board like the rest of the surfers, but her balance was off and the board wobbled in the water. She gripped it tightly. *Balance*, she thought. *Keep centered*.

"Linnea!" John called out, and pointed to the two surfers to his left. "Meet Richie and Trey. They're my buddies who live over on Sullivan's. And over there"—he waved to two men at her right, who had longer, graying hair and sat on their boards with the attitude of kings—"that's Mickey and Danny. They taught the rest of us how to surf. We call them the Godfathers."

Linnea returned their waves, careful not to upset her balance. "Who's the girl?" she asked. Next to Mickey sat a smashing girl with long blond hair who had an enviable confidence and ease on the board.

John leaned over to look. "That's Carson Muir. Wait—it's Legare now. That's her husband, Blake. Lucky guy." He cupped his hands around his mouth. "Hey, Carson!"

The woman turned her head and, seeing John, returned a warm smile and a relaxed wave. It was clear she felt as at home on a surfboard as the guys. Linnea wanted to feel that confidence on the water someday.

"You all know each other?"

"A lot of us do, yeah," he answered. "We've been surfing this same stretch of beach most of our lives. Bumping into each other, literally. Plus, there's always an element of danger in the sea. The unexpected. We have each other's backs."

She looked around at the vast sea that seemed to stretch to the sky and realized her vulnerability out here. And her lack of knowledge.

"I can see why. It's a little scary way out here."

John quietly slipped off his board and swam to grab the edges of her surfboard, holding it steady in his strong hands. His face was solemn and she felt the intensity of his gaze.

"Don't be scared, Linnea," he said seriously. Droplets of water hung from his lashes and sparkled in the sun, making his eyes appear as green as the sea. "I have your back."

She saw in his eyes that he was watching out for her. She felt safe with him. Their eyes lingered for a second, and she felt the heat warm her body.

"Remember why you came out here," he continued. "Why we all come out here. You know that euphoria you felt riding over the wave?"

She nodded.

"We call that surfer's stoke. It might look like we're all just sitting out here waiting for a wave, but it's a kind of meditation. We're taking it all in. There's this sense way out here that we're part of something bigger than ourselves. There's this overwhelming sense of peace. Time seems to disappear and nothing matters but the sea and the sky and that we are alive."

Linnea stared at him, appreciating his words and that he'd lowered his guard to bring her into his world. She didn't know what to say. Didn't feel the need to say anything.

A profound silence followed as he continued to hold on to her board and they rocked in the water. She heard the splashing of water, the cry of an osprey overhead. Her senses came alive, attuned to the moment.

John looked over her shoulder, and his expression suddenly focused. "Okay, Gidget. This might be a good wave. Listen to my cues and paddle as hard as you can till you catch the wave."

Uncertainty reared its head. "How will I know?"

"Believe me, you'll know. Just don't rush it. One of the biggest mistakes is to stand too soon. Be patient. Wait those extra couple seconds, and then pop up." He patted her board. "Big Blue is a steady steed. You just take all the time you need to stand up. He'll take you in. Here's your wave!"

Linnea gripped her board tightly as he turned Big Blue around to face the beach. Everyone else in line was getting into position. She spread her arms out, ready to paddle.

"When I say so, start paddling."

She looked forward, holding her breath. Listening.

"Go!" he shouted. "Paddle, paddle, paddle!"

Linnea felt a giant push that she thought was the wave until she realized it was John pushing her. All five of her senses heightened, and her mind focused. She felt the board catch the wave, gliding, gaining speed. She raised herself to her knees, counted to two, then popped up to her feet. She was up! Euphoric! For a fleeting second, she was flying. Her whole existence was soaring on this single wave!

Almost as quickly as she got up, she fell off, tumbling into the white water as if she were stuck in a washing machine on permanent press. She felt a tug on her right ankle and surfaced, breaking free of the wave. Gasping for breath, she climbed back on the board.

She swiped her streaming hair out of her eyes and lifted her face to the sun, blinking in the light. She heard John hooting and shouting her name behind her. Her heart expanded, and as she waved back she grinned so wide her cheeks hurt.

Euphoria, she thought, feeling like she had entered a new world of indescribable beauty. *This is my ocean.* She turned her surfboard, knowing which direction she wanted to go. She began paddling hard, feeling no fatigue, only a driving desire to get back out on the breakers.

"Come on, Big Blue. We've got this."

Chapter Twelve

*Turtles do cry, but not because they're sad. They have
glands that help empty excess salt from their eyes,
which look like tears.*

"YOU'VE GOT COMPANY," said Emmi.

Cara leaned over the counter and looked out the
kitchen window to see a black Land Rover pull up the drive. She
felt a flutter of anticipation at seeing David, not that she'd ever
admit that to Emmi Baker Peterson.

"It's David and Rory."

Emmi lowered her coffee mug with interest. It was Emmi's free
day, and they'd been catching up over coffee and a seven-layer caramel
cake from Caroline's Cakes. Cara never took a bite of her favorite cake
without remembering Caroline Ragsdale Reutter. She missed her former Ashley Hall friend. As she tasted the cake's sweetness she thought
how sad it was that the best—like Caroline and Brett—went young.

"This has become a regular thing, hasn't it?" asked Emmi. "It's been, what . . . a few weeks now?"

"Yes," replied Cara, opening the cabinet and pulling out a fresh mug.

"And you're still calling it playdates?"

Cara looked at her askance. "What do you mean, *calling it playdates*? That's what they are."

"Come on," Emmi chided, nudging her. "We both know he's coming to see you. Rory is but a hostage to his romantic schemes."

"That's a terrible thing to say," Cara scolded her. "If you think that, then you're saying I'm holding Hope hostage too."

Emmi wiggled her brows.

"You're hopeless. David and I are simply taking the children out together." She set the Juliska mug on the table beside a matching white plate. "You know, I had no idea there was this whole other side to the Charleston area."

"The one meant for little kids and their parents," Emmi said sarcastically, biting into her cake. Some of the cake flaked off onto her shirt, and she nonchalantly brushed the crumbs from her chest.

Cara laughed. "Exactly. This whole being a mom thing is new to me, and it's so much nicer doing these outings with a friend. David is a font of knowledge about wherever we go. You know," she said in a distant tone, "it's been a while since a man's intellect challenged my own. And we enjoy each other's company. David's a very nice man."

"Uh-huh," Emmi drawled. She looked out the window and watched as David pulled Rory out of his car seat. "He's dreamy.

That's what he is." She straightened. "And he's got a nice butt." She popped the last of her cake into her mouth.

Cara snorted and leaned over the counter again. She watched David with Rory in his arms swing the car door shut and walk toward the house. He was wearing black jeans that showed off his long legs and a plain white button-down shirt, sleeves rolled up. He'd told her he had a closet full of Brooks Brothers button-downs from his working days that were the most comfortable shirts he owned. So he wore them rolled up at the sleeves and didn't care if they got stained.

"Yes, he is," Cara admitted with a sigh. "And I don't quite know what to do about how he makes me feel."

"Honey, you don't have to do anything."

Cara looked at her best friend and wanted to share with her how these feelings for David made her feel like she was somehow betraying Brett. But the doorbell rang, cutting off further conversation.

Hope looked up sharply from her high chair, eyes wide and alert. Cara pushed off from the counter. "Watch her a sec, will you?" Cara asked Emmi, and hurried to the front door.

"Right on time," she said, swinging wide the door.

"I take no credit," David said, walking in with Rory in his arms. "The ferry leaves the dock at nine o'clock sharp."

As he walked by her, she caught the scent of his cologne. It was very subtle and, she knew, expensive.

"I've got cake and coffee in the kitchen," she told him. "And Emmi's here."

She followed David into the kitchen and watched as he walked straight to Emmi and planted a kiss on her upturned cheek. Cara smiled as they exchanged pleasantries, glad he got along with her friends. Then he bent toward Hope.

"Good morning, Miss Hope," he said, and gently kissed the top of her head.

Hope leaned far back against the chair and lowered her chin, looking up at him coyly. Her dark lashes fluttered.

"She's such a flirt," Cara said with a light laugh. "And how are you, young man?" she asked Rory. Rory looked back at her with his round blue eyes. "Would you like a piece of caramel cake?" She turned to David. "Oops, is that all right, Pops?" she asked, using the name Rory called him.

He grimaced. "Maybe just a bite. He's got a real sweet tooth and Heather's pretty firm on her no-sugar policy."

He set Rory down in the booster seat Cara had set up and buckled him in while Cara went to pour his coffee. It was a comfortable routine they'd fallen into over the past several weeks. Coffee and a morning snack for the kids, diaper changes, load up the car, and off they went on a new adventure.

Cara and David had become quite comfortable with each other as they minded the children. Since Brett, she'd been cautious with men, not wanting them to get too close and holding back on anything important or personal. With David, however, the children had established a common bond. They had each other's backs and had reached a comfort level she'd never experienced with a man before. Not even with Brett. Children changed everything.

And she'd needed that change.

Cara handed David his steaming mug of coffee.

"Smells great. Thanks," he said, his eyes glittering at her over the rim of the cup. After a swallow he added, "Mmm . . . tastes great too."

Emmi drew closer with the cake and offered some to David. He accepted it with thanks. She set the box on the table. While the children nibbled fruit snacks, the adults stood in a circle with their coffee.

"So, where are you heading to today?" Emmi asked.

"Yes," Cara echoed, turning to David. "You said you had a surprise for today. Where are we going?"

David leaned over the table to set his half-eaten cake on the plate. "Well, you know how we've talked about taking the kids on my boat?"

Cara nodded slowly. "Yes," she said guardedly. "I thought we'd decided they were too young."

"Right," David replied readily. "So instead, I got us tickets on a boat tour. There's a company right on the island I heard good things about." He pulled tickets out of his shirt pocket and held them up in the air. "Coastal Ecotour."

Cara felt her stomach fall along with her face and stared back at David, speechless.

Seeing her reaction, his thick brows drew together in concern. "Don't worry. It's large and only goes out on the Intracoastal Waterway. It's very smooth. Perfect for the children. I checked."

Cara looked to Emmi for support. She stood silent with her fingertips pressed against her lips. Cara looked again at David and swallowed hard. "You didn't know?"

"Know what?"

"My late husband. Brett. He owned Coastal Ecotour. That was our company."

David's face paled. "Oh, Cara, I'm sorry. I had no idea. Forget I suggested it. I'll give these tickets away. We can go—"

"No, don't do that," she interrupted, shaking her head. She took a breath, considering her words carefully. "No. You know what? I should go. To Capers Island. I've been meaning to go for years. And I want to take Hope. It's a very special place with a lot of beautiful memories."

Emmi drew closer and put her hand on Cara's arm. "But only when you're ready."

"Right," David agreed. "When you're ready."

"I am ready," Cara said with a shaky smile. "As ready as I'll ever be. And honestly . . ." She looked into David's dark brown eyes. She felt safe in the depth of concern she saw there. "I'd like to have you with me when I go."

~~~~~

CARA FELT HER stomach clenching during the slow drive north on Palm Boulevard toward the Isle of Palms Marina. The large, open gravel parking lot was half-filled with parked cars and boat trailers. David hunted for a spot with shade, and finding none open, opted for a spot close to the water. Once he'd parked, he leaped from the car to help Cara from the passenger seat.

"I'm fine," she said with a soft laugh. He was being exceedingly solicitous. "My heart hurts, but the rest of me is good. Let's get the kiddies."

She heard every crunch of gravel like a drum pounding in her ears as they walked with the children toward the dock. A new sign, slightly bigger and with bright lettering, read COASTAL ECOTOUR. She immediately spied the *Caretta*, moored by the small wooden office built on pilings. The *Caretta* was a long, flat, creamy-white pontoon tour boat with steel railings, a metal roof, and narrow benches on either side. Her mind flashed to the day the boat had been christened after her. She'd stood in a white dress and hat, beaming into Brett's eyes under a cerulean sky, surrounded by friends and family. He'd been so proud. Then, on the count, she'd swung the bottle of champagne and broken it against the hull. She'd given the *Caretta* and Coastal Ecotour ten of the best years of her life. And then she'd sold it and moved away. She felt the ensuing three years' time like an invisible barrier she had to cross.

She swallowed hard and, lifting her chin, followed David to stand with a cluster of people at the dock entrance. She knew she could stroll over to the office and say hello, and there would be hugs and tears. *No waiting for you!* But she couldn't. She wanted to hide in the group of strangers dressed in pastel T-shirts and Bermuda shorts with phones out clicking pictures. Suddenly she didn't know if she was ready. She leaned against David, and he wrapped his free arm around her shoulders and squeezed.

The line began to move forward. Two young boys raced down the ramp, hooting and hollering, to grab front seats. A man's voice called out, "Hey, no running! There's plenty of room."

Cara bit her lip, recognizing Robert's voice. They inched forward. She stood behind David as he handed Robert their tickets. Robert was chatty, calling Rory a young pirate. She followed his gaze from Hope's face to her. His words stopped short, and his smile dropped into a gape of wonder.

"Cara!" Robert exclaimed as his expressive blue eyes moistened. "I didn't know you were coming. No one told me."

"It was last-minute."

"And you waited in line?"

"Felt like old times," she said, looking into his eyes. The silence that followed spoke volumes.

"But hey, you're going to have a great time. You'll see a few changes, but nothing major. Brett created a well-oiled machine. I just keep it going. Though I've got to confess, I sure do miss you handling the books. I try, but . . ." He shook his head.

She knew he was being modest. He'd been with Brett from the beginning and had helped build the business. It was her great joy to help Robert buy the company after Brett's death.

"Business good?" she asked.

"Very. We keep growing. Did you see our new boat yet?" When she shook her head, he waved her closer to the ramp. "Come take a look. It's a beauty," he added, and she couldn't miss the pride in his voice as they walked down the wooden ramp to the dock. Beside the *Caretta* was a slightly smaller, flashier blue-and-white pontoon boat.

"It's fabulous," Cara said, admiring the blue padded seat backs, something she and Brett had talked about. "What do you call it?"

Robert looked out at the boat and said, "*The Salty Captain*."

Cara sighed. That was Robert's nickname for Brett. "That's perfect." She looked at Robert. He had the wiry body of a seaman. His blond hair was salt-stiff, his tan deep and ruddy, and around his neck and up his arms were handcrafted macramé and beaded jewelry pieces made by his wife and daughter. Robert was a good man.

"You're the new Salty Captain."

His eyes sparkled with gratitude. "Aye, that I am," he replied with a pirate's growl. Then he looked at the large diver's watch on his wrist. "And being captain, I have to get this boat moving. Let's get on board."

She and David took seats in the rear of the boat, steering clear of the two rowdy boys, who were pinching and jabbing at each other. Robert's assistant, a stocky young woman with her brown hair pulled back in a ponytail, jumped to and from the boat with ease, if not grace, to untie the ropes. This had been Linnea's job once upon a time. She had been a natural teacher, trained by Brett. Cara smiled, remembering the first time she watched Brett leap like Douglas Fairbanks, counting on his impeccable timing as he brought the boat out of dock. When the big engines roared to life the children on the boat all sat up, eyes wide, and leaned over the railings to watch the water churn. Robert guided the boat at a snail's pace along the no-wake zone, until they entered the Intracoastal Waterway. Then he opened it up to full speed. The boys were, for the first time, speechless as the whitewater caps pushed out a wide wake and sprayed the air with droplets of water. Robert could spin a good tale as he explained how the Intracoastal Waterway extended from the Florida Keys all the way north to Boston. Cara listened and remembered how it had been a dream of hers and Brett's to take that journey one day, maybe for their twenty-fifth anniversary.

Robert spoke to the children and adults alike with the passion of a teacher who loved his subject. As he talked about the dolphins, the sharks, and the different species of fish that swam in these waters, everyone could hear in his voice how much he loved all marine life. He stood with his shirttails flapping in the wind and his hands always moving as he showed them the intricacies of shells and pulled up live snapping crabs from the sea. As he educated them, he helped each of them understand what they could do to make a difference. He'd learned these lessons from Brett. Listening to Robert, she heard Brett's expressions, his jokes, the passion that had guided his life.

David leaned closer and said, "If I come back in another life, I want to be that guy."

She looked at him, his eyes sparkling like the water around him. He had no clue about all the memories flitting through her mind now. To all outward appearances, she sat calmly with a mild smile on her face, observing the scenery through her large, dark sunglasses.

"Why?"

"Look at him. He's doing what he loves. What more can anyone ask from life?"

Cara saw that David was being sincere. He'd worked long and hard for many years, had been enormously successful, and now, a widower and a grandfather, looked at what life offered differently.

She turned her head and looked at Robert, but in her mind she saw Brett. He'd always known this was the life he wanted. There'd never been any question in his mind. He was happiest on the water, on the *Caretta*, teaching visitors to the lowcountry all about her charm. She was awash in memories as the boat swayed in the current.

At last they reached the small island of Capers. Robert pushed the growling engines up into the sandy edge of the beach. The engines quieted suddenly, and he let out the anchor.

In the resulting peace, Cara could hear the gulls cry overhead and the sound of the waves lapping the shore and against the boat. Robert lowered the gangplank, and in friendly order, everyone disembarked. Cara brought up the rear. David stepped off first and stood in the watery sand of the shoreline, then reached for Rory, then Hope. Cara took a breath and stepped once again onto Capers Island.

Capers had always been her and Brett's place. They'd courted here, made love here for the first time, and returned many times over their ten years of marriage. Miles of white sand sparkled under a brilliant blue sky, welcoming her back. The tide was low, so the beach was streaked with long gullies that coursed through the sand like rivers. Cara knew Rory and Hope would love splashing in the sun-heated pools. She'd always felt a million miles away on Capers Island. Today, however, she was crowded by memories.

"Shall we go?" David asked, not wanting to rush her.

The other boaters were already far ahead. Some had disappeared around the bend; others were slowly strolling, inspecting shells, taking photographs. All enjoying the remote, idyllic island. A squeal caught her attention, and turning, she spotted the two mischievous boys swimming around the rear of the boat, up to no good. Robert was already trotting toward them, calling them back. Cara held back a smile, knowing he'd have his hands full for the next forty minutes. She adjusted Hope's sun hat and, catching David's eyes, smiled and took a step forward.

The sand was warm, the sun was hot, and there was just enough of a breeze to keep the insects at bay. David and Cara walked at the children's slow pace. Hope's steps were faltering, especially in the soft sand. The tide line was covered with shells of all sorts. Cara kept her gaze to the ground, bending from time to time to pick up a shell, poking in each to make sure she wasn't stealing the home of some snail. Hope mimicked her, picking up a shell and delighting in putting it in the bag, over and over. The rest of the boaters had moved far off across the island, leaving them the wide swath of beach to themselves. Cara looked around and spied a shallow gully of water beneath the shade of the trees.

"David, there's a sweet little pool of water in the shade. Let's let the babies play here. It's perfect for them."

David asked Rory, "What do you say, champ? Feel like a swim?"

Cara was restless and not in the mood to talk. David sensed this and didn't press. After a while of tending the children splashing and crawling, Cara pulled Hope from the pool and dried her.

"David, if you don't mind, I'd like to go ahead on my own. I need some time alone."

"Of course," he replied. "Would you like me to take care of Hope?"

She shook her head. "I'd like to keep her with me. But thanks."

"I'll meet you at the boat, then."

She was grateful for his understanding. David was not the type to sulk.

Cara picked up Hope and began walking along the seemingly endless stretch of narrow beach strewn with large, dark, fallen trees.

A few of the dead trees still stood tall like ancient monoliths, their curled and gnarled roots twisting around sand and shells in the open air. It was a ghostly place, desolate in its stark beauty. Brett had thought it the most beautiful spot in the world.

She found what she was looking for. A small creek cut through the sand, a favorite spot of Brett's to cast a net for shrimp. She turned inland toward the shelter of the trees to a place she knew well. Not too far in, a large dune crested to a flat plateau. It was hard going with Hope in her arms, but Cara dug in her heels, climbed the dune, and stood panting at its peak. The ocean's breeze caressed her skin, and she looked out over the thicket of shrubs to the mighty blue ocean beyond. This was Brett's favorite place to pitch his tent. Here was where he'd first made love to her, and it was here, too, that she'd fallen in love with him.

She felt his presence keenly around her. She could almost hear his voice in the wind whispering her name in the trees. Cara lowered to sit on the dune beside Hope. She wanted to lay her head on the sand, stretch out her arms, and weep, as one would mourn at a grave site. Her chest ached from holding it in. But Hope needed her. She was a mother first.

So instead she began to dig a hole to entertain her daughter. She idly scratched the surface with her fingertips, then a bit deeper, when some unexplained urge took hold of her. She began digging, deeper and deeper, clawing the sand, her tender fingertips scraping tiny bits of shell. Putting her hands in the sand grounded her, gave her a place to let her anxiety flow from her brain and her heart out through her fingers into the beach. This was not a game, nor was it like digging a turtle nest. This, she knew, was a kind of grave, the grave she'd never dug for her husband. Brett had been cremated, his ashes sprinkled on the water off Capers, straight out from where she sat now.

Cara's fingers dug deep to where the sand was cool and moist. Earthy. Beside her, Hope was mimicking her, picking up handfuls of sand and throwing them into the air. The gold band on Cara's right ring finger caught the sunlight, and she stilled. She held her hand up, her eyes filling with tears.

"Brett," she called out to him, her voice breaking with emotion. Hope turned her head to look at her, attuned to her mother's tears. Cara took a breath to try and contain herself for Hope's sake.

"I love you," she said aloud. "I miss you every day." She paused, lowering her hand. She needed to say the words out loud. "Your presence is still so very real. You're everywhere I go. Everywhere I look." She reached over to stroke Hope's arm. "I have a child. At last. And I need her. She's a gift. Her name is Hope. You would love her."

Hearing her name, Hope's eyes grew expectant. Cara reached for the bag of shells and emptied them out in front of the baby. Immediately Hope was enthralled with them.

Cara spoke again. More deliberately. "I'll always love you. But I have to accept that you are gone. And that I have to move on." She paused. "I've found someone who I think I could love. He's a lot like you, in so many ways. Good. Kind. Honest. But he's different, too. He's not you. And he's not a substitute you, either. I like him," she confessed. "Very much."

It was so hard to say the words aloud. She felt a pang of guilt and it wasn't fair. Cara brought her hand to her heart in a fist.

"You're not even alive, but I feel like I'm cheating on you! What should I do?" she asked, tears flowing down her cheeks. "Please, Brett, let me know it's okay to say good-bye. To move on."

Hope lunged forward to hug her. "Mama!"

Cara hugged her back, knowing the child sensed her sadness. "Mama's fine, sweetheart. These are good tears," she said, then pulled back and wiped her eyes. "Mama knows what she has to do."

Cara looked at her hand and, without hesitation, slid the thin gold wedding band from her finger.

"Here, Hope."

Hope reached over and, with her chubby pincer fingers, picked up the ring.

"Can you put the ring in the hole? Go on, it's okay. Put it in."

Hope delicately, obediently dropped the ring in the center and watched as it fell deeper than she could reach. She immediately looked to Cara for approval, and seeing her mother smile, she clapped her hands and burst into a joyful "Yay!"

"Good girl, Hope. Thank you for helping Mama."

Together they filled the hole with sand and patted the top flat like a turtle did its nest. Finally, Cara chose the best shells and formed a circle over the smooth sand. She leaned back on her arms and looked at her work. There was symmetry to the project, a synchronicity about being here today, with Hope and David, that made the circle feel binding. She felt sure she was heard.

She lifted Hope into her arms and with a determined stride left the hidden dune in the pines and walked from the shade into the open, sunlit beach.

Chapter Thirteen

Sea turtles swim at a leisurely pace but are capable of moving at
great speeds for short distances with their long, broad flippers.
Leatherbacks can dive to a depth of a thousand meters.

W ORK WAS BEGINNING to take off and Cara was hitting her
stride. The cloud of worry dissipated with the steady
income. Each morning she awoke and said a quick prayer of
thanks that her life was her own again. She volunteered to share
Linnea's turtle team schedule so she could walk the beach with
Hope in the mornings. It was like old times slipping into her
turtle team T-shirt, lathering on sunscreen, and stepping out into
the placid air while the day was young and the sky was still
blushing.

This morning, as always, Hope was wide-eyed and silent as
they walked the beach. The sand was rippled by the outgoing tide.
The muted colors of shells added texture to the scene, and there

were the usual clusters of shorebirds and the skittering of crabs. She walked at a power pace, her long legs covering the distance in easy time. At first Cara had been shocked at how winded she was at the end of her turtle walk. But now she was enjoying the exercise, doing it for herself as well as Hope. She was bonding with her daughter. Her head was cleared out of doors, and she could solve the problems playing in her head. And she was feeling more fit. More herself.

She finished the walk without spotting tracks. But she did spy Linnea and John out in the surf. The waves were modest, but they looked like they were having fun. Cara had never surfed, though Palmer had surfed avidly when they were growing up and Brett had loved the sport. She admired Linnea for deciding to follow her bliss and just do it. She watched her ride a wave, her arms outstretched like a bird in flight. Cara's heart swelled with pride. "Good girl," she said aloud. Then promised herself she'd give Hope the chance to take lessons in the future.

She was showered and dressed and had a snack packed by the time David arrived. They loaded up the big car with children and gear and headed for Magnolia Plantation. They drove in a companionable silence. Hope and Rory babbled in the backseat. Cara stared out the window, lost in her thoughts.

"You seem fired up about something," David said, glancing over at her.

"Do I?" she said, thinking how perceptive he was. "Actually, I do have a lot on my mind. A chance at a new account."

He turned his head briefly and she saw that his eyes brightened with curiosity. "I'm glad. Care to talk about it?"

His voice was pleasant. Interested. She welcomed his opinion and explained.

"The client is the owner of a restaurant chain in Charleston. Chic, high-end. I'm sure you've eaten at one of them. They're expanding beyond Charleston and looking for fresh marketing ideas. I knew someone who knew the owner." She glanced at him. His eyes were on the road. "That's one of the perks of living in a small town. I'm meeting with them tomorrow afternoon. I've been putting together my ideas. I have to admit, I'm a bit nervous."

"You've had big clients before."

"I have. Very big. But it's only me now, and the stakes are high."

"Do you feel prepared?"

She took in a breath, considering. "I do. I really think my ideas are good ones."

He seemed impressed. "Then my money's on you."

She looked at his hands on the wheel. Long-fingered, tanned. Clean nails. Brett had worked with his hands, and like a worker's hands, they were always chapped, stained, and scratched. But he'd taken care to keep his nails clean.

"Think twice," she told David. "I'm an independent consultant up against major, high-powered consulting firms. They have money to spend on flashy presentations. All the bells and whistles. My presentation will be, shall we say, only me and my ideas."

"Isn't that what matters?" He threw her a smile. Looking back at the road, he said, "I don't know if you realize how persuasive you are."

~~~~~~~

CARA FELT LIKE a million dollars as she strode up King Street. It was an overcast day and the streets were crawling with cars. But to her, the day was sunny. She was wearing a new Ralph Lauren summer suit with a pencil skirt that fit her lean body and long legs like it was designed for her. She'd styled her hair, which was growing longer, to tuck it behind her ears, and wore her mother's large pearls. In her briefcase was a neatly typed presentation that gave her the confidence in her step. As she swung her arms, she noticed the glances she was getting from strangers. It fueled her fire. *This is my town*, she thought. *And I'm back.*

Hall's Chophouse in the Upper King District was a bastion of Charleston where the old guard met young pages and squires to eat, drink, and do business. She opened the heavy doors and paused to let her eyes adjust to the dim lighting. At once, Billy Hall stepped forward and greeted her warmly.

"Cara Rutledge." The lights went on in his eyes and there was the instant connection of old Charleston. "It's so grand to see you again. I remember you coming in here with your father and mother."

"This was Daddy's favorite place."

"You moved away, didn't you?" His tone held a hint of scold.

"Yes," she replied, holding her own but smiling. "But I came back years ago. I live in my mother's beach house on Isle of Palms. I've kept pretty much to the islands."

"I'm glad you're back. You can't ever really leave Charleston, can you?"

She shook her head. "No. Charleston is my home."

"Your brother's here." Billy looked across the red-bricked room to the gleaming bar. "There he is."

Cara looked over and saw Palmer sitting on a stool with a few friends. She smiled, delighted to see him. Then she spotted the glass in his hand, and her gut clenched.

"You're a bit early for our meeting," Billy said. "Why don't you say hello to Palmer? Meet us upstairs when you're done. We're in the private room."

Cara affixed a smile. "Thanks, Mr. Hall."

Cara hadn't seen her brother in several weeks. It was odd, but living out on the island she sometimes felt like she was a hundred miles from the city rather than a quick trip over the bridge. For her, going to the city meant wearing nice clothes, proper shoes, makeup. Her mother had pummeled into her the message that ladies didn't stroll a city like Charleston in beachwear. Whenever Lovie had passed a young woman in cutoffs and a T-shirt on East Bay, she'd rolled her eyes and muttered, "Raised by wolves."

Life on the islands was more laid-back than in the city. City and island, each had its charms. Having lived in both places, having been both city mouse and country mouse, Cara appreciated each unique lifestyle—and the proper clothing for each.

Palmer was leaning on one elbow on the bar. His cheeks were flushed and he was staring down at his almost empty glass of what she knew was bourbon. Linnea had mentioned that she was worried about how much her father was drinking lately. Cara's mind flashed to her father's heavy drinking, and she wondered if Palmer was suffering late-onset alcoholism. She told herself not to scold. That wouldn't help—and besides, she wasn't his mother. She was his sister and friend. *Just breathe*, she told herself.

"Palmer," she said softly when she reached him, and touched his sleeve.

He jerked around and seeing her, his blue eyes widened with surprise.

"Cara!" he exclaimed, and rose to his feet. His joy at seeing her was palpable. "What are you doing here? And looking so fine."

He leaned forward to kiss her cheek, almost bowling her over with the fumes of alcohol.

"I'm here for business," she said, taking the stool beside his.

"Business, eh?" Palmer asked, seemingly impressed. "Well. Let me buy you a drink." He lifted his hand to flag the bartender.

"No," she said, putting her hand on his arm. "I'm working."

"Never stopped me," he said with a laugh.

She thought, *I can see that*, but kept her smile tightly clenched. It was just after five and Palmer was already well into the sauce.

"Palmer, what brings you here today?"

"Business." He shrugged. "Or the lack of it."

"Is there a problem?"

He stared into his drink and laughed without humor. "I guess you could say that."

"What? Can you tell me?"

"Aw, it's just business. Ups and downs. That sort of thing."

"I understand business, you know."

He looked at her and smirked. "Yeah, that's right. You're the smart one. You're the one Daddy should've left the business to. You don't fail at anything, do you? I bet if he had, it'd be thriving now. Not near bankruptcy."

Cara's heart chilled. "Bankruptcy?"

Palmer quickly shook his head and waved his hand sloppily in the air in a sign of dismissal. "No. Not that. I was just using words." He paused to finish his drink in a single gulp.

"You can tell me."

He slammed the glass down on the bar so loudly other guests looked at him with disapproval. He didn't seem to notice. "A few investments have gone south." He shrugged. "It happens." His cheeks sagged.

Cara drew closer. "Palmer, you're my brother. I love you. You were there for me when Brett died. I couldn't have made it through the financial mess if it weren't for you. Let me help. Is there anything I can do?"

His blue eyes melted with affection as he gazed back at her. Then he shook his head. "Nah, I'm fine. Nothing I can't handle. Daddy told me the business was like being on a ship. You have to roll with the ups and downs." He moved his hand as if it were a ship riding the waves, then let it land on the bar. "I've been through this before. Soon we'll be on calm seas again. Don't you worry."

Cara looked at her watch. "Palmer, I'm sorry, but I have to go. My meeting . . ."

"Sure. Off you go. Good luck, sister mine."

"Palmer, why don't you go home? Julia must be worried."

A glance was exchanged, and Cara knew her brother understood her meaning.

"I'll settle up and go. Don't be a stranger. Come visit. The house feels so empty."

"I'll try. But you should come to the beach house. It's summer! And you need to see Linnea. She's a surfing prodigy."

Palmer's face lit up. "Is she?" He burst into a genuine grin. "That girl's a spitfire. Just like you." Then he shook his head in mock ruefulness. "What is it about the Rutledge women? Y'all seem to have gotten the best the gene pool has to offer."

Cara laughed and bent closer to kiss his cheek. "It's just being a woman, brother mine."

～～～～

AN HOUR AND a half later, Cara walked out of the private meeting room and down the stairs. She paused to take a deep breath, then made her way through the shoulder-to-shoulder crowd to the bar. She felt her news bubbling in her like fine champagne and she had to move deliberately to keep herself from jumping up and down. The bar was packed, too, but she got lucky when a man rose. She grabbed his stool and pulled out her phone. She dialed the number of the person she most wanted to share her news with.

"David Wyatt."

"David? I got the job! They loved my ideas and decided at the table!"

"Congratulations! I'm not at all surprised."

"Come meet me for a drink. Let's celebrate!"

There was a moment's pause, and she knew he was looking at

his watch. "If I hurry, I can make the next ferry. I'll be there if I have to swim."

She laughed, feeling the joy of it. She cradled her phone to be heard over the jazz band that had started playing. She felt her lips move against the keys.

"I'll be waiting."

Chapter Fourteen

Sea turtles that arrive at sea turtle hospitals most commonly suffer from debilitated turtle syndrome, shock from exposure to cold temperatures, injury from a boat strike or shark bite, and consumption of marine debris like plastic bags or fishing line.

Over the next few weeks, John showed up at seven every morning that the surf was good, and if Linnea was free from baby duty they took off together. He brought the boards and Linnea brought the coffee. His knocks on the door became customary. John often dropped in for no particular reason. Sometimes he'd show up with lunch or coffee, or occasionally in the evening with a bottle of wine. They would sit at their laptops, he working, she searching for jobs. Cara had already declared he was a "lovely young man," and felt comfortable having him around. The fact that he often sat on the floor and played with Hope helped solidify that opinion. Hope couldn't pronounce his name and it came out "Don," so John's nickname around the beach house became Uncle

Don. Emmi was over the moon about their friendship and her matchmaking arrows were flying.

Linnea wasn't interested in falling in love this summer, however. This brief period at the beach was becoming an extraordinary time of self-discovery. A hidden self was emerging—independent, courageous—that had previously been tucked away by a lifetime of feminine inhibition.

Part of this awakening came from her time out on the ocean. She found that being on the water heightened her perceptions and her senses. She carried the peace of the sea with her throughout the day, tackling tasks with an ease that brought tranquility not only to her but also to the household. Cara had commented on it several times: "You have such a lovely calm about you," she'd say. Or, "I never for a moment worry about Hope when she's with you."

John's coming and going also added a new dimension to her life. She'd always felt she had to be "on" with other men. With John, it was refreshing to share a common interest rather than a drink. They were friends first.

On such a day in early July, it was Linnea's day for turtle duty so she couldn't go surfing. The team was busy morning and night, since the females were still nesting and the earlier nests were beginning to hatch. When she stepped out of the house in her uniform T-shirt, Linnea was surprised to find John waiting by the door. He was clad in his usual swimsuit, but instead of a rash guard, he wore a turtle team T-shirt.

"John, good morning! I'm sorry, but I can't go surfing this morning. I have to walk the beach for turtle duty."

"I know," he replied easily, reaching out to take her turtle team bag. "I thought I'd tag along, if that's okay." He pointed to his chest. "I even wore my turtle shirt."

"I saw," Linnea said, raising one brow with amusement. "I have to say, I'm surprised you have one."

"Are you kidding? My mom's on the team, remember?"

She laughed. It was just like Emmi to give her son a Turtle Team shirt every year, convinced he'd want one as much as she did. As far as Emmi was concerned, nothing was cooler than being on the turtle team.

"So, no surfing today?" she asked.

"It's a lake out there today. We're not missing anything. Shall we go? Mom's already sitting by the phone, waiting for calls."

They walked along the beach in the same relaxed manner in which they paddled out on their boards. Completely at ease, they talked about anyone and anything. Linnea always started her walk toward Breach Inlet. Then she'd turn around and head all the way north to Ninth Avenue. Beyond that was someone else's area to monitor. It was an easy walk, no more than half an hour, designed to get all the volunteers' turtle track sightings reported by seven o'clock.

"Have you found any leads yet for a job?" he asked.

"No," Linnea replied. "But I've narrowed my search."

"Location-wise?"

"No, I'm pinpointing what part of the field I'm most interested in. As for location, I'm open to moving, but I've concentrated on the South."

"Do you want some help?"

She turned her head, curious. "You know the business?"

"No. But I'm a whiz at search engines. And . . . you might consider broadening your location search. California might be someplace to start looking. Lots of opportunities."

"Thanks. I'll take you up on that."

He looked at her and said, "What are friends for?"

Linnea swiped a pesky mosquito from her face, then stopped to tuck her hair into her turtle team cap. Something at the water's edge a distance away caught her attention. She squinted at the large, dark shape.

"John!" she called out, pointing. "Do you see that?"

Not waiting for an answer, she took off at a clip toward the bridge at Breach Inlet. Her heels dug into the soft sand along this always-changing section of beach. The turbulent water of Breach Inlet roiled as she trotted toward the mysterious shadowed hulk that lay unmoving near the base of the bridge.

It was a sea turtle! Her breath caught in her throat, and she ran faster, her heart pounding in her chest. An adult. Probably a female. As she drew closer, her heart nearly broke at the tragedy of losing a nesting female holding future generations.

John came to a stop behind her and whistled softly. "That's a big one."

"Yeah," she said, and began rolling up her pants. It was the biggest she'd ever seen, a full-grown turtle, maybe three hundred pounds and three feet long. It was unmoving and covered with barnacles. Not a good sign. The first thing she had to do was drag it ashore before the current towed it off into Breach Inlet. She stepped into the chilly water and felt a yank back on her arm.

"You can't go in there," John said, holding her back. "It's like quicksand, and the currents in Breach Inlet are deadly."

Linnea jerked her arm free. "I'm getting that turtle. It'll get swept away, and we'll lose it."

"No," he said sharply. "I'll get it. Wait here. I'll push it to you."

Before she could stop him, he stepped into the sloping sand of the shoreline. She held her breath as the gelatinous sand sank around his feet. Fortunately, a motorboat sped by, creating a strong ripple that pushed the turtle closer to shore. John took a few more slow steps out along the shallow slope. There was an abrupt drop-off not far offshore, she knew, and the water roiled beyond, deathly and dark.

"Be careful, John!" she called, clutching her hands.

But John was already at the turtle's side, a few feet beyond the shore. Any farther and they wouldn't be able to fetch her. They only needed to get her a few feet farther up on the sand. John stood behind the turtle and grabbed hold of the shell. With a guttural grunt, he pushed her forward, and like a surfboard, the turtle sailed closer to the beach. Linnea rushed into the water, the sand sucking at her feet. The turtle's shell was slimy with barnacles and algae, but it was the chunk of shell missing from her rear that stole her breath. But there was no time to stare. John was already at the turtle's back. They had to lift the turtle up the sand. He gripped the opposite side of the carapace and, looking up, met her gaze, his eyes shining with determination.

"Ready?"

When she nodded, he shouted, "Lift!"

John gave another grunt, and his arms strained under the tremendous weight of the turtle. But Linnea could barely move it.

"Wait," she called, catching her breath. She hurried to the front of the turtle. It wasn't smart to stand near a loggerhead's jaws, but she wasn't even sure this one was alive. John moved to the back of the shell. As she bent to grab the front of the shell, she saw one of the eyes flicker open a slit.

"John, she's alive!"

His face focused with new intent. "All right then," he said. "Ready?"

Linnea pulled and tugged, leaning back to add her body weight to the effort. Her arms strained so hard she thought they'd pop from their sockets. Even still, she knew the real effort was coming from John. His face was red, his muscles bulging, and his heels dug deep into the sand like a great beast of burden. The huge turtle scraped the sand as it slid uphill, victory gained by inches, until they pulled the massive creature the final few feet onto dry sand.

Linnea plopped down, gasping. "I'll never watch a turtle drag her shell ashore without remembering this," she said.

John was bent over, wiping his hands on his shorts. "That's a big turtle," he said again, sounding winded. She noticed he was missing a sandal, but he raised his hands before she could speak. "I'm not going back in there after it."

"I have to call this in," Linnea said, and scrambled to her feet. She wiped her hands on her shirt, then retrieved her phone from her bag and dialed Emmi's number. She answered on the first ring.

"Emmi, we've got a stranded turtle. A big one. And she's alive!"

"Oh my God!" Emmi took a breath, and Linnea imagined her grabbing a pen and paper. "Where is she?"

Linnea passed on all the details. Emmi would call the Department of Natural Resources, which would contact the South Carolina Aquarium. All Linnea had to do now was wait for the cavalry and guard the turtle. She released a long sigh, feeling the tension slowly leave her body. This was a first for her. One for the books.

"Your mom's coming," she said to John as she walked back to the turtle's side and crouched to inspect the damaged shell. A few large, crusty barnacles clung to the carapace, and smaller ones were scattered in a splay pattern. A jagged-edged half-circle had been chomped out of her carapace.

"Looks like a shark got a good bite out of her," said John, joining her at the turtle's side. "But she was lucky. She saved her rear flipper."

It pained her to see it. "Poor mama," Linnea said. "This turtle has survived unimaginable odds just to reach maturity. Then she traveled thousands of miles to return to this area to mate. She's already crawled up these beaches a few times this season carrying that shell. Now she's back."

"How do you know it's a female?"

"Because it has a short tail. But, also, a mature turtle near shore right now is probably a female with a body full of eggs to lay. What a waste. Damn shark. There's plenty of fish out there. Why'd he have to pick on this mama going about her business?"

"A shark's got to make a living too."

"I hope they get here soon. She doesn't look too good."

"Turtles have been around for millions of years," he said, putting a hand on her shoulder for comfort. "They've got to be resilient."

She leaned against him, feeling the warm water and gritty sand against her shoulder. "Thank you, John. I couldn't have gotten her ashore without you." She laughed shortly, remembering the weight. "No way."

"We make a pretty good team." He snorted. "Plus Mom will be thrilled I helped the turtle team. She's been angling to get me to help on the team since I was a kid. I've successfully avoided it until now. And it's all because of you."

Linnea smiled and looked up at him, squinting in the sun.

Emmi came running around the bend of Breach Inlet, her red hair flying in the wind, a red bucket banging her hip. Not far behind her was Flo, walking swiftly for her age, her arms pumping the air. Linnea knew nothing would keep that old turtle lady from a live turtle on her beach.

Before long, a group of eight people from the SCDNR and the South Carolina Aquarium, all in branded T-shirts, converged around the turtle. Strandings were common along the coast, but the appearance of a mature sea turtle that was alive was cause for excitement. Michelle Pate, the head of the SCDNR turtle program, pulled out a measuring tape and bent over the turtle, calling out measurements to another on her team who wrote the information on a clipboard. They confirmed Linnea's estimates, and she smiled each time someone new arrived and exclaimed, "What a big turtle!"

"Well, lookee here," Michelle said, crouching over a flipper. "This turtle's been tagged." This caused a flurry of excitement as team members gathered around.

Toy Legare, who'd arrived with the aquarium crew, quietly

drew near the limp turtle's head. Linnea watched as she gently poured seawater from the red bucket over the turtle to keep her cool and hydrated. The turtle had been lying on the sand passive and unmoving. Toy crouched close, which was cumbersome with her pregnancy. When she knelt and lowered her head to peer at the turtle's face, the creature moved a flipper and opened her eyes.

Toy looked into the turtle's eyes, and a slow smile spread across her face. "I know you," she said with wonder. Looking up, she called out, "It's Big Girl!"

Emmi stepped closer, squinting at the turtle's face.

"How can you tell?" she asked doubtfully. "They all look alike to me."

"Oh no, they don't," said Toy, her eyes set on the turtle. "Each one has a different look, a different personality. Big Girl is special. I'd never forget her."

"Well, we'll know for sure when the tag numbers check out," said Michelle, rising. "She *is* a big girl, I'll give you that. And fast. The shark got only a small chunk. Her rear flipper is intact." She looked to her team. "We're done here," she said as she stepped away from the turtle. "She's all yours, Toy."

"Thanks, Michelle," Toy said, rising to shake her hand. "We'll do right by her. Not too many organisms on her carapace. I don't think she was out there floating long. I think she'll make it. We got her in time. Or rather"—she turned to Linnea—"you got her in time. Good job."

Linnea felt extraordinarily pleased at being singled out. She looked for John and smiled at him with gratitude.

Toy turned to her team members from the aquarium. "Let's carry her up to the van." She looked back at Michelle, a grin across her face. "I don't need an ID to tell me that's Big Girl. She was my first turtle rescue, the one that founded our hospital. I pulled this turtle out of the ocean myself. When was it?" She scratched her head. "Had to be more than ten years ago." She shook her head with wonder. "We had to put her into a kiddie pool. There's going to be a lot of people stoked to see this turtle come back."

Michelle laughed. "If you're right and that *is* Big Girl, that's a huge success. The first drink's on me."

"You're on!" Toy said. Then, tapping her belly, "As long as it's juice."

"Be sure to call Cara," Flo said before she left. "She'll want a full report." Then, in a softer voice, she asked, "Do you really think it's Big Girl?"

Toy's eyes lit up. "I do."

Flo shook her head in disbelief. "Big Girl back . . ."

"I know," Toy said. "I'm sure she has lots of stories to tell us."

~~~~~

CARA AND DAVID were enjoying a second cup of coffee while the children played at their feet. Rory was pushing a wooden train around the track, but Hope was more interested in the trees and people that stood around the tracks. When the phone call came from Toy, Cara bolted to her feet, electrified.

"I'll be there as soon as I can," she told Toy. She looked out at the commanding vista of marsh and sea from David's window, her mind clicking fast.

"Is everything okay?" David asked. He'd set his mug on the table and stood beside her, his face etched with concern.

"Oh, yes," she replied. "It's actually great news. A turtle has been rescued and sent to the aquarium. Toy thinks it's one we rescued years ago. A very special turtle. David," she said, deciding. "I have to go."

"Of course."

"I'm sorry to cut our playdate short." She looked at her watch. "But if I leave now, I can make the next ferry."

"Cara . . ." He touched her sleeve, stalling her. "Before you go—I wanted to let you know I'll miss our playdate next week. I have to go out of town on business."

"Nothing bad, I hope?"

"Something came up. I have to fly to London. I'll only be gone a week."

"Goodness. You go to London on business?"

"I told you I have other business concerns. Some of them are in London. What I wanted to ask you . . ." he said, and his voice lowered. "When I get back, I'd like to take you out to dinner. Not a playdate. Just you and me and no distractions."

Cara swallowed, feeling the force of his intent.

David misunderstood her hesitancy. "I know going out on a date is a major step for you. I've tried not to rush you. But"—he smiled at her—"we *have* been seeing each other a couple of times a week for over a month."

She smiled then, too. "You're right. It is a big deal. But I'd love to go out to dinner with you."

His smile broadened, and his dark eyes lit up. "I'll call you with the details. But for now, you've got a ferry to catch."

～～～

A FEW HOURS later Cara reached the impressive steel and stone structure of the South Carolina Aquarium. She never failed to feel a deep flush of pleasure at seeing the harbor's crown jewel beside the sea, a proud symbol of preservation, education, and conservation for all the marine creatures that called the ocean home. She walked at a brisk pace through the park leading to the aquarium's front gate. It had been several hours since the turtle was rescued. She hoped they'd be finished with the intake procedure. The security officer checked her in, then notified Toy of her arrival.

"Take the elevator to your right to the third floor," he instructed her. "She'll have to buzz you in."

Cara walked to the stainless steel doors of the private elevator, then decided instead to enter the aquarium through the public entrance. She made her way along the entrance walkway, then paused at the top veranda overlooking Charleston Harbor. From this high point, the wind gusted salt-tinged air and she heard the raucous cries of seagulls. This was a commanding view teeming with sailboats, pleasure cruisers, and great cargo ships heading to the world beyond. And just in view was Fort Sumter, a place rich in history. *The harbor was the heart of this historic city,* she thought. Where the past had been forged and the future promised. Not far from the docks she spied the quick arch of a dolphin, its gray skin gleaming in the sun. As quick as she saw it, the dolphin disappeared.

Entering the aquarium gave Cara a sense of déjà vu. Suddenly she was back at the Tennessee Aquarium as their public relations director. Seeing the bustle of visitors, hearing the buzz of excitement, witnessing the level of learning, she felt an unexpected, thus all the stronger, wave of longing to return. She looked around at the gleaming tanks filled with colorful fish and at the people watching, transfixed, and realized that she missed being involved with an aquarium. Every day presented new challenges, new opportunities. Each day was an exercise in giving back and bettering the lives of animals and the people who learned from them. She thought of Linnea's comment about wanting to educate, and realized that she did, too.

She watched the fish swim around the coral and reflected on why she so enjoyed working for a nonprofit. She'd had a long and successful career in the corporate world, had enjoyed the excitement, the demands. In these regards, however, nonprofits were companies too. Certainly her time at the Tennessee Aquarium had brought creative challenges. In fact, because it was a small operation, she'd had to wear many hats and do so much hands-on work that each day was a surprise.

Cara began to walk toward the elevator where she was to meet Toy. She'd just had a successful client meeting. Her consultation business was on its way. Why then did she feel so nostalgic about her former job?

She knew the answer. Working for a nonprofit had given her a strong sense of purpose. Nonprofits had a mission. And the aquarium's mission was to preserve and protect marine life—something she believed in and that gave her a personal motivation. What she sacrificed in a paycheck she made up for in satisfaction. And they needed good people running them.

"Cara!"

Shaken from her thoughts, Cara turned quickly to see Toy walking toward her. She was wearing jeans and a loose SC AQUAR-IUM shirt that couldn't hide her pregnancy. Despite her snappy gait, as she drew nearer, Cara noticed gray smudges under her eyes and a lackluster skin color that spoke of her exhaustion. But her eyes gleamed with the news. They hugged warmly, as sisters would.

"Is it Big Girl?" Cara asked.

"Come see for yourself."

Toy led her on a tour of the turtle exhibit and recovery area. Cara was deeply moved at having witnessed the hospital evolve from a dream and a makeshift hospital in the basement to this magnificent recovery center. Its growth, she felt, was a reflection of the growing concern about issues surrounding coastal development and ocean conservation.

"I'm so proud of you," Cara told Toy, meaning it. "You've been here since the beginning. You've come a long way."

"Thanks."

But Cara saw the fatigue etched on Toy's face and felt a sudden concern for her. "Are you taking on too much?" she asked gently. "You look exhausted."

"I am. But it was an unusually busy day. Speaking of which, let's go see Big Girl. She's not up here. We still have a hospital in the basement. We use it for intake and critical care."

Toy led her down the gray back stairs to the aquarium basement, a far cry from the sleek exhibit upstairs. Down in the bowels of the building was where the power of the great aquarium hummed. Giant pipes and wires snaked along the ceiling, and red-painted pumps with shiny black valves and rows of gray steel fuse boxes lined the walls.

"There she is." Toy pointed to a large cylindrical tank.

Cara approached tentatively. The blue tank wall was solid, with a single window through which to view the turtle under the water. From the top, however, she had a full view of the sea turtle, its shell dusky brown and covered with nasty-looking barnacles. They even clung to her head and near her eyes. The turtle was motionless.

"She's alive?"

"Oh yes," Toy replied, drawing closer. "She's had a busy morning. We scrubbed as much of the slime off of her as we could. Those barnacles will come off in time."

Cara felt sorrow, seeing the ragged edges of the broken shell. "Look at that shark bite," she said. "You can see the teeth marks."

"I've seen worse. A lot worse. She must've tucked tail and skedaddled, because she got away without losing a limb or her tail. Experience."

"Can she be released?"

"Oh, sure. We release turtles that've lost flippers."

Cara looked at Toy. "So, it's really Big Girl?"

A smug smile spread across her face. "It sure is. The tag was confirmed. I don't know why anyone doubted me."

Cara scoffed, "Maybe because I sure couldn't tell if it was her . . . except for her size. I hate to say it, but it's been years, and they're not that different. Though she's still the biggest sea turtle I've ever seen."

Toy crossed her arms, her face soft with affection. "She sure is. And she's even bigger after ten years."

"Has it really been ten years?"

"I was putting this together in my mind. I was living in the beach house at the time. And Little Lovie was about five."

"That's right," Cara recalled. "Brett and I had moved out of the beach house into his house."

"And I had started working at the aquarium. They didn't have a sea turtle hospital yet. Remember?"

"How could I forget? We had to put Big Girl in a blue plastic kiddie pool under the porch of the beach house for the night."

Toy chuckled. "Do you remember we took shifts sleeping next to her in case she decided to crawl off?"

Cara barked out a laugh. "Oh, yes. What a miserable night! So hot and humid. And the mosquitoes!"

"As if you or I could have held back a three-hundred-pound sea turtle anyway." They both laughed again at the absurdity. "It was a good thing she was so sick."

"But we got her into the hospital," Cara said smugly.

"Yes, we did. And she was the aquarium's first official sea turtle hospital patient. It's pretty amazing to realize that our first rescue turtle, the turtle that founded this hospital, that was healed and re-leased, is back again. After a decade, she's still laying eggs. Think of all the turtles this one produced."

Cara perked up. "You know, this is a phenomenal PR moment for the aquarium. Big Girl is living, breathing proof of the importance of sea turtle hospitals. This rehabilitated nesting female has been out in the ocean laying new generations of turtles for ten years because you saved her."

"Because the aquarium's hospital saved her."

"Right. But it's nice to have a face with the story."

Toy looked at the turtle. "That is a great idea." She turned to Cara and said thoughtfully, "You really do have a knack for this."

Cara rolled her eyes. "That's why they pay me the big bucks. Tell you what, let me play with the idea a bit and I'll submit it to Kevin. He's still the CEO around here?"

"Absolutely. Stop by his office before you go. He'd love to see you."

Cara felt the kick of exhilaration she always did when she came up with a good idea. Something would come of it, she felt sure.

Chapter Fifteen

*Loggerhead eggs incubate for fifty to sixty days, depending on
the heat and location. The sex of the turtle is determined by the
heat of the sand. If the sand is hot, the turtles will likely be
female. If the sand is cool, the turtles will likely be male.
Thus the saying "hot chicks and cool dudes."*

L INNEA WAS ON baby duty. Breakfast had been eaten and
cleaned up after, Moutarde had fresh seed and water and was
nibbling a stalk of kale, Cara had headed off to meet a client, and
Linnea was sitting on the back porch with Hope coloring the new
princess coloring book. Or rather, Linnea was coloring in the book
and Hope was making jabbing motions at the paper. It was a nice
morning to sit outdoors on the windward porch and let the heady
breezes keep the insects at bay.

But the peace was short-lived. Hearing footfalls in the gravel,
Linnea looked up and was surprised to see John Peterson approaching, holding two Styrofoam cups. His shorts and shirt were
both wrinkled, as if he'd just fallen out of bed and slipped them on.

"Good morning!" she exclaimed with a short laugh. She felt a bit odd seeing him out of a swimsuit.

"Morning," he said. "I went for some coffee and brought you some."

"Thanks, but I've already had two cups."

"But this is a latte. From Paname."

"Oh, in that case, thank you." She reached out to take the cup. "Come sit," she said. "We're coloring."

"Can't. I have to work. Just wanted to bring you coffee." He caught her gaze and his smile deepened. "Thought it was neighborly." He lifted his hand in farewell, then turned and headed down the steps.

She smiled, thinking it could be a very nice thing having John Peterson as a neighbor. She hurried back to Hope.

"Oh, Hope," she moaned as she saw Hope drawing blue marker all over herself.

She ran to grab the marker from her grip. Hope immediately began to fuss. Linnea scooped her up and carried her directly to the kitchen sink. "Thank goodness this stuff washes off," she said, turning on the water. Cara wouldn't be happy to see blue tattoos on her baby. Hope became fascinated with the water coming from the spigot and forgot all about the marker. Linnea finished washing off the blue ink, and just as she was drying the baby, the doorbell rang. She smiled, wondering what John's excuse was this time.

She carried Hope with her as she hurried to the door.

"Yeeeees," she sang out in an exaggerated drawl. Her mouth snapped shut when she saw it wasn't John Peterson standing on the porch, but Darby Middleton. Carrying an enormous bouquet of stunning white roses.

"Darby? What are you doing here?" she said, blinking into the morning sun.

His blond hair captured the sunlight, and his eyes were so large and blue, she felt mesmerized. He was well aware of this effect and used it to his advantage. He smiled, revealing beautiful teeth.

"I've tried texting you but you ignored me. So I had to come to see you." He reached out to hand her the roses. When she didn't move to accept them, he continued, his face contrite, "White roses imply pureness of heart." He looked at his feet. "You know, I searched online and found stuff about the language of flowers. I wanted to find out what flowers would say *I'm sorry*. I discovered purple hyacinths mean *Please forgive me*. I looked everywhere—and I mean everywhere—but I couldn't find a single hyacinth. Done in April." He shrugged. "The florist told me white roses were the next best thing to tell you how very sorry I am." He extended the flowers again.

She didn't take them.

"Please, Linnea. I was a complete idiot. I was drunk." When she frowned, he lifted his palms and hurried to add, "Not that that's an excuse. But it wasn't the real me. Linnea, you know me. You know I respect you. I'm so sorry, and I'm asking you for the chance to make it up to you. Lin, we've known each other for so long. Please. I don't want to lose our friendship."

Linnea looked at him, beyond his imploring blue eyes. In so many ways he was still the little boy she'd had a crush on in grade school. The boy who'd placed her first kiss on her willing lips in the coat closet at cotillion. Her steady boyfriend throughout high school. He was the first man she'd made love with. They had real history. There was a time when she'd been madly in love with Darby, even thought she would marry him. At the very least, she didn't want to lose their friendship either.

Linnea reached out and accepted the gorgeous white roses. She brought them close to her face. "They smell lovely."

"That's one for my side."

She released a slow smile and carefully brought the flowers close to Hope's nose. "What do you think, baby? Do they smell good? Should I forgive him?" She leaned lower and showed Hope how to sniff. Hope tried to mimic her, blowing air out of her nose. Linnea laughed.

She tilted her head, then with a slight smile stepped aside. "Do you want to come in?"

Darby walked past her, arms tight at his sides. She was sorry to see him feeling awkward around her. It wasn't right for people who'd been best friends since childhood. He followed her through the foyer and the living room, which was currently covered with toys. Darby lived in one of the great historic houses of Charleston. And, like so many Charleston families, the Middletons had a quaint, fairly rustic beach house on Sullivan's Island. His beach house had been built in the same era as this one. Darby would notice that the floor was antique heart pine, the mantel was original, what artists were collected.

Linnea set Hope down among her toys, then headed toward the kitchen to find a vase for the roses. "You were a rat, you know," she said over her shoulder.

"I know. I'm sorry."

She didn't know how many times he'd have to apologize before she really forgave him.

"How did you know where I was?" she asked, adding water to the vase.

"Your mother told me."

Of course, Linnea thought. Her mother would've been only too happy to tell Darby Middleton where to find her daughter. Linnea was surprised she hadn't sent out an all-points bulletin. Made him a map with little hearts pointing the way.

"Uh-huh," was all she said.

"In her defense, I showed up at your house and begged her to tell me. She was hesitant until I told her I needed to beg for forgiveness."

Linnea knew he could be quite persuasive. She placed the roses in the vase. "And so you have. Apology accepted."

Darby, instantly more relaxed, leaned against the marble counter in the galley kitchen and crossed his arms against his chest. "I haven't been here in years. Not since high school. Nothing's changed."

"That's part of its charm. The sunroom is new," Linnea said, setting the flowers on the table in the living room. Darby followed her. "Cara freshened up the house with paint, new fabric. But other than that . . ."

"So, you're babysitting now?"

"Actually, I'm a nanny."

"Oh. Right."

She didn't like his tone. "Did you know Princess Diana was a nanny?"

"Sounds like a romance novel. *The Princess Nanny*."

"She wasn't a princess when she was a nanny, silly," she said. "She was eighteen and a part-time nanny for five dollars an hour."

He snorted. "That much?"

"And you?" she asked. "What are you up to this summer?"

"I'm interning at my father's law office."

"Oh yes," she said, remembering their earlier conversation. His father was a U.S. senator and a senior partner in his family's influential Charleston law firm. "You start law school in the fall." She thought of her brother spending the summer working in their father's business. "Do you want to be a lawyer?" she asked him. "Or do you feel you have to be a lawyer?"

Darby smiled, understanding the question all too well. "In college, I felt squeezed into the decision. My father can be very insistent."

"Yes, I can imagine the orations at dinner."

"And my mother. She likes living in Washington, DC. But now . . . yeah," he said with heart. "I want to go to law school. I want to go into politics. There's a lot I feel I need to do. This country is going to hell in a handbasket."

Linnea looked at Darby, tall and handsome, even elegant. He'd do very well for himself. His future was glittering with possibilities. It was no wonder her mother wanted her linked with this rising star. Linnea wondered about his politics. If they were like his father's, he'd be conservative.

"You'll only get my vote if you defend the environment," she said. "Your father, bless his heart, hasn't voted on the right side of the aisle there." She shook her head when he opened his mouth to defend the senator. "Darby, we're the ones who will be living in the mess climate change is creating. And our children. We need strong men like you in politics. Someone who will stand up and protect our environment. I'm just saying I hope that's you."

"I'm not a senator yet," Darby said, dodging the subject. He drew closer. "I didn't come here to talk politics. Let's save that for dinner."

"Dinner?"

"Yes. I'd like to take you to dinner. How about tonight? Let's go to the Boathouse."

Linnea gazed at Darby, and despite his good looks and stunning future, she felt nothing, no spark or interest, just bored. He'd always been narcissistic. She'd just been too infatuated with him to see it. He'd tell her where they were going, and she'd follow along. She couldn't remember him ever asking what *she* wanted to do. When she went to USC, he'd stopped calling. It had hurt her deeply. Out of sight, out of mind. And here he was again, knocking on her door, telling her where she was going. Except, Linnea didn't want to go where he was going. She was mapping out her own direction. She might not be sure where she would end up, but she was sure it wasn't with him.

"I'm afraid I can't. I have plans."

He frowned. "With who?"

She smiled and looked at Hope. "My cousin."

He made a face. "Tomorrow night, then?"

Linnea reached out to touch a delicate rose petal. It was truly beautiful. But the bloom would wilt in a few days' time.

"Darby," she said, dropping her hand and looking into those impossibly beautiful blue eyes. "I appreciate that you came here to apologize. It speaks volumes about you. And our friendship. But I want to keep you as a *friend*." She emphasized the word. His expression shifted, so she knew he understood her meaning. "I don't want to start dating you. We're not the same people anymore. You have your future planned." She smiled. "I'm winging it. And I like it that way."

"But, Linnea, we're so good together."

"No, Darby. You liked that I was willing to do what you wanted me to do, and that our mothers think we're perfect for each other—we have the right pedigree and our children would be beautiful."

"Come on, that's not fair."

She knew it wasn't fair, just as she knew it was true.

He took her hands. "Lin, say yes. Give us another chance."

She slipped her hands away. "I'm sorry, Darby. I'm saying no."

She waited to see how he'd react, her muscles tightening.

He laughed shortly, like he'd just caught the joke a beat late. "Got it," he said, and pursed his lips. He tilted his head, studying her. "We could've been something special."

"You'll always be my first love," she told him.

His face softened, and in that smile she caught a glimpse of the young boy she'd been best friends with for so long.

Hope began fussing on the floor, tossing her toys.

"Well," he said by way of finality. "It looks like you've got your hands full. I'll get going."

"Okay, but I'll see you around."

Linnea picked up Hope and walked Darby to his sleek navy car. He climbed into the front seat and started the engine. It purred into action.

"Bye, Lin-Lin."

Linnea smiled, touched that he'd used his old nickname for her. As she waved, and watched the car drive off, she heard water sprinkling behind her. Looking over her shoulder, she saw John standing in front of Flo's roses, watering them with a green garden hose. He lifted his hand in a silent, neighborly hello.

She strolled over to the iron fence and prickly pink rosebush divider.

"Hi," she said.

"Hi," he said over the fence. His tone was flat.

"*You're* watering the flowers." Linnea knew Flo doted on her roses and took great pleasure in watering them and checking for black spots or insects.

"Yep."

"Where's Flo?"

"At the doctor's. Mom drove her to an appointment. She asked me to water the flowers for her and . . ." He lifted the hose up for her to see.

"That's nice of you."

"Not really. It's called indentured servitude. I'm called upon to change lightbulbs and furnace filters, clean the garage, take out the trash. . . ." He motioned to the bins at the end of the driveway with the hose, accidentally spraying Linnea with water. She squealed and jumped back.

"Sorry!"

She wiped drips of water from Hope's face, as she scowled and whined.

"Really," John said, horrified. "I'm sorry, sweet baby. Is she okay?"

"It was just a few drops. We're fine. My shoes, on the other hand . . ." She looked down at her vintage white patent-leather loafers. They were wet.

"Again, sorry. But you know you should wear sandals at the beach."

"Now you're telling me what shoes to wear?"

He smiled and shook his head. "Sorry," he said again.

It seemed to Linnea that a lot of people were telling her *sorry* today.

"Boyfriend?" he asked.

So he did see Darby, she thought. "No. Yes. Well . . ." She tried to explain: "He's an old boyfriend, and now he's just a friend."

"You're going out with him?"

She appreciated his tone of jealousy. "I don't know. Maybe."

John stared at the flowers. Then with a decisive movement he turned off the spray nozzle.

"What are you doing tomorrow at seven?" he asked.

"Surfing?"

"Not this time. Seven at night. For dinner."

～～～

LINNEA SIPPED HER second vodka martini, a little dirty, extra olives, and luxuriated in the feeling of being a young woman out in the evening, sitting across a candlelit table from a handsome man, instead of being a nanny, niece, and daughter.

They'd walked the short distance to the Boathouse restaurant on Breach Inlet. The outdoor bar was jam-packed, but inside they were lucky to get a small table by the window overlooking Hamlin Creek. The Boathouse was comfortably decorated in shiplap and parts of old wooden boats. Across the small table lit by a votive candle, John was talking about surfing the mighty Jaws waves in Maui. She liked the sound of his voice, low and melodic with a faint southern inflection. He had the deeply tanned skin, casual style—an open checked shirt over a T-shirt—and that indefinable something else that marked him as a lowcountry man. His auburn hair was sun-starched from his morning ride on the waves. What attracted her most was his laid-back air of confidence, which spoke loudly: *This is my turf.*

They'd ordered Clammer Dave oysters, crab fritters, and local shrimp in the shells. John stuck with India pale ale, she with martinis.

"You know, for all the time we've spent together, there's still a lot I don't know about John Peterson," she said.

John tilted his head and raised his eyebrows. "What do you want to know?"

She shrugged lightly, feeling her silk blouse slide against her shoulders. "Where were you born?"

"Atlanta."

"Really?" she said, surprised. "I thought you were born in Charleston."

He shook his head. "My parents were born here. They met as kids and were high school sweethearts, dated through college and married right after. My dad works for Coca-Cola, so we moved to Atlanta and that's where I was born. But my mother's family kept their beach cottage on Isle of Palms and she brought us here every summer." He looked at his glass. "I've spent summers here my whole life. After their divorce, my mother sold her family cottage and bought Flo's house and moved here permanently. I was already in California so . . ." He spread his palms.

"It's sad that high school sweethearts who hung on all those years could ever fall out of love and give it up so late in the game."

"It was my dad's fault. He traveled a lot and cheated on my mother. What an ass."

She heard the twinge of anger still smoldering. "You never know. It takes two to tango."

John shook his head. "I always thought they should've tried harder to work things out, but what do I know? My mom, though, she's true-blue. You don't cheat on a good woman."

She pulled an olive off the cocktail stick with her teeth, thinking John had just risen several notches with that comment. She chewed the briny olive, sipped the cool martini, then licked her lips, aware he was watching her.

"So," she continued, putting down her glass. "What took this southern boy to California?"

A wry smile creased his tanned face. "I went for school and stayed for work," he replied simply. "Since I'm into computers, it was a no-brainer. California is where it's happening."

"Then what brought you back here this summer?"

He leaned back and his fingers tapped the table. "That's more difficult to explain."

"Try me."

He laughed and rested his elbows on the table. "Well, the startup I was working on failed, which happens. I'm pretty confident I'll find something, but while I was looking I thought why not come home for a while, visit my mom, see friends. So I did."

"I know Emmi is over the moon you're here."

His face softened at the mention of his mother, and she could tell how much he loved her. "She'd love it if I moved here permanently."

"My parents live in fear I'll leave."

Their eyes met, and they smiled in mutual understanding.

She said, "But you're moving back to California?"

He nodded. "Eventually."

"Any luck on the job market?"

He smiled ruefully. "Well, yes and no. My plans have changed." When she didn't speak, he continued, "I came back months ago, back in early spring. There've been some interesting developments."

"Oh, I thought you'd only just arrived in June."

"At my mother's house. Before that, I rented a room for a while in a house on Sullivan's Island that my friends own. Surf buddies— Richie and Trey, you met them. We go way back," he added by way of explanation. "It turns out a lot of my friends are in real estate now."

The waiter stopped at their table to freshen their waters. "Anything else I can get you?"

John looked at Linnea questioningly. She shook her head.

"No, thanks," he said.

The waiter left, and John took the moment to drink his beer. Putting the glass back on the table, he looked at her with uncertainty. "Are you sure you want to hear all this?"

"Very. I want to learn about those interesting developments."

His eyes sparked. "Anyway," he began, "hanging around together, I heard my friends talking about work and realized real estate in Charleston was still an old-school business." He leaned forward, intent. "That's when it hit me: I could apply new tech practices to transform the local real estate market."

She smiled, stirred by his enthusiasm. "John, that's very cool."

"Yeah," he replied, grateful for her response. "That's what I thought. I'm figuring out a way to make a real estate platform that's going to generate leads to home sites. It will help agents, sellers, and buyers—with data analysis to boot. I can apply technology that's already being used in other industries to leverage tools and marketing practices to increase profitability."

Linnea wasn't entirely sure what all that meant, but she did understand that there was a whole lot more to this guy than his mesmerizing eyes. John relaxed and went into greater detail about his project. She learned a lot about him not only from his words, but from watching him. He began gesticulating as he talked, his eyes brightening as he explained a point.

It occurred to her that she'd never met anyone quite like him before. He was older, true. He'd had more experiences and was more worldly than the men she knew in college. But even that wasn't unusual. It was his brilliance hidden behind his casual, laid-back style that appealed to her. He didn't need to advertise. He knew who he was, his worth, and he didn't seem to care if anyone else did. And he had passion about his idea. She liked that about a man.

"It's been done in other industries," he concluded modestly, then flattened his palms on the table. "But not in real estate. I'm psyched. It's a real opportunity." He laughed, and she enjoyed the sound of it. "I had to leave San Francisco and come to Charleston for the best idea I've ever had. Go figure." He reached for his glass. "So that was a long way of telling you what I'm doing."

"That's all?" she asked teasingly. "You're creating a computer program that's a game changer for an industry." She looked at him obliquely. "Me? I'm a nanny."

"I'm living in my mother's house," he countered.

"And me in my aunt's."

They both laughed, sensing the attraction between them growing.

The waiter returned and discreetly left the black padded folder on the table. Linea looked around the restaurant as John took care of the bill. It was nearly empty. They were closing down the place. It had been a long time since she'd had such a good conversation that time flew by so fast she didn't notice.

"Shall we go?" John asked, extending his hand.

~~~~~

IN A COMPANIONABLE silence, they walked along the narrow beach at high tide. Overhead a full moon rose high, its golden light a shimmering ribbon across the sea. Linnea took his offered hand and slipped off her sandals, letting them dangle from her fingertips.

"That's the Sturgeon Moon," John told her, pointing to the moon. "That was when the American Indians near the Great Lakes knew it was time for fishing."

She stared, feeling the majesty of a full moon rising. "I used to wonder if more sea turtles came to shore during full moons," she said. "You know, with the tides and all."

"And do they?"

She laughed lightly. "No. It's a myth. Like more women having babies during a full moon. It seems to make sense when you think of the pull of the moon and tides. But babies and turtles both come during all phases of the moon."

"I love it when the moon looks like a golden road on the water," he said, stretching out his arm to indicate the light over the ocean. "It always makes me want to try to walk it."

"Like following a rainbow to the end."

"Right."

"When I see a moon like that, I think of a poem I read as a girl. It's so dramatic and I've never forgotten it. There's this great beat to it, like hearing the horse galloping. It's called 'The Highwayman.'"

John cleared his throat and recited in a baritone:

"The moon was a ghostly galleon tossed upon cloudy seas.
The road was a ribbon of moonlight over the purple moor."

Linnea, delighted he knew the poem, joined in:

"And the highwayman came riding—
Riding—riding—
The highwayman came riding, up to the old inn-door."

They both laughed when they finished, and Linnea leaned against him.

"My heart still breaks for the lovers."

"You're a romantic," he said.

"Everyone is a romantic under a full moon."

"So"—John stopped and faced her—"let's do something romantic."

"Like what?"

"Go for a swim."

Linnea looked at him guardedly and took a step back, dropping his hand. "I don't have a suit."

John's eyes lit up. "You don't need one."

"Uh-uh, I'm *not* going skinny-dipping with you. First of all, it's illegal."

"So swim in your underwear. It's no different than a bikini."

"Who says I'm wearing underwear?"

John's mouth hung open. Linnea laughed, pleased she'd got him. "Secondly, I never swim in black water. Nighttime is feeding time for the sharks."

"We're not their prey."

"So I've heard. But it's dark in there and they can make a mistake. I've released a lot of hatchlings and I know how many sharks are out there." She turned and started walking away, calling flirtatiously over her shoulder, "But nice try."

John trotted to catch up with her. "Linnea, I think this neighbor thing has made things awkward between us."

"Awkward?" she said, looking at her hands. "I thought it's been nice."

"It has, but I feel like we're like . . . pals who surf together. Hang out at each other's houses. Laugh at each other's jokes."

"Friends," she said.

"Yeah."

She was keenly aware of his closeness.

John reached over to take her hand. Looking at it, he gently rubbed his thumb over her tender skin. Linnea's attention was focused on the small patch of skin, each neuron aflame as the ball of his thumb grazed over it, sending sensations throughout her body. She stared at her hand too, holding her breath.

"Here's the thing," he said in a low voice. "I like having you as my friend. But that's not what I want."

Linnea felt a thrill ripple through her body; spreading her arms out, shoes dangling, she swirled in a circle. "What do you want?"

His eyes were the dark green of a stormy sea. She felt she could drown in them. She felt the heat between them, felt his arms slip around her. She began to tremble with anticipation and her breath held as he lowered his head.

"This."

Linnea opened her lips slightly and felt his lips, warm and trembling, gently graze hers. She lowered her lids and leaned in closer, hungry for his kiss. The moonlit world was dreamlike as he left a moist trail across her cheeks, her neck; then, at last, he returned to her lips and crushed her against him. She whimpered as she brought her arms around his neck and pressed herself against him. She felt the heat spark into a raging fire that swept through her body, consuming her.

At the sound of her deep-throated moan, he pulled back to catch his breath. They rested their foreheads against each other, breathing hard, then both laughed lightly, knowing the other had felt the explosion too.

John leaned his head lower and said in her ear, "Want to come over to my studio?"

Linnea took another breath with a step back and looked up into his green eyes.

"Yes."

~~~~~

THE MOON LIT their way home.

The garden's iron gate squeaked when John opened it. Linnea cringed at the noise, feeling sure Emmi would hear it and come to a window. The last thing Linnea wanted was for her and John to become the hot gossip topic for the ladies. The gravel crunched beneath their feet as they walked through the moonlit garden. Flo's roses filled the night with their heady scent.

He led her past the main house to the rear, where the period carriage house sat nestled among hydrangeas, their white mopheads resembling smaller moons in the distance. It was a classic Victorian design with a gambrel roof and a railed upper porch. The ground level never housed a car because it was crammed with storage. A long flight of stairs led to the second-floor apartment that Flo had lovingly remodeled as her mother's art studio. It was Miranda, however, who'd insisted on the flamboyant Moroccan double-door entry. When Emmi purchased the 1930s Victorian from Flo, she'd painted the houses turquoise and the gingerbread trim a pale coral. Looking at the colors, Flo had shaken her head and said, "Miranda would have loved it."

"The house used to be white," Linnea told John as they climbed the stairs. She couldn't resist adding, "How do you feel about living in a turquoise and pink house?"

He didn't miss a beat. "It's sea blue and coral," he replied, straight-faced. "Caribbean cool."

"Ah," she said in mock understanding. When they reached the door, Linnea marveled at the intricate trompe l'oeil tile pattern that Miranda had drawn around the doors.

John opened the door and she stepped into a single large room with a vaulted ceiling and large, multipaned windows. Moonlight poured in through them, blanketing the floor in silver. She had to blink when John turned on the electric lights, so harsh in contrast.

"I'll get the wine," said John.

While he went to the tiny galley kitchen across the room, Linnea slipped off her sandy sandals and looked around. It was surprisingly neat for a man's apartment. She clasped her hands behind her back and strolled around, captivated by Miranda's murals. Linnea had visited Flo and Emmi's house for many years as she grew up, but she'd never been inside the apartment. After Miranda died, it had been used for more storage.

Cara had described Miranda as a charming eccentric, an artist with flamboyant strawberry-blond hair that was, in fact, alarmingly pink. She wore flowing clothing, long shawls, and dangling earrings. Everyone adored her. She'd taught Emmi and Cara art in the studio in the summers. The girls had sat behind easels with the big Moroccan double doors flung wide open, looking out at the sea.

Miranda would encourage the girls to ignore the rules and paint whatever they felt in their souls. That was a far cry from the school art teachers of the time, who scolded them if their trees didn't look like trees. Miranda was larger than life, and Cara had confessed that she better understood Flo's penchant for plain pants and T-shirts.

Miranda's other passion had been sea turtles, something Flo claimed was imprinted on their DNA. Turtles had bonded them with their neighbor, Lovie. So it was no surprise to see that Miranda had painted the walls of the studio in a glorious ocean theme. Nothing Disney-like here: the dolphins, loggerheads, pelicans, jellyfish, and shrimp were incredibly lifelike, swimming around the blue walls of the studio. Linnea thought it would be like living under the sea.

She ran her fingers over the old Victorian sofa covered in green velvet, worn and no doubt lumpy from years of use. Most of the furniture in the studio had been Miranda's collection of mismatched favorites, and they weren't all old-fashioned. The artist had a modern streak. Breuer cane chairs clustered around a painted farm table. And she'd bet money that was an original Mies van der Rohe chair. Her vintage antennae were twirling.

Linnea walked to the large desk that sat in front of a window overlooking the side yard. Peering through the window, she was intrigued to see that it provided an excellent view of the beach house—her bedroom, in particular.

John returned with the wine and handed her a glass. She took a sip and relished the cool, citrusy flavor of the sauvignon blanc.

"Thanks. It's perfect." She swirled the wine and said, "I can't help but notice your view."

John looked out the window, then back at her with a sardonic smile. He had the grace to laugh. "I sometimes just stare out the window. I mean, the beach house happens to be right there."

"Uh-huh . . ." she said, not buying it.

He shrugged in a French manner. "I admit that—occasionally—I'm hoping to catch a glimpse of you."

"That's sweet, if a bit voyeuristic."

"Not at all," he said, putting his hand over his heart in a wounded display. "I don't have X-ray vision and can't see through your bedroom curtains. I assure you, all is completely innocent."

"That's good to know."

"Though when the windows are open, I can hear Cara's canary singing."

She laughed. "We all do."

"It's that neighbor thing again," he said in a more serious tone. "You're so close. And yet . . ." He let the familiar phrase dangle.

She felt the change in tone thicken the air between them. They were back here . . . the reason why they'd strolled from the sea to this small studio. He was waiting for her decision. Linnea took a small breath.

"I'm here now."

His eyes kindled and he set his wineglass on a nearby table. Without speaking he reached out for her glass, and likewise set it down. She wasn't the least bit nervous. She felt comfortable here, in this place, with him. It felt right.

He took her hand again, the same hand he'd held on the long beach walk. In a flash the memories converged—the connection she'd felt matching the rhythm of her step to his, bumping hips and shoulders, the sound of his voice against the rumble of the waves, the feeling that they could keep on walking all night. He brought her hand to his lips, looking into her eyes, then turned it over and kissed the palm. Linnea sucked in her breath. She'd never realized how sensitive that patch of skin was. Then he let his fingers slide up her arm to cup her face. He smiled at her, a smile of promise and reassurance.

She smiled back, coy, flirtatious, her eyes signaling *yes*.

His head slowly lowered, his gaze holding hers until, at last, his lips met hers. This second kiss was more assured, more demanding. A moan rose in her throat, and again she leaned into him, surrendering.

Once more he took her hand, and led her to the back corner of the studio. Under a dramatic round window and a mural of dolphins arching was an antique sleigh bed made of beautiful mahogany with ball-and-claw feet. The bed was unmade, the pillows dented with the memory of his head.

Her fingers nimbly undid the covered buttons of her pale-pink blouse. He stood motionless watching her, his arms hanging at his sides. When she was finished, he stepped closer to bring his fingers to her shoulders and slide the blouse away. Then, in a rush, he pulled his own shirt off over his head and reached again for her.

"Wait," she whispered against his lips.

He froze, uncertain.

"Turn off the lights," she said, yearning for the moonlight.

He took a few steps away to flick off the lights. Instantly the room was once again flooded with silver light. Looking at him now, standing motionless with his finely muscled chest creating shadows, he was like a marvelous statue carved from a single piece of marble.

"Linnea?" He asked so much in saying her name.

"John." Her answer spoke volumes.

He stepped forward, wrapping her in his arms. This kiss ignited a fire that went beyond foreplay. Now they lunged for each other, tearing off clothes, kissing bare skin revealed. They fell back onto the bed, never for a second releasing each other. His hands trembled as they rounded bare shoulders, slid along the curves of her back, then up again.

In the moonlight Linnea felt part of the mural, floating in the sea. As the kisses deepened, she felt the smaller waves hit. She let them glide over her, gasping for breath. Higher they rose, steeper and steeper. She felt herself paddling hard, moving forward with strong, deliberate strokes, closer to the breaker. His lips were everywhere, his hands holding her firmly, guiding her to catch the wave. Suddenly she felt it coming. She moved faster, pacing herself to his cues. When the great wave hit, she let go, and with a gasp, she caught the wave. She was riding high, soaring, letting the wave take her home.

Chapter Sixteen

Twenty inches under the sand, the hatchlings begin to pip, or break out of their eggs, using a small temporary tooth called a caruncle. They work together to rise up like an elevator. Once at the top, they remain for a number of days and absorb their yolk, which is attached by an umbilical to their abdomen. Often called the lunch pail, this yolk will provide them the much-needed energy for their first few days when they make their way from the nest to offshore waters.

A TRIPLE-DIGIT JULY HEAT wave hit Charleston, and the turtle team discovered that the nests were hatching early, some as early as forty-seven days. And as always, whispers of warm water fueled fears of hurricanes.

On the first day the heat wave broke, dropping to the low nineties, Linnea hopped into her Mini Cooper and met her brother for lunch at Saffron Café on East Bay, not far from the family business. It was part bakery, part restaurant, and they'd eaten there for as long as she could remember. Linnea welcomed the blast of air-conditioning as she stepped into the café. Cooper was already there, flagging her down from a table by the window. He was dressed in a faded dress shirt and black jeans, his effort at respectability at the office, and his dark hair was longer than usual, curling around his ears. He already had a tray full of food.

She grabbed a tray and hurried down the refrigerated section, pulling out a dish of Saffron's delicious hummus and pita and an iced tea, then paid for it and met Cooper at the table.

Cooper rose as she approached and kissed her cheek. "Nice outfit."

Linnea put her tray on the table and showed off the adorable pleated white top with red piping and the crisp red cotton skirt. "It was Lovie's. Isn't it amazing?"

"Really?" He laughed. "Only you . . ."

"Only me what?"

"Only you could pull that off."

"Thank you very much," she said, not sure if that was a compliment. As she sat, she glanced at Cooper's plate. Philly cheesesteak, fries, a chocolate fudge brownie, and sweet tea. Despite his clearly healthy appetite, he looked like he'd lost some weight, and his skin was as pale as paper.

"How are you doing?" she asked.

"Okay."

"I've been expecting you to show up at the beach house, but summer's half over and we haven't seen you."

"I've been busy," he said as he bit into his cheesesteak.

"Come to the beach," she implored him. "You look like you could use some sun." She held out her arm on the table next to his. "Next to me, you're a paleface."

"How are you so tan?"

"I've been surfing."

Cooper's sandwich stalled before it reached his mouth. "Surfing?" he asked incredulously. *"You?"*

She would've been insulted, except that his reaction was spot on. At least for the old Linnea. "Absolutely! I'm getting pretty good, too. John's been teaching me." When she saw his brows knit, she added, "He's Emmi's son. He's living next door for the summer. And Cara gave me Brett's old board."

"No way. That board is sick."

"I call him Big Blue. I go out whenever there are waves. John said he'll teach me kiteboarding next."

Cooper set down his sandwich. "Okay, now I'm getting jealous."

"Don't be. Come out and join us. You're a good surfer."

Cooper scoffed at that. "Not really. I'm probably not as good as you now."

"You just need practice. Come on."

"I'll try to get out there."

His voice had a lackluster tone that told her he would not. She was filled with a sudden fear for her brother. His pale skin, lost weight, lack of enthusiasm for life . . . He was dramatically changed from the buoyant, popular boy she was used to being with.

"Coop," she said in all seriousness. "What's the matter? You're not yourself."

"Come around more often and you'd know."

That was a deliberate slap and it stung. She had been lost in her own world on the island, her worries for her brother on the back burner.

"I deserved that. I'm sorry. What's going on?"

He pushed his plate away. "It's a freaking nightmare at home, that's what's going on. Don't let Dad know I told you this, but the business is going under. Sales are down, and he's not getting any new orders. And he's drinking more than ever."

"That might explain why he's not getting new business."

"Maybe. I don't think so. He's still on board every day at work. He's good at what he does. But his heart isn't in it. Something else is going on."

"What?"

"Hell if I know. He doesn't confide in me." He grabbed his iced tea. "I'm only his son."

"What does Mama say?"

"Mama? She's MIA. I mean, she's there in the house, but it's like she's some ghost. She sneaks around, walking on eggshells when he's drinking. And when they're together?" He shuddered. "It ain't pretty. They scream at each other like it's World War III."

"Mama? Screaming?" Linnea couldn't imagine it.

"It sucks. You wouldn't recognize home."

"I'm sorry."

"Why are you sorry? You couldn't change anything."

"I feel like I abandoned you."

"No, you got out. I don't blame you. It's every man for himself on a sinking ship."

Linnea couldn't believe what she was hearing. This was so foreign to the household she'd grown up in. Sure, her daddy enjoyed a drink at night, but nothing like this. She felt frightened, not only for her parents, but for Cooper.

"How do you deal with all that?"

"I leave as often as I can. I go to my friends' houses, the hunting lodge." He shrugged. "I don't think they notice."

Linnea pushed his plate back toward him and shifted the conversation back to surfing. She'd heard enough to know that she had more digging to do, and to feel relieved she'd escaped. If she'd stayed at home, she would have been fighting with her father too. Probably screaming like her mother. And that was not the woman she wanted to become.

"Cooper, no ifs, ands, or buts about it. You're taking a few days off and coming to the beach house. For me. It's our last summer as kids, right? We're both going off again, you to college, me . . ." She shrugged and laughed. "Somewhere. Please say you'll come. This weekend. Please?"

"Yeah, I've got some vacation days. I'll come."

"You better, little brother, or I'll sic Aunt Cara after you!"

~~~~~

AFTER LUNCH, LINNEA went directly to Tradd Street to talk to her mother. The gate was open, and after parking her car, she walked through the garden. She found her mother there in her broad-brimmed straw hat and gardening gloves. A basket sat at her feet, but she wasn't working. She was standing, cross-armed, staring at a bed of annuals that looked like they needed a good weeding. If anything was a red flag for her mother's health, it was weeds in her garden. Linnea had arrived all bowed up and ready for battle, but now her battle cry dissipated, replaced by a real concern.

"Mama?" she called gently, walking up to her side.

Julia startled and swung her head around. "Linnea! What a surprise! What brings you here?"

"Can't a girl visit her mama when she misses her?"

Julia's face crumpled, and she leaned in to hug her daughter. Pulling back, Linnea was caught off guard to see tears gathering in her mother's eyes.

"What's the matter, Mama?"

Julia exhaled heavily and, lowering her head, removed her gardening gloves. "Oh, Linnea. I don't know where to begin."

"Let's sit down in the shade."

"Do you want some tea?"

Linnea shook her head. "I just came from lunch with Cooper."

Understanding flickered in Julia's pale-blue eyes. "I see."

"Mama, he's not looking good."

"No." She bent to pick up the empty garden basket and led the way to the stone bench under the live oak for a respite from the southern July sun. Julia removed her hat and set it on the bench beside her.

"Child, what are you wearing?"

Linnea looked down at her skirt and top. "Don't you like it? It's vintage fifties. Cara gave me some of Lovie's old clothes. I think they're gorgeous."

Julia smiled softly. "I thought I recognized them. Sweet Lovie." She sighed. "I surely do wish she were alive today. We all could use her wisdom. She had a way with your father."

Linnea sat down on the bench beside her. "What's going on?" she asked. "Cooper said all hell's breaking loose here."

Julia laughed shortly. "That about describes it."

Linnea didn't speak.

Julia sighed again, then filled the silence. "He probably told you that the business isn't doing well?"

Linnea nodded.

"Poor Cooper. I'm sorry he has to witness this. But a mother can only protect her children from so much."

"It's not the business that has him worried. Or me. It's Daddy's drinking. I noticed it at the party last month. Daddy has always liked his drink, but not like this."

"No," she agreed in a soft voice. "Not like this. Linnea, I can't protect you from the truth either. It doesn't matter, really. It's all going to be public soon enough."

"What?" Linnea asked, truly alarmed now.

"It's not just the business that's failing," Julia began. "He's invested most of our savings in a real estate project and even borrowed from our friends. He was so sure this one deal was going to make his fortune. He's always wanted to surpass his father's successes, you know." She paused. "He really didn't care for his father."

"Yes. It's no secret."

Julia scowled. "Stratton Rutledge was not a very nice man. And a worse father. He made your father's life a living hell while he was alive. I never liked him, and to be honest, I was a little afraid of him. I can't bear that portrait of him hanging in the living room. I feel like he's staring down at us, finding fault. Cursing us. The old son of a bitch," she murmured under her breath.

Linnea had never heard her mother swear or speak ill of another person.

"What about the investment?" Linnea asked, bringing her mother back to the point.

Julia sighed again, this time with disgust. "I don't know for certain, but I suspect"—her eyes flashed with import—"strongly, that there's trouble. Your father is terribly worried."

"What did he invest in?"

"I can't remember the name. Something to do with mermaids, I think. It's in real estate. Here in Charleston."

Linnea shook her head. "I remember talking to him about a big project at the beginning of summer. Or rather, I asked, but he shifted the conversation away. Makes sense now. What happens if Daddy loses his investment?"

"Oh, darling," Julia said, a tinge of frustration in her voice. "What do you think? We'll be bankrupt."

A stunned silence followed. For a moment Linnea thought she'd misheard. Not in trouble. Bankrupt. Could it be possible, or was her mother exaggerating?

"But that's ludicrous! He can't be that badly off. He has the business, even if it's not doing well. He's always managed to stay afloat." For a dreadful moment Linnea thought she might burst into tears. Instead, she put her forehead in her palm to calm herself. "Mama, you've got to stop Daddy's drinking. It has to be affecting his business."

"I'm trying, Linnea!" Julia said, her voice rising with her temper. "We argue about it all the time. But he won't stop! What can I do? I've thrown away bottles of bourbon, and he just goes out and buys more."

Linnea held back, seeing how exhausted her mother was. How brittle. "Daddy didn't always drink like this."

Julia heard the change in tone and shook her head. "Not always," she said more calmly. "But there were times . . ." She paused, then pushed on. "He drank a lot before you were born. It became a serious problem for us. I almost left him."

Linnea had had no idea her mother was capable of such a thing.

"I told him he had to get help or I would leave. And to his credit, he did. I was proud of him. He didn't get any support from his father, naturally. His mother tried, of course, but by then she was spending most of her time at the beach house. His father . . ." Julia's face filled with resentment. "Hardly the example for his son. And now here is Palmer, repeating the same pattern for his son."

Linnea heard the desperation in her voice, and remembered Cooper telling her their mother was screaming at Palmer. She reached out to touch her mother's arm. "I know you're trying, Mama." There was a long silence, each of them lost in their own thoughts. Eventually Linnea spoke again. "I'm worried about Cooper. He doesn't look good."

"I don't think he's happy working with his father. He adores him. Too much, perhaps. Cooper's always tried to please him. But it's difficult."

"Mama, is Cooper . . ." She paused, trying to couch her words so they didn't sound accusatory. "Do you think he's doing drugs?"

"What?" Julia's head snapped up. "Why would you ever say that?"

Linnea realized that her mother wouldn't recognize the signs of drug use that she'd spotted in Cooper: pale skin, dilated pupils, lost weight, changed personality.

"I'm just asking," she said in a calm voice.

"Well, don't," Julia said brusquely, adjusting her position on the bench. "Your brother doesn't have a drug problem. I would know."

"He has a drinking problem." Linnea stated the obvious.

A cloud crossed over her mother's face, and Linnea saw that her skin was as pale as the alyssum in her garden and new lines were carved deep into her forehead. Worry lines, her mama always called them.

"Yes," Julia admitted in a resigned voice. "He drinks too much. But I don't know that I'd call it a problem. All boys drink. . . ."

"Mama, I think he's doing drugs."

"Well," she scoffed, "he might be experimenting a bit. You know, with marijuana. But that's normal, isn't it?"

"That's where he might've started. But I'm worried it's something more serious."

"Oh, Linnea, you're such a worrywart about your brother. You always were, you know. Hovering over him like a second mother. It's sweet, but I'm telling you he's right as rain."

Linnea knew there was no point in arguing with her. She refused to see the truth because she wouldn't or couldn't.

"Mama, promise you'll keep a close eye on him. And you'll call me if you see anything. Make sure he eats. And look at his pupils."

"His pupils! I'm not going to stare into his pupils. What do you expect me to see?"

"If they're dilated," Linnea explained. "That happens with drug use." She was having a hard time not letting her frustration flow into her voice.

"Really, Linnea," Julia said with a huff, and gathered her garden gloves as if to stand.

Linnea put her hand on Julia's arm to hold her back. "Mama, you're always making excuses for Cooper. You did all his art projects for him and helped him with his homework. Cooper's not a little kid anymore. It's not helping when you cover up for him or look the other way when he's drinking too much. Or doing drugs. This is too serious. Too dangerous. And it's called enabling."

"Now I'm an enabler?" She rose abruptly. "I think I've heard quite enough."

Linnea hurried to her feet. "I'm not saying it's your fault. I'm just asking you to pay attention." She reached for her mother's hand to stop her. "Mama, I'm really worried."

Her mother's face softened. "Honey, don't you worry. I'll keep my eye on him. Cooper's a good boy. Why, he starts at the Citadel next month. They'll keep him on the straight and narrow." She patted Linnea's hand on her arm reassuringly.

Linnea stared at the hand till she could assuage her disappointment. When she looked up, she met her mother's smile with one of her own.

"I've invited Cooper to the beach house this weekend. Please make sure he comes. He looks like he could use some sun."

"That's an excellent idea. I surely will. I think some time at the beach is exactly what he needs. He spends far too much time holed up in his room." She patted Linnea's hand again. "And just forget what I told you about your daddy's business. I shouldn't have burdened you with my worries. I'm probably overreacting. You caught me at a weepy moment in the garden. Everything will turn out fine."

"You're doing it now."

"What am I doing?"

"Trying to protect me. Closing the curtains."

"Nonsense." Julia leaned forward to kiss her on the cheek. Then she glanced at the gold and diamond watch at her wrist. "Forgive me, precious, but I have to rush. I'm due at the Junior League in half an hour. I really must change." She rose to a stand.

Linnea felt shoved out the door like some unwanted peddler. She also rose to stand beside her, piqued. "All right, then," she said, bending to grab her purse. "Bye, Mama."

She turned on her heel and headed toward the driveway, but stopped when she heard her mother call her name.

"Linnea!"

She turned.

Her mother's smile was starched and pressed across her face. "Don't be a stranger, hear? And don't worry!"

~~~~

LINNEA WORRIED ALL the way back to Isle of Palms. The sun was setting as she crossed the Ben Sawyer Bridge. Surreal streaks of magenta, purple, and orange filled the sky and shimmered in the high tide. Usually she felt an emotional separation from the mainland as she drove over the bridge. Tonight, however, her heart lay heavy in her chest, and her mind was weighed down by family issues. She took heaving breaths so she wouldn't cry.

When she got home, she immediately went to Emmi's to see John.

A light was burning near his desk window in the apartment

above the garage, signaling he was home. Linnea climbed the stairs to the double doors with a heavy tread and knocked softly.

She could hear his footfalls coming to the door and the click of the lock, and the door swung wide. His face immediately eased into a grin when he saw her.

Linnea stepped in and wrapped her arms around him.

"What's the matter?" he asked, his voice rich with concern.

"Just hold me a minute."

He tightened his arms around her and placed his lips on her head. "I take it you had a bad day?"

Her laugh was short but filled with relief, as he'd intended. She released her hold and stepped from his arms.

"The worst."

"Wine?"

"Please."

"Do you want to talk?"

They sat on the green velvet sofa. Linnea tucked her legs beneath her and told him about her lunch with Cooper, her worries about his health, and her visit with her mother, sparing no details. When she was finished, she felt some relief at hearing herself explain it all without emotion. She could think more clearly.

"My mother won't confront the problem. She doesn't want to see that Cooper might be using drugs."

"She's in denial. She may never see it. Until it's too late."

"Don't scare me." Linnea leaned against him on the sofa, needing his comfort. "I'm worried both my parents are so focused on financial ruin that they won't notice what's happening with Cooper right under their noses."

"What did you say your father invested in?"

"Some real estate deal in Charleston. A big one."

John unwound his arm from her shoulders, rose, and walked over to the big desk. "Let's take a look. Grab a chair." He shoved aside a pile of papers to clear room for her and fired up the computer, tapping his fingers on the edge of the desk in impatience as it powered on.

"What was the name of the company?"

"She couldn't remember the name. She said it had something to do with a mermaid."

John raised a brow. "A mermaid?"

Linnea shrugged. "I've been trying to remember the name of a company my father and I talked about early in the summer. He was invested in it. Mama said it had the name of a mermaid . . . or something like that."

"Hold on," John said. He closed his eyes and pinched the bridge of his nose in concentration.

She waited in tense silence as he muttered, "Maybe a siren? I recall something about a siren in Germany. She lured fishermen to their death. What was her name . . . ?"

"It began with an *l*."

"Lorelei!" he exclaimed. "That's it." He straightened with alacrity and began searching the program he'd created for his real estate project. His fingers flew over the keyboard. "I should've thought of that right away. It's the name of a huge project on Laurel Island off Charleston. Okay, here it is." He moved over so Linnea could read the information.

She read, stunned by the breadth of the project. Lorelei was the name of a billion-dollar development going into a prime piece of real estate on Charleston's Upper Peninsula. The plan was to transform the site into an upscale, mixed-used community.

"It's a mammoth project. I can see why Dad was interested."

"A landmark opportunity. That's one of the last premier waterfront parcels on the peninsula. Solid gold. He must've gotten in early." He returned to reading the screen. "Says here the project was announced in 2016, so your father must've invested earlier than that. But look here," he said, moving back so Linnea could read. "The project is stalled. City Council hasn't signed off on the plans."

"Oh no." Linnea leaned back in her chair. "Stalled indefinitely."

He scanned farther and whistled softly. "Here, read this," he said. "This will give you some more info on the boatload of problems they're facing. I'm going to make a phone call to a friend of mine who's involved. See what I can find out." He backed out his chair and walked off in search of his phone.

Linnea scooted closer and continued reading, hearing his sonorous voice behind her. She looked up a couple minutes later when she felt him standing beside her chair. His expression was grim. "What?"

"It's bad," he said. "Word on the street is they're shutting the project down. They should be making a formal announcement soon. I'm sorry, Lin."

"Oh no." She put her head in her palm. "Poor Daddy." Suddenly all the worry and grief she'd held inside all afternoon bubbled up. Tears began to well. Embarrassed, she covered her face.

"Linnea," John said. Placing his hands on her shoulders, he

gently guided her to a stand and enfolded her in his arms once more. He moved a lock of hair from her face and tucked it behind her ear. "This is a tough lesson to learn, but you should know," he said in a low voice by her ear. "We can't raise our parents."

She laughed.

"I'm serious," he said. "The older we get, the crazier they seem. I remember when my parents got a divorce. I was still in high school, and man, I was pissed, especially at my dad. He was the one who was fooling around. My mom took it really hard. I worried about her. Stayed by her side when she cried, which, by the way, was all the time. I listened to her rants. One night she got so angry she started throwing all his stuff into the yard. That's when they saw the lawyers. But eventually they figured things out. She moved here. My dad bought her family's beach house for an exorbitant price. He remarried. We hardly see him anymore. Everyone's moved on. It's hard, I know, but you just have to let them figure things out on their own." He lifted her chin with his finger so he could look into her eyes. "They're stronger than they seem."

She laughed again, then sniffed and wiped her eyes.

"Come on," he said, taking her hand. "Since the computer is up and running, let me show you a company I found that's looking for someone with an environmental science degree to do public education programs for their products."

Linnea's eyes widened with hope. "That sounds too good to be true."

"It is. The job is in California."

Chapter Seventeen

The hatchlings stay below the sand's surface until it cools,
usually indicating night. They emerge in a rush, tumbling over
one another in a sprint past predators such as raccoons, crabs, and
birds. Those that make it to the sea now begin a treacherous jour-
ney to the Gulf Stream where floating Sargassum provides
protection and food. It's survival of the fittest.

TONIGHT WAS HER first real date in three years. Cara had
soaked in the hot, scented tub till her skin was pink. It was
luxuriously decadent and calmed her nerves. She couldn't believe
she was as nervous as a teenager.

That in itself was rather a shock. She didn't think she'd ever
felt like this, the way the songs lyrics described: dreaming of him,
counting the hours till she saw him again. Perhaps it was because
she hadn't fallen in love at an early age. She was forty when she fell
in love for the first time with Brett. It wasn't a gush of feeling, but
rather a sense of knowing.

She lifted the loofah and let a stream of hot water trail across
her breasts, lost in thought. Was this the different kind of love

David had talked about? Brett had raised the bar very high, but with David, it was a different bar. She did feel a gush of romantic feeling with him, and it both delighted and disturbed her. She knew this feeling of awkwardness at dating again, feeling love again, would persist for a long time. How could it not? She had to cope with loving two men at the same time. But one was no longer a part of her life. The other was asking to be.

And both her mind and her body were telling her she was ready to try.

Cara took extra time applying her makeup, aware of the glimmer of excitement in her eyes. She'd been extravagant and purchased new undergarments, very good, elegantly sexy as only the French could design. Luxurious underwear gave her a private confidence, even if no one ever saw it but herself. She pulled the sleek white silk sheath dress out of the closet and over her head. The dress slid down her body like water. Her skin was so tan from her walks on the beach that the contrast was stunning. Finally, she selected a strand of sizable pearls for her neck and more for her ears. She looked in the mirror. A woman knew when she was looking her best. Cara smiled with satisfaction, then reached for her scent. It was new. Chosen for a new man.

When the doorbell rang, she felt a shiver of anticipation. She stepped into her heels and hurried to the door.

"You look stunning!" Linnea said with a gasp.

Cara turned to see her standing near the foyer, Hope in her arms, waiting. Her hair was pulled back in a ponytail and she wore baby-doll pajamas and fuzzy slippers, a look straight from the sixties.

"Thank you. As do you."

Linnea laughed. "Don't worry, I'm going to duck. Have a good time."

"Mama!" Hope called, reaching for her.

"Night-night, baby," Cara said, hurrying to kiss her once more. Predictably, Hope began to cry as the doorbell rang a second time.

"Go on, we'll be fine," Linnea said, then hurried down the hall with the fussing baby.

Cara took a final breath, then opened the door to see David standing under the light in a crisp, beautifully cut tan suit and a pale-blue shirt with a gorgeous tie. She felt a sweep of happiness seeing him at her door again and realized she was feeling what they wrote about in songs after all. She'd missed him. In one hand he carried a bouquet of local summer flowers, her favorite. Cara opened the door wider, aware that though she'd opened this door for him many times this summer, tonight's welcome felt decidedly different from the playdates.

"Come in."

"You only have time to put these in water, I'm afraid. Our reservations are for seven and I heard there's traffic on the bridge."

"All right. Come in for just a minute, then."

She walked across the living room, dimly lit by two lamps, toward the kitchen. Moutarde was silent in his cage. She reached up to grab the vase from a high shelf, but David was quick, his long arm grasping it and handing it to her.

Their eyes met and for a second she thought he was going to kiss her.

Footsteps caught her attention and she turned to see Linnea hurrying in, arm outstretched.

"I'll take those," Linnea told her, and took the bouquet. "Ooh, pretty."

Cara held back a smile. "Hope's asleep already?"

Linnea put the flowers in the vase. "Out like a light." She stopped in front of David. "Hi and good-bye, David. I just came in for a glass of water." She poured herself a glass of water and with a final wave scooted from the room.

David's brows rose with humor at Linnea's pajamas. "Déjà vu."

"Quite. Well," Cara said, "I guess we can go."

~~~~~

CHARLESTON BOASTED MANY exquisite restaurants, and this small enclave was one of her best-kept secrets. They were seated in an exquisite walled garden filled with flowers in bloom. Small garden tables draped with thick white damask dotted the patio, each with candles that flickered in the dusk. Edith Piaf sang in the background.

David consulted the wine list with the sommelier. She let her gaze float about the garden. Other couples, young and old, filled the tables, enjoying a haute cuisine meal on a soft summer night. Inside the house, candles glimmered and more couples dined. She smiled to herself, realizing that David had selected a romantic, quiet restaurant rather than a showy one. Her attention shifted to the man across the table.

David had become so much more than the friendly, good-looking man who'd delivered Heather to the beach house a few years back. He'd become an important part of her and Hope's lives. Cara was a woman who enjoyed handsome men and had dated many in her life, discarding them without a second thought. Only Brett had risen above the pack to claim her heart. She sensed that David could—if she would let him—claim it as well.

He handed the wine list to the waiter and, eyes gleaming in the candlelight, focused his attention on her. "I think you're going to like what I selected. I had a little fun with wine pairing. I hope you'll enjoy it."

"In that case, I'd best pace myself."

"Why? I'm driving."

"I'm a terrible drunk. I get all weepy."

"You? I can't imagine you weepy. In that case, I hope you do get a bit tipsy so I can witness the other side of the usually implacable Cara Rutledge."

"Implacable? Me? My dear boy, you have a lot to learn about me."

David grinned. "I look forward to it."

The waiter arrived at the perfect moment.

"Champagne," Cara exclaimed, pleased. "I love good bubbly. What's the occasion?"

"Isn't being together enough of an occasion?"

She gazed at him over the glass as she took a sip. "Tell me about London," Cara said, moving the conversation in a new direction. "It's been ages since I've been. How is the queen?" she asked jokingly.

"In residence. The Union Jack was flying."

"What was the urgent business?"

"Oh, you don't want to talk about my business."

"Actually, I do. You may not believe this, but there are women who have a good mind for business. I happen to be one of them."

He appeared chagrined. "I didn't want to start expounding. Once I do, it's hard to stop me. I'm much more interested in you."

"I appreciate that. However, I'm interested in you, too. I want you to tell me everything. Every last detail."

Gradually, haltingly, David opened up about his business venture. As he began to expand on what his work in London entailed, she became aware for the first time of how involved he was with his company. She'd fallen into the mistaken impression that David was retired, dabbling in stocks and enjoying time with his grandson. Tonight she listened, spellbound, as he spoke with confidence and authority.

"The phenomenon of unmanned aerial vehicles is pretty exciting. We've taken the stuff of sci-fi movies and books and turned it into reality."

"You're in *drones*?" she asked, stunned.

"Yes. Or rather, my company makes the small cameras that are attached to drones. Drones are not only for hobbyists and tech-savvy enthusiasts anymore. Businesses and decision makers worldwide are seriously interested. The technological developments and advancements in the field of smart electronics are breathtaking."

"But, you're a lawyer. How did you get involved?"

"I've always loved electronics as a hobby. And I flew . . . still do on occasion. This seemed a natural fit. I invested in this small startup years ago. We went public in 2016, and since then"—he spread out his palms—"the growth has been exponential. And it's still expected to skyrocket. The more involved I got, the more interested I became. So much so that I retired from my law practice to focus on the company."

She sat back, astonished at how little she really knew about this man. As he went on to explain details of his cameras, she realized the scope of his intelligence, and more, his influence. He transformed from a friendly retired lawyer into a successful international businessman right before her eyes.

"That reminds me," he said, reaching down beside his chair to grab a bag she'd been curious about since she'd seen him carry it into the restaurant. "I have something for you. A little souvenir from London."

"You shouldn't have," she said politely, envisioning a tin of tea or a box of sweets emblazoned with images of Big Ben. She took the large bag from him, noting that it came from Harrods, and spread open the tissue paper.

"It's a Burberry bag!" she exclaimed, stunned.

"Do you like it?"

"Of course. It's beautiful."

He appeared pleased with her response. "I remembered you broke the handle of your tote bag at the park and thought this one could replace it."

Cara looked at him, moved that he'd think of such a thoughtful gesture. "But, David, that was a little nothing bag I bought at Target. This is a Burberry tote." She exhaled slowly. "I can't accept this."

"Of course you can. You love it."

"No, I can't. You already do so much for me. You pick up my tab when we're out, buy our tickets, drive us everywhere. That's already a lot. But this . . ." She shook her head. "This is too much. I really can't accept it."

Cara gave one last loving look at the gorgeous Burberry tote and slid it back into the paper bag. She was about to reach for her glass, but David was faster, putting his hand over hers on the table.

"Cara, please accept the bag. I don't mean to sound crass, but it's really not that expensive for me. And the fact that you like it so much makes it worth every penny." His gaze was penetrating. "Let me give you gifts or do little things for you. And can I say, it's insulting to a man not to let him pick up your tab when we're out together."

"But a tab for ice cream is not this year's hottest Burberry bag."

"What's the fun of having money if you can't spend it on people you care about?" He looked down at their hands, then back at her. "I hope you know I care about you."

She studied his dark eyes, illuminated by the flickering candle, and heard his words again in her mind.

David continued, his expression vulnerable, "I hope, too, that I've come to mean something to you."

She was surprised by the strength of the emotions welling up inside her. She looked down at their joined hands. "You mean a great deal to me," she told him. "More than I thought I'd feel again." She turned her palm up and wrapped her long fingers around his wrist. "Thank you for the beautiful bag. And . . ." She raised her eyes to his. "Thank you for bringing me back to life again."

She'd asked for a sign to make it clear she was ready to let go of her grief and find love again. To be loved again.

She'd never thought it would come in the form of a Burberry bag.

~~~~~

LINNEA HEARD THE front door open, the click of high heels on the wood, and the plunk of a purse on the foyer table. She smiled, hearing Cara hum as she walked into the living room.

"You're glowing," Linnea said. "And it's not from the sun."

Cara startled at seeing Linnea cozy on the sofa. Sade sang on the speakers, and on the cocktail table were two wineglasses and a bottle of red.

"Am I?" Cara asked, putting her long fingers to her cheek. "It's probably the alcohol. Lord, I'm tipsy."

"Uh-uh, that ain't it," Linnea said, then patted the sofa. "Join me? I have a nice bottle of Malbec."

"Oh, no, I've had too much wine already. David ordered a wine pairing and it was heaven. But no more wine for me."

"Glass of water then?" Linnea asked, rising from the sofa, her tan legs showing under the baby-doll pajamas.

"Perfect. Thank you." Cara slipped out of her heels, pulled the pins from her hair, and ran her fingers through her mop of hair, giving her head a good scratching.

Linnea returned with a tall glass of water, glad to see Cara relaxing. The ice chinked in the glass as the two women sat on the sofa, each with her chosen drink in hand, and settled in the pillows.

"So, you had a nice dinner?" Linnea asked, raising her eyebrows.

"It was more than nice," Cara said. "I feel like I'm still floating. It was . . ." She looked up as though searching for the right word. "Transformative."

"That's a pretty powerful word."

Cara sighed. "I know."

Linnea leaned forward. "Well, c'mon, what makes an evening transformative?"

"I don't know if I can explain it."

"Try."

"Well . . ." Cara began. "The setting was perfect. Candlelight, heavy white linen, the scent of flowers, fabulous wine, and delicious food."

"Enter handsome man, beautiful woman. Sounds like a Hallmark movie."

"It was," Cara said with a slight shrug. "We talked about anything and everything. We have this comfort between us, a lack of inhibition that allows us to tell each other things that we might choose not to tell anyone else. The kind that comes from trust."

Linnea thought of John and felt another notch of surety about him. "I know that feeling."

"David is an extraordinary man. I've never met anyone quite like him. He's just returned from London on business and brought me a sweet souvenir," she added with a smile. "I'll show you later. Anyway, while I listened to him talk about his business and how much he loves what he does, it was so strange—it was as if a different person was sitting across the table from me. Someone formidable. Someone I was suddenly very interested to know more about."

"I know what you mean!" Linnea said, sitting upright. "The same thing happened to me. With John. We were having drinks and he was talking about his new project and I realized he wasn't just some laid-off surfer dude. He has real depth . . . and I found that attractive." She smiled seductively. "Very, very attractive."

Cara laughed lightly. "I've always found intelligence to be an aphrodisiac."

"Oh yeah? Is it a coincidence, then, that both the men you fell for were tall and handsome?"

"Strictly a coincidence."

"Or luck."

"Luck had nothing to do with it." Cara laughed. "Truly. I like to think it's fate."

"Or good karma."

Cara tilted her head. "I like that better. God knows I've paid my dues."

Linnea watched Cara closely. So elegant and strong, yet behind the façade she presented, Linnea had seen her broken, too. Brett's death had done that. Frozen her heart for three years. She was happy and relieved to see the thaw.

"So, you're ready for love after love?"

Cara's face grew thoughtful. "It's very strange to go from tears for Brett to smiles for David. I've had to accept that my divided heart is normal. Intellectually it all makes sense, of course. But emotionally . . ." Cara shook her head. "It's very hard. Nothing makes much sense in the heart. I have to go with how I feel. My instincts have always been pretty good, and over the years I've learned to listen to them. If I don't, I make errors and fall into regret."

"So what does your gut tell you?"

"Not to be afraid," Cara replied. "I've found someone who

loves me, scarred heart and all. The love I have for David is different than the love I had for Brett. But I'm different, too. So, yes, I believe I am ready."

"Oh, Cara, I'm so very, very happy to hear that."

"Me too," she replied. "And you? Are you ready? I can't help but turn the tables and tell you I've watched you and John together. You seem to be a good fit."

Linnea paused, feeling again the confusion that overtook her whenever she thought about her relationship with John.

"You might be ready for love, but I'm not. Not the happily-ever-after kind. I'm only twenty-two. I don't even have a real job yet. I haven't tested myself yet. Aunt Cara, I want to get married and have children someday. But one thing I learned this summer. As much as I adore Hope—and you know I do," she asserted.

Cara smiled. "I know."

"Being a nanny this summer showed me I'm not ready to settle down and be a mother yet. I've got things I want to do. Places I want to go. I don't even want to get tied down to a serious relationship."

"Then don't."

"You make that sound so easy."

"I didn't say it would be. I'm saying you have the choice. Linnea, you're only young once. Take it from me, life speeds by, and if you don't enjoy your freedom while you have it . . . Too soon you may make a commitment, have children, have a house and debt, all of which is wonderful on its own merit. But be ready for it. Go into it wholeheartedly. Then you'll never live your life wondering about what could have been." Cara leaned far over to take hold of the bottle of wine and poured herself a glass. "I'm talking too much."

"No, you're not," Linnea said. "Please go on. You're like a second mother to me. I've always admired you. How you up and left at eighteen and never looked back. I mean, you were only eighteen!"

Cara settled back on the sofa and brought her long, slim legs up to stretch out beside Linnea. It was an intimate move, one a mother might make with her daughter.

"Linnea," Cara began, "don't glamorize what was a sad situation."

"I know—but be honest. It took courage."

"I had to make a choice. My father drew his line in the sand, and I crossed it. Let's just say he made it impossible for me to stay."

"But you left Charleston," Linnea persisted. "Went all the way to Chicago. Did you have money?"

"I had my savings. It wasn't much. But it bought me a train ticket. I knew a girl from school who went to Northwestern, right outside of Chicago. It was one of the universities I'd applied to." She snorted. "And gotten in." She brushed a bit of lint from her dress. "I remember being so jealous that she could go to college and have an apartment, all paid for by supportive parents. While I . . ." She set her glass on the table and said without self-pity, "I looked for a job. I always loved school, you know. Learning. I still love walking through libraries and bookstores, just to let my fingers run along the spines of books."

"And you got a job."

"I did. There are more ways to learn than in school. 'Experience is the best of schoolmasters.' I think Thomas Carlyle said that. It's true. I figured if I couldn't go to school to learn, I'd get a job in the area I wanted to learn. I started as a receptionist in an advertising agency, but I always asked questions about the job and worked late. People noticed. I learned so much on the job, but I also went to night school, got my degree, and earned several promotions along the way. All in all, I did quite well for myself. And there's no small degree of satisfaction in knowing that I did it all on my own." She sighed and placed her palms on her thighs. "Then I got laid off. I came running home and my life changed in ways I never anticipated. Or wanted. I never expected to fall in love." She lifted her shoulders and took a sip of the wine. "The rest you know."

Linnea admired Cara's resilience. And more, her independence. She'd thumbed her nose at her father and taken off for Chicago. She was a role model. Someone Linnea could always count on to be honest.

"I want an adventure like that."

"Hardly an adventure."

"Well, to test myself, then. Sometimes I lie on my back and think, where would I go if I could go anywhere?" She laughed self-consciously. "Of course, at first I come up with ideas of Paris or San Francisco . . ." She paused, thinking of John.

Cara caught the reference and arched a brow. "San Francisco?"

Linnea nodded. "There's a job possibility there."

"Really? That's exciting. Hallelujah!"

"I don't know. There's a lot to consider."

"Like what? Frankly, my dear, you don't have a lot of other offers."

"But what will Daddy say? And . . . it's not a good time to leave home."

Cara paused, looking at her askance. "Excuse me. But didn't you just tell me you admired me for leaving home at eighteen? You're twenty-two. What are you afraid of? Certainly not my brother . . ."

Linnea shook her head. "Aunt Cara, I haven't been completely open with you."

Her gaze sharpened. "About what?"

"About Daddy. Cooper. Mama." She closed her eyes to collect herself. "They're all one hot mess. I'm afraid for them."

Cara sat up and set her glass on the table. Linnea felt a new tension in the room as Cara set her razor-sharp focus on her.

"I know your father's been drinking more than usual."

Linnea snorted derisively. "A lot more. Every night he gets drunk. Cooper said living at home was hell."

Cara swallowed hard and her brows knitted. "I see. And Cooper?"

"He's the one I'm most worried about. He was supposed to come here last weekend. He promised." She shrugged. "But he didn't. He's dodging me. He's drinking too. I think . . . no, I feel sure he's doing drugs."

Cara inhaled sharply. She thought for a moment, then asked, "What kind of drugs? Marijuana?"

"I don't know, but it's more than pot. I tried to talk to him about it, but he denies it. He's so unhappy, Cara. He feels trapped, and I think drugs help him escape."

"What's he feeling trapped about?"

"Everything. He doesn't want to go to the Citadel. That's a biggie. Mostly he doesn't want to disappoint Daddy. Which means he'll be trapped in the family business." She laughed harshly. "He might not have to worry about that."

"What's that?" Cara's voice was sharp.

"According to my mother, they're on the verge of bankruptcy."

Cara's face registered shock. "Good God!" she exclaimed. "The family's gone to hell in a handbasket, and I'm only just hearing about it?"

"The Rutledges are very good at covering up."

"No," Cara snapped. "We're very good at lying. There's a difference." She rose and began pacing the room, her fingers tapping her crossed arms. She stopped before Linnea, her dark eyes flashing.

"First, I have to tell you I'm hurt you didn't come to me with this sooner. I thought we had a stronger relationship."

Linnea felt crushed by the criticism. "I'm sorry."

"I'll go see my brother. Try to talk some sense into him." She stopped and exhaled. "But you know him. He holds his feelings in like Fort Knox. And with good reason. In all fairness, when I left home all those years ago, I left him to deal with the mess at home. You may think that I'm the brave one, but I say it was your father. He held the family together and dealt with our father. He's the one you should admire. Palmer is not a bad man, Linnea. I fear if what you say is true, he's simply lost."

Linnea had never heard her aunt speak like this before. And she'd never thought of her father in this light.

Cara came to stand in front of Linnea. "Regardless of what Palmer does or says, regardless of what happens with your brother, Linnea, you have to make your own decisions for your own life. You're not a child any longer. Nor are you your brother's keeper."

"But you just called my father a hero for staying."

"I did. But Cooper is not alone. He has his good parents. And he has me. Let *us* be there for him." She reached out to place her hand on Linnea's shoulder. "My darling girl, I love you too much to allow you to throw your life away. I'm not saying go to San Francisco. I'm saying don't feel compelled to stay here. Do you understand?"

Linnea nodded. "What if that means going with John?"

Cara took in a breath and straightened, lifting her hand. She asked urbanely, "As a lover? A friend? A traveling companion?"

"All of the above."

"Not as a husband."

"No."

Linnea knew that Cara understood the ramifications of that decision with regard to her father, her mother, her reputation.

"Then I'd say be very careful. Not only of your own feelings, but of his."

Chapter Eighteen

*Veterinarians at sea turtle hospitals diagnose each turtle
and work with staff and volunteers to provide treatments and
care. Patients are given IV fluids, antibiotics, vitamins, and other
medications, similar to any human patient. Based on the sea turtle's
condition, a variety of procedures may be performed, such as X-rays
or ultrasounds. The goal is rehabilitation and release.*

A s THE DOG days of August plodded on, the female turtles ended a productive season. They had been nesting on these local beaches since early May, going back and forth from sea to beach every fourteen days to lay another clutch of eggs. Their instincts fulfilled, their bodies empty of eggs, the tired and hungry turtles swam home to the sea to forage and gain strength before they returned in three years to repeat the cycle again.

One female turtle was not leaving. Not yet. Toy and Cara stood shoulder to shoulder in the great exhibit hall before Big Girl's tank. She had been moved to the main exhibit when her health improved, and being so large, she was a star attraction.

She enjoyed the larger tank, but today she seemed restless, swimming round and round the tank, her flippers stretching wide. Her carapace was gleaming, free of barnacles, and her eyes were bright and aware. Still, there was a frantic quality to her swimming.

It was early and the crowds had not yet been allowed in. Toy administered the medications and made notes. Flipping her clipboard closed, she looked at Big Girl.

"She wants to go home," Toy said.

"I know. Poor girl, it wasn't a good season for her," said Cara.

"She laid more than seventy eggs in that tank. We did our best to catch them and bury them, but none of them hatched. No surprise there, but still . . . we hoped."

"When will you release her?" Cara asked.

"As soon as the blood work comes back clear and Dr. Shane gives her the okay. Her shell will never heal, but there are a lot of sea turtles in the ocean living productive lives with shark bites. It's got to be a badge of honor to survive it, right?"

"I was kind of hoping she couldn't be released. That we could keep her."

"I know. But our Caretta in the big tank wouldn't like that. Remember—"

"I know. They're solitary swimmers."

"And that's not our mission, is it? It's like you said, Big Girl's a prime example of the resilience of turtles and what we do here." Toy looked at the turtle. "She'll go back into the ocean where she belongs, and in a couple of years, hopefully she'll lay thousands more eggs."

"What a girl," Cara said, and crossed her arms. The size of Big Girl's head gave new meaning to the word *loggerhead*. "I really love this turtle."

Toy grew serious. "This turtle was here for me when I needed her most. Remember how we examined her on a makeshift table of cardboard boxes? And look where she is now," she said, indicating the gleaming new sea turtle recovery center. "When I look at her, I'm reminded of why I went into this line of work in the first place. She taught me so many lessons about life. Resilience. Big Girl was my teacher. And this place," she said, indicating the aquarium, "has been my school." She took a breath and tilted her head. "Having her come back into my life now was providential."

Cara turned to face Toy. Her face wasn't as pale and tired as a few weeks ago, and her golden hair had a brilliant sheen. She seemed healthier. Happier. Her baby bump was larger, too.

"How so?" she asked.

Toy watched Big Girl make another circle in the tank. "Big Girl helped me to realize how much I love working with turtles, all the animals in the aquarium, really. And how passionate I am about protecting them and their natural habitat. That's why I was so excited about the new position as conservation director."

Toy looked up at Cara. "But I know now that I don't want to leave the sea turtle hospital," she concluded. "I've watched it grow from a kiddie pool to a state-of-the-art hospital. I still have so much to offer. So much I want to do here." She shrugged and smiled in sweet surrender. "I don't want to leave."

Cara was stunned. "You're not taking the position?"

Toy shook her head. "The more I thought about it, the more I realized I don't enjoy public speaking. I'm more a behind-the-scenes person. And the hours would wreak havoc on my personal life. Especially with this new baby." She gently patted her belly. "I had to think long and hard about this decision. It didn't come lightly. My biggest concern was that I'd end up failing both at work and in my home. Part of my strength is knowing what I'm good at and where I belong. And I love doing it. And Lovie used to say, 'If it ain't broke, don't fix it.'"

Cara smiled, remembering.

Toy cleared her throat and stepped closer. "Cara, would you be interested in the position?"

Cara wasn't prepared for that question. "As conservation director?"

"Yes."

Cara blinked. "This is so sudden. So unexpected."

"Is it? You know how much the PR department and Kevin have appreciated all your ideas about the campaign for Big Girl."

"They've done a great job with it."

"It's wildly successful. You're like a never-ending font of ideas. It's just what the position needs. And you're an excellent public speaker."

"More a salesperson," Cara said with a wry grin.

"Don't shortchange yourself. I'd say you know how to deliver a message."

"Isn't it a full-time position?"

"Yes. For the first few months while you launch it, I suspect it will be time and a half."

Cara brought her fingertips to her lips and began tapping in thought. "I have to admit, I've been dreaming about coming back to work at an aquarium. I miss being around the ambience. But to be totally honest, Toy," she said, "I'm building my own clientele as a consultant. In fact, I've just taken on a new client. I've worked hard this summer. I'd have to think long and hard about that." She turned to look at Big Girl swimming in an endless circle in the tank. She felt like she was swimming with her, going around and around the same questions endlessly, eager for release. "And there's Hope. I left the aquarium in Tennessee to come home and raise Hope. This would mean going back to work full-time. I have to consider this very carefully."

"Of course." Toy paused. "Cara, just for the record. You know I'm working full-time, and I'll be having a new baby in the fall. You can make it work. Lots of us do." She grinned. "Want to know the secret of being a happy mother?"

Cara laughed. "Of course."

"If mama is happy, the family is happy. It's that simple. And there's no one way to make mama happy. Stay-at-home or working mother, there's lots of struggling to be organized and moments of exasperation and exhaustion." She rolled her eyes. "Lots of those. But there are so many more moments of joy and satisfaction. It's all about quality time when you're home. Turning off the TV and sharing. That's one of the lessons that Big Girl taught me. You keep swimming forward, pushing hard, but at the same time, you appreciate each moment."

Cara said, "Is this a serious proposition, or are we just chewing the fat?"

Toy smiled. "I've been authorized to talk to you and make the offer. Kevin is waiting for you in his office whenever you're ready. But, Cara, don't wait too long."

~~~~

CARA CAME TO a stop before the imposing black wrought-iron gate that blocked the driveway to her old home on Tradd. Linnea had told her about the gate. It was handsome, true, but also a pain in the neck. She rolled down her window and punched the intercom button. Then she waited. It was hot outdoors, and she was losing air-conditioning.

"Hello?"

"Palmer, it's me. Cara."

There was a pause; then she heard a click, and the big gates swung open. She parked and made her way along the familiar path through Julia's gorgeous garden. She spotted Palmer waiting for her at the door, a grin on his face.

"Alert the news! Cara Rutledge deigned to make an appearance at her brother's house!"

She gave her brother a kiss. "It's so hot—why would I come to the city? You should hightail it to the beach. These are the days our forefathers built the summer homes for. To escape!"

"I wish, sister. Some of us aren't so lucky to live on an island."

"You could," she shot back with a nudge. "You have a house on Sullivan's."

"Yeah, yeah," he said, dismissing the discussion about the rental house they'd had so many times before. "I'm about to fix some lunch. You hungry?"

She shook her head. "No, thanks. I'll eat when I get home. I was in town at the aquarium and thought I'd stop by."

"Glad you did." He looked at her with affection. "Real glad. I've missed you. Iced tea?"

She smiled and felt her heart expand for him. "Love some."

"It's not as good as yours, of course. Julia only makes the unsweetened tea." He patted his belly. "She thinks it's going to make a difference." He laughed and shook his head. "I try to humor her where I can."

She girded her nerves for what she was about to say. She waited until the tea was poured and they sat together at the big scrubbed wood table in the kitchen like they did when they were children.

Cara let her gaze sweep the kitchen of the great old house with its wooden beams, heart-pine floors, and brick fireplace. "I'm so glad that when Julia redecorated the house, she didn't throw the baby out with the bathwater."

"Nah," Palmer said, resting his elbows on the table and lacing his fingers. "She has more sense than that. Plus Mama would never have allowed it. She was still alive and kicking when most of the work was done." He paused, squinting his eyes. "I still miss her."

"Me too."

"Do you still smell her perfume out there?"

"I did when I first arrived. Quite strong," she said, omitting the ghost story. The more time went by, the more she was beginning to doubt she'd really seen her mother. To wonder if she'd just been tired from the long drive and it had simply been her imagination. "Not lately, though. I'm disappointed, truth be known."

"I'd like to be there when it happens. Just to see what I felt, you know?" He paused and clasped his hands together tightly. "I never got to say good-bye to her. That thought still haunts me."

Cara's heart ached for her brother. "Mama knew you loved her. You were a good son, Palmer. The best."

Palmer looked at that moment like the little boy she remembered. He'd adored Lovie, but even still, he had been as much an authoritarian with her as their father had been, controlling her finances with an iron hand. Cara suddenly recalled, with a stab of worry, that he had taken money from Lovie's bank account to help support his business back then, too. That meant this wasn't the first time the family export/import firm had had financial trouble.

"Palmer . . ." Cara hesitated to break his reverie. "I want to talk to you about something."

His pensive gaze suddenly sharpened. "Oh?"

"I understand that the Rutledge Export/Import is in trouble."

"Who told you that?" he asked, his voice sharp, tilting his head as though to better hear.

"You told me that, you alluded to it the day at the bar."

"Oh, yeah . . ."

"And from Linnea. She heard it from Julia. And from Cooper."

Palmer sat back in his chair and rubbed his jaw, clearly agitated.

"We're all family, Palmer. No one is talking out of turn."

"My business is no one's business but my own," he said. "And it's doing fine. I told you that."

"You did. And I don't believe you."

He glared back at her.

"Palmer, I've known you all your life. You can't fool me. You're doing what you've always done, trying to cover up any unpleasantness and bear the trouble alone. Why? We're family, Palmer. You shouldn't feel a responsibility to bear this weight all on your own."

"You should've thought about that before you left thirty years ago. Left everything squarely in my hands."

"I deserve that. But since we're being honest . . . we both know Daddy wasn't going to leave the business to me even if I did stay. Even if I wanted it. I know you never wanted to take over the business. Daddy forced it on you. And you've taken care of it—and this house—ever since."

"He never asked me if I wanted it. Not once. I wish he had given it to you."

"As your sister who loves you very much, I'm telling you that it isn't your responsibility to keep that firm afloat."

"That's what men do," he said with an air of bluster. "We keep the ship sailing."

"Spare me the platitudes. You're not a captain. You don't have to go down with the ship. And if you call me a little lady, I'll kick you so hard you won't be able to walk for a week."

Palmer guffawed and slapped the table. "There she is. There's my sister." He stood up and walked to the cabinet. "I could use a drink. Want a drink?"

"It's three in the afternoon."

He pulled out a glass and a bottle of bourbon. "I'm running late, then." He chuckled as he poured himself a liberal amount. He looked up. "You sure you don't want any?"

Cara didn't reply.

Palmer came back to the table with his glass and sat with a heavy thump in the chair. "Oh, stop giving me the stink eye," he said with a dismissive wave. "I'm too old to be lectured by my baby sister. Don't worry. I've got everything under control."

"Really? Do you have your drinking under control?"

Palmer's face darkened. "Don't meddle, Cara."

"'Meddle'? That's not the word I'd use. 'Intervention' is more like it."

"Shit," he drawled, and slammed his palm down on the table. "That tears it. I'm sick to death of you women hounding me for having a few drinks."

"'A few drinks'?" Cara said, her voice rising. "Is that what you call getting drunk on a nightly basis? Fights with your wife and son? Palmer, you need help. Let me help you, whatever you need me to do. It's you and me, remember? We swore after Mama died we'd take care of each other. You were there for me when I was falling apart after Brett died, and I'll love you forever for that. And I'm prepared to go to hell and back to help you now. You can beat this curse, Palmer. You don't have to end up like our father."

"I'm not like him," Palmer roared. "I'm nothing like him!"

"Are you so sure? Palmer, you're becoming just like him."

His face went pale.

Cara pressed on. "Don't you remember what he was like? Yelling at Mama, browbeating her till she near broke. And me? He drove me away. I ran so hard and fast I couldn't stop till I crossed the Mason-Dixon line. And you . . ." Cara's face softened with love. "You got the worst of it. He came down on you so hard if ever you crossed him. He browbeat you too, but you stood and took it all. For me and for Mama." Her eyes filled with tears, and she took a long, shuddering breath. She couldn't allow herself to get emotional.

Palmer softened. "I don't want to be like him. But I just don't know what to do about it. The business is a mess. I admit it. There doesn't seem to be a way out for me."

She heard the desperation in his voice. "There is," she said urgently. "Palmer, I'm not here for an intervention. Let's just say I'm here for a conversation. The first of many, okay?"

"Okay."

She took a breath. "You have to break this destructive pattern. Daddy started it with you, and now you're continuing it with Cooper. If you don't stop it, Cooper will continue with his son."

Palmer looked at her, stone-faced. "What pattern is that?"

"First, you have to stop drinking. We'll stand behind you. And second, take the burden of all this"—she gestured to the house—"off the shoulders of your son. Don't do to him what Daddy did to you."

"What?" Palmer looked at her with confusion in his eyes.

"The whole Rutledge male beating-of-the-chest thing. It's positively tribal. Cooper doesn't want to go to the Citadel," Cara told him. "He doesn't want to work in the family firm. Don't force him to feel responsible for all this."

"I'm not forcing Cooper to do anything! As a matter of fact, he's off picking up his uniform now. Tomorrow he enters the Citadel. Becomes a knob. He's right excited about it too. His mother and I are taking him out to dinner. A kind of farewell celebration."

Her eyes captured his. "Are you so sure he's excited? Or is it panic you see in his eyes?"

Palmer frowned, and his eyes flashed with anger. "Don't go too far, sister. He's my son."

"That's my point." Cara rose and leaned forward on the table, closer to her brother. Her voice was low and firm. "You forget—I was there when you went off to the Citadel. You smiled for Daddy, put on the good show." She tapped the table hard with each syllable. "But I know how you felt inside."

She straightened and took a breath, hoping she could convince her brother. "That's how Cooper feels. He's trying to do the right thing, Palmer. He's trying to do what you want him to do. To make you proud. And it's killing him." She straightened, collecting her calm. "He's drinking too much. We're worried about drugs." She saw with frustration that Palmer waved his hand in denial and leaned back in his chair. She pressed on. "And he's going out to the hunting lodge on weekends. I know what happens out there all too well. As do you."

Palmer remained silent, but his gaze burned back into hers with fury.

"I'm not here to badger you. I'm here to ask you, to beg you, to break the cycle. To stop drinking and consider what kind of an example you're setting for your children."

Palmer rose slowly and leaned forward on the table. "What kind of an example did our father set for us?"

Cara didn't budge. "Exactly."

Palmer lifted his chin and crossed his arms tightly against his chest. When he spoke, his voice rumbled from his chest.

"Go back to your beach house, baby sister," he said with a tight smile. "Where you belong. We're all just fine here."

Cara smiled back at him with genuine affection, but her voice rang with firmness. "You're not getting rid of me so easily, brother mine. I'm on your side, whether you choose to believe me or not. I'll go. But I'll be back. Again and again. Because I love you."

~~~~~

DAVID CAME WHEN she called. Cara walked along the crooked walkways and cobblestone alleys of Charleston to burn off some of the excess frustration bubbling in her veins. August might not have been the hottest month, but it was the most humid. She was moist by the time she arrived at The Chophouse. Harold greeted her warmly and secured a table for her in the bar. The jazz piano player had just started playing.

She just had time to sit and sip some water before she saw David enter. He was not an easy man to miss. She waved, and his face lit up at seeing her.

When he came to the table, he bent to lightly kiss her cheek in welcome. The move surprised Cara, in a good way.

"I'm so grateful you could meet me," she said.

"Of course. It was fortunate I was already in the city."

A waitress came quickly for their order.

"A Campari and soda," she said, looking forward to the bubbles on this hot day.

"Bourbon. On the rocks. So," David said as the waitress left, folding his hands on the table. "What's up?"

"More family drama, I'm afraid." She filled him in on her discussion with Linnea, then followed up with her visit with Palmer.

Their drinks came. They each tasted theirs and returned to the conversation.

"Palmer's put you in a tough spot," David said. "You see what has to be done, you've offered to help him, pointed out the damage he's inflicting on his son, and he refuses to listen. So what can you do? Is that right?"

"In a nutshell, yes."

"The answer is—nothing."

"Nothing?"

"You have to let him fail. To hit the proverbial rock bottom. It's tough love, but remember, you are not being cruel by doing this. It's a last resort. Ultimately you're helping him to help himself."

"But what about Cooper?"

"You said he was entering the Citadel?" When she nodded he said, "They do have a reputation for making a boy a man."

"But he doesn't want to go."

"Then talk to him."

Cara closed her eyes, inexplicably weary. "What a tangled web we weave . . ."

"When we practice to deceive," he finished for her. "Who are we deceiving?"

"Not us. Palmer," she said. "If I could just get him to recognize what he's doing. To himself. To his family."

"Who's to say he doesn't know? He might be so depressed he can't change."

"There's that web."

"Point well taken."

Cara sipped her drink, braced by the bitterness and the chill of it. "Speaking of change," she said, switching subjects, "I had another meeting today."

"You've been a busy lady."

"I went to the aquarium to see Toy and Big Girl."

"How are they both doing? Fecundity reigns."

"Very well, thank you," she said, amused. "Actually, Toy made an interesting proposal. She asked if I would be interested in the new position of director of conservation."

David put down his glass. "But isn't that to be her new position?"

"It was. But she's decided she doesn't want it."

"Really . . ." He considered this. "I thought she did. Is it because of the baby?"

Cara shook her head. "That was my first thought. The baby plays into it, I'm sure, but she said she's come to realize that she doesn't want to leave her position with the turtle hospital. That's what she loves doing. So she's decided to stay on at the hospital and offered me the position."

"She *offered* it to you?"

"Yes. She said she had the authority. Now I have to decide if I want it."

"And do you? Do you want the job?"

"I think I do. I could let my clients know in plenty of time for them to find a replacement. My ideas will be my farewell gift to them. My chief concern is Hope. Whether I should take a full-time job. I worry whether I'll be able to handle working with a child at home. I'm new at it. And I did come here to be a stay-at-home mother. That was the plan." She exhaled and looked into David's eyes. He was listening, biding his time.

"Can I tell you something, and you have to promise you won't think I'm a terrible mother?"

He laughed and said, "Sure."

"I like working. I love coming downtown to meet with a client. I feel so alive. My brain is firing on all synapses. And when I work on my ideas, I feel energized, bursting with creativity. David, I get bored playing with Hope all day. That's the simple truth. I don't think I was cut out for it."

"And you feel guilty."

Cara put her cheek in her palm. "Yes."

"Don't."

She made a face.

"Do you think you're the first parent who feels guilty for going to work and leaving his or her child behind? Join the club. Don't forget I was a single father after Heather's mother died. She left me alone with a daughter who had anxiety problems. I didn't have the luxury of deciding whether I would stay home with her or not. I had a career. A job to do to keep the family afloat. And so do you. Sometimes you just need to do what you have to do." He raised his glass. "No guilt. No blame." He took a sip of his drink, then put his glass back on the table.

"I'm hungry," he said, and signaled for the waitress.

Cara sat quietly and considered what he'd said, as well as what Toy had said. *If mama is happy, the family is happy.* She didn't need to belabor this decision. That wasn't her style, anyway. Cara knew what she was going to do.

"I'm going to take the job," she said.

David grinned. "Good! Congratulations."

The waitress showed up with her pad and pen.

"Champagne," he ordered.

Chapter Nineteen

An innate instinct leads hatchlings in the direction
of the brightest light, which in nature is moonlight reflecting
off the ocean. Lighting from man-made sources such as street-
lights, city sky glow, lights from commercial establishments,
beachfront homes, and pool lights disorient sea turtles. People
on the beach carrying flashlights, lighting bonfires, and using
landscape lighting can also disorient hatchlings and send
them racing toward land and certain death.

SEPTEMBER CAME AND Cara felt the change of seasons in her marrow. The sky was still crisp blue, the air balmy. If she stepped into the ocean she knew it would feel like bathwater. But there was a subtle shift she couldn't explain. There was the hint of fall in the air. And with September, the world of the island changed.

Peace was restored on the small island for its approximately four thousand residents. Tourists visited year-round, but the heavy toll came during the summer months. Cara, like every other resident, welcomed the easing of congestion. But the peace came at a price: with September came the peak of the active hurricane season. Right on schedule, a tropical storm was brewing in the Caribbean. Weather forecasters were watching this one and already creating computer programs of potential routes the storm could take.

The weather on Isle of Palms, however, was still blissful. The ferry ride to Dewees was as smooth as silk. Tonight a merry group was heading for a small preview show of Heather's paintings at the Dewees Community Center. Emmi and Flo sat with Cara and Hope inside the ferry in companionable silence, each enjoying the magnificent view of the sun setting over the Intracoastal Waterway. They were dressed to the nines for the event, Emmi in emerald green that complemented her fiery hair, Flo in crisp white linen and pearls. Cara wore a dress she hadn't worn in more than ten years—a long black silk ablaze with Hawaiian red hibiscus flowers. Lovie had thought she looked so chic in this dress, with her dark hair worn up and a bit of red lipstick. Cara had seen the dress in the back of her closet and, thinking of her mother, slipped it on.

The rest of the troupe was sitting on the upper deck. Linnea and John had joined their coterie of friends, a group Linnea liked to call the Islands Surf Team. The boys had all known one another from childhood, and the women had found they had a lot in common. Toy and Ethan were having a rare night out without their kids. Cara was delighted to see Toy resplendent in red silk that delicately showed off her baby bump. Ethan's cousin, Blake Legare, had joined them with his wife, Carson. Linnea had become especially close with Carson, a fellow surfer. Toy, meanwhile, had formed a tight friendship with Heather. Toy was teaching Heather about turtles, and Heather took Toy out for birding events. Cara smiled, thinking how nice it was to see the young people form friendships that could last lifelong. Sometimes life worked out that way, she thought. They all seemed to get along famously.

September was bringing changes for her as well. She stared out at the water and brought to mind for the hundredth time the long conversation she'd had with Kevin Mills at the South Carolina Aquarium.

"Penny for your thoughts," said Emmi.

Cara swung her head around to meet Emmi's green-eyed gaze. She smiled, knowing her best friend knew her so well she couldn't keep anything from her.

"I was thinking about the job offer again."

Flo overheard and leaned forward on the long, padded bench to speak past Emmi. "You should take it," she said in her matter-of-fact manner.

Cara and Emmi shared a commiserating gaze. "I'm considering it," Cara said, shifting Hope from her lap to the padded seat beside her. "Kevin was very complimentary. Still, that means working full-time with a child at home. I don't want to fail."

"You've never failed at a thing, from what I can tell," Flo said.

"You're working all the time anyway," Emmi argued. "You call it part-time, but we both know you're giving your consult business one hundred percent."

"What's holding you up?" asked Flo.

"Nothing's holding me up. Kevin and I have begun a discussion in earnest. It's an honor to be asked to head up a new department and it's truly an exciting position. It's as though all the years of advertising and marketing in Chicago, running the ecotour business for Brett, and doing public relations for the Tennessee Aquarium have prepared me for the breadth and scope of being conservation director."

"You're uniquely qualified," Emmi said. "They're lucky to have you."

Cara loved Emmi for being her best cheerleader. "I'm the lucky one. Toy would have been an asset too. Still . . ." She paused to gaze at Hope, who had climbed to her feet and was looking out, spellbound by the scenery flashing by her window. Cara put her hand on the baby's bottom to steady her, her heart pumping with affection. "There are ramifications to be considered for Hope, for our future."

"Like what?" Emmi asked.

"You know how long I waited for a child. It's hard to leave her behind." She sighed and said, almost to herself, "I know she'll be fine. I found a wonderful day care for her. So far she really likes being there. I think all the playdates with Rory made a difference."

"Of course she'll be fine," Flo said. "She'll be surrounded by love. From all of us. No child will be loved more." She paused, reflecting. "I never had children," she said. Her blue eyes were as bright as torches. "It was my decision. And I love children. I spent my adult life in social services helping them. In one way, I had hundreds of children—I gave my life to them. But I knew myself. I needed to work in a bigger picture. I wasn't fit for staying home. Knowing that, I made choices. I've no regrets. And," she said with a softening of her expression, "I had two special little girls who were like my own daughters."

Emmi and Cara both chimed in with declarations of affection.

Emmi wiped her eyes. "Please, stop with all this emotion. You're going to ruin my makeup."

Cara laughed fondly at her bighearted friend.

Flo, by contrast, was never comfortable with displays of emotion. She shifted the sweater in her lap, then looked up again, her gaze clear-eyed.

"What I'm trying to tell you," she said in all seriousness, taking time to look at both Cara and Emmi, "I've known you both all your lives. Cara"—Flo focused her attention on her—"you've always been an academic. A real go-getter. And frankly, you're a bit citified too." She put up her hand. "Don't get riled. It's who you are. You won't be happy staying home, talking to children and baking cookies. Unlike Emmi, who was always good with art and crafts. She thrived being a full-time mom. And she was fortunate to have a husband who could support her.

"Cara, dear, you thrive in the business world. Ignore comments from others about how a good mom stays at home. You need to experience the personal satisfaction that your decision is best for you and your child. Heavens, millions of children with working parents have grown into successful, loving adults. The same goes for children with a mother—or a father, for that matter—staying home. Even if you feel confident today about whichever decision you make, there will be days doubt creeps in. You'll feel you've made a mistake, or that you're getting the short end of the stick. Just know that your decision doesn't have to be permanent. You can always go back to work, or you can leave your job later if now's not the right time. Look at Emmi. Her children are grown, she's single again, and now she's happy managing a shop. Life is a long series of choices. All we can do is make the best decision we can at every turn, hope for the best, and deal with the consequences."

Emmi turned to Cara, for once speechless. There was nothing left to say.

Cara felt Flo's words were swirling in her mind and taking root. "Thank you, Flo. I needed to hear that."

Hope squealed and started pointing. They all turned to see what the fuss was about. Out in the lavender water that reflected the changing skies, three dolphins frolicked in the boat's wake, arching and diving, creating a show for Hope, who watched, utterly thrilled. Cara joined in with the chorus of "Look!" and "Ahhh!" Watching the dolphins, laughing with her loved ones, she felt the weight of her thoughts dissipate into the air like the droplets of water outside the window.

David and Bo met them at the dock with golf carts to take them to the Dewees Community Center. David drove the large "limo" cart to handle the group. The center was bustling with a good crowd. Judy Fairchild welcomed them at the door and guided them to the drinks and refreshments.

Heather floated across the room to greet them all with a great show of welcome. She wore a blush-colored lace dress that swirled around her ankles, and her blond hair was loosely curled and flowed past her shoulders. At her neck she wore an impressive necklace of diamonds, with more diamonds in her ears. Cara remembered the painfully shy girl who had come to the beach house only four years earlier. It was a joy to see how she'd blossomed. Marriage and motherhood suited her, and tonight she was celebrating the preview of her first art show.

David came to Cara's side, debonair in a formal dinner suit and carrying a flute of champagne. Her heart skipped a beat.

"Don't you look handsome," she commented, taking the wine.

He nodded, smiling. "Thank you. And may I compliment you on your dress."

She sipped her wine and their eyes met over the rims of their glasses.

"Shall we take a spin around the room?" he asked.

Cara was eager to see the collection. For this exhibit, Heather had culled from her larger collection only paintings of shorebirds, knowing that the residents of Dewees were proud to house a major shorebird sanctuary. The songbirds and other pieces she was reserving for her Charlotte show. There was a buzz of excitement in the room, lots of exclamations.

"I'm so happy for Heather to see such a turnout," Cara said.

"And all the red dots," David added, pointing out the small red dots in the corners of the painting labels that indicated a work was sold.

"Already?" Cara was a little stunned. She felt a thread of trepidation. The show had only just opened. And yet, she wasn't surprised. She paused before a painting of a heron spreading its wings in the sunlight. The feathers appeared almost transparent. "Heather's talent has grown exponentially," she said in hushed awe. "For one so young . . ."

They moved on, each painting more beautiful than the last. Cara kept her eyes open for one painting in particular, however. And when at last she spied it, she tugged at David's sleeve. "Over there," she said, urging him along. "There's the one I've come for.

The roseate spoonbills. I saw the beginnings of it in the tree-house studio, remember? I haven't been able to get it out of my mind since then. Hurry!"

They cut across the room to where two couples stood admiring the painting. Cara and David were tall enough to look over their shoulders.

"Oh, David," Cara said on a sigh.

"Like it?"

"Love it. I am overwhelmed. It's beyond my expectations." She let her gaze wander the brilliantly rendered painting of a trio of roseate spoonbills standing in the water, their pale-pink plumage catching sunlight, and their reflection mirrored in the water. The cluster of people moved on to the next painting, allowing Cara space to walk to the small cream-colored card describing the painting and the price. The price was surprisingly steep. Cara hadn't realized Heather's art had reached that level already. But her breath caught when she saw the small red dot in the corner of the card.

"Oh no. It's sold," she said, feeling crushed.

David looked around the room. He was a head taller than most of the people and had a clear view. "Most of them are. It's like a fire sale. People are rushing to find something available. Isn't it marvelous?"

"Yes, of course." She made a resigned face. "But I'm so disappointed *this* painting was sold. I meant to buy it."

"Did you?" he asked, surprised.

"Don't you remember? I saw this painting in its early stage up in the studio. I came here tonight secretly hoping to buy it. But it's already sold." She sighed heavily and looked around the room for Heather. "Do you think she'd do another? On commission?"

"I would think so, but she's very busy now, of course."

"I know, but I could discuss it with her. Heather introduced me to the roseate spoonbills and I've been mad for them ever since. Maybe she'll give me a friends-and-family discount. Where is she?"

"Cara . . ."

"Oh, there she is," Cara exclaimed, spotting Heather standing with a group of admirers, probably new patrons. "Let's go find out."

David reached out for her elbow and gently held her back. "Cara . . ."

Cara turned and looked into his eyes. His heavy brows were knitted, and he seemed unsure about something. She felt suddenly awkward. "I was only kidding about the friends-and-family discount," she said.

David laughed lightly and shook his head. "No, I'm sure that's not a problem. You make this difficult."

Cara stepped closer, intrigued. "What's that?"

David sighed with mock exasperation. "I bought this painting."

"*You* bought it?"

"Yes. As a present. For you."

Cara stared back at him, speechless.

"It was meant for your birthday. So . . ." He smiled. "Happy birthday, a few months early."

"You bought this for me?"

"Yes. I remembered how much you loved it."

Cara stared at him. He'd noticed how much she loved the painting. . . .

"Please don't tell me you can't accept it," he said.

"I shouldn't."

"But you will."

She couldn't stop the smile from blooming on her face. "Only if you tell me you got the friends-and-family discount."

"Of course."

"Then yes. Oh, David, I love it. I can't remember the last time I loved a gift more. Not even my Burberry bag. And not just for the gift, but because you noticed. You really are spoiling me."

"That is my intention." His eyes kindled and he captured her gaze as he leaned forward.

Cara's breath held as she lifted her chin. Their first kiss. She felt his approach in millimeters. The buzz around them silenced in her ears as all her senses were focused on the man before her. The sight of him, the scent of his cologne, the feel of the wool of his jacket as she lifted her hand up to lightly touch his arm that slid around her waist. When his lips touched hers, she felt a searing heat shoot through her, igniting her. Ice broke around her heart as it began beating rapidly. It was the softest of kisses, one of great restraint. One that held promise. A whisper of a moan escaped her throat when David pulled back. Blinking, she looked at him again and saw that he was as shaken by the kiss as she.

"Excuse me."

Cara tore her gaze from David and turned to see Emmi standing at her side. In her arms Hope was chewing one of her teething biscuits, looking tired. The old matchmaker was smiling like the Cheshire cat.

"I hate to interrupt," she began teasingly. Her wide mouth

couldn't suppress the grin. "But this little one is conking out. Her awnings are lowering."

"Yes, of course," Cara said, and reached out to lift Hope into her arms. Hope cuddled up and laid her head on Cara's shoulder. "We should go. What time is it?"

"Seven forty-five," Emmi said. "If we leave now, we can make the next ferry."

Cara turned to face David, her gaze imploring. "I hate to ask you to leave your daughter's party . . ."

"The party seems to be breaking up," he said.

Cara looked around and saw that many of the visitors were saying good-bye and leaving for home in a rush. In fact, it looked rather like a mass exodus.

"What's happened?" she asked.

Heather approached, her eyes wide with fear. "We just heard. The tropical storm was upgraded to a hurricane. They're calling this one Irma. And it's headed straight for us."

~~~~~

THE STORM HAD begun as a tropical wave off the coast of Africa. Over the next few days it coalesced into a tropical storm and was given the name Irma. During the next twenty-four hours the storm grew highly organized and met with favorable warm surface-water temperatures and low wind shear. Shortly thereafter the rapidly intensifying storm developed a distinct eye feature with sustained winds up to 115 miles per hour. The storm, now Hurricane Irma, was fast becoming an extremely powerful and possibly catastrophic Cape Verde–type hurricane, the strongest and potentially deadliest observed in the Atlantic in more than a decade.

The hurricane was driving everyone in the Caribbean and along the southeastern coast of the United States frantic. It kept shifting directions, sending the experts back to their computers to reveal new tracking cones, which in turn sent another group of residents panicking and laying in supplies. The only thing the experts agreed upon was that Hurricane Irma was heading toward Florida, but where exactly they couldn't predict.

On Isle of Palms, Cara felt a distinct heaviness in the air. It was not something she could describe, but she knew it when she felt it. She called it *hurricane air*. It might've been the barometric pressure, or possibly the dense moisture in the air. Or, too, it could have been her instincts rearing up from a lifetime of experience. Regardless, an uncomfortable panic was building in her chest as she raced from store to store gathering emergency provisions.

Linnea, however, was ecstatic. She and John joined a legion of local surfers and hit the ocean to ride the "hurricane waves." Waves of this height and strength only came during storms. Among the surfers there was lots of bravado talk about riding out the storm. There was always the one who claimed he never left the island for a storm and never would leave. There were others who wanted to ride just one more of the good waves before they had to hurry home and shutter up the house. Regardless of their evacuation plans, everyone acknowledged that this monster storm that had been upgraded to a Category Five was not to be ignored.

John and Linnea strapped their surfboards on the roof of his truck and were headed back home when they met up with the bumper-to-bumper traffic on Palm Boulevard heading toward the Connector for points north. Since most of the tourists had already left at the first whiff of the storm's approach, all the cars were likely local residents. John turned on the radio.

"I wonder if they called mandatory evacuation," Linnea said, feeling the age-old chill run down her spine. "Lord, we'd better get back. Cara must be frantic."

John was looking at the weather alert on his phone. "The current cone of travel has Irma heading up the coast. I heard from Ethan that the governor called for mandatory evacuation for barrier islands south of us. So far, Isle of Palms seems to be dodging the bullet, at least for a head-on collision. But the storm's still coming so he's racing back to the aquarium. They have a mammoth job ahead of them getting the place battened down."

Linnea felt herself shrink inside, like a turtle seeking safety.

They waited at the STOP sign for what seemed forever, but the train of cars kept coming.

"Won't they let us in?" Linnea asked, exasperated and anxious.

John lowered the window and waved his hand. At last a Good Samaritan slowed to a stop and let him make his left turn onto Palm Boulevard. John waved his arm in thanks, pulled out, and hit the gas.

"It's a good thing I postponed my flight," he said with a shake of his head at the sight of the long line of cars on Palm Boulevard. "There's no way it would have gotten out. They're going to shut down the airports."

"Is your mother all packed up?"

"Yeah. I got all the shutters up. We're tight and secure," he said with satisfaction. "But, damn, there're a lot of frigging windows in that house. As soon as we get back I'll get started on yours."

"No worries. David and Bo said they were coming to finish the beach house for Cara today. Other than that, we got all the emergency supplies—we have food and water, and Cara's packed her photographs, important papers, and insurance records. Our suitcases are by the door, ready to go."

"When do you leave?" he asked.

"As soon as Cara does. I'm going home first. Daddy and Cooper are closing up the house and then we're all meeting up at the lodge. We'll be safe upstate. The worst we'll get there is a lot of rain and mud. And you?"

"Mom and Flo made reservations at some hotel in Columbia. I'm guessing we'll head out tonight."

She reached over to put her hand on his knee. He swung his head to look at her, his eyes meeting hers.

"Do you want to come with me?" he asked.

He'd asked her several times to join him, as had Cara. "No, thanks, I want to be with my family."

They pulled into John's driveway and parked the truck. There was an anxious silence. Both of them were aware that they were going soon to different places, that it was the end of the summer, that John would leave for California in a few days, and that they didn't know what the future held.

Linnea looked out the window and spotted Cara carrying a box to her red Volvo.

"I'd better go," she said. She didn't move.

John reached across the seat and took her hand. She looked

over to him. His red-tinged hair was still wet, slicked back, and a drop of water trailed down his temple. She felt the energy pulsing in his green eyes.

"Linnea," he began tentatively. He looked at their joined hands. "Regardless of what happens, whether we get clobbered with a Cat Five or we amble back home after dodging another hurricane, we both know I have to leave for California. Time's run out, Linnea." He looked up, his piercing gaze pinning her. "Are you joining me?"

Linnea puffed up her cheeks and blew out a plume of air. "Oh, Lord, John, don't ask me now."

"I'm not trying to pressure you," he said with a gentle tug on her hand. "But I'll say this one more time. You should go after that job in San Francisco. At least take the interview. It's the best offer you've had. Plus, you know you have a place to stay."

"I know. . . ."

"What are you afraid of?"

"I told you," she said with emphasis. "Daddy will go nuclear that I'm running off to what he thinks is Sodom and Gomorrah without being . . ." She stopped. She couldn't say the *m* word. "You know."

"Married."

The word dropped like a bomb. Linnea felt blown to bits, but only shrugged. "Yes. That's what he wants for me." She glared at him. "I didn't say it's what I wanted."

John's expression changed, and Linnea could see he was struggling.

"I care for you, Linnea," he said. "A lot. You know that."

She didn't respond.

"But marriage is a big step," he continued. "I don't think either of us is ready for that."

"I'm not." She said it defiantly. Though in the most secret spot of her heart, her feminine pride was hurt that he didn't at least offer to marry her.

"Come to California," John told her. "See how you feel. Check out the job. You might not want it. So much is up in the air. No pun intended."

She smirked.

"Let's take it one day at a time."

She looked at their hands, thinking of all he'd said, but couldn't think of a thing to say. So she remained quiet.

"Lin," he said, emotion sliding into his voice. "Look at me?"

She lifted her gaze. His eyes were pulsing with sincerity.

"I think we have something very special between us. Let's give it a chance. See where it takes us. And who knows? We might end up coming back here." He laughed shortly. "You'd like that, wouldn't you?"

"Maybe," she conceded, looking at their joined hands and trying not to smile.

John reached out to lift her chin. Reluctantly, she looked into his eyes. His green eyes . . . She'd fallen in love with his eyes first. She didn't want to fall in love. Not yet. Why did he have to come along when she was least ready for him? He clearly wasn't ready for her. *Just go*, she cried in her breaking heart.

"You're my best friend. My surfing buddy. The first person I think of when I wake up and the last person before I sleep. I love you," he said.

Linnea crumbled. Her defenses were destroyed. She knew what it took for him to utter those words. Her heart rallied and joyfully surrendered. She wasn't ashamed of the tears that flooded her eyes.

He saw the tears and grinned. "Does that help?"

She stared back at him for a moment, making him wait. Then she lunged forward to wrap her arms around him. "Yes," she said, kissing his neck, her tears mingling with the ocean's salt water. She laughed out loud and looked into his face. "Took you long enough."

"What?" he asked, incredulous. "You're the first girl I've ever said that to. Other than my mother."

Linnea softened and leaned back against the door, facing him. "Really?" she asked dubiously.

He looked sheepish, having said too much. "You know it's true," he said. "You're driving me crazy, Linnea Rutledge. And I love you!" he said louder. "There. I said it again. So now, what do you say? Will you come to California?"

Linnea nodded and whispered, "Yes." Then with a hearty groan she put her face in her hands. "Oh, God, now I have to tell my father."

Chapter Twenty

All six sea turtle species found in U.S. waters or using U.S. beaches are designated as threatened or endangered under the Endangered Species Act. Endangered status means a species is considered in danger of extinction. Threatened means that a species is likely to become endangered. The ESA provides penalties for taking, harassing, or harming sea turtles and affords some protection for their habitat.

CARA LOOKED UP in the sky and saw the telltale thin, watery clouds stretching from the ocean toward the mainland. These were hurricane bands, and they looked like no other. To her, they resembled fingers reaching out in a menacing grasp, as though the storm were clawing its way inland. She felt an involuntary shudder and clasped her arms around herself.

David came up behind her and wrapped his long arms around her. Perspicacious as usual, she thought, and leaned back into his strength. She closed her eyes, relishing the safety she felt there, something she never thought she'd feel again.

"Don't be nervous," he told her. He leaned down and put his mouth by her face. She felt the faint scratch of stubble against her tender cheek. "The last shutter is in place. You're all safe and secure."

"Thank you," she said with a weary exhale.

"Did I tell you how much I hate those aluminum shutters?"

"Twenty-two times," she replied. "Once for every window."

"You need to get roll-downs. Or replace your windows with hurricane glass. That's what my house has. Makes hurricane season a breeze. Pun intended."

"Oh, sure," she replied, turning in his arms. "As soon as I win the lottery." She looked over at her little house, all boarded up with the aluminum shutters at every window. It looked cold and dreary, not at all the welcoming beach house.

"I shouldn't be so jittery," she said, a bit embarrassed. "I've been through hurricanes all of my life. It's part and parcel of living along the coast. Back in the day, we put plywood up on the windows." She laughed. "If you think aluminum shutters are tough, try those. I still have slivers. I don't remember my parents doing much for the house in Charleston. We may have moved furniture to the upper floors and taken mirrors off the wall, that kind of thing. Mostly we just hopped in the car and headed for the country. My daddy liked to say that's what he had insurance for. For better or worse, Charleston's endured a long history of hurricanes."

"Maybe. But not a whole lot of Cat Fives."

She sucked in her breath. "No," she agreed. "The last big one was Hugo. And remember what that storm did." She shuddered. "Every summer when the hurricane forecasts come out, we all shake our heads and say we're due for another big one. It's not if but when." She looked at David, sought his understanding. "That kind of thinking takes its toll over time. The tension and fear . . ." She paused. "They slowly build up like a disease until, smack, one year hurricane season hits and you're paralyzed and you realize that you have PTSD. That's what I have. Really. Too many years of trauma from staying on this island and weathering storms."

"Why did you stay and not evacuate?"

"Brett," she answered succinctly. "He never left. Not ever for Category One hurricanes. He had his fleet of boats to take care of. That was his livelihood. They had to be battened down or moved to a different location. Every fall we lived listening to the weather reports round the clock. Even now, the TV is on, blaring the weather stations. The meteorologists all say the same thing over and over, but each time a bulletin is released we come running like it's the first time we've heard it. I live in constant readiness to flee."

"That's how you're supposed to feel. It's not smart to get complacent."

"Well, this time, I'm running," she said emphatically. "I've got Hope to think about."

"Right." He narrowed his eyes. "Where are you headed?"

"To some hotel in Columbia. Emmi made the reservations. I've got it all written down inside."

David put his hands on his hips. "Why go to a hotel? Come to my place in the mountains. It's right outside of Asheville."

Cara was taken aback. "You've never mentioned before that you have a house in Asheville."

"It's never come up till now." Seeing her dubious reaction, he grinned and said, "For the sake of transparency, I have a house in Costa Rica, too. Look, it's no big deal. Lots of folks from Charlotte have cabins in Asheville or a house near the lake. My wife loved the mountains, so we went there." He rubbed his jaw. "I haven't been in a while. I'm pretty content on Dewees. But Heather and Bo have gone up a few times this summer. She's always loved it there, which is the main reason I hang on to it. They're on their way now, as a matter of fact. With Rory."

"That's good. I'm glad they've left." She rubbed her arms in anxiety. All this talk of evacuation was making her nervous.

"It's a place you can go. Will you come? Bring Linnea, too."

"But I'm supposed to meet Emmi and Flo."

"Bring them, too."

"Is there room for us all?"

"We'll squeeze you in somehow. It'll be better than a hotel."

Cara put her fingertips to her forehead, gathering her thoughts. "Linnea is going home, so she won't come. The family will go upstate to the hunting lodge. I was invited, of course, but . . ." She looked up and saw David standing like a mountain against the changing sky. He was offering her safe refuge.

And, she knew, so much more.

"Thank you. Yes. I'll go with you."

~~~~~

LINNEA WOKE WHEN her phone rang. She reached out to grab it, her first thought being not to awaken the baby. The house felt muggy, the air thick. She put the phone to her ear, noticing that the night was still black. Good news never came in the middle of the night.

"Hello?" Her voice was scratchy for lack of sleep.

"Linnea? It's Mama."

Linnea heard something in her mother's voice that had her sitting bolt upright in the bed, clutching the phone. "What's the matter, Mama?"

"It's Cooper," she said in a hoarse voice. Linnea heard the tears in it. "He's in the hospital. MUSC."

"What?" Linnea said on a breath. Her mind was spinning as fast as her heart rate. She envisioned a car accident. Broken glass. Blood. "Is he okay? What happened?"

"Yes. No . . ." She choked back a cry. "It was an overdose."

It took a few moments for Linnea to take that in. "I'll be right there."

"Don't come yet. They won't let you see him. He's still in treatment. It could be hours yet."

She had thoughts of coma and brain damage. "How bad is he?"

"We don't know yet. Oh, Linnea . . ."

"I'm on my way."

～～～

LINNEA DRESSED QUICKLY, then hurried down the dark hall to waken Cara. She roused with a start, immediately on alert.

"What?" she said with alarm. "Is it Hope?"

"No, nothing like that."

Linnea's voice was shaky as she told her the news. Cara bolted from the bed.

"I can dress quickly. Would you get Hope ready?"

"You don't have to come to the hospital."

"But of course I'm going to the hospital." In typical fashion, Cara began making quick decisions as her hands dug through her drawer. "We'll caravan to the hospital," she told Linnea. "We'll go on to evacuate afterward. It's good the cars are already packed up. Let's just close up here and leave now. I'll call David later and let him know what we will do once . . ." She paused to find the right words. "Once we know the situation."

"Cara, wait."

Cara stopped and turned toward her, underwear in hand. Her face was puzzled.

"It could be hours before they'll even let us see Cooper. You can't wait in the hospital with Hope that long." Cara opened her mouth to argue, but Linnea pushed on. "Second, the storm is coming. You need to get out."

"There's time."

"Cara, don't wait. Go back to sleep and leave in the morning with David, as planned."

"I can't just leave y'all for North Carolina. You're my family."

"Hope is your family. Your child."

Cara took a step closer to Linnea and put her hands on her shoulders, looking her directly in the eyes. "Linnea, you and Cooper have been my children all your lives. A natural mother couldn't love you more. I'm going."

Linnea stepped into Cara's arms. "A daughter couldn't love her mother more."

～～～

THE NIGHT WAS as dark as pitch and so humid Linnea could hardly catch her breath. Not the moon, not a beam of light from the stars, could penetrate the heavy cloud cover over the lowcountry. The house next door was dark. John and his mother had left for Columbia with Flo. She suddenly missed John and wished he were with her now. She felt terribly alone in her little car.

Linnea followed the tiny red brake lights of Cara's car as she drove over the murky blackness of the Connector. It was eerie, like driving into nothingness. Her hands gripped the steering wheel, and she counted the minutes.

The traffic was light at this hour and they made it to the hospital in good time. Though the parking lot was packed, many of the cars belonged to locals seeking high ground in case of flooding. Linnea circled the lot in search of a space, cursing. At last she found a spot that was debatably illegal, but she could just squeeze her Mini Cooper in.

She met Cara and Hope at the entrance. They raced through the halls to the emergency-room waiting area. The few people sitting in the chairs either looked sick or seemed to be waiting for news about someone who was sick. They sat with vacant stares or their heads resting in their palms.

Cara and Linnea went directly to the nurse sitting behind the wide, polished entrance desk, a heavyset woman with a cup of coffee by her side. When she glanced up, her cold eyes revealed that she had seen it all. She promptly directed them to a different waiting room. A security guard opened the door into a wide and long cream-colored hall branching off into a maze of other corridors. They walked in silence, their heels clicking on the polished floors. Linnea's heart was pounding and she felt each step like she'd run a mile. At last they pushed through a set of heavy doors into a second waiting room. Linnea immediately spotted her mother and father sitting in chairs some distance from each other, neither one speaking, staring into space.

"Mama!" Linnea began running.

"Linnea!"

Linnea felt her mother's arms around her and held her tight. "Mama," she cried again. At last she could let the tears flow. "I've been so worried." She took a step back and wiped her eyes. "How's Cooper?"

"No further word. We're just waiting."

Across the room, Cara was talking to Palmer in hushed tones. When their eyes met, he held out his arms. Linnea ran into them. These were the arms she was accustomed to, warm and strong.

"Oh, Daddy," she cried.

Palmer released her and put his hands on his hips. His face was flushed, his eyes glazed with disbelief, like a man in shock. "This is so terrible. A drug overdose! *My* son . . ."

"How did he get to the hospital?" Cara asked. "Was he home?"

"No," Julia spoke up. "His friends brought him in."

Palmer screwed up his face and looked at Linnea. "Did you know he was using drugs?"

Linnea shifted her gaze to her mother. Julia stared back at her with a sunken, haunted expression. Linnea was filled with a sudden fury. She wanted to scream at her, *I told you to watch him!* But how could she blame her mother? What had she herself done to intervene?

Cara stepped in. "We all wondered if he was using drugs. I told you we were worried last time I saw you. And you brushed me off. Told me to go home."

He stared back at her blankly, then his shoulders slumped and he put his hand to his forehead. "I didn't believe you. Damnation. How could this happen to a family like ours?" he asked, anger seeping into his words. "How could Cooper do this to us?" Palmer paced the room, restless. He stopped before Linnea. "I can't imagine you doing something like this. You've always been a good girl. A real comfort to us."

"He didn't do it to hurt the family," Linnea cried. "He did it because he was hurting. He tried to tell you, Daddy. And you too, Mama." She burst into tears. "But you didn't listen."

Palmer swung his head to pin Julia with his stare. "You knew about this?"

Julia, pale and drawn, had no will to fight. She just turned her back on him.

"Palmer, this isn't the time for blame," said Cara. "I'd say this was the time for prayer. Let's all sit down and silently say our own prayers for Cooper."

Palmer's face sagged as if the wind had blown out of him. He nodded in agreement and walked with the stooped pace of an old man to an empty chair.

They sat in relative silence for another hour and a half. Linnea crossed her arms and leaned back in the remarkably uncomfortable chair. Hope was asleep in Cara's arms. Julia had turned down the volume of the television in the waiting room so they could close their eyes.

At last a nurse came out to talk with them. Beside her was a man in blue scrubs who was so thin and young that Linnea couldn't guess whether he was a resident or a physician. He was carrying a clipboard in one hand. His other hand he stretched out in greeting. Julia stepped forward to take his hand, followed by Palmer.

"I'm Dr. Foster, the resident on call tonight. You must be the Rutledges."

Palmer cleared his throat. "Yes."

Dr. Foster lowered his clipboard. "The good news is your son is doing well. He was admitted with opiates on board. We administered a shot of Narcan, which woke him up. He wasn't very coherent. But he did say it wasn't a suicide attempt."

"Thank God," Julia said.

"Of course it wasn't a suicide attempt," Palmer blustered, but his face had grown ashen at the suggestion.

"Has he been depressed?" asked Dr. Foster, pushing on. "Is there any family history of suicide or depression? Drug use?"

"No," Palmer said with alacrity.

"Well, actually . . ." Linnea spoke up. She walked toward the doctor, avoiding looking at her parents. "I thought he seemed depressed. Not his usual self."

The doctor wrote in the file, then looked up and asked Linnea, "And you are?"

"His sister."

Understanding reflected in the doctor's face.

"He wasn't depressed," Palmer repeated.

"He's being stabilized now," the doctor continued, unfazed by Palmer's insistence. "Psychiatry is coming to see him. Whether they'll decide to keep him or not, we don't know yet."

"Psychiatry?" asked Julia with alarm. "But you said it wasn't a suicide attempt."

"My son doesn't need to go to a psych ward," declared Palmer.

"Your son was in pretty bad shape when he arrived," Dr. Foster said. "He wasn't awake enough to get much information from him. He'll stay here until he's seen by Psychiatry and . . ." He paused and looked at Julia. "As soon as he is, he'll be transferred to the psychiatric hospital."

"But—" Palmer began, his face coloring.

"Palmer . . ." Cara said softly in warning.

"Mr. Rutledge," Dr. Foster said with compassion, turning to address him. "Cooper is denying that this was a suicide attempt. But he could easily have killed himself. He doesn't appreciate the gravity of that. The fact that he doesn't concerns us. He needs to be observed for a while. He'll also get some needed therapy." He glanced briefly at Linnea. "His friends who brought him in also reported that he'd been depressed."

Palmer didn't speak.

"Can we see him?" Julia asked, stepping forward. "Please. We've been here all night."

The doctor looked at the nurse and nodded. He spoke kindly to Julia. "He's awake. He may not be terribly lucid. But yes. You can see him. For a short visit. The nurse will give you information about the psych hospital and visiting hours." He raised the clipboard to his chest. "Okay then," he said by way of conclusion. "I'm glad this was good news. There've been far too many cases of opiate overdoses brought in. Not all of them end up nearly so well."

With a final nod, the doctor turned and hurried through the double doors.

The nurse was a short, slender woman with tight black curls. Small, but she gave off a vibe that you wouldn't want to cross her.

"This way, please. I'll bring you to your son."

Julia hurried to grab her purse and sweater. Cara rose slowly so as not to wake the baby. Linnea followed her mother and father through the double doors and down a wide, brightly lit corridor with white and pale-blue flooring. Emergency room beds lined the walls, and around each were curtains that could be drawn shut when privacy was needed. A few were closed, and Linnea could hear soft voices emanating from behind. Men and women in blue scrubs with stethoscopes around their necks were all hard at work.

Their nurse stopped in front of one curtained cubicle in the middle of the room. It looked like so many others. Her stern expression slackened some.

"Right in here. As the doctor said, this can only be a short visit. We're expecting the psych eval any moment." She extended her arm, indicating they should go in.

Julia rushed to the side of the bed. Cooper's eyes appeared sunken but they followed his mother, filling with tears.

"Cooper," Julia said in a choked voice, grasping his hand. "My baby."

"I'm sorry, Mama," Cooper said, his voice thick and raspy. "I'm so sorry."

Palmer stood at the end of the bed with Cara. Cooper looked over to him and cried, "I'm sorry."

Palmer stared back at his son, working his mouth, but words didn't come.

Linnea followed her mother to the side of the white plastic bed and leaned over the metal side rail. She let her gaze travel to her brother's, and her voice caught in her throat. She didn't recognize him. Cooper was rail thin; his dark eyes seemed huge in his face. But most shocking, his hair, his beautiful dark curls, had been shorn off like a sheep's coat. His scalp was pale against the stubs of dark brown.

"They shaved your head," she said sorrowfully, shaking her head.

Cooper looked at her drowsily. "Yeah. I'm a knob."

Linnea tried to laugh, but it came out more of a choked sob.

Cooper's face scrunched up, and it embarrassed her to see him cry. "I . . . I didn't try to hurt myself," he forced out. "I swear I didn't."

"I know, honey," Julia said, wiping the tears from his face with a handkerchief. "Of course you didn't."

"What happened?" asked Palmer.

Cooper's eyes darted to the bottom of the bed where his father stood. Linnea saw fear shift in his eyes.

"I don't know. Sir."

"What do you mean, you don't know? You OD'd! You were doing drugs."

"Yes, sir."

"Palmer, let's not get into that now," Julia said tersely, delivering Palmer a fierce look. If she were a tigress, she would have been snarling.

"This is going to be a problem," Palmer told Cooper. "I did what I could about that DUI. But this . . ." He shook his head and gripped the metal railing of the bed. "Hell. This is the kind of thing that can get you bounced from the Citadel."

"Daddy," Linnea said sharply. She leaned over her brother toward her father, tears flooding her eyes. "Aren't you listening? He doesn't want to go there."

"It's okay, Lin," Cooper said, reaching for her.

"Sure he does. Tell them, Cooper. Tell them you want to go back."

Cooper held his sister's hand and looked squarely at his father. "No," he said in a steady voice. "I don't. I'm not going back."

Palmer leaned forward, staring into his son's eyes. "What was that?"

Cara stepped into the argument. "Palmer, don't."

"I'm not going back," Cooper said again, with a fierceness born of desperation and determination.

The room fell into a stunned silence.

Palmer stared hard at his son. He said in a gravelly voice, roughened by emotion, "I'm disappointed in you."

Cooper's eyes reflected his crushed spirit. His whole body seemed to go limp, and Linnea realized he'd been holding himself stiffly the whole time they were there. She stared at her father, equally crushed. At any time such cutting words would be horrible, but now, when Cooper was so fragile, they were plain cussed cruel.

"How could you say such a thing to sweet Cooper?" she cried.

Cara faced her brother with Hope in her arms. "I'm disappointed in *you!*" she told him. "And I know Mama would be, too."

Palmer swung his head around and glared, shocked at her words. Then, without a word, he turned on his heel and walked away.

Chapter Twenty-One

*Marine debris comes in many forms, ranging from
small plastic cigarette butts to 4,000-pound derelict fishing
nets. Plastics in the ocean take days, weeks, and even decades to
break down. Debris may also be mistaken for food by marine
animals. Nets and fishing line negligently left in the sea
trap animals, which leads to injury and death.*

CARA SIGHED WITH relief when she turned off the highway toward Tryon, North Carolina. The traffic had been brutally slow. As feared, it was bumper-to-bumper with cars, campers, and trucks with southern license plates fleeing the hurricane. Hope was good, considering, crying herself to sleep for this final leg of the journey. They'd caravanned, pausing at gas stations for pit stops when the baby refused to settle. David was eminently patient, never checking his watch. Cara was grateful to be following David's massive Range Rover. He took it slow along winding, wooded roads through small mountain communities. Small shops and restaurants, each more charming than the last, lined the roads. From the looks of it, many people were stocking up after a long journey.

At last he turned off the main road to a narrow road that led through a bold wooden gate. Up they climbed, deeper into the woods, past tall hardwoods, dogwoods, pines, and Cara's much-loved rhododendrons. When they reached the top of the hill, suddenly the land cleared and in the center of soft green grass sat a massive log house. It was stunning, surrounded by broad porches replete with rocking chairs overlooking breathtaking long-range mountain views. A fleet of thunderclouds hovered low and fat, promising strong wind, thunder, and lightning. Cara drove around the circular gravel driveway to park near one of the front porches. She pulled the parking brake, then slowly climbed from the car. She leaned against the door, weary beyond words. She felt she had little left to give.

She heard the other car door close and turned her head to see David walking toward her across the gravel. He wore boots, dark jeans, and a white shirt rolled up his arms but his face appeared tired from the long, stressful drive.

"We made it," he said, stopping before her.

She offered him a crooked smile and gestured at the huge house. "You think you could squeeze me in?" she asked, teasing him with his own words.

His eyes crinkled at the corners. "How are you?"

"Tired. Sad. In need of a bath and sleep, in that order."

"And Hope?"

"Asleep in the backseat."

"We're all pretty tired. We can rest now."

Her gaze swept the magnificent log home with its long mountain views, the fenced pastures and barn. "It's stunning," she said. "I feel a million miles away from the beach. And from the storm. Thank you for inviting us to come."

"I'm glad you like it. I hoped you would." There passed a quiet communication between them that it was also important to him that she liked it. "Let's get you inside. Those clouds promise rain."

On cue, the wind gusted, tossing leaves and bits of dirt into the air. Cara looked out over the mountains toward the sea. An armada of clouds was traveling north. She said a quick prayer that her brother and the family would hunker down and be safe. The storm was upon them.

~~~~~

HURRICANE IRMA'S PREDICTED path shifted again in what the meteorologists called a wobble. The storm no longer had the Charleston coast in its sights and there was hope there'd be fewer calamities than predicted.

At least weather-wise.

It was late morning when Linnea and her mother walked the few short blocks from the hospital to the Institute of Psychiatry. The skies were overcast, the winds were blowing hard, and rain had started falling. But they weren't afraid. It seemed like any other serious thunderstorm.

The streets were deserted. Charlestonians were staying indoors as directed, hunkering down for the oncoming storm. Once in the psychiatric hospital, the two women stoically sat in the waiting room until Cooper was admitted. Julia needed to see for herself that her son was in good hands. When they were allowed, they met

Cooper in the dayroom where he would spend most of his day under observation. This was an airy, brightly lit community room with two-story windows. Cooper appeared calmer now but more despondent. The doctors assured them that this was normal as he began to comprehend the ramifications of his actions.

Linnea was exhausted and emotionally drained. She'd awoken at two in the morning. It was almost eleven. She needed to sleep. And so did her mother.

"Mama, there's nothing more we can do for him. And he's currently getting a lot more sleep than you and I combined."

"I'm not leaving him," Julia said stubbornly, shaking her head.

"I get it. But we have to take care of ourselves if we hope to help him. Let's go home, just for a little while. We can shower, grab some food, and pack a bag. Then we'll come back."

Her mother stared at her, numb with indecision.

"Please, Mama."

"Yes, fine," Julia said wearily. She clutched her purse close to her chest as she looked longingly over her shoulder at the dayroom. "But I do so hate to leave him here."

Linnea looked at her mother with almost maternal tenderness. She'd never seen her so disheveled. Not in public. Her usually impeccable appearance was altered—her ashen face was void of makeup, her hair in a haphazard ponytail, and she was wearing a lived-in sweater and jeans. Linnea was shocked to see she'd aged, too. Her face sagged with grief.

They walked the short distance from the Institute of Psychiatry back to the hospital garage. Linnea was stunned by the increased power of the storm as it moved closer. The wind was blowing so hard they had to raise their voices to be heard. When they reached the garage they decided to leave Linnea's Mini Cooper and drive Julia's substantial Mercedes. It was clearly the better choice to navigate Charleston's flooded streets.

"I'll drive," Linnea said, and she slipped in behind the wheel of the car. Julia offered no argument and slumped into the passenger seat. The garage was deserted as they drove to the exit.

The security guard looked at them like they were crazy. "You're not going out in that?"

"Not far," Linnea called out.

"We're coming back," her mother felt compelled to tell him.

"Be careful, ladies, and get home quick. And stay put. The storm may not be hitting us directly, but a king tide is predicted to combine with the storm surge. They're expecting a four- to six-foot surge. That means we're going to have some serious flooding, the worst since Hurricane Hugo. Yes, ma'am. I don't know about you, but I wouldn't want to get stuck in this hospital. It'll be a lake out there."

"Thank you," Linnea called out as they exited, feeling her heart rate accelerate with the engine.

Leaving the garage, they entered a storm whipping the air, stirring up debris. Rain began to beat the roof like a tom-tom. Neither woman spoke as Linnea crawled south along Rutledge Avenue toward Tradd. The water of Colonial Lake appeared as dark as steel.

The mile-long trip took twenty minutes. Linnea parked the car in the driveway and they scurried to the front door, ducking their heads and pushing through the squall. Once inside, they both sighed audibly when they closed the door against the tempest. The house was dim and quiet. Not a light was on. The storm made the skies as dark as dusk. They removed their damp shoes at the door and slipped from their raincoats without speaking, tacitly understanding that neither of them wanted to disturb Palmer. Linnea felt her eyelids drooping with fatigue as she wiped a damp lock of hair from her forehead.

"You're back."

Linnea startled at the sound of her father's voice and spun around. She didn't see him and was momentarily confused. Across the foyer, the living room was dark. Nonplussed, she looked to her mother. Julia was putting her purse on the small Hepplewhite table in the foyer. Her hand stilled and her face hardened at Palmer's voice.

"Where are you?" Linnea called to her father.

"Let him be," her mother hissed as she lifted her hands to her rain hat. She shook the water off with brusque, angry strokes.

"In here," he called back.

Linnea walked to the living room, following the sound of Palmer's voice. The thick silk drapes were closed against the storm. Not a gleam of light came from the large crystal chandelier hanging in the middle of the room. Only the small light positioned above the portrait of her grandfather Stratton Rutledge shone on the massive, ornately framed painting.

Linnea had never really known her grandfather. He'd died while she was young. Nonetheless, she'd heard the stories of his ruthlessness, and thus was a little afraid of him. She'd often wondered why her mother never took the painting down after he died, knowing how she felt about the man. One of a pair of blue velvet wing chairs had been moved to sit in direct line of view of the portrait.

"Daddy?" she called softly, approaching. She peered around the tall back of the chair, and then her shoulders slumped. Palmer was sitting in the chair, his meaty hands on the armrests. In one of them was a tumbler half-filled with a brown liquid. "What are you doing sitting here alone in the dark?"

Palmer glanced up at her briefly, his eyes red and swollen with grief, then turned his gaze back to the portrait. "I'm ruminating."

She'd never seen him like this. Almost manic. He'd obviously hit the bottle the moment he got home. Linnea didn't know if she was more annoyed or frightened.

"Julia!" he bellowed.

Linnea startled at his outburst and swung her head to look at her mother out in the foyer. Julia straightened, but her face was impassive. Cold. She stood staring into the room but didn't reply.

"You've been gone all day," Palmer called to her in a belligerent tone.

"You left," Julia said accusingly. "You left your son lying in the hospital."

Linnea stood frozen between her father and her mother. Outside, the wind was howling. Inside, Linnea felt a storm building in the room, as fierce as the one outdoors. The tension was thick and conditions were tempestuous. Her mind flashed warnings.

"Do you hear me, woman?" Palmer shouted, rising to a stand. He rocked on his heels with the effort, sticking out a hand to balance himself on the tall back of the wing chair.

Something in Linnea snapped. She couldn't take any more. She threw caution to the wind and reared up. "She's not some woman. She's your wife!" she shouted. "She spent the whole night and all morning with Cooper. Leave her alone!"

Palmer rounded on her. "Watch your mouth, little girl."

"I'm *not* a little girl and I will *not* watch my mouth!" she cried. She wiped a droplet of rainwater from her forehead. "In fact, I wish I hadn't been so meek before. Maybe if I'd spoken up, Cooper wouldn't be in the hospital now."

"Linnea . . ." her mother said in a warning tone. She moved into the room to stand a few feet from them.

"I knew he wasn't himself," Linnea cried. "Yes, he was drinking. But it went way beyond social drinking. And it wasn't *boys will be boys* drinking, either. He was drinking to get drunk. He was taking drugs to escape. He was doing it because he couldn't face his life." Her chest rose and fell with emotion, making it difficult to get the words out. "You told him all that bullshit about what it meant to be a Rutledge. How you went to the Citadel and Granddad went there. Why couldn't you just once ask him what he wanted to do?"

"He wanted to go," Palmer countered, almost pleading his case. "He enrolled, didn't he? He's just having a tough first week. Knobs have it hard. But, hell, it's part of the system. Makes you a man."

Linnea put her palms to the sides of her head and shrieked as loud as the howling wind: "You're still not listening! *He. Did. Not. Want. To. Go!*"

No one spoke. Behind the curtains, the windows rattled from the force of the wind. It sounded like some ghost trying to get in.

Linnea felt spent. Her hands dropped to her sides. "You never listen. That's the problem. Neither of you," she said, turning to include her mother. Julia's face drooped.

"And I'm no better," she continued. "I pretended it wasn't my problem. That he was a big boy now and could figure this out for himself. I should have helped Cooper find a way to speak up for himself. To stop hiding his feelings and tell you how he felt."

The vision of Cooper sitting in the dayroom of the mental hospital, blankly staring out the tall windows, haunted her. Tears flooded her eyes. "He's lost." She hastily wiped her eyes. "You know what I think?" she asked her parents. "I think he did take an overdose deliberately. It wasn't an accident. And do you know why? Because if he did overdose, he'd get kicked out of the Citadel. Cooper was willing to risk his life rather than tell you face-to-face how he felt."

"Linnea, don't say that!" Julia cried, her voice broken.

"You're making this all up," Palmer said belligerently. His hands fisted and relaxed nervously at his sides and he stuck his jaw out in defense. "Cooper said he didn't try to hurt himself. The doctor confirmed it. You heard it." He turned to Julia for confirmation.

Linnea shook her head and huffed out a short laugh, feeling some of Cooper's hopelessness. "It doesn't matter, does it? It almost killed him. But, hey!" She lifted her palms with exaggeration. "He got you to listen."

Her father's hands went still.

"And you know what?" she said by way of challenge. "I'm going to speak up too."

Palmer's eyes flashed like lightning. He crossed his arms as though to barricade against more hurt coming his way. "All right, missy. I'm listening."

It was said as a threat. Linnea's mind screamed out warnings to stop, but she'd gone too far. Cooper was strong; now she had to be. It was now or never. She steeled herself, lifting her chin.

"I've got news," she announced. "I've found a position in my field and I have an interview. And if they offer me the job, I'm going to take it."

Palmer's face reflected his surprise. Clearly this wasn't what he'd expected to hear and it took the wind out of him. "Well," he said, and wiped his face with his palm. He looked exhausted, and seemed at a loss for words. "That's good. Real good."

"Let me finish," Linnea said.

Palmer's smile froze and he tilted his head, puzzled.

"The job is in California," Linnea continued. "San Francisco, to be exact."

"What?" Julia's voice was stunned. "When did you decide this?"

"Just this week."

"Why didn't you tell me?" she asked, sounding hurt.

"Oh, Mama, you had Cooper on your mind today. I didn't want to add to your burden."

"You don't have to protect me," Julia said, standing straighter. "I should protect you. I should protect both my children."

Palmer broke through with bluster, having caught a second wind. "You're *not* going to San Francisco."

"Yes, I am," she replied, facing him with equal conviction.

Julia stepped closer. "Where would you live?"

"I have a place to stay," Linnea said.

Palmer frowned. "Where is that?"

The wind gusted again, stronger now, whistling outside the

windows. The brittle branches of the old oak tree rattled like claws at the window. Linnea felt her courage waver.

"A friend's."

"Who?" he asked, stepping closer.

Linnea met her father's unblinking gaze. "Emmi Peterson's son, John."

She heard her mother suck in her breath.

"I'm not a little girl anymore," Linnea rushed to say.

Palmer's eyes widened. "You're going to California with a man?"

She swallowed hard. "He has an apartment there. I'm going to crash at his place until I find an apartment of my own. He's being a good friend."

Palmer snorted unkindly. "I'll just bet he is."

She tried for reason. "That's all we are. Friends. But if I want something more, you need to trust me that he's a good man and I'm making the right decision."

He shook his head. He was having none of it. "You're not going! And that's that."

Linnea felt no fear and spoke in a monotone that was, oddly, more effective than a shout. "I leave as soon as the storm is over."

The tension skyrocketed with a sudden fierceness. He was blowing up, his rage building to a tipping point, and she felt her own anger swell like feeder bands of the hurricane.

"Hell, no!" he roared, stung to the core. The wind gusted, rattling the window, and the lights flickered. The storm was upon them.

She stared at him, mouth agape. She didn't know this man, and he frightened her.

He pointed to her, his face red, spittle at his lips. "You're not going anywhere! Who do you think you are? Goddamned beach house. What happens to women out there? My mother. My sister. Her damn friends. And now you? A bunch of radicals, all of them! Enough, I say! I'm your father, and I want you back home under my roof, hear? Where you belong."

Linnea glared at him, then turned away. "I'm out of here."

"Don't you dare turn your back on me!"

It was all so fast, Linnea would never recall exactly what happened.

From the corner of her eye she caught sight of her father raising his hand in anger. Her breath hitched.

At the same moment, a deafening crack erupted just outside the house, and amid the terrible sound of ripping wood she heard her mother cry, "No!"

Linnea yelped and cowered, arms up over her head. Her heart pounded wildly.

Julia stood in front of her daughter, shoulders back, fists at her sides, eyes blazing. "No!" she shouted again in a resounding voice.

Palmer stared back at her, eyes wide, his hand still in the air. His face sagged and he staggered forward like a speared bull. His hand dropped to reach out to Linnea. "I'm sorry."

"Don't touch her!" Julia shouted at him.

Linnea straightened, staring at her mother. She was a lioness, roaring, empowered.

Palmer had the thousand-yard stare of shell shock. His gaze drifted from Julia to Linnea, then back to Julia. His face contorted with anguish. In a sudden, swift move he turned and grabbed the crystal glass from the table and, with a guttural cry of anguish, hurled it at the portrait. It hurtled, spewing a trail of bourbon, to crash against the painting. Glass splintered and the seeping brown liquid spread over the old man's face.

Linnea slipped her arm around her mother.

Palmer staggered across the foyer to the front door and opened it. The wind howled through the room like the cry of a ghost. He turned and looked once more at his wife and daughter.

"I'm sorry," he said, and stepped out into the storm.

Chapter Twenty-Two

*Florida is the most important nesting area in the United
States for loggerhead, green, and leatherback turtles. A staggering
80 percent of loggerhead nesting occurs in six Florida counties. A
twenty-mile section of coastline from Melbourne Beach to Wabasso
Beach comprises the Archie Carr National Wildlife Refuge, the most
important nesting area for loggerhead turtles in the western
hemisphere. A thousand nests per mile are recorded.*

Two days later the storm had passed and the sun rose on a
calm but changed shoreline. Cara hovered over news reports,
shocked at the photographs of waves crashing the sea wall of Rainbow Row in Charleston, the severe flooding and the battered
dunes on Isle of Palms.

As soon as the all-clear for Isle of Palms was declared, she packed
the car back up, eager to return to the beach house. David asked her
to stay in the mountains longer, but with Cooper in the hospital and
Linnea not answering her texts, Cara was anxious to get home.

Her fingers were dancing on the wheel by the time she drove
up to Primrose Cottage. Her eyes hungrily devoured it, scanning
quickly. There were the usual fallen palm fronds and torn screens

on porches, but she blew out a plume of relief at seeing no damage. She realized how very much this house meant to her—no, even more, what the beach house *symbolized* for her: a strong foundation, grace under pressure, continuance, resilience.

"We're home!" she called out to Hope.

Moutarde chirped from his travel cage at hearing the joy in her voice.

The front steps were still damp and covered in leaves and mud. The torn front porch screens flapped in the wind and her plants had been knocked over, spilling dirt and geraniums. These she scooped back up as best she could; then she laid a blanket on the front porch for Hope to play on while she unscrewed the aluminum panels covering the front door. It didn't take too long. Lifting Hope into her arms, she pushed open the front door.

Inside, the house was dark and humid and had that shut-in staleness of an attic. She flicked a light switch. Nothing. *So,* she thought with dismay, *the electricity is out.* She couldn't open a window because of the hurricane shutters. Still, enough light peered through the cracks that she could tour the house with Hope in her arms, searching for any leaks or damage. Her last stop was the rear porch. This had been Brett's last project. He'd been very proud of the design of the sunroom with a wide deck in back. Cara sighed with relief to see that all was intact. No puddles on the floor.

She settled Moutarde back in his large birdcage, then went outdoors and around to the back to remove the shutters from the sunroom. Her eyes scanned the roof, the trees, and the broad deck that Bo had constructed. Thank God all was unscathed. There was work to be done to get the house opened, but they were blessed.

From around the house she heard the rumble of tires in the driveway next door, followed by car doors slamming, then footfalls in the gravel.

"Hello! Anybody home?"

Cara walked toward the voices. "I'm in the back!"

Emmi rounded the corner of the house first, her mouth stretched across her face in a grin. She looked disheveled and wan, but ran to Cara to embrace her in a sisterly hug. Flo ambled up more slowly, but her arms were strong with emotion. The three women formed a circle, arms around each other, love flowing from one to another.

"We made it through another one!" Flo exclaimed.

Lastly John stepped onto the deck like a knight in shining armor, brandishing not a sword but a battery-operated drill. He grinned, his cheeks shadowed in stubble. "I'll get those panels down for you in no time."

While the other women opened their house and John was busy removing shutters, Cara sat on the deck while Hope played and tried to reach Linnea, then Julia, and finally Palmer. But none of the calls went through. She ran her hand through her hair, sick with worry. She'd seen on the news the terrible flooding the city had, especially around the hospital. She could only hope they'd all had the good sense to stay home and wait out the storm. There was some comfort in knowing that Cooper, at least, was safe in the hospital.

Before too long the hurricane shutters were removed, the electricity had been restored, and a fresh pot of steaming coffee was made to bolster the troops. The first thing Cara did was to go from room to room and push open all the windows of the house. The musty odor dissipated as salt-tinged ocean breezes blew through, balmy and fresh. She enjoyed the domesticity of sweeping the deck and walkways, dragging yard debris to the street. There was a serenity to everyday chores, a kind of Zen. Cara laughed as she worked, watching Hope try to keep up with her on her chubby legs. Cara began feeling that peace had been restored at Primrose Cottage.

She was preparing a picnic dinner of food scavenged from the fridge and cabinets when she heard more car wheels in the driveway, followed by the honking of a horn. *Who could that be?* she wondered as she put down the bread slices and walked to the kitchen window to peer out. Her heart skipped in joy.

"Linnea!" she called out. Cara rushed to pick up Hope from among her toys. "Linnea's here," she told her, and scurried out the back door to meet her on the deck.

Linnea ran to kiss Cara, then swept Hope up in her arms and twirled her around, squealing with happiness.

"I was so worried!" Cara said, her gaze hungrily devouring every inch of Linnea's face. "I couldn't reach you. I didn't sleep a wink for worry."

"I'm sorry. We couldn't get service or the Internet. I tried texting you on the way over."

"How did you get here? I saw the flooding on TV. It's horrible."

"I know," she said wearily. "Some of the roads are like rivers. Mama called the city Venice. But there were side roads that we could use to get through the city. It took forever." She kissed Hope and handed her back to Cara. "Thank goodness we were driving Mama's tank. My little Mini Cooper would never have made it."

"Linnea, how's Cooper?"

Her smile slipped. "He's doing better. He's in the psych ward."

Cara frowned with concern. "Oh."

"It's really okay. We couldn't get back to the hospital because of the flooding." She rolled her eyes. "Mama was fit to be tied. But we called this morning and he's doing better. There's a big bright room where they can keep an eye on him. It's not like he's locked up in a cell or anything. Cara, I'm glad he's there. He'll get the help he needs right now. And he can't go anywhere even if they released him. The hospital area is a lake. We got out just in time, or we'd still be stuck there. The doctors and nurses are coming in by boat!"

"It was unbelievable. I—"

She stopped when she heard her mother's voice.

"Hello?" Julia rounded the house. Despite the long, ragged night, she appeared strong and steady, dragging two suitcases. She stopped when she saw Cara and Linnea grinning and laughing.

Cara hurried to her side with Linnea. "Welcome," she said warmly, leaning forward with Hope in her arms to offer a kiss of greeting.

Tears filled Julia's eyes. It seemed as though she'd been holding herself together by a thread and now for the first time she felt she could let go and that one, slender thread tore and released the flood of anguish.

Cara understood and handed the baby to Linnea. She wrapped her arms around her sister-in-law. "You're safe now," she told her softly. "You're with us."

Cara took Hope back in her arms and was guiding the women indoors when they heard the husky sound of John's voice.

"Linnea!"

Turning, they saw John racing around the corner of the house. His hair was tousled, red stubble framed his face, and his green eyes were pinned on Linnea. He took the stairs in two leaps and ran to scoop Linnea into his arms and plant a breath-sucking kiss.

Emmi hurried around the corner after John and, seeing the two locked in an embrace, stopped short. Then, her face glowing, she fist-pumped the air. Flo followed at a slower pace, blinking up at them in confusion.

Cara took in the scene, holding Hope close, and leaned against a porch pillar, swamped by a wave of memories of another such day. Another aftermath of a storm. Only that time, it was Brett who had come running. For her. Closing her eyes, she felt again his arms around her, tight and sure and strong. The feel of his lips claiming hers. It was so real she could smell him. Brett's presence was strong, and her heart ached for him. Hot tears seeped from the corners of her eyes, and she squeezed Hope tight and took a ragged breath to stop them.

Then she felt an arm wrap around her shoulders and two short, reassuring pats. Cara opened her eyes to see Emmi standing beside her.

"I know," she said in a low voice.

She sniffed, bolstered by her friend's understanding. Emmi remembered, too.

John's arms tightened around Linnea. "You didn't answer your phone!"

Linnea hiccuped a laugh that sounded more like a cry. "No service," she choked out.

He rocked her in his arms, his relief palpable. "Don't ever leave me again."

"No," Linnea said, smiling into his face.

Cara looked to Emmi, a sympathetic smile easing across her face. The old matchmaker was grinning with pleasure. When their eyes met again, Emmi gave her a thumbs-up.

"Mercy!" Julia exclaimed. "I guess that's why Linnea calls this the Social Club."

"That would be my house," Emmi said, stepping forward to help with the suitcases. "Next door. I've got a mountain of food. Come on, everyone. Let's eat."

<hr />

EVERYONE FOLLOWED EMMI over to her house. Linnea took Hope along when Cara asked for a few minutes alone.

She still felt Brett's presence keenly. He was here with her, she knew it. She went to the pergola and laid her hand against the wood, patting it with appreciation. She thought back on hurricanes past that had ravaged Lovie's pergola. Each time, Brett had faithfully rebuilt it for her. It had become both a tradition and a family joke.

This one Brett had built for Cara. He'd chosen the best wood, thick and strong. "Built to last," he'd declared. Cara looked up and saw that the canes of the roses were twisted and broken. More red petals had drifted down to dot the deck. But this time, Brett's pergola had persevered.

"Oh, Brett," she said, and hugged the pillar of the pergola. *This* was her sign. "Strong and sure. I know what you're trying to tell me. And I hear you. No more tears. I'll weather the storms. I'll persevere. Live again. Love again. I will treasure each day."

She reached up to wipe away the last of her tears. "And each day," she said, looking out at the endless sea, "I'll remember you."

～～～

THE SUN WAS setting on an emotional day. Hope was asleep in her crib. The canary was back in his cage. All the debris had been swept and the windows were free of shutters. Cara felt a sense of peace she hadn't known since Hurricane Irma threatened the Atlantic.

The three Rutledge women sat together under the pergola, all in their pajamas, sipping wine, finding comfort in one another's presence. It was a typical post-storm night. The humidity had blown off and the sky burst with unusual brilliance. Lovie had always claimed it was God's way of reassuring them that all was well.

They did what women have done since the days of hunters and gatherers. They shared their stories, their fears and triumphs, finding both solace and support in the process. Julia spoke of the exchange with Palmer in front of the portrait of Stratton. Linnea told Cara of her decision to go to California and how that had sparked her father's fury. Finally, Cara confessed the depth of her feelings for David. There was laughter amid the tears, too. Especially when Cara described David's log house in North Carolina.

"Shades of Pemberley?" Linnea teased.

So much has happened, Cara thought. It would take days, weeks, to sort things out. Foremost on her mind, however, was her brother. No one had heard from Palmer since he'd rushed out of the house into the storm. The reports of the flooding in Charleston were alarming, but Julia had remained stoic, praying, convinced Palmer was all right. Cara never allowed such things to chance, however. She'd called all the hospitals and the police, but no one had seen him.

Cara asked, "Julia, have you reached Palmer yet?"

She nodded pensively. "Finally."

"For heaven's sake! Why didn't you tell us?" Cara asked, anger rising in her chest. "We've all been so worried. Where is he?"

"Forgive me for not telling you. I only just talked to him, and I've been sitting here in a stew, trying to figure out what I'm going to do next. I was going to tell you."

"When?" Cara blurted.

"Mama, tell us now," Linnea demanded, sitting up in her chair. "Where is he?"

"He's at the hospital," she said in a tone of disbelief.

Cara felt alarm. "Is he hurt?"

"No, no," Julia said in a rush. "In the psych hospital. With Cooper."

Cara was astonished.

"With Cooper?" Linnea asked, worry ringing in her voice. "Is everything okay? Is that good for Cooper?"

"Yes," Julia said with reassurance. She swallowed and took a breath. "He went to apologize. He's been talking with Cooper. Making peace somehow."

There followed a stunned silence.

Cara was much relieved. Then she knew a moment of pride in her brother. It washed over her, sweeping away all the resentment lingering from the last exchange.

"You see why I needed to digest that before I told you. I needed to know my own mind, my own heart." Julia spoke levelly, without apology.

"Mama, I'm so happy," Linnea said, and came over to the settee to rest her head on Julia's shoulder.

Cara was still peeved that Julia hadn't told them instantly, but that was overcome by her pleasure at the outcome and seeing the new bond established between mother and daughter. She was glad she hadn't charged off and started a row. Emotions still ran high and they needed to be supportive now, not combative. She thought of her brother, and wondered how he'd managed to fight his way through the raging floodwaters to reach the hospital. His determination was staggering. It gave her hope to contemplate the implications.

"This is important," Cara said, sitting up.

Julia and Linnea, interrupted, looked up.

"He did it!" Cara said. When the two women stared back at her uncomprehendingly, she added, "He broke the cycle. Thank God."

"I couldn't have stayed under the same circumstances," said Julia with conviction.

Cara saw the new strength in Julia's eyes. "I wouldn't have either." Then she smiled. "But look at you! You stood your ground. You can't know how proud I am of you."

"Me?" Julia asked. "I only did what any mother would do."

"No," Cara said, and it near broke her heart to say it. "Not every mother. My mother didn't."

Julia looked stunned. "Lovie?"

Linnea lifted her head, listening, her gaze on Cara.

"You broke a cycle too," Cara said to Julia.

"I don't understand."

Cara took a sip of her wine and set the wineglass on the table. She shifted to a comfortable spot and crossed her legs. This story would take strength to tell.

"I was a little younger than you, Linnea," she began. "Just eighteen. I was telling my father I wanted to go to Boston University. He said I couldn't go." She glanced up at Linnea. "It went very much like what you experienced. Only my father was crueler. Harsher." She glanced away in shame. "When I close my eyes, I can still see his belt flying in the air, feel the snap of leather like a bullwhip."

"He beat you?" Linnea blurted in a shocked whisper.

Julia's eyes also widened. This part of the story Cara had never shared.

"Just that once. But I'll never forget the humiliation. It's hard to speak of it even now. But it's important you know." She shuddered. "The ghost of that horrible man still lives there, I swear it. That's why I don't like to step foot in that house."

"I know," Linnea said in a soft voice. "I felt him too."

"Palmer certainly did," said Julia. "He hated the son of a bitch." She ducked her head. "Excuse my French."

"But that means Daddy is like him," Linnea said in a quiet voice.

Cara straightened, unable to let Linnea think that about her brother. "No, he's not," she said with conviction. "He proved to you that he's not at all like him. He was stuck in a family pattern. A bad habitual resolution of his anger and his deep sense of failure."

"But—"

"Listen to me," Cara interrupted. "Don't you understand what happened? Last night your father broke that cycle!" She paused, trying to find the right words so that Linnea would comprehend the vital truth. "When my father hit me, my mother cowered in the background. I looked to her for help." Cara swallowed. "But she didn't come to my rescue." She released a long sigh. A lot of water had flowed under that bridge.

"I understand her reasons now, but then I felt abandoned. Alone. But, Julia," she said, focusing on her sister-in-law. "*You* intervened! You stood up for your daughter. You said no." Cara felt her emotion welling up. "I am so proud of you. And of Palmer, too."

"Palmer?" asked Julia with indignation.

"Yes. You not only shamed him. You forced him to see who he was becoming."

Julia's eyes glimmered in understanding. "His father."

"Right," Cara said. "The one man he never wanted to be like. Don't you see, Linnea, if we didn't stop this cycle, Cooper would treat women like his father did. He'd become the worst of Palmer."

"Not Coop . . ." Linnea said, shaking her head.

"Yes. That's the power of the cycle. Honey, you didn't know Palmer at Cooper's age. He was every bit as sweet. And conniving . . . Let's not make Cooper out to be an angel here. He's made some pretty big mistakes, for himself and for his family. He has to take responsibility for his own actions. And you"—she looked at Linnea and then Julia with a meaningful gaze—"you have to let him fight those battles. And not try to fix things for him."

The women went quiet, listening to her.

"But the work isn't done yet. We have to help Palmer find the strength to really change." Cara looked at Linnea with an unwavering eye. "This is the time for understanding. And compassion. And love for your father." She turned to Julia. "And your husband. I assure you, he doesn't feel any of those emotions for himself. I wager he feels pretty badly right now. He's hit rock bottom. And that's good. That will help motivate him to break the cycle for himself."

A gentle breeze wafted through the air, carrying the scent of jasmine. Cara inhaled the sweetness, eyes closed; opening them again, she saw Julia and Linnea, her family. She leaned forward and stretched out her arms to the women. It was impossible to keep the optimism from her voice.

"Are we in this together?"

Linnea and Julia reached out to take her offered hands to form a united circle.

Chapter Twenty-Three

Thanks to the efforts of experts like Sally Murphy,
SCDNR, shrimp boats in the United States and countries
that export shrimp to the United States are required by law to
use turtle excluder devices (TEDs), trap-like doors on nets
that allow turtles to escape. South Carolina was the
first state to mandate TEDs.

HURRICANE IRMA WAS a fading memory. The floodwaters had abated and residents had returned home. Cara stood on the beach where, only a week earlier, rolling dunes draped in golden, cascading sea oats had dominated the border. It was stunning to see them all gone, wiped clean away by the force of the storm. The previous year's hurricane had leveled the dunes too, but this time there was nothing left. The rippled sand stretched flat, littered with trunks of palm trees and driftwood and gouged by an unusually large number of gullies.

Cara wrapped her arms around herself and stared out at the wild beauty of the wide open beach, untrammeled by crowds, colored towels, and umbrellas. She could see miles away tonight, the visibility was so clear. The sun had set on another day, leaving the earth blanketed in a soft lavender and purple light. The sea turtles were gone, she thought, looking out at the swells. It had been a good year. Most of the nests had emerged by the time the dunes were swept away. John and Linnea were gone, too. Flown off to San Francisco. That Palmer had shaken John's hand at the airport spoke volumes. There was no assurance that they would end up together for life, but Cara was hopeful. It was a happy ending to this chapter in their lives, she thought. And, perhaps, the first chapter of what was to come.

Cooper, too, was turning a page. He'd dropped out of the Citadel and was living at home, enrolled in the College of Charleston. He was also in therapy—as were Palmer and Julia. There were many changes coming for the Rutledge family. Significant transitions.

Which was where Cara came in.

She walked the beach for half an hour, all the way to the pier, then turned around and headed back. Her mind was working out questions and seeking solutions. Her heels dug deep half moons in the damp sand, making the effort strenuous. By the time she returned to her beach path, Cara was tired but felt at peace with her decision. Her gaze shifted to the small yellow house in the distance. Her beach house. The light was on, shining like a beacon in the darkening sky. It had withstood many hurricanes and family upheavals. It would, she thought, have to be strong for one more.

She walked to a particular patch of sand and grass that had once been hidden behind the great dunes, situated on the lot in front of her beach house. It was a sweet place. Bits of seaside fall flowers colored the area—sea lavender, white oxeye, goldenrod, and the yellow primrose for which her cottage had been named. The plateau of sand dipped softly. Still, it was but a remnant of the haven it had once been for Lovie when she had a rendezvous with her great love, Russell Bennett.

Cara sat on the sand, stretched out her long legs, and leaned back on her elbows. The air smelled delicious. She heard the plaintive cry of an osprey and, looking up, saw the great fish hawk circling overhead. She closed her eyes and let her hands stroke the sand, feeling its coolness slide through her fingers. This spot had been her mother's favorite place to sit after Russell died. Flo had told Cara how Lovie used to come out here to talk with him, or perhaps to feel closer to him. He'd died in a plane crash out in the ocean not far from here. Lovie liked to think of him out there with the turtles, waiting for her. It made sense to Cara that she'd visit his memory here, where once they'd been so happy.

After Brett had died, Cara had come to this same spot to find comfort. She had tried to speak to him, but never truly sensed his presence. Not that she'd expected to be visited by him, but she felt the consolation one felt when visiting a grave site.

Tonight, however, Cara had come to this spot with a purpose. She needed to communicate with her mother. Although Cara had seen her mother's ghost the night she arrived, not once since May had she so much as caught scent of her signature jasmine perfume. So Cara had come to Lovie's dune, at the bewitching hour that Lovie had favored, with the express desire to be heard. She had things to say.

Cara opened her eyes, brought up her knees, and wrapped her arms around them. She felt the chill of dusk. It was time.

"Mama!" she whispered. "Please, listen to me. I need you to hear what I have to say. So you'll understand what I've decided to do." She paused. "Years ago, you told me your secret. And you said no one was ever to find out. You paid a dear price for your secret and trusted me not to tell. I promised I never would. And I haven't. Mama . . ." Cara took a breath. "I must break that promise now. I'm sorry. I've gone over and over this in my head, and each time I come to the same conclusion. I must tell Palmer."

There, she'd said it aloud. Her intention was in the universe. She ran her hand through her hair, feeling both relief and a kind of despair. "Mama, secrets are no good for families. They're destructive and divisive and always come out in the end. But that's not why I'm breaking my promise. I'm telling Palmer so I can help him. So you can help him. Oh, Mama, he so desperately needs our help. And isn't that what families do for one another?"

A sudden breeze swept over her, cool and fresh-smelling. Cara sat bolt upright and sniffed. Then she laughed out loud. It was the unmistakable scent of jasmine.

"Thank you, Mama!"

~~~~~~

A WEEK LATER the doorbell rang, launching Cara from her chair where she'd been tapping her foot in anxiety. Moutarde began chirping at the bell. She looked at her wristwatch. "Right on time," she murmured. She tugged at the sleeves of her white silk blouse. She'd deliberately chosen to wear her mother's sizable pearls at her ears and neck. Today would be an important discussion. She'd said as much to Palmer when she invited him over. She walked briskly across the polished wood floor, clenching and unclenching her hands at her sides. She wanted everything to go just right today. Taking a breath at the door, she swung it open.

Palmer stood on the porch in khakis and a polo shirt, his expression wary. He looked so much like his old self that she burst into a wide grin of pure pleasure. Seeing it, Palmer opened his arms. Cara stepped into them. Brother and sister hugged each other, laughing with the joy of it.

"Oh, Palmer, it's so good to see you."

"Cara . . ."

"Come in, come in," she said with exuberance.

"It's been ages since I've been in here," he said, following her through the living room, his gaze darting about. "Nothing's much changed."

"No," she repeated. "No changes for Primrose Cottage. But there might be a few changes elsewhere." She threw him a glance, her brow arched.

Palmer caught the reference and tilted his head, curious.

They headed for the kitchen table, as was their habit as children. She wanted to surround him with as much relaxed, family comfort as she could muster. Two glasses of iced sweet tea were served in tall cut-crystal glasses. On the table lay two folders. The navy one bore the insignia of Morgan Grenfell Trust Limited in the Channel Islands. The white one was blank.

Palmer eyed the presentation and looked at her quizzically.

"Please, sit down," Cara said, indicating a chair. After he sat, she joined him at the table.

"What's this all about?" Palmer asked. "Everything is so formal. I feel like I'm being sent to the executioner."

"Hardly," Cara said with a short laugh. "This is more likely your release from prison."

Palmer shook his head without understanding. "Okay then, sister mine. I raise the white flag."

"I know you do," she said gently. Cara paused, then began, "I've asked you here to tell you a story. I'd appreciate it if you'd just listen to the whole story before you interrupt with questions."

"A story? About what?"

"Palmer . . ." Cara said with exasperation.

"Sorry."

She folded her hands on the table. "This is a story about our mother."

Palmer's eyes flared with interest.

Cara cleared her throat and began to tell her brother about the great love story of Olivia Rutledge and Russell Bennett. She told it as she herself had heard it, simply and without embellishment. The love story was so profound, it didn't need any. Then she moved on to the more difficult part.

"When Mama gave me the beach house," she said, "she bid me to keep her story secret. From everyone, including you. I agreed. When I did, Mother entrusted me with the rest of the secret. One that had been troubling her, knowing her death was imminent. You see, her love story and what I'm about to tell you are intricately connected. One can't know one side without the other."

Cara reached out to move the two folders to the middle of the table. She pushed the navy folder with her fingertips toward Palmer.

Palmer didn't move. He simply stared at it.

"Read it."

Palmer flipped open the folder and read. She watched as he leaned forward over the papers . . . as his face colored. When he finished, he closed the folder and laid his palms upon it.

"Let me get this straight," he said, aghast. "*You* own the beach-front lot?"

"Yes. Mama left it to me with the beach house."

Palmer leaned back in the chair as if he'd been dealt a blow. "I can't believe it. After all these years of begging you to sell the beach house, to build another house, you were sitting holding that lot. You knew I was digging to find out who owned it!"

"Yep," she said with a short laugh. "It used to drive Mama crazy."

"Well, shit." Palmer burst out laughing, slamming his hand on the table. "Sister mine, you're one helluva poker player."

"I know. But, Palmer, I haven't yet played my final hand."

Palmer's expression shifted. Cara saw again the vulnerable child in the man. The brother she'd grown up with. A curious boy, even hopeful. One without a scheme.

"You see, I promised Mama I would never tell anyone about the land. To do so would force the story of her love affair with Russell to become public. At least to her family. She paid the highest price to keep that secret. She let Russell go. He was the love of her life."

"I've got to say, that makes me happy to hear. I'm glad she found some happiness."

"You know Mama. She didn't want to hurt Russell's reputation or his wife's. Or bring shame to us, her children. So she stayed with Daddy. I think we know what a sacrifice that was. But that's why she came to the beach house. It was her sanctuary. Knowing that, Russell left her the land so that she could, if she ever chose, leave Daddy and provide for herself. A private form of insurance. Before she died, she instructed me to put it into conservancy."

"But you didn't."

Cara shook her head. "I tried. As it turned out, to do so I would have had to expose her secret. I made an executive decision. I decided to keep the land as though it were in conservation. Unsullied. Open to the countless people who walked past it on the way to the beach every day. Palmer, I did my best to keep her secret."

For a long time Palmer said nothing. Then he asked, "Why tell me now?"

"Because it's time for you to know. I gave this a great deal of thought. I wrestled with it for many nights. But I believe it's the right thing to do. Palmer, you're my knight in shining armor. I'm so proud of you. Of what you've done for yourself and for your family. Mama would be proud, too. You're truly the patriarch of the family now. One we all look up to and admire."

Palmer put his palms up. "Hold on. While I appreciate the kind words, let's be realistic. I've fallen off the white steed. I'm flat on my back, broke, and, I don't mind telling you, a little bit scared."

"That's a good start."

He laughed. "You always were a ball-buster."

Cara laughed too, owning it. "Seriously, you've made some great strides. Joining AA—"

"Cooper joined with me."

"I know. How did your meeting with Bobby Lee go?" she asked, referring to the family's longtime lawyer.

"As good as a meeting with Bobby Lee can go, under the circumstances. He's a good man, served our family well. I'm in a fine mess, but we'll sort it out. I'll sell the business. The name and the history associated with it hold value. And . . ." Palmer paused, and rubbed his palms together. He appeared guilt-ridden. "Julia and I have decided to put the house on the market. I'm sorry, Cara. I feel like I let you down. Let the whole family down. But I had no choice. I can't afford to maintain it, and I need the money. I've lost most of our savings. My inheritance is gone. And now the house."

"To hell with the house," Cara said.

Palmer's eyes widened.

"Come on, Palmer, Mama and Daddy bought that house in the sixties. It's not like it's been in the family all that long. And frankly, I always hated it. It was never a happy home. And besides, it's haunted."

"What?" Palmer was both surprised and amused. "You sensed it too?"

"Why do you think I don't come around?"

Palmer barked out a laugh. "So that's why." Then his smile fell, and he said ruefully, "Julia loved it."

"She told me she's glad to be moving to Sullivan's Island. She's tired of tending that big old house. And she's especially happy you ruined the portrait of Daddy."

He paused, comprehending the magnitude of the words. "She did?"

"Yes. Do you think she's been happy watching you sink under the weight of it? She loves you, Palmer. Why, I don't know."

They both laughed, knowing Cara was joking.

"I'm going to have to sell the lodge too." He looked at her sheepishly.

Cara shrugged. "It's yours to do with what you will. Besides, I don't hunt."

Palmer smiled gratefully. "Well," he said, "I guess that's that."

"Not quite." Cara drew herself up and addressed her brother as she would a client. She moved the white folder with her index finger across the table toward him. Palmer looked at it, then at her, curiosity shining.

"I've come up with a proposal," she said. "We both know you've been after me for years to sell the lot and build a house on it."

Palmer's brows rose in surprise. "Yes," he drawled, and leaned forward over the table. "Like I told you, I've got plans—"

Cara lifted her palm. "Hold on, brother. This time, *I've* got plans. This is going to be a joint project. Here's what I propose. I'll provide the land. You'll use your money from the sale of the Tradd Street house and whatever else you choose to sell to build the spec house. We'll work out an LLC with Bobby Lee. Each of us will, hopefully, see a profit. That should, at the very least, buy you time to decide your next venture."

Palmer sat back in his chair, stunned. "I don't know what to say."

"You don't have to say anything. We're family. You were there for me when I needed you. I'm only glad I can be here for you with meaningful support. Mama loved us both equally. You know she didn't have a mind for figures. As bright as she was, she was naïve about such matters. I suppose many women of her generation were. But she was very smart and had her own set of values that didn't always equate with dollars and cents. When you got the house in Charleston, Mama was pleased because she knew it mattered to you and Julia. It made you happy. She gave me the beach house because she knew I loved it. She never took into consideration the monetary value. For her, it was the emotional value that mattered.

"The land, however, posed more of a problem at her death, because of the secrets it shrouded. But times have changed. We have changed. It feels right to use the land to help you too," she said, tapping the white folder, her eyes gleaming with satisfaction. "It's all detailed in that folder. Take your time reading it. Palmer, if we use the land in this way, the secret will be kept between us. The land is in my name, not hers. When I sell it, we'll both be bequeathed a final gift from Mama."

Palmer brought his fingers to pinch the bridge of his nose. She saw the tears squeeze out of his eyes.

Cara said, "Russell Bennett wrote to Mama that he believed the mind often dictates to the heart. But he believed the heart was the truer guide. He was a very wise man."

The chair creaked along the floor as Palmer stood. He brusquely wiped his eyes, then held out his hand.

Cara rose to take it. They shook on the deal.

He led her to the sunroom. The sun poured in, and beyond, the mighty Atlantic rolled in and out in its predictable manner. Moutarde, still in his molt, began chirping at the presence of humans, curious, delighted.

Palmer went to stand before the windows and, crossing his arms across his barrel chest, stared out.

Cara joined him by the windows, but watched her brother instead. She imagined he was visualizing, as he always had, the house the two of them would build on the lot. One house, slightly to the left so that she could keep her view. She smiled to herself. That had always been Palmer's biggest selling point in all the years he'd tried to convince her to sell the beach house. It was funny how life turned out, she thought. She felt lucky to be here, alive and well, to witness the end of this chapter of their lives.

"Can you see it?" she asked him.

Palmer turned his head. "You want to know what I see?"

She nodded.

"I see Linnea and Cooper surfing out there. And someday, their children. They're my real treasures. The best things I've ever done."

Suddenly the room was filled with the scent of jasmine. It was pervasive, stronger than ever before. Cara looked at her brother to see his eyes widen with wonder.

"Is that it?" he asked in a whisper.

Cara smiled and nodded. "Yes."

Behind them the canary began to chirp insistently. Curious, Cara turned her head to look. Moutarde was hopping back and forth on his perches, clearly excited. She looked beyond to the living room. The bookshelves, the fireplace and mantel, the paintings. Suddenly she gasped. There was a shimmer of light, ethereal as a sunbeam, coalescing in the center of the room. The floating dots flittered like dust motes, then gathered to form a hazy image—

transparent, vague, but unmistakable. Cara clutched her brother's arm tight and pointed.

Palmer turned his head. She heard his sharp intake of breath.

"Mama . . ." he breathed.

Brother and sister stood together, hand in hand, lost in their own thoughts as slowly the ghost began to dissipate, gradually disappearing.

Palmer took a step forward, hand outreached. "Good-bye, Mama," he said in a choked whisper. It was a farewell more than a decade in the making.

There followed a deep silence, eerie yet comforting. All that was left of the vision was the scent of jasmine. They each took a deep breath. Then Palmer turned to Cara. His eyes were filled with light.

"You can't ever sell this place!"

Epilogue

"For, lo, the winter is past; the rain is over and gone;
The flowers appear on the earth;
The time of the singing of birds is come,
And the voice of the turtle is heard in our land."

SONG OF SOLOMON 2:11-12 KING JAMES VERSION (KJV)

I T WAS A morning for second chances.

The Rutledge family had come together to support Cara's first event for the South Carolina Aquarium. The summer was behind them and they faced a fall of change when all the world turned gold. Though the island's beach season was over, word of the aquarium's sea turtle release had brought hundreds of people to Front Beach on Isle of Palms. They were lined up on either side of an open swath of beach where the sea turtle would make her final crawl to the sea. Mothers, fathers, children, grandparents, news people with cameras—everyone was claiming a spot to see the turtle.

Palmer and Julia stood in the front beside Cooper, all wearing

ISLAND TURTLE TEAM shirts. Palmer's arm was around Julia. Cooper's hair had grown out enough to cover his scalp. Most of all, he appeared relaxed near his parents, smiling behind his sunglasses.

Cara felt the excitement building in the group. This wasn't just any sea turtle being released today. It was Big Girl. The press had ballyhooed the success of this turtle's second chance at going home, and she'd become the darling of Charleston, her big block head on posters everywhere. In her heart, Cara had always known this was a special turtle.

A murmur rose up from the crowd as the aquarium's van drove onto the beach. The TV cameramen trotted closer and the crowd inched forward. The turtle team volunteers in yellow shirts, including Flo and Emmi, rallied, keeping the spectators back with friendly reminders that they'd get a chance to see the turtle as she crawled past. Little children clapped their hands and jumped up and down in anticipation.

A small group gathered at the back of the truck. A man with a microphone was talking to Toy. Cara watched her expertly answer the questions and tell the story of Big Girl's rescue and recovery. She was a natural on camera. Cara smiled, thinking Toy was wise to stay where she shone in her work.

Cara, too, was happy in her new position at the aquarium. She was here in an official capacity. She'd worked furiously putting out press materials and doing presentations, educating the public why this particular turtle was so meaningful to the rehabilitation effort.

When Toy finished her interview, she turned and gave the signal for the turtle to be lowered from the truck. The huge white crate was lifted to the ground by six strong men. She could only imagine how much heavier Big Girl was at nearly three hundred pounds than the juvenile turtles or Kemp's ridleys that were usually released.

Toy waved a group of people to the front.

Little Lovie and Danny were shy and proud in equal measures as they stepped forward carrying signs. They looked adorable, and Toy beamed with pride. Danny's sign had the turtle's name written on it. Little Lovie's gave her weight. Then Linnea stepped forward, beaming, wearing her T-shirt.

Cara laughed out loud at seeing her niece back from San Francisco and called her name. When she caught her eyes, Linnea pointed in a *got-you* signal. Beside her, Toy was laughing, pleased she'd managed to carry off her surprise.

"Okay, Big Girl," Toy said. "It's time to go home."

Cara moved closer to the crate, not wanting to miss a moment of the release. This one was personal. There were grunts as the men lifted Big Girl from the crate and set her on the sand. Her throat bellowed as she lifted her head, smelling the sea. The crowd oohed at the first glimpse of her size. *That's a big one*, she heard repeated in the crowd.

Cara watched Big Girl study her surroundings—people to the left and to the right. An open path to the sea straight ahead. Her heart skipped a beat as Big Girl made her first move forward on the sand after months in the tank.

"Go, Big Girl!" she shouted.

She was on her way. The children walked ahead of the turtle with their signs, all the way to the shoreline.

Big Girl knew what to do. This wasn't her first rodeo, Cara thought. She was strong and healthy and headed for home. Her powerful flippers dug into the sand, one after the other, in a straight path to the shore. Linnea walked behind her with Toy, her honor guard. It was a privilege, and no two people deserved the honor more. As Big Girl passed she elicited gasps, and phone cameras rose into the sky as people saw the shark bite on her gorgeous, reddish-brown shell.

That's right, Cara thought on seeing the reaction. *This girl's been through some tough times, taken a few knocks, but she's moving forward, as steady and relentless as a tank. She's going all the way home.* That, she knew, was Big Girl's most important lesson.

From time to time Big Girl paused, resting under the weight of her carapace. When she did, the ancient mariner lifted her head as though hearing the clarion call of the sea urging her home. Then she pushed forward again, flipper after flipper, scraping the sand on her long trek across the beach. When at last she reached the water's edge, she paused one more time and let the gentle waves cascade over her, cooling her.

"Just a bit farther," Cara said, clasping her hands tight. She saw the renewed urgency when Big Girl pushed forward, feeling the familiar salt water of the Atlantic. Onward she pushed into deeper water until, with one final push of her powerful flippers, she was swimming.

The crowd surged forward in jubilation, cheering her on, clapping their hands, and rejoicing in Big Girl's return to the sea. Cara stood at the water's edge and felt the warm water swirl around her ankles. She brought her fingers to her mouth to still the gush of emotion rushing through her like a wave. She watched as Big Girl swam farther out, her great head visible in the murky water.

Cara felt an arm slide around her shoulders, and looking up, she saw David standing beside her holding Hope in his arms. They stood together until the turtle had vanished from sight and the crowd gradually dispersed. Linnea came running from her spot a bit deeper in the sea, squealing like a girl, to hug Cara with joy at seeing her again.

Soon everyone in the Rutledge family had gathered together at the water's edge. They laughed and hugged, buoyed by Linnea and John's presence. Toy moved slowly from the water, her belly preceding her, to join her children and Ethan. Bo and Heather approached with Rory in arms. Finally, Emmi and Flo found their way into the circle.

Cara stood back and watched this glorious reunion of family and friends, all the people she loved most in the world. She captured the singular moment in her mind, with the sun shining on their faces, knowing she'd keep it in her memory forever like a treasured photograph. To remind her of how blessed her life was.

Suddenly Linnea grabbed her hand. "Come on!" she shouted, laughing. Julia was holding Linnea's hand as well. Emmi rushed forward to grab Julia's other hand, then Flo, then Heather, finally Toy and Little Lovie. They stood in one long line, hand in hand, facing the sea.

"Ready?" Linnea shouted. "On the count of three. One . . . two . . . three!"

In a chorus of squeals, laughs, shouts, and giggles, the women rushed forward as one, hands held, heads high, eyes glistening, into the sea. Cara felt the warm water swirl around her as she ran through the oncoming waves in a baptism of sisterhood.

Inevitably they reached the point where they could walk no farther. Beyond was Big Girl's world. Shouting their farewells to the sister turtle, laughing, hugging, they released hands and turned back toward the beach.

Cara was soaked through, her hair plastered against her head, her mascara running, and she'd never felt more beautiful. She looked ahead and saw the line of men waiting on the shore. They were laughing too, no doubt at the antics of the women they loved. Cooper and Palmer were daring each other to run into the surf. Ethan was holding back a crying Danny from running in. Bo hoisted Rory to sit high on his shoulders and search for Heather.

Cara caught sight of David standing at the tide line with Hope in his arms. In his eyes she felt welcomed. Loved. She saw the possibility for her second chance. She felt pulled forward by a compelling magnetism. Brett had been her sun, but David was her moon. Moving toward him, her steps were sure, one foot after the other, and her fingers gliding above the water. He was smiling now, waving. Hope spotted her and began kicking her legs in excitement. Cara laughed, enjoying the sound of it.

Cara Rutledge was coming home.

Acknowledgments

Tʜɪs ʙᴏᴏᴋ ᴍᴀʀᴋs a return to my beloved sea turtles. Every year I've marveled at the new information gathered by experts in the field. And too, I've wept at the continuing degradation of our oceans and nesting habitats. Hope springs eternal. Over the course of these twenty years, I've been blessed with great mentors and friends. I send great love and gratitude to my fellow Island Turtle Team members: Barbara Bergwerf, Mary Pringle, Tee Johannes, Beverly Ballow, Barb Gobien, Linda Rumph, Jo Durham, Cindy Moore, and Christel Cothran.

I am especially grateful to Sally Murphy, SCDNR Wildlife and Freshwater Fisheries Division, retired—my mentor and friend—for reading the manuscript and fact-checking all my turtle-related information, and for catching those pesky grammar errors, too. I'm truly grateful to all at the South Carolina Department of Natural Resources for great work on land and sea, especially Michelle Pate and Charlotte Hope.

Acknowledgments

I am eternally grateful to the South Carolina Aquarium for years of support and dedication, especially my friends and leaders in conservation Kelly Thorvalson and Kevin Mills. I hope I did this fabulous institution justice.

Sincere thanks to The Leatherback Trust for continuing inspiration and education on the great leatherbacks, in particular friends Jim Spotila, Maggie Kruesi, and Frank Paladino.

Hugs and a humble bow of gratitude to Cynthia Boyle, Patti Callahan Henry, and Gretta Kruesi for inspiration, plot ideas, and helping me through difficult stages of the book. Your wisdom and support mean the world to me.

Love and thanks to Andie MacDowell for her friendship and support of sea turtles and my novel *The Beach House*. Thanks, too, to Hallmark for creating with Andie the beautiful film for Hallmark Hall of Fame which illuminates not only the story of a mother and daughter reconciliation but the plight of our beloved sea turtles.

My heartfelt love to my dear friends Linda Plunkett, Leah Greenberg, Marjory Wentworth, Signe Pike, Cassandra King, Patti Morrison, Lindy Carter, Kate Pittman, and Hope Rechea for moral support, wise advice, encouragement when I needed it, and cheers when I deserved them, and for gathering when the call went out.

A special thanks to my incredible Advance Readers Team. I'm especially grateful this year to those who convinced me that I needed to write a follow-up in the Beach House series—immediately. I hope you enjoy seeing your ideas come alive in this book!

How many ways can I thank my wonderful editor Lauren McKenna for guiding me with her critical eye and her editor's ear, and for asking the insightful questions that helped shape my characters and storyline? The story sings because of you! And to Sara Quaranta and Joal Hetherington for sharp-eyed line editing and follow-through on all the details of getting a book to publication. At Gallery Books I'm so fortunate to have Jennifer Bergstrom as my publisher and a dream team of support—Jennifer Long, Abby Zidle, Michelle Podberezniak, Jennifer Robinson, and Diana Velasquez, and all. And a respectful bow to Carolyn Reidy.

I am beyond lucky to have my incomparable Home Team. My love and heartfelt thanks to Angela May, without whose friendship and brilliance I don't think I could function. At Magic Time Literary, Kathie Bennett and Susan Zurenda; at Tandem Literary, Meg Walker; at Authorbytes, Steve Bennett and the team; and for keeping me afloat, Lisa Minnick, Max Glenn, and Mary Steele.

With this book I begin a marvelous journey with my agent Faye Bender of The Book Group. Thank you for your wise guidance, thoughtful support, and warm smile. I'm also very grateful to Jerry Kalajian at IPG.

And the last is always first in my heart—Markus. You know I couldn't continue without you.

Beach House
Reunion

Mary Alice
Monroe

THIS READING GROUP *guide for* Beach House Reunion *includes
an introduction, discussion questions, and ideas for enhancing
your book club. The suggested questions are intended to help your reading
group find new and interesting angles and topics for your discussion. We
hope that these ideas will enrich your conversation and increase your en-
joyment of the book.*

Introduction

Home is where the heart is. Returning to the idyllic Isle of Palms three years after losing her husband, Cara Rutledge is ready to embark on a fresh start.

Moving into the beach house once owned by her mother, Cara finds everything and everyone on the island to be comforting and familiar. Yet at the same time, heartbreaking memories often resurface. Only through reconnecting with friends, family, and the beauty of the lowcountry does Cara find the strength to release her painful ties to the past and welcome the opportunity for a new love, career, and hope for the future.

Meanwhile, Cara's niece, Linnea, is a recent college graduate unsure of where her life will take her. Rather than live with her parents in their historic Charleston home, filled with entitlement and expectations, Linnea heads to her aunt's beach house for the summer. At the house, the presence of her grandmother Lovie, the original "turtle lady," can be felt all around her. Linnea remembers the lessons her beloved grandmother taught her as a child, which encourages her to rediscover her passions and pursue new possibilities. Rejoining the turtle team, learning to surf, and falling in love, Linnea finds the strength to break from tradition and find her own purpose.

In this heartwarming novel, three generations of the Rutledge family come together to break destructive family patterns, resulting in new bonds that will last far beyond one summer reunion.

Topics & Questions for Discussion

1. Each chapter of *Beach House Reunion* opens with a fact about sea turtles. Discuss how the information increases awareness of the species. How do they relate to either Cara's or Linnea's story?

2. Cara moves back to Isle of Palms after making significant changes in both her personal and professional life. What's the motivation behind her return? Do you find too much change at once to be overwhelming, or exhilarating? Discuss the role of family support in the life of a new mother. How do friends fill the role of family? Do you agree with Flo that "it takes a village"?

3. "Make do" is a phrase that Cara's mother, Lovie, used to say. What does it mean? How does this expression

relate to Cara's life? Do you incorporate a similar mantra into your life?

4. What traditional roles in Charleston society do Palmer and Julia expect their children to follow? Do you think their convictions of how young men and women should present themselves are outdated or sexist? Discuss how Cooper and Linnea break from their parents' conventional values. How are traditions and values changing for the young in your area?

5. Motherhood came as a surprise to Cara: "This opportunity to be a mother came out of nowhere. I was speechless. A deer caught in the headlights. I swear I couldn't breathe for days while I agonized over the decision" (p. 34). Consider the unique challenges she faces as a single parent in her fifties. What advantages might she enjoy?

6. Lovie has a significant presence in this novel. How does she help navigate the choices of the Rutledge women—Cara, Linnea, Julia? And her son, Palmer?

7. For Cara, Capers Island holds precious memories that tie her to Brett. Describe the pivotal moment when Cara buries her wedding band in a sand dune. How was this act transformative for her? Why do you think she felt it imperative in order to move on?

8. Consider the dichotomy between Cara and Linnea's feeling of home. Cara relocates her life to move back to her mother's beach house for a sense of ease and belonging, while Linnea is eager to leave Charleston for a chance of possibility and hope. How can home feel protective for some, and obstructive for others? What symbolizes home to you?

9. Cara begins to accept that her "divided heart" (p. 279) is normal, and admits she is ready to fall in love again. "The love I have for David is different than the love I had for Brett. But I'm different, too. And it doesn't mean there can't be love after love" (p. 280). What's so enlightening about Cara's breakthrough? How does she come to this place of understanding? Do you think a person can feel different kinds of love?

10. Explore the significance of the rescue and rehabilitation of Big Girl. What does Big Girl symbolize for the Rutledge women, and for Toy? How is she a pillar of strength and resilience? Is Big Girl's rehabilitation a metaphor for what the women are each experiencing in their lives? The final release?

11. Discuss the impact of the water/ocean in this novel on the Rutledge women, even the baby. Cara goes to the sea "to relieve stress, to gather her thoughts, to recharge

her batteries" (p. 98). And Linnea finds joy riding the waves. "The ocean awakened her, leaving her feeling invigorated, confident, like she belonged here" (p. 180). Do you believe in the healing power of nature?

12. Discuss how surfing (and being near the ocean) changed Linnea. What is your favorite body of water—the ocean, a lake, a pool, a bath?

13. Cara is torn about accepting a full-time position at the aquarium, until Flo put things into perspective for her: "Life is a long series of choices. All we can do is make the best decision we can at every turn, hope for the best, and deal with the consequences" (pp. 309–310). How does Flo's advice help Cara? Do you find that her words can guide you in your own life?

14. The issue of destructive family patterns is revealed through Palmer's alcohol abuse and trend toward domestic violence. In this book he follows the same trajectory as his father, Stratton. And in turn, the pattern is repeated in his son, Cooper. How has Palmer's drinking affected his family? To what degree are he, Julia, and in a lesser respect, Linnea, contributing to Cooper's drug use? And how do Palmer—and Julia—ultimately break the destructive family cycle that began with Stratton and Lovie?

15. In *Beach House Reunion* the character Palmer Rutledge completes a five-book character arc that began in *The Beach House*. He relentlessly pushed, even bullied, his mother, then his sister, to sell the beach house. In *The Beach House*, Palmer laments, "I never got to say good-bye" after his mother's death. Discuss how his character grew in each subsequent novel. How did brother and sister persevere, heal and finally unite in the novel? In the series?

Enhance Your Book Club

1. In this novel, readers learn so much about sea turtles and the importance of protecting their habitat. Check out the following resources for more information on conservation efforts and how you, too, can help.

   http://seaturtle.org/: information on sea turtles

   https://conserveturtles.org/: discover how this organization ensures the survival of sea turtles

   http://www.scaquarium.org/conservation/: learn about South Carolina Aquarium's conservation initiatives

   https://www.worldwildlife.org/species /loggerhead-turtle: learn how the World

Wildlife Fund is helping to protect sea turtles' habitat

2. Research reveals how our brains are hardwired to react positively to water. Being near the ocean can be calming, inspire us to be creative, or help us feel more connected. Take a walk, go for a hike, visit the water, spend some significant time outdoors—even just for a few minutes each day. Do you feel differently? Is being outdoors particularly nurturing or peaceful? Consider having a water feature at your book club meeting or hosting at a lake or beach house.

3. Linnea discovers her passion for surfing—a hobby she's always wanted to learn. Do you have any interests that you haven't yet pursued? Take a class, learn a new skill, or try something you've never done before. It's never too late!

4. Friendship and family is the heart of this novel and unfortunately, many of us don't take enough time to express our appreciation to our loved ones. Show your friends or family how you care about them. Consider writing cards, inviting them over for dinner, giving them a phone call, or, better yet, organizing a trip.

5. *Beach House Reunion* can be read alone, but it is also the fifth book in the Beach House series. To go back and learn more about the Rutledge family of Charleston read Mary Alice Monroe's *The Beach House, Beach House Memories, Swimming Lessons,* and *Beach House For Rent.*